ICE
LAND

ICE
LAND

BETSY TOBIN

First published in 2008 by
Short Books
3A Exmouth House
Pine Street, London EC1R 0JH

This paperback edition published in 2009
10 9 8 7 6 5 4 3 2 1

A CIP catalogue record for this book
is available from the British Library.

ISBN 978-1-906021-34-4

Printed in

For Bruce, with love

For this is an island and therefore Unreal.

W.H. Auden & Louis MacNeice
Letters From Iceland

And there where the glacier touches the sky,
the land ceases to be earthly.

Halldor Laxness
Under the Glacier

FREYA

When I was sixteen, I was given a cloak made entire-ly of feathers. It was made from pale grey falcon wings, unthinkably soft, with no more weight than a handful of ash. I remember the sensation as Odin first laid the cloak across my shoulders. His hands brushed too long against my skin, but even as I noticed this, something else was happening deep inside me: a sudden narrowing, as if I was being squeezed from within. In an instant, I too felt weightless, and in another second I was airborne. I looked down to see them all staring up at me: my father, his expression vexed with disapproval; my twin brother Freyr, his dark eyes pools of envy; Odin's wife, her smile frozen with complacency (surely she must have seen his lingering caress?) And Odin himself, staring too intently with his one good eye, as if he could divine all the secrets of my adolescence. With relief, I turned my gaze from them and flew towards the hori-zon, the wind rushing at my face. And for the first time in my life, I felt free. At sixteen, I'd not yet learned that it takes more than wings to release one from the bonds of kinship.

❧

They say this island sprang from the armpit of a giant. That his sweat turned to rivers which in turn begot the land. It is a jagged place, scarred by ice and fire, and perpetually torn by pale green rivers that refuse to stay their course. Long ago, the forests were thick here. Wild beasts stood quietly, as if waiting to be shot. That was before men came and culled them, using broad axes and fine-tipped arrows. Now trees are scarce and the animals hide, but the land remains generous. Each spring, the farmers toil in the fields to clear lumps thrown up by frost. In summer, they drive their herds deep into the highlands, where the grass is sweet and the sun never dies. In winter, darkness descends upon us like a shroud. Men wrap themselves in furs, huddle around fires, and tell stories from the past.

Water surrounds us. To the north, the frozen sea is but one day's sail. To the south, the long fingers of Norway and Denmark are eight days' journey. The sea offers us food and protection, but takes many lives in return. Despite its peril, the men here are of a wandering nature. They look to the horizon and refuse to let it lie. But they always return, if the sea or the sword does not claim them, for this island pulls on its people. Once settled they are bound, both by its beauty and its harshness.

I was not born here. I left the land of my birth as a young girl, and came to dwell in Asgard with my father and brother. We were a peace offering, my family and I, a gesture of conciliation between the Aesir and the Vanir, my father's people. My father was already a widower, saddled with the burden of two young children, so he had nothing to lose by throwing his lot in with the Aesir. In return, they made us certain promises. Njord, my father, was given control of the seas. Freyr, my brother, was given control of the harvests. And I was left with the tainted realm of love.

Over time, I've come to represent love's failings. Men and women turn to me in equal numbers. They bring their broken engagements, their shabby infidelities, their star-crossed romances, their spent marriages, their unrequited passions, in hopes that I will have a cure. Sometimes I do. More often I do not. For what they don't know is that our world is an elaborate conceit. The gods have no real influence over the lives of men. We are nothing but totems: we occupy the space that men create for something larger than themselves. Few who dwell in Asgard understand this. Fewer still would admit to it. But false belief underpins us all.

And, as for the sharp spear of love, it too is a deceit. Long ago, in another life, I was wounded by its impact. Now I know that solitude and self-reliance make far more loyal bedfellows. Though I've been married once before, now my bond is to the earth and the sky and the mountains that surround me. My home, Sessruminger, lies in the south of Asgard, snugly in the lee of Mount Hekla. Her vast glacial peak rises up behind me like the imposing neck of a triumphant queen. Hekla's moods can be capricious: one moment she is stark, calm, majestic; the next wild, dark and menacing. But I am thankful for her presence, for it is she who orients me when I take to the skies, and she who brings me back to earth. My tale starts and ends with Hekla, and I will tell it as it happens, in the manner of the bards.

FULLA

She craves the unexpected. Each day, she rides her horse across pock-marked fields of blackened lava to the hot pool, her servant Helga two strides behind. And each day, she prays her life will somehow burst its narrow banks.

But the gods do not listen.

Her future was set out long ago, like runes carved in stone. She will reach the age of consent, marry a man of her grandfather's choosing, and bear him as many sons as she can endure. She will watch her boys grow into stout young men, learn to wield the sword and axe, and die violent deaths. Just as her father did.

Already there is talk of such a marriage. Fulla hears them murmuring by the fire, her grandfather and the other godi of the region. They huddle together, their eyes wet with drink, and speak in hushed tones that she must strain to hear. Again and again, she hears the same word issue from their lips: Norway. A place she has heard of but never seen, eight days' journey across the sea. A lifetime away. She hardly dares consider what they are planning: marriage to a foreigner, a man of unknown age and temperament, whose name she cannot pronounce. She loves her grandfather, but she does not know whether she can live the life he has ordained for her.

In a sudden fury, she leans forward and urges her horse into a run. He leaps ahead, happy for the opportunity to sprint. She gallops as hard and as fast as she is able, her teeth clenched tight, the ground beneath her a blur of motion. But, after a minute, she hears the strangled wail of Helga far behind her.

Perhaps just once, she'll ignore Helga's calls. No, not today, she thinks resolutely. For the pull of duty is like a weight about her neck. She slows to a walk and waits for Helga to catch her up. The older woman shoots her a look of consternation.

"What race is this?" Helga demands.

"We saw a snake," she says. "My horse frighted." Helga eyes her for a moment, weighing her words. Fulla does not remember when she learned to lie. Only that she is surprisingly adept at it.

After a few minutes, they reach the end of the lava field and begin the ascent over the last hill. The ground is studded with a thick carpet of dwarf birch, no taller than her knee. From a distance, the trees form a shaggy layer of fur. Up close, they appear stunted and gnarled, as if the effort of growth is too much for them. A well-worn dirt path snakes its way through the scrub land over the hillside, and when she reaches the top she can see the hot springs a short distance below, a distended ring of dark water surrounded by tall marshy reeds. The water bubbles up from some hidden source, giving the impression that beneath the valley is a vast simmering cauldron. She sees at once that the pool is deserted, and cannot help but feel a twist of disappointment. Her daily ride here is one of the few sources of contact she has with those outside her grandfather's farm.

She reaches the stand of birch trees and dismounts. Helga arrives a moment later and climbs down from her mount with a grunt. Her figure is too stout for horses. "Looks like we'll have the baths to ourselves," says Fulla, tethering the ponies to a tree.

"Just as well," Helga says. The older woman scratches at her midriff, then frowns at the darkening sky. "Weather's coming. We'd best hurry."

Fulla is already disrobing as she winds her way down the path. To one side of the pool lies a long stone wall with a bench running along its length. Her grandfather built it partly as a place to rest, and partly as a wind-break. Fulla drops her clothes in a pile on the stone bench, then advances through the marshy reeds towards the water. The cold wind bites at her flesh. Helga is right, she thinks. They should have come earlier, before the storm. No wonder the pool is deserted. But then she is sinking into the hot warmth of the waters, her feet sliding across the smooth stone floor of the pool. She moves out into the centre, where the pool is deepest, and immediately sinks down beneath the water.

Even before her head breaks the surface, she hears Helga's words of disapproval. "You'll catch your death, missy." Helga is standing a few feet from the pool's edge in waist-high water, her hands upon her hips. Her large breasts hang free like two ripe marrow. Fulla watches as Helga lowers herself carefully into the thermal waters. Her fleshy arms caress the water's surface. She opens her mouth to speak just as Fulla submerges herself once more.

Beneath the water, all is dark green and luminous. She can just make out Helga's shape, a bulbous mass of light in the distance. She turns away, moving her hands in front of her face, her fingers splayed and glowing eeri-ly. The water is clouded with thousands of tiny particles. Small fronds of weed drift past her eyes. She can hear nothing but the sound of her own heart. Perhaps this is what death feels like, she thinks. Perhaps this is where her parents are right now, floating together in some vast, warm pool of darkness.

A moment later she bursts to the surface, gasping for air. She circles in the water, expecting to see Helga's disapproving frown, but instead the older woman is staring into the distance, her face creased with concern. Fulla swims towards her, her feet scrambling for a footing on the stone, then pulls herself up out of the water and follows her gaze. Over the stone wall, at the top of the hillside, two strangers on horseback look down on them. A split-second later, they are joined by three others. Even from here she can see the men are heavily armed. She lowers herself into the water up to her shoulders, just as the riders begin to pick their way on horseback down the hillside. Helga too drops into the water, glancing at her uneasily.

As the two lead men draw near, Fulla recognises them as the eldest sons of Skallagrim. She is surprised to see them, and not a little wary. Their farm lies just over the hills to the east. Her grandfather has forbidden Skallagrim and his clan from setting foot upon his land, ever since a dispute over boundaries led to her own father's death.

Both riders drop from view for an instant as they near the wall, then reappear, their horses halted just the other side. The two men stare down at them, and the others join them one by one. Fulla's eyes travel down the line until they reach the fifth and final rider: a youth not much older than herself. His hair is a tangled auburn mass and his eyes are a pale shade of brown. The boy stares back at her brazenly.

Helga makes a strangled noise in her throat, and Fulla shifts her gaze back to the lead man, whose horse is moving uneasily behind the wall. He reins it in repeatedly with short, sharp jerks. He is darker than the others, with eyes set deep, like a hawk's, and a beard so full it obscures his mouth entirely.

"I am Thorstein, son of Skallagrim," he announces loudly. "Tell your grandfather that Skallagrim is dead," he continues. "We will meet him on the boundary at noon tomorrow."

Fulla hesitates. The words are angry ones, the sort of words that killed her father. She does not feel like offering condolences. "You can tell him yourself," she replies, in a voice as loud as she can muster. "I'll not be your messenger." A tiny cry escapes from Helga's lips.

Thorstein exchanges looks with the man next to him, then turns back to her. He raises his eyebrows, scrutinising her more intently. She shifts uneasily under the water, aware of her naked flesh just beneath the surface. "As you wish," he says with the thinnest of smiles. "But we are coming, just the same." He whips his horse around abruptly and urges it into a gallop up the slope. One by one the other riders follow. But as the last rider turns his mount, his gaze snags on hers. She sees a flicker of something in his eyes, but does not know what it signifies.

They stay until the riders are out of view, then scramble quickly out of the water, not waiting for the wind to dry their skin before they hastily pull on their clothes. Helga is talking in short bursts, but Fulla does not listen. She has one thought only: of reaching her grandfather as quickly as possible, so she can carry their message back to him, just as they knew she would.

FREYA

ll my life I have waited for Hekla to unveil herself: even on the clearest day she wears a ring of cloud. This morning is no different. The air is cold and bitingly clear but Hekla remains wreathed in white. I pull my woollen cloak more tightly around my shoulders and walk outside to draw fresh water. But as I reach the spring, I hear a long, low roar – like the dying throes of some enormous animal. The noise is deafening. It washes like a torrent down the mountain and sweeps right past me across the valley. A moment later it is gone. Terrified, I turn and scan Hekla's flanks. But I see no beast, nor any other living soul, not even a bird. And then the ground beneath me lurches violently, as if shaken by the hand of a giant. The wooden bucket flies from my hands as I am thrown forward onto the grass, where I wait for the earth's trembling to subside. Only then do I realise that there is no animal. There is only Hekla.

The earth calms and the air is deathly still. I stare up at the sky. Far off in the distance, a cock crows. I listen as it calls twice more. The sound stirs something deep inside me. A crimson rooster, I think, biding its time in the halls of Hell. For that is how the poets said it would begin: with the rooster's rousing call. Now their prophecy comes back to me in fragments, each one clinging like a shard.

Though we may be a divine race, the poets have long warned that our world is on the brink of destruction.

19

One day, according to the prophecy, our families will be torn asunder. Brothers will do battle to the death, and sons of sisters will fight their own kin. When this happens, the sun will turn black and great flames will lick the sky.

We have lived with their dark promise all this time: now I can almost feel the wolf's hot breath upon my face. For it is the wolf that will bring about our downfall, say the poets. *A storm age, a wolf age.* That is how our destruction will begin. *The fetter will break and the wolf will run free.*

FULLA

Hogni emerges from the house at the sound of Fulla's calls, his laboured movements those of an old man. He walks slowly towards her, one hand absently pulling on his greying beard. Fulla rides breathlessly into the yard, and before she can dismount, blurts out the tale of her encounter with Thorstein. Hogni stares up at her, nonplussed. His large eyes are of a pale blue colour and, despite his age, they remain surprisingly clear. When she has finished, he grunts in acknowledgement, and motions for her to climb down. He takes the horse's reins and begins to lead it away. "Grandfather?" she calls after him, puzzled. He stops and turns back to her. "Shouldn't we call in the men from the boundaries?"

He raises an eyebrow. "There's been a death, not a murder," he says.

She stares after him, speechless, as he leads her horse into the stable.

That night, sleep does not come easily. Inevitably, her thoughts turn to her father, and the day he was found half-dead by one of Hogni's farmhands. When they brought him into the yard, Helga had to drag her from the doorway so she would not see his injuries. Three days later, he was dead. Only then was she allowed to enter his bedchamber. By then, he was so altered that she refused. Now she regrets her cowardice.

Fulla closes her fingers around the small bronze amulet he gave her when she was five. "Here," he had said, placing it around her neck. "Keep this close. Then your mother will be with you always."

She'd studied the amulet, tracing her fingers along the delicate shape of the patterned serpent curled around the base of a tree. "Where is she now?"

Her father had hesitated. "She is with Odin and Thor and the others. They will feast together, until the day we meet again."

"When will that be?"

"Later. When you are grown. Until then, we must be patient." Then he'd held up his own amulet, identical to the one around her neck, and kissed the top of her head.

Now, all these years later, she has lost both of her parents. And not all the patience in the world will bring them back.

Thorstein and his men come the following day. Shortly before noon, Fulla climbs the hill behind the house to watch for them, her gut twisted in a knot. The storm has passed and the weather is clear and mild. When the sun is at its highest point, she catches sight of them, tiny dark specks on the horizon. She watches tensely as they take shape. After a minute, she sees that this time there are only three riders. Once again they carry weapons, but now they are dressed like those riding to battle, in tight-fitting leather caps and chainmail shirts. Each man carries a broad sword and round wooden shield.

Scrambling down the hill, she shouts for her grandfather. He emerges from the forge with soot on his face, and pauses briefly to wash himself with water from the well. Then he puts on his cloak and waits for the riders, with Fulla by his side. The three men ride into the yard, Thorstein at the fore. They dismount from their horses and turn to face Hogni. Thorstein steps forward, the two men flanking him, and clears his throat. "My father is dead. We have business to discuss."

Hogni frowns in disapproval. "The business of grief?"

Thorstein shifts uneasily and exchanges a look with his brother. "We wish to discuss the boundaries."

"Now is not the time," Hogni replies. "We will come and pay our respects to the dead. Fulla, make ready your things." And with that, he turns and strides off in the direction of the barn.

This time, Thorstein blinks in perplexity. He looks at Fulla, who meets his gaze only briefly. She turns and goes inside to fetch her things. Once inside, she closes the door and leans against it with a smile. She washes her face, grabs her cloak and pulls a comb quickly through her hair, before going back outside, where the stable boy is standing with her horse. Her grandfather is already mounted, as are Skallagrim's relations.

They set off at a brisk trot, Fulla and her grandfather in front, the other three just behind. They ride for nearly two hours without a word spoken between them. When they reach Skallagrim's farm, Fulla is struck at once by its size. There are more than a dozen buildings, all with turf roofs, tucked into the lee of a broad hillside. A small stream tumbles from a waterfall halfway up the hill and meanders to one side of the yard. The farm looks well-tended and prosperous. At least half the buildings appear to be dwellings. At the sound of the horses, several people come out to meet them in the yard. One of them is a fair-haired woman wearing a linen dress and a goatskin kirtle, with a large bunch of iron keys hanging at her waist. The woman greets Thorstein with an anxious look, and Fulla realises she is his wife.

They climb off the horses and Thorstein explains their purpose. Thorstein's wife turns to them without hesitation. Her face is lean and taut with tiredness, but she nods to them graciously and beckons them inside. "Come and rest from your journey," she says. They enter the largest house, where more than a dozen people are already gathered around the long trench of fire. Benches line the carved wooden walls. They have been strewn with a colourful array of woollen blankets and animal furs. The roof timbers are large and richly decorated with the carved figures of animals. Fulla looks quickly about the room at the range of faces she does not recognise. These people are our enemies, she thinks. She accepts a cup of ale from a pale young woman with auburn hair and freckled arms, who smiles shyly and nods to her.

Thorstein stands a little awkwardly to one side, and for a few moments, no one speaks. "My father passed on quietly during his sleep," he explains somewhat hesitantly. "He had not been well of late." Thorstein's voice cracks slightly at this last. He clears his throat before continuing. "His body is laid out within." He gestures towards a bedchamber at the far end of the room.

"It is a blessing that he went peacefully," says Hogni judiciously.

"May Christ receive his soul in heaven," says Thorstein.

Fulla watches Hogni stiffen. She steals a glance at Thorstein. She did not know Skallagrim and his family were followers of the new religion. For an agonising moment, she fears her grandfather's anger. The two men eye each other silently.

Hogni finishes his drink and hands the cup back to the pale woman. "We will view the body now."

Thorstein motions for them to follow. At the doorway to the bedchamber, he stands to one side and Hogni ducks inside the narrow doorframe. Fulla hesitates, then follows. The room is small and dark, lit by a single iron lamp that hangs suspended from the wall. Skallagrim lies fully clothed upon the narrow bed, his hands folded over his chest. His skin is grey and there is a slightly sour stench in the room, intermixed with the smell of burning tallow from the lamp, but otherwise there is little to suggest that he is not safe in repose. Hogni stands silently by the bed and bows his head. Unsure what she should do, Fulla follows suit. After a few moments, the air in the tiny room becomes dense and cloying, and the body of Skallagrim seems to swell in the half light. She is relieved when Hogni finally raises his head and clears his throat, turning to go.

Once again, they duck through the doorway, and this time, when Fulla comes into the main room, she sees the auburn-haired youth amongst the others. The boy watches her as they move through the room, until her grandfather lays a hand upon her arm and steers her towards the door.

Hogni pauses in the doorway and turns to Thorstein. "Our business is complete," he says with an abrupt nod. Thorstein opens his mouth to speak but Hogni raises a hand to silence him. "I am an old man, just as your father was. I am past the age of argument. The boundary lands you dispute shall be yours. I give my permission for you to move the markers, but should you or your kin ever cross onto my land again, then I must warn you our response will be swift and merciless. These are my conditions."

"Very well," Thorstein says in a guarded tone. "We accept. The markers shall be moved at sunset this evening."

Hogni gives a wave of his hand and turns to go. Fulla follows him out into the sunlight, where their horses are waiting. Thorstein stands to one side as they mount.

Several members of Skallagrim's family file out of the house to watch them depart in silence. Hogni turns his mount and walks the horse slowly out of the yard, with Fulla right behind. When they are several paces from the house, Fulla hears a shout.

"Hold up!"

She turns to see the auburn-haired youth running after them. Fulla halts her horse, but Hogni rides on unaware.

"Vili!" Thorstein shouts at the youth.

He calls back over his shoulder. "Her girth is loose."

Fulla sees Thorstein frown. By now, her grandfather has halted his horse several paces ahead of her. The boy reaches her saddle and bends his head to her girth, pulling at the strap with a grunt. As he leans into the horse, Fulla looks down at him. He is thin and muscled and wears a generously cut dark red tunic that hangs loosely from his frame. Her eyes stray to the bare skin exposed at his neck. Inside the tunic, a tiny silver cross swings freely from a cord.

The boy finishes adjusting her saddle and raises his head to look at her.

"Thank you," she says a little stiffly. He nods, and seems on the point of leaving, when his eyes drift down to the amulet around her neck. He stops short, and a look of confusion crosses his face.

Almost without realising, Fulla raises a hand to the amulet, as if protecting it from his gaze.

"Vili!" Thorstein calls from behind. After a moment, Vili tears his eyes from the amulet and turns away, nearly stumbling. Then he jogs back to where Thorstein is waiting.

"Fulla! Are you all right?" Hogni calls to her. She is staring after the boy, one hand still holding the amulet.

She turns her horse towards Hogni, nodding. He

urges his horse into a lope, and after a moment's hesitation, she follows.

That night, two godi from neighbouring farms arrive. As is their habit, they plant themselves around the hearth, clutching drinking horns of ale and debating the merits of Hogni's decision. Hogni is unrepentant. "I shall brook no more arguments over land rights," he says, motioning for Fulla to join them. Reluctantly, she seats herself on the bench at his side. "All these years we have lived and died by the sword. And we have little more to show for it today than when we first set foot upon this land thirty years ago." He breaks off to cough for a moment, and Fulla steals a sideways glance at him. She sees a face that has been ravaged by age and exposure, yet with the eyes of a younger man.

Ulf leans forward and points a drunken finger at him. "You cannot afford complacency, Hogni. Not now. Not with Olaf's men scouring the land looking for converts, and threatening to burn down our temples."

"Let them come," says Hogni with a dismissive wave. "Let them bring their bells and their crosses and their incense. They will never win the hearts and minds of our people." He stares into the flames morosely. "We came here to be free of them," he adds, almost to himself.

"They say this Thangbrand is a dauntless sort of man," says Ulf. "He is passionate and ungovernable. And clever of speech."

"He is even cleverer with the sword," interjects Thorgillson. "He has killed two men already who dared mock his beliefs."

Hogni snorts. "Yes, yes, I have heard all the chatter.

Thangbrand sleeps with a crucifix in one hand and a dagger in the other."

"Nine godi have been converted already," says Ulf pointedly.

Hogni stares into the fire. "Not me. I'll not take the fly that Thangbrand casts."

"If King Olaf has his way, Iceland will become the spawn of Norway. Reading its laws, preaching its faith, worshipping its idols," says Thorgillson.

"I came to Iceland seeking refuge from their god," says Hogni, shaking his head. "I'll not wait to see my adopted homeland bow down before a Christian king." He lays a bony hand on Fulla's knee and squeezes a little too hard.

"What will we do?" she ventures.

He sighs. "A good question. What indeed? We are a tolerant people. But they push us too far."

"Pray to Thor and Odin," says Ulf. He raises his drinking horn with a lopsided grin. "And sharpen our swords."

❧

Later Fulla slips away from them, relieved to be free of fighting talk. She has seen nothing of these Christian missionaries they speak of, though secretly she would welcome the diversion. She finds her cloak and slips out to the stable to say goodnight to her horse. Outside, the night is cold and clear. The sun has long since dropped beneath the horizon, but the sky is not yet fully dark. She makes her way in the deep blue light across the yard to the stable and ducks inside, pausing for a moment as her eyes adjust to the darkness. A few slivers of evening light come through the cracks in the building, and after a pause she begins to move about, filling a wooden bucket with some oats from a barrel in the corner, and calling softly to her horse.

The horse moves forward in its stall and nickers softly. She comes to the door and he pushes his nose against her chest, while she reaches up to scratch behind his ears. Then she picks up the bucket and hangs it on an iron hook.

"Here you go, Bor. Eat well, my handsome warrior."

"A lucky fellow, to garner such fine praise."

Fulla spins around in the half light with a gasp, her heart beating hard. A figure steps out from the shadows. She stares at him for a moment.

"Do you not know me?" asks the auburn-haired youth. He takes a step forward.

She takes a deep breath and lets it out. "Of course I do. You startled me, that's all," she says tartly. He holds up his hands in apology. "If my grandfather sees you here, he'll have your flesh roasting on a spit," she continues.

He raises an eyebrow. "Bold words. Are they yours or his?"

"It won't matter when you're dead," she counters evenly. "Why have you come?"

"I've brought you something." He holds out his hand. Something dangles from it, but in the darkness she cannot see.

"You bring nothing but trouble," she says coldly. "Why would I accept a gift from you?"

"Because this is no gift," he says, holding it out to her. "It belongs to you."

She hesitates, then reaches out for the object. He drops it into her hand, and at once she recognises the feel of it. She looks down: the amulet matches her own exactly. Her fingers close around it instinctively, even while her stomach plummets. Her voice drops to barely more than a whisper. "Where did you get this?"

"I found it with my mother's things after she died."

She reaches inside her gown and pulls out her own amulet, holding the two next to each other. "They were commissioned for my parents as a wedding gift, but my father's was lost. It was taken from his body... " Her voice trails off.

Vili stands silently for a moment. "My father gave it to my mother," he says finally. "Before his exile."

This last word stretches out between them. It takes a moment for his meaning to reach her. "No!" she says hotly. And in the next instant she reaches out and slaps him hard across the face. A bright patch of crimson appears on his cheek. "The blood of a murderer flows through your veins!" She says through clenched teeth.

"I am not my father's keeper," he replies, "any more than you are. His sins are not my own."

For a moment, they stand facing each other in the darkness. Her eyes come to rest on the tiny silver cross at his throat.

"You follow this Christian god?" she says in disbelief.

"My mother's family is Christian. They came from Norway. Her people converted."

"And you?"

"I follow neither."

"You wear the cross," she says accusingly.

"It was my mother's."

They hear the sound of shouting in the yard. Fulla hesitates, then crosses to the stable door, peering outside. She sees two farmhands running towards the house, and further behind, a third man follows across a field, leading a horse. Vili peers over her shoulder.

"They've found your mount," she says turning to him, a note of triumph in her voice. "Your fate is sealed. I cannot help you now."

"Fulla!" he says urgently. "They'll kill me!"

"Pray to your Christian god. Maybe he will save you." He nods towards Bor. "Give me your horse!"

She stares at him incredulously. "You must be mad! Why should I help the son of my father's killer?" She turns to go.

Vili lunges forward and grabs her arm. "Why should I die for the sake of a trinket?"

"You should have asked yourself that before you set out!"

Vili hesitates, still holding her arm. "Go on, then," he says, nodding towards the house. "Raise the alarm." He pauses, watching her defiantly. "What are you waiting for?"

She glowers at him for a long moment, her face burning with anger. "His tack is in the corner."

Vili drops her arm and moves at once to the corner. Within moments, he is saddling and bridling the mount. "Is he fast?" He asks from inside the stall.

"That depends on the skill of the rider," she says sharply.

"No need to worry on my account." He flashes her a grin.

"My only concern is for the horse," she counters. She steps in front of him. "Swear you'll bring him back."

Vili stops. "What? And risk my neck again? Now it's you who are mad! Anyway, my mount is worth twice yours."

"Swear now," she counters. "Or I'll scream so loud you'll wish you'd stayed in bed this night."

He looks at her aghast, then shakes his head. "All right, I swear," he says finally.

She steps aside while he finishes cinching the saddle. "Bring him back in three days' time," she says, "at midnight. I'll wait for you here." He nods, swinging himself up into the saddle. "There is another door at the back," she continues. "Go as quietly as you can over the hill, then circle round to the east. I'll distract them at the front of the yard."

Vili hesitates briefly. "Thank you," he says.

"You can thank me in three days," she replies swiftly. She moves to the far end of the stable and unlatches the door, quickly peering outside, before motioning him to come. Vili guides the horse through the narrow opening, ducking his head. She watches as the horse trots silently through the tall grass and disappears, then latches the door and dashes out of the opposite end of the stable and into the farmyard. She pauses for a long moment, then screams with all her might.

FREYA

ekla's outburst leaves me numb. For some time, I do not move, the damp grass slowly seeping through my cloak. Is the prophecy true? I do not know. Even as a child, I understood the Aesir were riddled with corruption. Envy and malice run right through us like a vein. So it is perhaps nothing less than we deserve.

I return to the house and go at once to the ornately carved wooden box that houses my feather form. The box is made of honey-coloured sandalwood, a gift from my father from a trader in Byzantium. The cloying perfume of the wood nearly overwhelms me as I lift the lid and peer inside. I have not used the form in many months; the pile of pale grey feathers lies inert. I reach inside and run my fingertips across the grain of their plumage. Taken separately, each feather is worthless. But joined together, they produce the miracle of flight. How can it be that something with so little mass can lend the feeling of weightlessness to something so much larger?

Minutes later, I take to the skies in search of Skuld. I have not yet formed the question in my mind, yet I know that I must ask it. Skuld is a seer: she can look through time as clearly as I can see through water, yet the enormity of this does not daunt her. She lives with her sisters on a small farm atop a pass on the northern edge of Asgard. By horseback it is a vast distance, but with the falcon cloak I can reach her in the space of an hour. As I approach the farm, I see her elder sister Urd in the yard, bent double beneath the weight of a wooden yoke. It has been almost a year since I was here last, and I am shocked by how much she has aged in the interim. I land softly behind her, and quickly shrug off the cloak before calling out a greeting.

Urd looks up from beneath the yoke, startled. Her face is long and round, like a generous wooden spoon, and her light brown hair hangs in untidy wisps about her face. Her forehead is smudged with dirt, and as she turns, the water slops over the top of the wooden pails, splashing her leather shoes. "Freya," she says breathlessly, her expression harried but no longer alarmed. Nothing truly surprises Urd.

"Greetings, Urd."

"Skuld is within," she says, nodding towards the house. She knows I have not come for idle talk. I smile gratefully and turn away. The house is set into the hillside, the doorway narrow and fringed with turf. I duck inside the dimly lit room, and take a moment for my eyes to adjust to the darkness. The room is long and low, with a thin trench of fire down the centre. Two small square windows are cut into the wall on my left, covered with the taut membrane from the sac of an unborn calf. Each emits a pale, ghostly glow of morning light.

The remaining walls are hung with thick tapestries woven from all the colours of the earth: deep russet red, nut brown, forest green and sandy ochre. The house feels both warm and alive, like the inside of some great beast. Someone has massed a pile of fir cones upon the fire; they spit and crackle in the flames, offering a faint smell of pine.

At the far end of the room, Skuld sits on a raised wooden platform, lost in concentration at her loom. Her dark tangle of hair shadows her face completely.

Her long fingers dart with alarming speed back and forth across the loom, like delicate spiders. I watch, fascinated, for when Skuld weaves, it is as if time itself pauses and waits for her to finish. Finally, I make a sound and she turns to me, her gaze unseeing at first. After a moment, a smile blooms upon her face. She rises and crosses to me.

"Freya." Skuld squeezes my hands with affection. Her face is thinner and more lined than I remembered, and there are dark circles beneath her eyes.

"You look tired," I say.

"I wove all night," she explains with a guilty smile. "Do not tell Urd."

We hear a noise at the door. Urd enters just then, her expression irritated. She shoots a dark look at her sister. "You've shirked your chores," she says.

"How so?" asks Skuld.

"The clay is too thin. Father said it should be to the depth of your wrist."

Skuld raises her eyebrows at me conspiratorially. "Father is dead, Urd," she replies. "The tree thrives, in case you hadn't noticed." She speaks of an enormous ash tree in the garden, a legacy remaining from their father.

"For how long, with you tending it?" retorts Urd.

Skuld shrugs. "Tend it yourself."

Urd purses her lips. "It's not my place and you know it," she says in a clipped voice. Skuld does not reply, and after a moment, Urd picks up a small axe and quits the house once more, the door banging behind her. Skuld turns to me with a smile.

"Poor Urd," I say.

"It's the tree I pity. She will kill it with care."

"Where is Verdandi?"

"Who knows? She is never at home. Urd says she has taken a lover."

"And has she?"

"Perhaps." She gives an unconcerned shrug. Skuld is unlike other women. She has a keen mind and a closed heart, and cares nothing for the world of men.

"You knew I was coming?" I ask.

"Yes."

"Then you also know why."

She looks past me. "You are afraid."

"Should I be?"

Skuld frowns. "Fear is like the beast that lurks behind us in the dark," she says slowly. "Sometimes it is real. More often it is imagined."

"And now?"

Her eyes roam towards the loom. "Now we must wait."

I am reminded that one must tread carefully with Skuld. The future is not hers to trifle with. "What does the loom say?" I ask. If Skuld will not tell me, then the loom may speak for her. I watch as she crosses over to the weaving. Her fingers reach out to touch the warp, as if they cannot bear to be apart from it. She plucks gently at the last thread of weft.

"Sometimes we cannot trust the loom," she says.

"What do you mean?" I ask. She says nothing so I move beside her, watching as her fingers gradually undo the last two threads of weft. I peer more closely at the tapestry. What strikes me first is the absence of beauty, for there is something jarring about what she has woven.

It begins normally, with a brightly coloured pattern of tawny oranges and yellow, arranged in a neatly plotted design. But halfway down the loom, the pattern becomes erratic. The colours bleed into one another, then gradually fade in their intensity, before turning suddenly to black. The bottom portion of the tapestry is a broad band of black. Something in the fabric catches my eye. I bend down more closely and see a tiny glint of gold, made by a lone metallic thread. "Gold," I murmur, surprised.

"Yes," she says simply.

"Where is it from?"

"The place of dwarves. In the mountains."

I stare at her in disbelief. "Nidavellir?"

She nods. Slowly I reach a hand out to touch the thread. It is hot, as if lit from within. I pull my hand back, alarmed. "What does it mean?"

"Go and see," she says intently.

"To Nidavellir?" I ask.

She nods.

The name sparks a memory. From the earliest age, we are taught to revere the stories of the poets, but not all of them are true. Still, as a child, there was one tale that caught my fancy. The poets said that deep in the mountains of Nidavellir, there was a necklace wrought entirely of gold. According to legend, just to gaze upon the necklace was enough to throw one's senses into disarray. Grown men would weep in its presence; women would fall to their knees with the blunt force of longing. To possess the necklace one became privy to the earth's secrets: the age of the mountains, the source of the rivers, the path of the sun, the depth of the oceans. But that is not all. The necklace had the power to alter the course of things, and to safeguard its keepers. They said it had been fashioned by dwarves, master goldsmiths who dwell in caves deep inside the belly of the earth. These dwarves are infinitely wise, according to the poets, but distrustful of the world outside the caves.

I have never believed in the existence of the necklace. But the look in Skuld's eyes is unyielding.

"How do I find it?" I hear myself ask.

"Ask for the Brisings."

The name is unknown to me. I fix it in my mind, even while my gaze is drawn back to the thread. For a few moments, I am entranced by the sight of it, as if everything else in the room has disappeared. Finally, with some degree of effort, I turn away from the loom.

"What of the black weft?" I ask. Black is inauspicious in her weaving. It signifies the dark face of death.

Skuld's face becomes a mask, her expression instantly unreadable. There is a limit to what she will impart, and I know that I have reached it. "Fate is woven," she says then. "But the future is uncertain."

FULLA

I t's a bad omen," says Hogni, the morning after Fulla's horse is stolen. They sit side by side on a bench by the fire, and eat skyr mixed with bilberries from wooden bowls. Fulla steals a glance at him: a large fleck of white rests on his upper lip.

"Skallagrim and his kin are land-crazed," he continues. "They will not rest until they have stolen everything that is ours."

"Skallagrim is dead," Fulla reminds him.

"Yes, of course," he says, with a wave of his hand. "But at least when he was alive, I could look him in the eye and hold him accountable. These sons of his, they have no code. The law for them is a plaything! Who knows what their intent was last night? We might have all been burnt alive in our beds!"

Fulla nearly chokes on her skyr. One hand inadvertently goes to the amulet at her throat. The one she wears this morning is her father's. Her own lies hidden beneath her mattress. Hogni continues speaking, unaware. "When I first came to this island thirty years ago, a man could ride for days without meeting a soul," he says, shaking his head. "Now every blade of grass is spoken for. Every tree." He lifts the bowl and drinks deeply, then wipes his mouth with the back of his hand. The fleck of skyr vanishes from his lip. "Perhaps our time here is drawing to a close," he says heavily.

"What do you mean?" asks Fulla with alarm.

Hogni regards her with a frown. "Maybe it is time we considered moving on. There is land for the taking in Greenland."

"And give up everything we've built here?"

Hogni casts his eyes about the room. "What good is this house, if they reduce it to cinder and ash?"

"They will not," she says earnestly.

"How can you know?"

She bites her lip, for she dares not speak of Vili or the amulet. "I do not think they will return," she says finally.

"And if they do? What choice have we, but to fight?"

She leaves him muttering oaths into his wooden bowl, and escapes into the scullery, where Helga is grinding grain in a large soapstone mortar. The older woman pauses from her labour. Her hair is bound tightly back in a pale blue headscarf, and her broad forehead is smudged with dirt. Fulla reaches into one of the earthen jugs that line the walls and fishes out a pickled walnut, popping it into her mouth. Its sweet syrup explodes with flavour.

"You look well enough this morning," Helga says, eyeing her closely.

"Why should I not?"

"For someone who's lost her favourite mount."

Fulla stops chewing. "Bor isn't lost," she says after a moment's hesitation. "Grandfather says we may be able to recover him at the Althing."

"Aye?"

"He promises to raise the matter with the lawspeaker." She reaches into the jar and picks out another walnut. "Anyway, the mount he's left behind is very fine."

"Who?" Helga fixes her with a questioning eye.

Fulla feels a flush rising in her cheeks. "The one who took Bor," she stammers.

40

"Then perhaps he will return," says Helga, "if his mount is so fine."

Fulla stares at her, speechless. Helga picks up the pestle and begins to pound the grain with renewed vigour. Fulla watches her for a moment, then slips outside, her heart racing. She runs across the yard to the stables and ducks inside with relief. The mare is in the corner stall. The horse shuffles uneasily, one eye fixed on her, as she approaches. "Good girl," murmurs Fulla. She raises a hand to the mare's shoulder and it flinches beneath her touch. Fulla picks up a brush and begins to comb the horse in long strokes, talking to it softly all the while.

Minutes later, she is leading the saddled mare out into the yard, when Hogni emerges from the house. He stops short when he sees her.

"What is this? One of theirs? Have you gone mad?"

"It's a horse, not a spy," she counters teasingly.

Hogni frowns. "Their animals are not to be trusted."

"Nonsense. She's a fine mount, you can tell by looking."

Hogni eyes the horse disapprovingly. "Perhaps," he concedes. "An even match for your Bor. Though we shall still raise the matter at the Althing."

❧

For three mornings Fulla takes the mare out, riding it harder each time. By the third day, the mare is no longer wary of her, butting her shoulder impatiently with its nose when she arrives in the morning. That night, Fulla feigns illness and retires early, shutting herself in her bedchamber. She dozes for a few hours, waiting for the household to settle for the night, before finally rising. When she emerges from her room, the large hall is lit only by the glowing embers of the turf fire. She treads carefully around the sleeping forms of her grandfather's manservants lying on made-up pallets near the hearth, and manages to slip silently out of the house. Outside, the night is cold and a light rain falls. The moon is barely visible through a dark haze of cloud. Vili will have a long, wet ride, she thinks with satisfaction as she crosses the yard. Inside the stable, she waits while her eyes adjust to the darkness, then crosses over to the corner stall and greets the mare affectionately. She settles herself on a haystack in the corner, pulling a woollen saddle blanket over her for warmth. She dozes fitfully, waking every few minutes, her limbs beginning to ache from the cold. When she wakes for the fourth time, she realises she has been sleeping deeply. She looks around her in the darkness; there is still no sign of Vili. Only then does she wonder whether he will come at all. Perhaps the prospect of the mare is not enough to lure him back, she thinks angrily. Perhaps she's been a fool.

She pulls another blanket on top of the first and succumbs again to sleep, dreaming of her father and a faceless woman in a long white dress, whose hands are pale and slender and icy to the touch. She wakes to find Vili standing over her, his chest heaving, his wet hair plastered to his skull.

"Sorry to disturb your rest," he says sarcastically, wiping the rain from his face. Fulla sits up quickly, brushing bits of hay from her hair.

"You're late."

"And you've not ridden half the night through sodden fields, so I'd not complain if I were you," he counters tersely, nodding towards the yard. "Your precious gelding is outside." He steps over to the mare and greets her fondly, reaching up to scratch behind her ears. "Hello, Trika, my beauty. They've looked after you well?"

"Well enough," says Fulla.

42

"Has she been ridden?"

Fulla instantly regrets riding his mount. "A few times," she answers evasively.

He raises an eyebrow. "By you?"

"Who else?" She scoffs. "No one else would touch her."

Vili frowns at this slight. He takes off his damp oilskin and shakes the water off, then hangs it on a post, before opening a wineskin slung beneath one arm. He takes a long pull from it and offers her a drink, which she refuses. He collapses heavily onto the haystack, closing his eyes.

She rises, and steps forward suspiciously. "What are you doing?"

He opens his eyes. "I need rest. We were hours coming. Your precious gelding lost its way." He pulls the woollen blankets on top of himself.

She looks at him, astonished. "You don't expect me to leave you here?"

"Stay, if you like. But you're in for a dull night."

She drags a stool over and sits down opposite him. "Half an hour. To catch your breath. That is all. If that mare is as good as you say, she can find her way home with you asleep upon her back."

"How very generous." He lies back again and shuts his eyes.

For a moment, she sits there silently, frowning. She takes a deep breath and exhales loudly. Vili does not respond. Fulla switches positions. "I'll have some of that wine you offered," she says finally.

Vili reaches to his side and holds out the wineskin, but never once opens his eyes. Fulla frowns and takes the wineskin, drinking from it. She wipes her mouth and replaces it by his side.

"That cross you wear," she says, after a moment.

He opens one eye. "I told you, it was my mother's."

"But your family, is it true they've all converted?"

"Most of them."

She hesitates. "What do you think of this Christian god?"

He looks at her askance. "I can only judge him by his representatives."

"Olaf's men?"

He nods. "They came in the spring and stayed for three weeks. It was then my grandfather took the oath of conversion and was baptised, together with my uncles."

"But not you."

"No."

"In spite of your mother's beliefs."

He scowls. "In *spite* of my mother's beliefs."

"What were they like?"

Vili grunts. "They were fine speechmakers. Men who hone their words like sharpened steel and were not afraid to back them up with a blade, if necessary."

"But they did not persuade you."

"I am not persuadable. What does it matter if we worship one god or many? He or they will still blight the harvest if they choose. Or bring down the side of a mountain. Or flood our grasslands in the spring."

"By these words, I take it you do not make offerings to Thor."

"Why should I? What has he given me in this world?"

"He has granted you life. And prosperity."

Vili fixes her with a stare. "When I was eight years old," he says slowly, "I watched my father ride out of my life for ever. Two years later, I nursed my mother to her death. And last winter, my only sister died giving birth to a stillborn child." He pauses. "Four lives he has taken from me."

She frowns. "You've been unlucky. But you are not alone. You still have your kin."

"I hardly feel that Thor has been working in my interests."

"My grandfather says a man is better blind than buried."

"'And a dead man is good at nothing.' I know the saying."

"You do not countenance it."

Vili pauses, gathering his thoughts. "I believe that we must all shoulder the burden of our own fate. We have no one to look to but ourselves."

"A lonely sentiment."

"Perhaps. But one I can rely on."

They sit in silence for a moment. "My people worship Thor," she offers.

"And you?"

"I lost my father when I was seven. I never knew my mother. By your standards, I am entitled to a degree of scepticism." She hesitates, plucking at the straw beneath her feet. "The old gods seem weak in the face of this new one."

Vili smiles. "Perhaps it is their followers who are weak."

She nods. "The godi are all old men now. When the last of them dies, what then?"

"Do not worry. If there is a gaping hole, Olaf will move swiftly to fill it," Vili says drily.

"No doubt he will plug it with a cross," she answers. They exchange a brief smile.

"Fulla," Vili hesitates, choosing his words. "I was too young to understand the circumstances of your father's death. Nor was I privy to my own father's motives. But... please accept what apologies I can make for the actions of my kin."

She shrugs. "It is as you said: your father's sins are not your own."

"No, but we are all strung together in our misdeeds. I will carry his crimes with me for the rest of my life, just as one day, my son will carry mine."

"Perhaps your son will have no crimes to atone for."

"Perhaps not."

Too late, they hear footsteps just outside. Before they can move, the stable door swings open to reveal her grandfather's figure in the doorway. He bears a torch, and a bleary-eyed farmhand stands just behind him. Both men are armed with swords. "Fulla!" her grandfather hisses.

She jumps to her feet. "It's not what it seems," she says quickly.

"It is everything it seems!"

"He's brought back Bor."

"Presumably because he stole him in the first place!"

Vili opens his mouth to speak but Fulla intervenes. "No," she insists. "It was one of the others."

Hogni eyes Vili. "Is this true? You've come to exchange them?"

Vili nods cautiously. "Yes."

"Does Thorstein know you've come?"

Vili shakes his head. "No."

Hogni steps forward and raises the torch. "I recognise you," he says slowly. "Your father was..." His voice fades to a stony whisper.

"My father was exiled," says Vili. "For murder."

"I should kill you here and now," continues Hogni.

"Grandfather!" says Fulla.

"Be quiet, Fulla!" Hogni takes a step forward and slowly raises the point of his sword until it rests lightly on Vili's chest. "No one would question my right to do so."

"No," says Vili evenly.

They stare at each other for a long moment, and Fulla sees the rise and fall of Vili's chest. After what seems like an eternity, Hogni allows the sword to drop to his side. "Take the mare and be gone," he says wearily, turning away. "I've no thirst for retribution this night."

Vili exhales, exchanging a glance with Fulla. "Thank you."

"If I set eyes on you again, you'll wish you'd died here and now."

Vili nods, then moves to saddle and bridle the mare while Fulla and Hogni look on. When he is finished, he leads the horse out into the yard and climbs on its back. He gives the briefest of nods to Fulla before turning the horse and setting off. They watch as he slowly disappears.

When they can no longer hear the thud of hooves, Hogni turns to face her. "I'll not ask how you came to be in the stables in the dead of night with the son of your father's killer," he says slowly. "No doubt your answer would be clothed in half-truths." He turns and crosses back to the house, leaving her alone in the darkness.

FREYA

ourneys make my blood quicken. Now as I approach Nidavellir from the air, I begin to feel a child's excitement. Beneath me, against a backdrop of mountains, the plains extend eastward as far as I can see, broad and grey and featureless. There is not a single tree or shrub within sight. I circle the area widely, taking stock. The ground undulates gently, pocked with small craters and rocky lava domes. From the sky it looks barren, but when my feet touch the soft earth, I see at once that I am mistaken, for a variety of plants grow here. Tiny red and purple flowers spring from cracks in the lava, and bright green moss grows ankle-deep in shallow craters, dotted with yellow buttercups. I stand for a moment, listening to the silence. A gust of wind blows. The sun emerges briefly from behind some clouds, and for a few moments, the earth glows.

I do not know what I am looking for. An opening in the ground, perhaps, or something more dramatic. Whatever it is, I do not see it. I choose a direction at random and walk in a straight line, scanning the ground as I do. After several minutes, I begin to despair, for there is nothing here but wind and moss and lava. And then I hear a sound, faint but familiar: the laughter of children. I glance behind me in the direction I have come from, but see nothing. I wait, and after another moment am rewarded with the noise again, this time ahead of me. I walk quickly in its direction, and nearly stumble into the hole.

It is small and perfectly round, about the diameter of a man's shoulders. I drop to my knees and peer inside. At first I see nothing but blackness. I lie flat upon my belly and thrust my head right into the hole, and after a moment, I see a vast, dark cave strewn with broken boulders and rubble. At the edge of my field of vision there is a blur of movement. Small shapes appear and disappear. I hear them call to one another: tiny children playing in the darkness, laughing and shouting, scrambling among the rocks, leaping from one to the next. I thrust my head even deeper into the hole, searching for another opening. How on earth did they get inside, I wonder? I look at them more closely, and decide that they are not as young as I had thought. I see now that they are dwarf children; they do not need a means of descent, for they already dwell beneath the ground.

A cry goes up from below. The dwarf children have seen me, and are standing in a small circle, their faces upturned like the petals of a flower. They smile and begin to wave their arms excitedly. They are not afraid, but curious, as any children would be. I wave to them a little tentatively, then sit back and ponder the hole. Even with the cloak it would not be straightforward, for I have little experience of flying in the dark and am unused to confined spaces. I peer through the hole, and as I do, one of the children signals to me. A young girl with piercing eyes and thick, straw-coloured plaits that fall like heavy ropes down her back. She points repeatedly in one direction and, after a moment, I leave the hole and begin to walk quickly in the direction the child has indicated. I am beginning to wonder whether I mistook her meaning, when I see an enormous gap in the earth some distance ahead, where the ceiling of the cave has collapsed inward, leaving a mass of broken rubble along the bottom and sides. With some difficulty, I scramble down the edge of the hole and, as I reach the bottom, I see the children approaching in the half-light, swarming like insects over the rocks. I stop and wait for them, and when they are several paces from me, they too pause, blinking rapidly in the daylight of the opening. I count them quickly: seven in all, with a few more lurking behind rocks. They are pale but perfectly formed: small replicas of myself at the same age. I smile at them.

"Hello."

The children titter and flush with excitement. The girl with straw-coloured plaits takes one bold step closer, but says nothing. She is eleven or twelve, but only waist-high. Her eyebrows are arched and sandy white; they shoot up with curiosity.

"Perhaps you could help me," I say gently to the girl. "I'm looking for the Brisings." The children burst into giggles and turn around in the darkness. The girl with plaits points to something, and after a moment a boy emerges a little sheepishly from the darkness. He is taller than the others, and older; perhaps too old to play at children's games. He walks slowly forward until he is level with the girl.

"My name is Brising," he says earnestly, squaring his shoulders and lifting his chin as he speaks.

"You?" My surprise is evident. I am struck at once by his looks, for he is an attractive youth, with soft brown hair that falls in curls about his shoulders, and wide, full lips. "I was expecting someone..." I hesitate, and the boy's face darkens.

"Taller?" he says crossly.

"Older."

"Oh." The boy's expression softens. "I am Berling. The youngest. We are four in all."

"Four brothers?" The boy nods. The girl with straw plaits nudges him.

"This is my cousin, Raiki," he adds grudgingly. The girl smiles. "Who are you looking for?"

"The eldest, I think."

"That would be Grerr."

"Can you take me to him?"

The boy nods and motions me to follow. The other children watch as we climb past them among the rocks. After a moment, Raiki follows at a little distance.

"Do you play here?" I ask the boy.

"They do," he says, nodding towards the others.

"But not you," I say teasingly.

He shrugs. "Sometimes."

"Is it safe?" I indicate the collapsed ceiling of the cave.

He shrugs. "It happened long ago." We come to a clearing in the cave, with tiny shafts of light coming through small openings in the ceiling. The tunnels branch off in different directions. The boy turns and heads into the darkness without hesitation. "Have you been here before?"

"Never."

"Then you must take care. The tunnels can be confusing if you do not know them."

This is an understatement, I decide, as there is little to distinguish one grey shaft from another in the darkness. "Who made them?" I ask.

"Some were formed by lava, some by water," the boy explains. "Others we made ourselves to suit our purpose. They join the caverns where we live and work."

I see light ahead, and soon we come to another open area, again with bore holes in the ceiling to allow sunlight through. Despite this, I find the atmosphere stifling. The air is heavy with the smell of damp, and in

51

the space of a few minutes it has crept into my lungs, causing my chest to tighten. "How many people live here?"

The boy frowns. "I don't know. All of us. Hundreds. Maybe more. The caves extend for many miles. Watch your head." He stoops through a small opening and I follow.

"Do you live with your brothers?"

The boy shakes his head. "I live with my mother. My brothers are older. They live nearby."

"Do any others come here?"

"Others?"

"Visitors, I mean. Like me."

He glances sideways at me. "Not often."

"Do you leave the caves?"

He frowns. "Not yet. I am too young. But Dvalin says he will take me when I'm grown."

"Who is Dvalin?"

"My brother. Half-brother. We all have different mothers. Except for Grerr and Alfrigg."

"I see. And where will he take you, your brother?"

The boy shrugs. "Outside. To the real world."

I laugh. "But your world is real."

The boy flushes. "You know what I mean."

"Does Dvalin travel in the real world?"

"Sure. He grew up there. His mother was one of them."

"And the others? Do they leave the caves?"

"No. Grerr doesn't like the outside."

"Why?"

"He hates the sun. But really, it's on account of being –" Berling stops. He stares at the ground in front of him, kicking at the dirt with his toe. I wait for him to finish. After a moment, he shrugs. "Dwarves do better underground."

We carry on walking in silence. I am impressed by the boy's honesty. And his humility. Both are qualities lacking in my own people. "We're nearly there," he says after a moment. Then he stops short and turns to me. "But I still don't know your name."

I am uncertain what to tell him. "I am Freya," I say finally.

He nods, his eyebrows knit together thoughtfully. He knows of me, I think. We come to another chamber, with tunnels leading in four directions. He points to one.

"My mother and I live here. The others live down the opposite tunnel. And this one here leads to the forge. We're goldsmiths."

"Yes, I know."

He stares at me for a moment. "You've come about the Brisingamen, haven't you?" he says.

I hesitate.

"The necklace," he says.

There seems no point in misleading him. "Yes."

The boy smiles ruefully. "Dvalin said it could not remain with us for ever."

"Why?"

"He said it was bound to find its way into the world."

I nod, unsure what else to say. "It must be very beautiful," I offer.

"Yes, of course," Berling says dismissively.

"What does Grerr say?"

"Grerr says the necklace is ours. He says it should remain with us for ever."

"I see. His attachment to it is very strong."

"The necklace is more his than anyone's."

"Why?"

The boy thinks for a moment. "Sometimes a thing owns a person. Rather than the other way around."

"May I see it?" I ask. "First, I mean. Before you take me to the others?"

A flash of doubt crosses the boy's face. I realise that I have erred, and raise a hand reassuringly to his arm. "Forgive me, Berling. I should not have asked."

He raises his chin defiantly. "No," he says. "I'll take you to the necklace. But you must give your word that you'll not harm it, nor tell the others what I've done."

I smile. "Yes, of course."

He glances quickly down each of the tunnels, and when he is satisfied that no one is about, motions for me to follow. We take the furthest, the one leading to the workshop, and after only a minute, turn off to the right into an even smaller channel. The opening narrows steadily, and soon we appear to be walking in almost complete darkness. I stumble on a rock and Berling pauses. "Are you all right?" His voice floats back to me.

"Yes."

"Grab on to my tunic. We're nearly there." I do, and we carry on for another minute, until he suddenly stops. He turns to the wall and I see him move his hands across the rock face in a smooth motion, as if he is seeking something. After a moment, he finds it. His hands lock tightly onto what appears to be a ledge in the rock and, bracing himself with his feet, he pulls it to one side. I see now that it is an enormous wheel of stone, cut so thin that it is imperceptible from the surrounding wall in the darkness. As the stone moves, light escapes from within. He pauses when there is a gap only just wide enough to squeeze through, and motions for me to enter. I duck down and go through the opening, relieved to be moving towards a source of light. Once inside, I stand. The cavern is small and perfectly square, as if hewn by hand, rather than formed by nature. A single torch is suspended from one wall, throwing flickering shadows all around the room, and in the centre is a pillar of solid rock no taller than my waist. My eyes are drawn at once to this pillar, for draped across its flat surface lies a vast square of black cloth. Berling seals the entrance to the cavern and stands behind me. I hear him take a deep breath, then he crosses to the pillar, and in one slow, deliberate movement, draws the black cloth to one side. He turns to me expectantly, the cloth dangling from his fingertips.

But I am not looking at Berling.

I am looking at the necklace. And all at once I feel ill. A wave of nausea sweeps over me and a dull pain bursts behind my eyes. I close them for an instant, wishing I had never come. When I open them a moment later, the necklace waits for me. It lies flat upon the smooth surface of the rock, arranged precisely, as if awaiting my inspection. I can see it perfectly from where I stand, for it appears to soak up all the light provided by the torch and hurl it back at me.

"Are you all right?" Berling asks.

I cannot speak. The necklace seems to mock me with its silence. Never in my life have I seen gold with such a lustre. Gold that surely must be warm to the touch, as if it had just been pulled from the fires. But it is not just the colour or the brilliance of the metal. It is the delicacy and the confidence with which it has been wrought, for the design of the necklace is unlike any I have ever seen. It lacks the bulky girth so often preferred by those keen to impress, and the frantic ornamentation that all goldsmiths seem to love. Instead, the necklace is made of minutely thin strands of gold interwoven like the tendrils of vines. At its centre is a small round pendant embossed with symbols of the sky.

I step forward. The necklace draws me in like a fish upon a line. I stop just an arm's length away, just as my legs give way beneath me. At once, Berling grabs my arm. "Hold onto me," he says. I clutch at him, breathing deeply, struggling to clear my head. But I cannot tear my eyes from the necklace. "Freya," he says urgently, his voice in my ear, "are you all right?"

I smile uneasily. "Should I be?" I ask. My voice floats down to me from the ceiling of the cave. He shakes his head slowly. A wise boy, I think, this handsome dwarf child. For he divines at once the secret that is only just forming inside me.

I will not rest until I have the necklace.

THE NORNS

When Freya came to us, we saw the dark fate of Asgard laid out before us like blackest obsidian. The Norns are time's witness: we have been here since the earth began. We have seen the continents collide then fracture, watched the oceans flood the voids and mountains rise and fall. We know the earth is like a gull's egg, its crust thin and breakable, a spectrum of layers buried inside. Deep down, the core is ferociously hot, beyond the reach of ordinary minds. It is circled by a swim of liquid rock and gas where heat runs in currents. It writhes and coils like a giant serpent that will not be contained. Men will never see this place of molten beauty, though it governs their existence. One day, it may surge and smother us all.

DVALIN

valin rides hard across the barren glacial plateau. All around him, the earth is dead. Little grows but an occasional splatter of yellow lichen that has attached itself to tiny fissures in the rock. To his right looms an enormous mountain of grey ice that towers above the surrounding peaks and craters. He has been riding for two days and nights, with only an occasional pause to rest and water his mount, ever since he received word of his sister's collapse. His head aches from lack of sleep and his hands are cracked and chafed from the cold.

He comes to a vast lava field, and the horse slows its pace, threading its way carefully around jagged rocks, sulphurous pools of mud and the occasional spiral of steam. The field is eerily quiet. No birds soar overhead, no lizards scamper among the rocks. Dvalin can feel the horse tense beneath him. He too feels uneasy, and will be glad to put this place behind him. Not for the first time, he curses Idun's husband for bringing her to this desolate corner of their land. He may be one of the Aesir, but as far as Dvalin is concerned, Bragi is a coward: a man of words rather than deeds, who closes himself off from society and flees at the first sign of danger.

After what seems like an eternity, they reach the far edge of the lava field, where the ground rises up in a steep bluff. The horse pants and blows its way up the slope, its head bobbing from the effort. At the top, they pause. The edge falls away sharply to reveal a wide green valley in the shape of an enormous bowl, the first habitable land they've seen all day. A glacial river cuts directly through the centre of the grassy valley. Even from a distance, he can see the river is deep and swift-running, the water eerily pale. Uncrossable, he thinks with dismay. One could perish trying. Beyond the river, he can just make out the edge of Bragi's farmstead, tucked into the base of the mountain. Dvalin traces the river up the valley to its source, where he can see it cascade down a series of waterfalls from a high granite cliff.

He urges the horse down the grassy slope, and at once can feel the animal's relief to be on soft turf again. The horse breaks into a swift trot, and after a few minutes they reach the river's edge, where Dvalin dismounts to look for a crossing point. The horse stares at the pale waters, its nostrils quivering, but does not drink. Instead, it turns back towards the long grass they have come through and begins to graze. Dvalin picks up a large rock and hurls it into the centre of the river, where it sinks without trace. He walks up the shoreline, a knot forming in his gut. He does not like fordings at the best of times. And his mount is already overtired from the journey. It would surely not survive the crossing. He therefore has two choices: he can leave the horse behind and swim. Or ride further south in search of a crossing point, but lose several hours in the process. Neither option is attractive. And somewhere beyond the river, his only sister lies unconscious, perhaps even dead.

Dvalin stares at the icy waters and remembers a time as children when he and Idun attempted to swim across a swiftly flowing river on a dare. They set off at the same time and within seconds were swept downstream. With some effort, he managed to reach the opposite shore, only to find Idun clinging to a large rock in the centre.

She was frozen with fear, unable to move. And for the next hour, he pleaded with her to release her grip and let the river carry her to safety. When he had nearly given up, an enormous swan the size of a small bull came out of the sky and swooped down, grabbing his sister in its talons and carrying her to safety. He watched as his mother, now in human form, laid Idun gently in the grass next to him. And then he vomited. Afterwards, he could not read the look in his mother's eye, could not tell whether it was anger or disgust. Now, without realising, he raises his face to the sky, just as he used to as a child. A lone bird soars overhead. An ordinary plover, he thinks, made of no more than bone and feather. Not a mythic woman-bird who appears without warning and disappears all too easily and for ever. After a moment, he forces his gaze back to the river. He will have to swim.

❧

Two hours later, Dvalin is sitting, half-frozen, in Bragi's large hall, but he has still not set eyes on Idun. Bragi rode off at dawn leaving strict orders that no one was to see his wife in his absence. Various servants and farmhands have come and gone from the big hall, but the chief enforcer of Bragi's orders is a tooth-sucking old woman with sunken breasts and a milky eye who busies herself running the household. Since his arrival, the old woman has wordlessly offered him bowls of curd and a change of ill-fitting clothes, but has refused steadfastly to let him see Idun.

But he is relieved to know that she lives. He is seated on a low bench by the large open fire. The hall is enormous, its walls made of solid wood panels and ornately painted roof timbers. A long, narrow strip of woven tapestry runs the length of the room, depicting

63

scenes of heavily clad warriors feasting in the Hall of the Slain. The room is richly furnished with several large chairs and a long wooden table, but there is little natural light and the air is heavy with smoke from the peat fire. At the far end of the hall he can see two small chambers: one for food storage, the other a bedchamber whose panelled doors remain firmly closed. Idun sleeps within the latter. He knows this from their glances. Shortly after his arrival, the old woman disappeared behind the panelled doors for a long interval, bolting them from within. When she finally emerged, he leapt to his feet, but she raised a finger to her lips and shook her head, as if he was a child.

And he looks like a child. As if his size was not enough, the garments she has given him are for a man two heads taller than himself. He feels a fool wearing them, and does not relish meeting Bragi in such a manner, but his own clothes are soaked through. He leans back against the wall. It would be so easy to sleep, he thinks, closing his eyes. Perhaps this is what happened to Idun. Within a few moments, he is dreaming of horses, of the clattering of hooves, and of men's voices as their mounts are pulled to. And when Bragi finally strides into the hall followed by his men, Dvalin has fallen off the edge of consciousness into sleep.

He wakes with a start. Bragi stands in front of him, arms crossed, head tilted. "Time to rise, Brother."

Dvalin sits up slowly, his head thundering with pain. He looks at Bragi, momentarily confused. Then he remembers Idun and the panelled doors. He struggles to his feet. "I came as quickly as I could," he says, glancing towards the bedchamber. "But I've not yet seen her," he adds with a hint of accusation.

"I went for advice. There is little to be done, it seems." The older man gives a long and weary sigh. He is exhausted, thinks Dvalin, and frightened for her.

"May I see her?" he asks.

Bragi nods towards the bedchamber. "Yes, of course. But I must warn you: she is not herself."

They walk towards the door and when Bragi opens it, Dvalin sees his sister's body laid out upon the bed. They have covered her with furs, and her dark hair is fanned out across the cushion, but what startles him most is the extraordinary whiteness of her skin and her wide-open eyes. He rushes forward in alarm.

"Idun!" He drops to his knees by her bedside peering at her face intently. He had not expected her to be awake. And yet she does not stir at the sound of her name, and takes no notice of his presence. He turns back towards Bragi. "But...she's awake."

Bragi sighs and shakes his head. "She neither sleeps nor wakes. She remains just so."

Dvalin reaches for her hand and holds it between his own. "Her hands are cold," he murmurs. "For how long has she been like this?"

"Nearly a week."

"You found her in this state?"

"I found her worse. Half-drowned. Her limbs nearly frozen. Only the ghost of a pulse. I pulled her from an ice crevasse."

"She fell?"

Bragi says nothing for a moment. He stares at the body of his wife, then raises his hands to his face and closes his eyes. When he speaks, his voice is barely audible. "She jumped."

Dvalin feels his heart leap. He turns to Bragi, aghast. "You know this?"

Bragi nods slowly. "I saw her. From a distance. Like some horrible dream. I could not get to her in time."

Dvalin reaches for his sister's hands, examining

each of her fingers in turn. Then he pulls aside the bedclothes to look at her feet. He pinches each toe gently,
studying the skin for signs of damage. Finally, he covers
her again. "You've done well, Bragi. Saved her life, no
doubt."

Bragi hesitates. "She breathes. Yet she is hardly alive."

The two men stare at Idun in silence. A farmhand
comes to the door and clears his throat. Bragi turns to
him and nods, and the farmhand disappears.

"There is one more thing you should know, Dvalin.
Some weeks ago she lost a child. It was the third time.
She was convinced there was a curse upon her womb.
Perhaps this is what led her to seek death. It is the only
reason I can think of. Prior to that, she seemed content.
We led a quiet life, but it was not without its rewards."
His voice trails off.

Dvalin looks at him and sees not one of the Aesir, but
a man tormented by the failings of his own life. "You've
done your best, I am sure," he says. But even as he
speaks, he is conscious that his words mock them both.
For a man whose wife is driven to suicide has surely
failed by any standard.

"I am needed elsewhere," says Bragi. "Please, stay
with her as long as you wish." He turns to go, but pauses at the door. "I am grateful you have come, Dvalin."

"She is my kin. I could not have stayed away."

Bragi nods and leaves. Dvalin turns back to the bed.
He stares at Idun intently for a long moment, then leans
forward and presses his lips to her pale, cool forehead.

"Take all the time you need," he murmurs. "We will
wait. Just do not leave us."

❧

Later that night, Dvalin and Bragi stare into the fire.

They share a drinking horn of mead that has been replenished many times by the cloudy-eyed serving woman. She moves silently about the hall attending to her tasks, and each time she approaches Dvalin, his eyes are drawn to the translucent frog-skin of her gaze. When Bragi speaks to her, she does not look at him, and when she fills the horn, her eyes are fixed on a point somewhere beyond the thing itself. And yet the horn does not overflow. And her movements are surprisingly deft. It is as if she sees, but does not see.

He is unused to drinking. At first, the mead seemed to ease the persistent aching in his temple, but now a somewhat duller pain has taken its place. They have eaten a meal of stewed calf earlier in the evening, and he feels desperate for sleep. But Bragi seems in need of companionship, so Dvalin endeavours to oblige, for his sister's sake at least.

"Why did you settle in this place?" he asks.

Bragi takes a large swallow from the horn and shakes his head. "I grew tired of life among the Aesir. There was so much deceit. So much corruption. When a race of people is universally admired, their hearts turn to stone."

"Perhaps not *universally*."

"Perhaps not. I should have mentioned their conceit." Bragi smiles. "And then I met Idun. She was young and full of hope. And she had something that the rest of us had lost. Idun had integrity. She carried it with her like a charm. And helped me to regain my own. When she agreed to marry me, I could not believe my good fortune. After all, I am more than twice her age. But you know this, of course."

He breaks off and Dvalin nods slowly. Bragi chuckles a little self-consciously. "Perhaps it was a father she was looking for, rather than a husband."

Dvalin returns the smile but says nothing, for Bragi's words strike him as only too likely. The older man stares into the fire, his expression sober. "I suppose I feared that if we stayed among the Aesir, she might come to see the folly of her choice."

Dvalin frowns. "Idun was always worthy of your trust."

"Yes, of course. But it wasn't her I doubted. It was myself."

"I don't understand."

"Jealousy is like a ghost that does not rest. I saw it everywhere among the Aesir. Even though she gave me no cause. I hoped that it would not follow me to this valley. And I was right. Away from others, I could devote myself to Idun and her happiness." He pauses for a moment, passing a rough thumb over the carvings on the horn. "But I could not give her all she wanted. We both longed for a child. An emblem of our love, and of the life we'd made together. But a child is not an emblem. I know that now. And we were not to be so lucky."

"I am sorry."

Bragi shrugs. "Once I lived for many things. Idun is all that matters to me now."

"She will recover."

"Perhaps. Perhaps I will join her, wherever she is. I have no wish to live out my days in solitude."

"You are a worthy husband."

"And you a worthy brother. Idun often spoke of you. She missed you terribly."

Dvalin stares into the fire. "She was ten when we were separated. When my mother left, she took Idun away with her to live among the Aesir. We did not see each other for many years."

"You were not bitter?"

"Towards Idun?" He shakes his head. "We had different fates, that is all. Hers was with the Aesir. Mine was with my father's people in the caves."

"I meant towards your mother."

Dvalin hesitates. "I was sorry to lose Idun. By the time I saw her again, our childhood was over." Dvalin's last words seem to hang in the space between them. He coughs a little self-consciously. Bragi takes another deep drink from the horn. He is the only one drinking now, and his face is flushed and pop-eyed from the mead. He wipes his mouth with the back of his sleeve. His expression brightens.

"Idun has often said that you should take a wife."

Dvalin smiles. "She is forever saying this. As a child, she made me act the groom to her bride." His smile fades as he sees a look of consternation form on Bragi's face. "It was child's play, nothing more," he adds quickly. Bragi looks at him a moment, then turns his face towards the fire.

"It is late," he says heavily, "and we must sleep."

"Bragi." Bragi turns to him, his expression distant. "Idun will recover. I am sure of it."

"I'm glad one of us is."

The old woman makes up beds for them on wooden pallets by the fire. Dvalin lies with his head near Bragi's feet and sleep takes him instantly. He is still exhausted when, many hours later, the old woman rouses him with her bony clasp upon his shoulder. Her face is so close that he can see the cloudy membrane stretched across her eye, and smell the vaguely sour scent of age. The old woman nods towards the bedchamber, and he is instantly awake. He rises and crosses to the doorway, where he sees Bragi kneeling by Idun's side, their hands clasped together.

"Please do not leave me again," murmurs Bragi.

"I will try not to." Idun raises her eyes, and a slow smile forms. "Dvalin," she says weakly.

Dvalin approaches the bed and kneels down by Bragi's side. "You're awake."

"I thought you were a ghost."

He smiles. "Not yet."

"How wonderful to see you. I've waited all this time. Bragi, he has finally come."

"Yes, my dear. He feared for you. We all did."

Her face creases with concern. "I'm sorry. So very sorry."

Dvalin kneels down. "Don't be. All that matters is that you are well."

"Dvalin, let me look at you. You've hardly changed."

"Not taller?" He asks with a grin. She shakes her head and they exchange smiles.

"When did you come?"

"Only last night."

Idun frowns and turns to Bragi. "How long have I been ill?"

"Nearly a week."

"A week!" She gazes down at the bedclothes and her eyes fill with alarm. "I remember the cold. It was so cold. I thought that I would freeze."

"Do not speak, my dear. You must rest."

"What happened?"

Both men stare at her for a moment, unwilling to respond. "You do not remember?" asks Bragi tentatively. Idun shakes her head slowly. He hesitates, then takes her hand. "You fell. Into a crevasse. Luckily, I saw you from a distance, and pulled you free."

"Oh." Idun frowns. "I remember the ice. It was so beautiful. I never realised how beautiful the ice could be." Her voice trails off, and for a moment she seems lost again.

Dvalin and Bragi exchange glances. "You must rest," says Bragi.

"Must I?"

"Yes. And take a warm drink. Something to strengthen you. I'll see to it now." He turns to go and Dvalin starts to follow, but Idun grabs his hand.

"Do not leave me!" Her voice is filled with alarm. Dvalin glances at Bragi, who raises his eyebrows briefly, then turns and leaves the room. Dvalin sinks down to the edge of the bed, still clasping Idun's hand. "Please do not leave me," she whispers. He bends forward and kisses her forehead.

"Be silent now. I am here." She takes a deep breath and lies back on her cushion, still holding tightly to his hand. They sit for a time, and she closes her eyes. After a few minutes, she opens them again.

"He thinks that I am well," she murmurs.

"You are."

She shakes her head slowly. "No."

"You need rest. And food. That is all."

"My mind is running swiftly now. Like a river. So many thoughts, crowding one another." She hesitates. "I am starting to remember."

"There will be time later, Idun. Right now, you must rest." He forces a smile, but the look on Idun's face alarms him, for she is clearly frightened.

"All these days, I have lain right next to death. Have felt its clammy touch upon my skin. But it is not death I am afraid of."

"What do you mean?"

"There is something evil inside me."

He frowns. "You are unwell, that is all."

"No. You must listen. While I slept, I dreamt a raven came to feast on my entrails. I watched it scavenge from my belly. Dvalin, the flesh inside me was rotten. I am rotting from within. That is why I cannot carry a child."

She begins to weep and he takes her in his arms. At that moment, Bragi enters carrying a dish of broth. He rushes forward with alarm.

"Idun!" Dvalin moves away and Bragi throws him a dark look. "Leave us now," he says. Dvalin slips out of the door, and goes to sit by the fire. He is relieved that his sister is awake, but also exhausted from his journey. The old woman wordlessly offers him a bowl of thick soup from a cauldron by the fire. He takes it and drinks deeply, all the while pondering Idun's words. Perhaps some evil has befallen her. Or perhaps it is her own conjuring.

When Bragi emerges from the bedchamber, his face is drawn with concern. He pauses in front of Dvalin and stares down at him. "She wants you," he says. The words are flung like stones. Dvalin takes a deep breath and rises, leaving Bragi standing motionless behind him. "Dvalin," he calls sharply over his shoulder, "please do not distress her."

Dvalin frowns, then enters the bed chamber. Inside Idun waits for him, her face composed but pale. She manages a half-smile. "I'm sorry." He shakes his head, lowering himself onto the bed.

"No. It is I who am to blame."

She glances towards the other room and lowers her voice. "He is prone to anger. And jealousy."

"I know. He told me himself."

"Sometimes the Aesir seem like children," she says conspiratorially.

"You forget that you are one of them."

She shakes her head. "No. I am neither one nor the other. Like you."

He smiles ruefully. "How can you be sure?"

"Because you told me so."

He frowns. "I said that?"

She nods. "When I was five."

"Wise words from a nine-year-old. And you heeded them."

"I always have," she says. He takes her hand and kisses it. "Dvalin, you must help me."

"Of course."

She hesitates. "You must go and see Menglad."

Dvalin takes a deep breath. He has not seen Menglad in many years. He had banished her entirely from his thoughts. Idun senses his reluctance.

"Please, Dvalin. You must go to her. You must tell her of my dream. And of my illness. She will know if something is wrong."

"But why me? Why not Bragi?"

"Bragi is an old man. Too old to travel to Jotunheim."

Dvalin rises and begins to pace the room. He knows that she is right. If Idun is unwell, Menglad may be able to help. But the thought of seeing her again makes his stomach roil.

"Will you do this for me?"

He turns to her. Her long, dark hair is fanned out across the bed linen, and a little colour has risen in her cheeks, perhaps in anticipation of his answer. But as he stares at his beloved sister, his mind has already turned to Menglad, has already drawn the fullness of her upper lip, conjured her laugh in his ear, and the scent of earth which clung to her always. Idun watches him with wide eyes, oblivious to the fact that he does not see her. For he is lost to that other place and time, and to that other woman.

"Of course I will."

THE NORNS

The people here do not realise that the land beneath their feet drifts on hidden tides. Our planet is a vast cauldron always on the boil, perpetually seeking to shed its terrible heat. Heat runs in currents: it seeps outwards from the core and travels towards the crust, then turns and journeys back again. The crust it encounters is not seamless, but a series of curved plates that fit together like a puzzle. As the currents circle and writhe they drag upon the plates, pulling them apart or thrusting them together. The plates buckle to form mountains, or slide beneath one another, melting back into the earth's mantle. When they are wrenched apart, new crust rises up from the fevered depths below. In this way, the crust of the earth neither grows nor shrinks, but continuously regenerates itself, like the skin of a lizard.

FREYA

hen Freyr and I were young, we once climbed to Hekla's summit. It took us many hours, and when we finally reached the snowline, we looked around us with dismay. Up close, the snow was brittle and grey, as if it had lain there for centuries. Undeterred, Freyr made a snowball and threw it at me. It hit my face, a hard ball of granular ice that stuck briefly to my skin, then fell to the ground. He walked over to me and raised a hand to my cheek, where an angry welt was already forming. We both looked down at the dirty ball at our feet, stunned by its violence.

Now when I think of Freyr, I imagine the youth that walked beside me that day, rather than the man he has become. Looking back, it is difficult to fathom how close we once were. We spent all our days together, and could read each other's thoughts without trying. Where is he now, the boy who threw the ball of ice that day? And what happens to our former self when we change? Does its soul hover around us, like an unseen mist? Or does it die and disperse, like ashes in the wind?

Adolescence wreaked havoc on my family. Freyr and I were torn asunder by the changes in our bodies. He grew restless and irritable, and I became rebellious. My beauty had fast become a burden. By the time I was thirteen, men halted mid-sentence when I entered a room, mouths agape, their thoughts momentarily forgotten. I fled from their attentions. The falcon cloak set me free:

with it I disappeared often, and at length.

My father too was disconcerted by the changes. He doted on me as a child, but his affection dwindled as I grew. As I approached puberty, my burgeoning sexuality alarmed him. One day, I emerged dripping from the baths, and he looked at my unclothed body as if seeing it for the first time. His face flushed and he immediately turned away. "Cover yourself, Freya," he said with an irritated flick of his hand, as if my nakedness was an insect that would not let him be. Gradually, it dawned on me that he did not know how to father a woman, only a girl.

But it was Freyr who was most affected, for my beauty tormented him. As children, we had tumbled like spring lambs, our limbs constantly entwined. And for much of our childhood we shared the same bed, often waking in each other's arms. But as puberty loomed, Freyr distanced himself. Suddenly, he could no longer abide my teasing, and if I laid a hand affectionately upon his arm, he instantly withdrew. His behaviour puzzled me at first, but I came to understand that Freyr could not reconcile himself to his own desire. He wanted me, just as all the others did, but dared not show it, even to himself.

Even Odin was not immune to my beauty. The day he gave me the feather form, he waited for me in the forest. I saw him from the sky, standing in a small clearing some distance from my father's house. At once I understood that the cloak was not a gift but a privilege I must pay for. I landed softly on the ground beside him, shrugging off the cloak in one movement. No words passed between us. The air was warm, but even so I trembled as his hands began to remove my clothes. He undressed me slowly, with quiet deliberation, as he'd done a thousand times before with a thousand different women.

When I was naked, he ran his hands down the length of my body, pausing at the join between my legs. Not once did he remove his gaze from mine. Did I want him? I was sixteen and still a virgin. Like most girls my age, I was obsessed with men. Though Odin was as old as the hills around us, he had the virility of a young man. His masculinity terrified yet enthralled me. I'd been taught from childhood that he alone had perfect knowledge. That day, I was frightened he would see right through me to the core of my desire, for I thought that I was somehow aberrant in my yearnings. But I wanted a clue to the mysteries that were unfolding in my body. So I lay with him on the damp, cool earth, thinking it was only right that he should be the one to have me. I knew as well that it would infuriate those around me: my own father, of course, but most especially, Freyr.

Afterwards, the spell was broken. I did not lie with him again, though he entreated me on several occasions. Soon, I realised that sleeping with him had conferred upon me a special power. When I returned to my father's house, Freyr looked at me and in an instant knew what had transpired. He stood in front of me, blocking my way into the house.

"Where were you?" he demanded.

"In the forest," I replied. I stepped past him and he grabbed my arm, pulling me around sharply towards him.

"Alone?"

I looked him in the eye. "With Odin."

He stared at me, his hand still tightly clamped around my arm. "You fool," he said bitterly. "The skalds will speak of this for generations."

"Your concern for my reputation is touching," I said drily.

"For nine months we shared the same womb, Freya!

What hurts you also damages me."

"Then perhaps it was you I should have slept with," I countered evenly. We looked at each other for a long, angry moment. I had spoken the unspeakable: Freyr could not abide such candour. He released my arm, pushing past me out of the door. Three weeks later, he met Sif and proposed to her at once. Now his love for her is all-consuming, just as his love for me once was. Freyr hates me now, precisely because I am not his.

After that, I avoided men altogether, until the day I met my future husband. Od was the first man I ever came across who did not stammer in my presence. He was indifferent to me, and I loved him for it. Instantly and blindly, and with a reckless abandon I have since become famous for. The day we met, I had flown deep into the central highlands, seeking a spot where I could be alone. I found it on a high desert plateau, where a hidden spring had forced its way up through the lava shield, forming an oasis. The water was a brilliant cobalt blue. It spread like fingers across the plateau, and all around it lay a bed of thick, luminous green moss. I lay upon the moss, turned my face to the sun and listened to the birds call around me. Eventually, I slept.

When I woke, it was to the sound of splashing. I sat up and stared at the spring, where I saw a man swimming. I watched in stunned silence, for the area was remote, and I could see no horse on which he'd travelled. At length, he hauled himself onto the moss some distance away from me, the water running from his chest in little streams. I could see he was not young, for his dark hair was streaked with grey. But he was fit and strong, and I liked the way he slid his lean frame into his tunic, and the care he took with his feet, which he dried separately, forcing the cloth in between each toe.

After he finished, I saw him finger something in the

grass, and when he stood, he held a flower. Curious, I walked over to him. He was staring down at the flower: a delicate purple blossom on the end of a long, slender stalk. He raised his head and looked at me without surprise. "Butterwort," he said. "Full of grace, yet it kills without mercy." He held up the base of the stem, which sprung from a small crown of hairy yellow leaves. Something moved in the leaves and I peered more closely. A tiny insect struggled in their centre, held fast by a sticky liquid. "Soon, the edges of the leaf will curl," he explained, "trapping what's inside. By nightfall, the insect will be gone." He handed me the flower. "You see? It's not only men who are murderous." Then he picked up his satchel and turned to go.

"How did you get here?" I asked.

He looked surprised. "On foot," he said. "How else?"

I was nineteen at the time, and Od was twice my age. He'd been married twice before. Both wives had died: the first he'd lost to illness, the second to the sea. Od had not mourned their passing, he told me, but rather, had wished them well on their journey to the afterworld, and turned his sights towards new horizons. I suppose this was an early warning I should have heeded: a red flag heralding his deep conceit and self-regard. But I was nineteen and naïve enough to think that I could contain Od's affections in a way his first two wives could not.

Ours was a brief courtship. At my insistence, we married quickly. By then I was anxious to escape the confines of my father's house. Od had travelled widely, had been as far east as Babylon, as far south as Bavaria, had sailed to Greenland and Vinland, and even to the Emerald Isles. He'd studied the runes, was fond of poetry, and had accumulated some degree of wealth on his travels. He was also a keen botanist.

"Look," he said one day, holding up a delicate fern we'd come across. He laid the long, slim tendrils gingerly upon the ground. "We shall call it Freya's Hair," he said, caressing each frond with the tip of his finger. And for the moment, I was pleased that his love of plants and his love for me had somehow merged. But some weeks later, when he discovered a tiny white flower and named it Freya's Tears, I grew unsettled, as if the flower itself was a portent of things to come

Only a few months into our marriage, I came across him in our bedchamber hurriedly stuffing spare clothing in a satchel. I was speechless at first, and in his haste he took no notice of my reaction.

"Where are you going?" I uttered.

"There's a ship on the coast bound for Alexandria," he said without pausing.

"Alexandria," I repeated dumbly.

"They say it has the finest turrets of any city in the world!"

"I'll come with you. We'll take the falcon suit."

Od stopped and looked at me with amused surprise. He stepped forward and planted a kiss upon my forehead. "Freya," he said. "Bird-wife. I shall not be gone long."

He returned four months later, as if only a night had passed during his absence. I had managed to busy myself over time, had tended his garden with care in the hope that his gratitude would prevent him from ever leaving me again. Still, I felt numb with relief when he walked through the door. "I've brought a gift for you, bird-wife," he said triumphantly, "from my travels." He removed a bronze belt encrusted with jewels of every colour from around his waist, and held it up for me to see. "Do you like it?" He was smiling now, his face an open question. I was too bewildered to answer, not by the generosity of his gift, but by his utter nonchalance in the giving of it. It was as if he'd been to market that morning and purchased me a trinket.

That evening, he made love to me for the first time in four months, not with eager abandon as I'd anticipated, but with restrained tenderness and studied affection. He used fine words that night, entreated me in the most exquisite terms. Indeed, his words shone like the polished gems on the belt he'd brought back for me. But even as he uttered them, I found myself wondering where, and from whom, he'd acquired them. And whether he'd paid dearly.

Afterwards, he slept like a dead man. I lay awake until dawn, wondering whether I should tell him about the child that had formed fleetingly in my womb during his absence, only to wither before its limbs had taken shape. I decided against it. We had not spoken of children, Od and I. He was a patient and attentive gardener, but I wondered whether his nurturing instincts would extend beyond seedlings.

Alexandria was his first sojourn. Two months after his return, he set sail for Constantinople, and the following spring, for Damascus. By then, I'd realised that Od could not stay in one place long enough to rear a weed, let alone a child. He brought me no more gifts after that first trip. Not the usual sort, at any rate. Instead, his bags were laden with exotic seeds and tiny cuttings, their roots shrouded in moss that he dampened each morning with sweet water on the long voyage home. Upon his return from Damascus, he spread them out upon the bed for me to admire, and I feigned interest, wondering which of us was mad. He held up a shrivelled stem. "The seeds of this can cure toothache," he said, cradling the dead flower head in his palm as if it held the secret to everlasting life. He laid the pod down and with two fingers picked up something I felt certain was mouse dung. "And this is a seed for an orchid so rare it has never been successfully cultivated. Ours would be the first!" I was incredulous. That night it occurred to me that the inevitable had happened: our marriage had begot nothing more than a plant.

The last time he left, I went with him. He did not know it, of course. He set sail one fine spring morning and did not see me soaring overhead. The journey nearly killed me. I was capable of faster flight, but did not dare lose sight of his ship, so I stayed aloft for whole days at a time, only resting after darkness fell, concealed in a dark corner of the stern. One night, he rose in the small hours to relieve himself, and I felt certain he would discover me. It was a still, cloudless night with a brilliant harvest moon, and as he finished his business and turned towards me, my heart was beating wildly. This is it and he will know, I thought. But then he looked right through me, and in that moment I came to understand that I was invisible to my husband, both as a bird and as a wife.

I flew home the next morning, determined not to follow him again, and resolved to finish with the marriage upon his return. But the days dragged into weeks and the weeks into months and nearly a year later, I broke my promise to myself and went in search of him again. After all, I thought, one cannot divorce a memory. It took me three months to find him. And when I did, he was sitting on a rock in the middle of a desert, sipping a small bowl of what looked to be wet leaves. I stared down at the bowl in disgust. He is even drinking plants, I thought. Od looked up at me and smiled. He showed no sign of remorse or even surprise.

"Our marriage is finished," I said.

"Of course it is," he replied.

Afterwards, I flew home. They said I wept along the way. They said my tears fell like rain and flooded the earth with my sorrow. If so, I have no memory of it. What I recall is a kind of blinding emptiness I'd not experienced before or since, during which I lost all ability to think or feel. Once home, I told my father Od was dead, which was the truth, as far as I was concerned. In fact, our marriage had foundered long before.

My first impulse after this was to renounce the world of men. This was quickly followed by a second, stronger impulse to embrace love in whatever form it came to me. I decided on the latter, telling myself I had a duty to fulfil. If I was not familiar with love in all its guises, how could I help those who came to me for assistance? That night, I donned my falcon suit and flew towards the coast, choosing a subject at random from the air. He was a fisherman: young, weathered and handsome, though his beard was littered with scales and he stank of the sea. We spent three days together, during which time he spoke only of tides and nets and gills. By the end, I could bear the sea no longer, much less his talk of cod.

Three days was too long, I decided, to be with *any* man. I invented a range of aliases: I was an escaped slave, an Irish princess, the wife of an outlaw, a wealthy widow. I travelled widely, taking lovers everywhere I went. I did not discriminate among them: they came in all shapes and sizes, young and old, rich and poor. I developed something of a penchant for the broken-hearted, lurking outside temples where they unwittingly sought my intervention. No sooner had they uttered their devotions than I'd appear, take them by the hand, and lead them away for comfort and solace.

Perhaps this was an abuse of my position. But how quickly the lovelorn forgot their purpose in my presence! So this is mortal love, I thought: weak-willed and short-lived. I decided to return to Asgard, to sample the delights my own race had to offer. It was here, practically on my doorstep, that I met Ottar. I hesitate to use the word love in connection with him. I don't know what it was we had. Lust certainly played a part. As did jealousy, anger and mistrust. Malice and betrayal made a brief, final appearance. In all, my relationship with Ottar was a long strand of ugly words that formed themselves into a bitter necklace.

But first, I should describe the man himself, for he had some unusual qualities. At times he was a boar. Not a *bore*, but the short, bristled variety with a snout and four legs. Like me, he could change shape, though in his case, the shape was less pleasing than my own. As a boar, he couldn't fly but he could run like lightning and could squeeze through very small spaces when he needed to, and could therefore disappear easily, especially in heavy undergrowth, which I discovered to my dismay towards the end of our affair. He was more attractive than most boars, as his bristles were made of gold. But while I'm partial to fine metals, I preferred him as a man.

He hated my falcon cloak. I think it made him feel inferior, an emotion that does not sit well among men in general, and the Aesir in particular. He was the patron of hunters everywhere and took his role so seriously that if a particular hunt was not successful, he felt compelled to intervene. Hence, stags would occasionally drop dead from muttered oaths. And migratory birds would fall, exhausted, from the skies. He had an inflated sense of his own importance, and refused to let nature take its course. But he was clever and virile. And exceptionally handsome, when not rooting about in the earth.

It ended badly. I went looking for him one day, and found his thighs wrapped around a swan maiden. He was so startled that he unwittingly changed shape. She got the shock of a lifetime, gold bristles or not. This last affair curdled something deep inside me. Afterwards, I shut myself inside the walls of Sessruminger with only my cats for company. Cats, I decided, had certain advantages over men. They were loyal without being sycophantic, independent without being absent, and affectionate without being rapacious. That they choke up balls of fur and leave dead rodents at my feet is unfortunate. But it is not grounds for divorce.

The last time I saw Freyr, he told me he was going abroad and that he might not return. And though I searched his face, I found no trace of sorrow or regret. That day he behaved towards me in a way that was both familiar and dismissive, as if our past was a cloak he'd worn for many years but was now happy to discard. I realised then that he'd been taken from me long before. As with Od, there was nothing left to mourn.

DVALIN

or two days, Dvalin stays by Idun's bedside. And though her condition rapidly improves, Bragi's creeping resentment of his presence threatens to snap the slender bond of kinship that lies between them. "He agitates with you here," Idun admits when she and Dvalin are alone. It is a rare moment of privacy, for Bragi has remained with them almost constantly.

"Agitates? His jealousy is like a boil that worsens by the hour. He'll soon burst if I don't leave."

Idun laughs. "It's true. You must go. But he's a good man, Dvalin. And his love for me is boundless."

"What of your love for him?"

Idun hesitates. "I used to think that love was like a small door deep inside us that we could open if we chose," she says finally. "Now I think it chooses us."

"If we're lucky."

"Yes," she concedes, frowning. "What of you?"

"What *of* me?"

"Have you never known a woman's love?"

He smiles wanly, and thinks of the women he has known: his mother, Idun herself, Menglad. "What face would it wear?" He teases.

Idun laughs. "I wouldn't know." Dvalin watches as she takes up a small piece of tapestry beside her bed and extracts a needle from a hollow birdbone hung about her neck. He is relieved to hear her speak lightly on such subjects. But his fears about her health are not completely assuaged. He lowers his voice.

"Idun. I am loath to leave you."

"And I am loath to see you go." She lays aside the tapestry and leans forward, grasping his hands in her own. "But you must. Please don't worry. There is much to live for, Dvalin. I am still hoping for a child. She smiles at him reassuringly, and gives his hands another squeeze before taking up her tapestry once again. "Perhaps Menglad can help," she adds, without looking up.

The mention of Menglad robs him of speech. He stares at her delicate fingers, at the deft way they work the thread, at the flash of sharpened whalebone as it disappears beneath the cloth. "Perhaps," he says finally. His voice rasps, but Idun doesn't notice.

Later that day, Bragi ferries him across the river in a small skiff. Dvalin can see his mount grazing at some distance on the other side. He whistles for her, long and low. The mare lifts her head and after a brief pause, comes slowly trotting towards the river. Away from the house and Idun, Bragi's mood has already lifted. He even smiles a little as he rows. By the time they reach the far side, the horse is waiting patiently, head still, nostrils quivering. Dvalin leaps from the prow onto the grassy bank, then turns and holds the skiff fast in the current. Bragi does not rise to clasp his shoulder in farewell. Instead, he keeps his seat, hands firmly locked upon the oars. "Take care of her," Dvalin says by way of parting. The older man's eyes narrow briefly before he nods. When Dvalin releases the prow, Bragi pulls hard on the oars, sending the skiff darting out into the current. Dvalin stands for a minute, following the boat's progress with his eyes. His words had somehow sounded like an accusation. Had he meant them to?

He mounts the horse and turns it south, intending to follow a different route on his return. He will travel via

Laxardal, where his father's closest friend, Hogni, lives. After a night's rest, he'll ride on to Nidavellir, then make the journey over the mountains to see Menglad. The prospect is not a happy one. The crossing itself is arduous at the best of times. But once over the pass, he must make his way through hostile territory, to the woman who once spurned him.

∽➁➁∼

Several hours later, as he approaches Laxardal, his mood lightens. His horse has begun to tire, but Dvalin urges him on, anxious to arrive at Hogni's farm before nightfall. He rides into the setting sun and all around him, the valley is transformed by the evening light. The mossy turf glows bright green beneath him, and the sun's rays shimmer like ice crystals on the tiny streams which cut across the valley floor. He feels suddenly elated as he lopes his horse across the valley, as if anything could happen in a world filled with such light. It lifts and carries him all the way to Hogni's farm, and his spirits are still aglow when he strides through the front door.

"Greetings, Hogni." The old man is seated by the fire tanning a deer skin. He looks up in surprise, then slowly rises, his eyes brightening.

"Welcome home, my son." The two men embrace warmly. Dvalin cannot help but notice the shortness in Hogni's breath, and the way in which his movements are laboured, as if he wears his age like a cumbersome suit of armour. It has been three months since his last visit, and Hogni seems a decade older. "We did not expect you so soon. You've come from Nidavellir?"

"From Idun. She's been unwell, but is recovering now."

"I'm sorry to hear of it. How long will you stay?"

"I can only stop the night, I'm afraid."

"Then we can at least furnish you with a warm hearth and a full belly."

"How are things with the farm?"

Hogni sighs. "Age brings no peace, I'm afraid. Skallagrim is dead."

"I can't say I'm sorry."

"His sons have raised the land claims."

Dvalin frowns. "They have no right. The claims were settled long ago."

Hogni shrugs. "The sword is law to them. They have no other."

"We have known this for some time," says Dvalin grimly.

"Skallagrim and I may have been enemies, but at least we understood one another," Hogni muses. "At any rate, I have granted his sons the lands they dispute."

Dvalin raises an eyebrow in surprise. "The eastern boundary? Why?"

"Please, Dvalin. I know what you are thinking. Jarl sacrificed his life for that land. But a plot of earth that has been soaked in blood holds little value for me now. I have seen too much of life pass by. Too much of death."

Dvalin nods thoughtfully. "Perhaps it is best to draw an end to the matter." He hesitates. "Perhaps we should have done so years ago."

Hogni places his hand atop Dvalin's. "Best not to speculate on what might have been. How goes life in Nidavellir?"

"My people prosper."

"Your father's legacy is a strong one."

"His successor is an able man in his own right."

"I miss his conversation," Hogni muses. "You too, no doubt."

Dvalin purses his lips but says nothing.

"I wonder what he would make of our present predicament," continues Hogni. "Olaf's missionaries are everywhere these days, preaching lies and blasphemy. They say nine godi have been baptised already, nearly a quarter of the parliament. In a few days we ride to the Althing, and there is talk of a separate encampment. They have even elected their own lawspeaker." He sighs heavily. "This island will be torn in two if they persist."

"You fear bloodshed at the Althing?"

Hogni shrugs. "It is possible."

"Does Fulla go with you?"

He nods. "Fulla will be at my side. She grows older by the hour. Fulla the child is no longer with us, it seems." He hesitates. "Sometimes I wonder who has taken her place."

"She will not disappoint you, Hogni."

"No, of course not. At any rate, we must look towards her future. I will not be here for ever."

"You forget that I am here," Dvalin reminds him gently. "I made a vow to Jarl to look after her."

"Still, it is my plan that she should marry. And soon."

"You have spoken to her?"

"Not yet. I've no wish to alarm her."

Dvalin raises an eyebrow. "It's her life we speak of, Hogni."

"Yes," he says. "Yes, of course. I shall raise the matter with her soon."

Later that evening, Dvalin finds Fulla alone in the stable, tending to her small chestnut gelding. She does not see him at first, and he listens quietly in the doorway as she murmurs to the animal, brushing down his sides as she speaks. The horse stamps its feet and nickers softly as she moves around his body. Dvalin lingers for a moment. The sight both pains and pleases him, for just as Hogni deteriorates with age, Fulla seems to grow increasingly into herself each time he visits. He has watched her from birth, has seen her transform from a red-faced infant to a smirking child, to an almost incandescent young woman. She is pale and small but no less striking for it, with wheat-coloured hair that hangs to her waist, and finely cut features. She moves patiently and confidently about the horse, reassuring the animal with her voice and her touch.

"You'll be riding him to the Assembly, I suppose," he asks finally. Fulla looks up in surprise, then breaks into a wide smile.

"Uncle." She crosses over to him and they embrace.

"Is it your first trip to the Althing?" he asks.

She shakes her head. "Father took me when I was five. I remember an enormous field of tents all draped in different coloured canopies, like a vast carpet of flowers. And more people than I'd ever seen. By the end of the week, there was so much mud I had to ride on Father's shoulders. You should come with us, Dvalin."

"I dislike mud," he says, smiling. "And people, come to think of it. Anyway, I am only passing through."

"I'm sorry we can't keep you longer." She picks up a brush and begins to groom the gelding, while Dvalin seats himself on a stool.

"Fulla, Hogni spoke to me of a betrothal."

She makes a face. "I fear he will present me with a crooked husband. A man thrice my age who speaks a harsh tongue and worships a strange idol."

"He merely wishes to secure your future, Fulla."

"I am not opposed to marriage, Dvalin. But I would prefer to have a hand in the selection."

"I do not blame you."

"Besides, I value happiness over security."

"One would hope for both."

She smiles. "Yes, of course."

"Your father set great stock by your happiness," he says gently.

She replaces the brush on a shelf and stares down at it thoughtfully, her back to him. "Do you miss him, Dvalin?"

"Very much."

"So do I. Grandfather rarely speaks his name."

"It is a terrible thing to lose a son."

"It is a worse thing to lose a father. Particularly when you've never known your mother." Her voice hardens slightly at this last.

"Fulla," he says softly. He takes a step forward, unsure what to say. She remains with her back to him, fingering the reins. It was easier when she was young, he thinks. A broken toy, a bruised knee – these things he could handle. But the uncertainties of adolescence. He is suddenly out of his depth.

"Anyway," she continues, "you are more a son to him than Papa was."

"No, Fulla. You are wrong. There is no substitute for blood in kinship."

She turns around to face him. "I am not so certain," she says slowly. Dvalin thinks fleetingly of his own father. Perhaps she is right.

"Fulla, your grandfather loves you very much."

She turns to the horse and places her hands upon its flank. "I know," she says pensively. He crosses over to her and lays a hand upon her shoulder. They stand quietly for a moment, and then Fulla recollects herself. She gives him a faint smile. "So we will journey to the Althing. And find ourselves a husband."

"Not just any husband," he admonishes. "A man of consequence."

"And good looks," she adds, grinning.

He raises an eyebrow. "Of wealth?"

She nods vigorously. "Naturally. And good humour."

"Not bent."

"Nor blind."

"Nor violent."

She looks at him in mock horror.

"Whose feet do not smell," he adds with a smile.

She laughs. "Precisely."

"Don't worry," he says reassuringly. "They will fall to their knees at the sight of you."

"I would rather they stood."

That night, on a made-up pallet by the fire, Dvalin cannot banish thoughts of Fulla's father from his mind. It is true that Jarl's relationship with Hogni was a turbulent one. They disagreed on nearly everything: the day-to-day running of the farm, the raising of Fulla, the precious jewel they shared between them, and the constant territorial disputes with neighbours that plague the settlers of this region. One day, Jarl rode off in anger to settle a problem over grazing rights at the eastern edge of the property. According to a farmhand, the boundary markers had been moved surreptitiously in the night. Against Hogni's counsel, Jarl vowed to resolve the matter once and for all. He rode straight into an ambush. Four riders lay in wait for him. He was a strong fighter but no match against four. Hours later he was found by a shepherd, unconscious but with the shadow of a pulse. The shepherd loaded Jarl onto the back of his horse and brought him home, where he died three days later, never regaining consciousness.

Dvalin stayed by his side until the end. The wounds he'd sustained were horrific, but Dvalin silently hoped Jarl would wake and speak his mind before he died. Years before, he'd promised Jarl that in the event of his death, he would see to Fulla's happiness. But Hogni was Fulla's only blood relation. When the time came, her upbringing was entirely in her grandfather's hands. Dvalin was powerless to intervene without risking offence to the one man who had been more of a father to him than his own. And yet he'd sworn an oath to Jarl to watch over her.

Dvalin turns on his side and stares into the fire. Hogni's decision to marry Fulla off quickly strikes him as impulsive, the whim of an old man in the twilight of his life. Dvalin closes his eyes, concentrates upon the heat of the fire on his face. Sometime during the evening his right temple has begun to ache again. He takes a deep breath and lets it out slowly, feeling his heart beat in rhythm to the throbbing in his head. Fulla must be allowed to choose her own husband, he decides. He resolves to speak to Hogni in the morning. But the prospect only sharpens the pain.

∽✦✦∾

Hogni's eyes darken with suspicion. The two men sit hunched over on the narrow wooden shelf that runs around the edge of the tiny bathhouse. Both are naked, their bodies flushed pink from the heat and covered in rivers of sweat. Beneath their feet is an open hearth and a pile of smooth, red-hot stones heated by a peat fire. Hogni reaches down and picks a large wooden ladle out of a bucket of water by his side. He tips the water onto the stones in a smooth cascading motion. At once, the rocks hiss and the steam rises up and envelops them anew.

He drops the ladle back into the bucket with a clatter. Both men stare down at the billowing clouds of steam still rising from the stones. The heat is intense and the air stifling. After a moment, Dvalin turns to him. "Hogni, you must listen. I am only suggesting that Fulla should have a hand in the decision. After all, it is she who must live with the consequences, not you."

Hogni shifts uneasily on the bench, moving a minute distance away. He swats at the steam with one hand, but does not meet Dvalin's gaze. "The man I choose for Fulla will be deserving. I promise you that much."

Dvalin nods. "Of course I know this. But she should be given a say. Her happiness is at stake."

The old man stands and reaches for a linen cloth hanging on a peg, signalling an end to the discussion. He wraps it tightly around his waist and steps down onto the warm flagstone floor. He shuffles the few steps to the bathhouse door, pulling back the heavy fur covering the entrance, and disappears, allowing the flap to shut behind him. Dvalin sighs with exasperation. He rises and grabs the other linen cloth and rubs himself dry, then hurriedly pulls on his clothes.

Dvalin returns to the house and begins to pack his saddlebag in preparation for his return journey. After a minute, Hogni emerges fully dressed from his bedchamber. He seats himself on the tanning bench in the corner and begins silently working on the deerskin. When Dvalin is ready to go, he crosses over to where Hogni sits. "Think on my words, Hogni. I will come again, after the Althing." The old man lays the deerskin to one side and slowly rises. He clasps Dvalin to him briefly.

"Go in peace, my son. May Thor watch over you," he adds.

Outside, a fine mist is falling. The early morning sky is a deep mossy green. Dvalin saddles his horse and rides off. When he is some distance from the house, he turns to see a lone rider galloping after him. He pulls his own mount to a standstill. It is Fulla. She wears a long dark blue cloak that flies out behind her, and her hair is clipped back in a mass of golden tangles. As she draws near, he can see the pale coldness in her face, and can just make out the mist upon her cheeks.

"You didn't say goodbye," she says a little breathlessly.

"I'm sorry."

"The two of you have quarrelled, haven't you? Over me."

He smiles. "I've achieved nothing, I'm afraid. Except to incur his wrath."

"You've won my gratitude."

He smiles at her weakly. "Then it was worth it."

She urges her horse forward until it is almost abreast with his own, then leans towards him, pressing something into his hand. "Goodbye, Dvalin." Fulla turns the horse back towards the house and spurs it into a gallop. Dvalin looks down at the object in his hand: a small bronze medallion with Jarl's mark stamped upon it. He closes his fingers tightly round the medallion, as if it can somehow bring him closer to its owner. In the distance, he can just make out the figure of Fulla as she reaches the house. Someone else waits for her in the yard, the lumbering form of her grandfather. Hogni holds the reins of the horse while Fulla dismounts, and Dvalin watches as the two embrace. The sight pains him, for in that instant they appear to recede, slipping even further away.

THE NORNS

The earth is inconceivably old. But Iceland is barely a child. We saw it burst and bubble from beneath the sea, a lump of smoking rock that grew and grew until it could no longer be ignored. This island is unlike all others, for it grows still, straddling two great slabs of crust that are slowly spreading, as if prized apart by giants. As the plates move, the earth's hot sap wells up from deep inside to fill the gap, forming a mountainous ridge along the sea floor that stretches for eternity. Iceland is the only point along this ridge that has risen above the waves. We have watched it build up over millions of years: ten thousand layers of overlapping lava flows.

FREYA

rerr plants his feet and crosses his arms defiantly. Next to him, Alfrigg twitches with apprehension, his head quivering from side to side.

"It's not for sale," says Grerr.

"Never. Out of the question," echoes Alfrigg.

"There's nothing to match it. Here or anywhere."

"It represents a lifetime's work. Many lifetimes. We... all of us... all of ours, I mean," stammers Alfrigg. He blushes.

"Four, in fact," adds Grerr pointedly.

I do not answer. Instead, I scrutinise them. All my life, I have found it easy to see into the minds of men. These two may be dwarves, but they are no different from the others I have known. *Smaller. Hairier.* The one on the left is obviously the leader. He is hairy even by the standards of his own people, with bushy eyebrows all askew, like the bristles of a boar, and a beard so coarse it leaps out from his chin and distracts me with its movement when he speaks.

By contrast, the other one is almost baby-faced. A thin, whiskery beard, and a wide, shiny forehead that occasionally creases with surprise. His eyes are large and round. They lack their brother's meanness, and dart about nervously while he speaks. Every now and then, they alight on the necklace, and he smiles with joy, as if he's seeing it for the first time.

The brothers shift uncomfortably under my gaze. I

tilt my head to one side and speak thoughtfully. "Your lives are not yet over. Indeed, you are still young."

Alfrigg colours anew, and even Grerr is forced to give a little cough. But then he shakes his head in protest. "You do not understand. It required all our skill as craftsman. And our cunning. I doubt that we will ever produce anything so worthy."

I realise then that he has little else. But my mind is latched firmly on the necklace, and I will not be deterred. "For whom did you labour so long and hard?"

Alfrigg blinks uncomprehendingly. Grerr narrows his eyes with distrust. "For ourselves," he says.

"But it is an adornment."

Alfrigg nods slowly. Grerr only glowers.

"You do not wear it," I continue.

"No one wears it." Grerr's tone is adamant. Alfrigg reaches out and fingers the necklace gently, as if to reassure both himself and it that nothing has changed. Suddenly, his face brightens.

"We intend to display it," he says proudly. "Just so."

"For yourselves?"

Alfrigg opens his mouth to speak, but Grerr cuts him off. "For whomever we choose."

At that moment, I walk the few steps to where the necklace rests atop the pillar and reach my hand out to touch it. Carefully, I lift it from the cloth, cradling the pendant in my palm. Both men lean forward anxiously. I can almost smell their apprehension. I do not blame them. The pendant is warm to the touch and seems to pulse gently in my hand, like the beating heart of a small animal. I long to close my fingers tightly around it and run. Instead, I force myself to replace the necklace on its cloth, then take a step backwards, turning to them.

"But you do not display it. You keep it locked away."

Alfrigg raises his hands in a conciliatory shrug. "It is too precious."

"It would be stolen," adds Grerr.

"Then it is no use to anyone."

I look from one to the next. They frown. Alfrigg shoots a worried glance at Grerr.

"Surely it was meant for more?"

"Such as?"

I flash him a smile. "The neck of a beautiful woman."

"Like yours." His tone is icy.

I shrug. "Or some other. Perhaps mine is not sufficiently beautiful."

Now both men stare at me.

"That would not be the case," murmurs Alfrigg finally.

I almost laugh. I cannot help but like him. There is something of the innocent about this man that is completely lacking in his brother. But it is Grerr who must decide, so I turn my attention to him. "I can pay well. In gold or gems. Or the currency of your choice."

"We've no need of your money," says Grerr. He has uncrossed his arms and has shifted his stance. I do not know whether it is this, or something in his tone, that tells me he has changed his mind.

"Perhaps there is something else," I say. The words spill softly from my lips, as if they have come from somewhere else. They tumble forth and come to rest in the empty space between us.

Grerr nods. Just once. "Perhaps there is," he says, inevitably.

And then I feel my stomach pitch. For I know only too well what they lack.

And that is the touch of a woman.

BERLING

few hours later, Berling sits opposite his mother on a wooden bench beside the fire. They play nine men's morris, a game he usually wins, though he has begun to wonder whether his mother really tries. For Berling, the approach of adulthood has been heralded by self-doubt. He can tell he's growing older, because with each passing day he loses another slice of youthful certainty.

His mother rolls a playing piece back and forth between her palms, concentrating on the three concentric squares in front of them. With his father's help, Berling carved the board directly onto the wooden bench when he was six. He still remembers how his hand slipped at one point and the knife leapt across the grain into his father's forearm. The six-year-old Berling watched with wide eyes as a small bead of crimson bubbled up from his father's skin. His father put a finger to his lips, raised his eyebrows conspiratorially, and nodded in the direction of his mother, who was working in a corner of the room. With a wipe of his sleeve, he swept all trace of the accident away, then reached forward to steady Berling's grasp with his own. Together, they finished carving the board. Berling still remembers the warm, meaty clench of his father's hand, and the sight of his swollen, mottled knuckles, for his father was already an old man by this time.

Not like a father at all, in fact. More like a grandfather, or an aging uncle, who stayed at home with them for interludes but was more often absent, and eventually disappeared for good. He remembers once tearing through the tunnels with some friends, when he barrelled around a corner and ran straight into his father's belly. The old man had been deep in conversation with his advisers, en route to an assembly. Somewhat winded, he stopped short and lifted Berling's chin in the palm of his hand. For a brief instant, Berling saw that his father did not recognise him. The two stared at each other for a moment, then Berling turned and fled, leaving his father speechless in his wake. Later that night, he had feigned illness and gone to bed early, rather than face his father's embarrassment.

Now he wishes he had more such memories, for they are all that remains. He sneaks a glance at his mother. She is still attractive, though her looks are somehow girded by her practical nature. *Does she miss his father?* He wouldn't know. Even when his father was alive, his mother had seemed self-sufficient. She worked hard, laughed if there was time for it, and saw to both their needs with utmost efficiency. Lately, he has begun to wonder who saw to hers. But such thoughts only make him feel inadequate.

His mother clucks with satisfaction and places the small piece of bone she is holding on a square. "Mill!" she says triumphantly, removing one of his opposing pieces from the board.

He studies the configuration for a moment, then plants a new piece in a threesome of his own, removing one of her pieces in turn. His mother frowns at the board, and after a few moments, makes a move of little consequence. He steals a glance at her, for she has missed something obvious. *Should he tell her?* But he sees at once that her mind has flown elsewhere. She does this constantly, steps in and out of his world with ease, and it confounds him. He looks back down at the board. The game has lost its edge now. It is little more than a scattering of bones on wood.

"So tell me about her, then," his mother says abruptly.

"Who?"

"You know who. Where does she come from?"

He shrugs. "South, I think. Somewhere in the mountains."

"Name?"

He hesitates. She is bound to discover sooner or later. But not from him. "She didn't say."

"And is she *very* beautiful?"

"Why?" He looks up at her, uncomprehending. His mother flashes him a smile, then deliberately looks back down at the board.

"You blush to speak of her, Berling," she says quietly.

He takes a deep breath and exhales slowly. The room does feel hot. His mother makes another pointless move, then sits back.

"So is she young? Old?"

"I didn't notice." He sees the corners of her mouth turn up slightly.

"And did your brothers settle on a price?"

Berling accidently drops the piece he is holding. He bends down to retrieve it, even as he feels his face go red. "I think so," he murmurs.

"And?" She looks at him expectantly.

He does not know what to say. They have sworn him to secrecy. He is not to tell a soul of the agreement. He is *particularly* not to breathe a word to his mother. "I don't know," he says lamely.

Gerd slaps her hand down hard on the wood. "The necklace is as much yours as theirs," she says crossly.

"You were instrumental in its making. You should get your share."

"I will, I will," he says, trying to appease her.

"When?" She waits for an answer.

He feels the burning once again in his face. His entire body is alight. "Soon."

His mother stares at him mutely.

"*Soon*," he repeats.

"Good." She leans forward and moves another piece, smiling now.

Berling looks at the board hopelessly, thinking of his brothers.

What *would* they have him do?

FULLA

he morning after Dvalin's departure, Hogni and
Fulla leave for the Althing. It is a perfect midsummer day. Large white clouds billow and drift aimlessly across a pale blue sky. From the farm at Laxardal,
they ride west across the grassy dales towards the sea. By
late afternoon, they reach the shores of Hvammsfjord,
where the Lax river meets the ocean. They turn south
and ride along the shore for a time, watching heavy
breakers roll in along the black sands. Far off across the
water, a dark purple mountain looms on the horizon,
signalling the furthest western reaches of the country.
The fjord is dotted with small dusky islands, barren out-
crops of rock, desolate and uninhabitable. Dozens of
swans and gulls wheel overhead, their cries at times
swallowed by the wind. Fulla relishes the sight and smell
of the ocean, for it has been many months, all through
the long winter, since she has been to the coast.

That night, they make camp within sight of the sea,
and are lulled to sleep by the sound of breakers rolling
into shore. The next morning they wake to heavy fog.
After a quick breakfast of flatbread and cheese, they turn
inland, heading south across the foothills of a vast range
of deep red mountains. Gradually, they leave the fog
behind them, and the sky above the jagged peaks warms
to a pale yellow. Three times that day, they must ford
rivers, searching for hoof prints in the riverbank
to find a safe crossing. The horses' nostrils flare when

they first enter the rushing waters; their eyes strain white with effort when they are eventually forced to swim. That second night, they reach a small farm on the banks of the Kvita River, old friends of Hogni's who welcome them with tankards of ale and a hearty meal of smoked mutton. Already Fulla is exhausted from two days' travel. Her legs are stiff and her backside is sore from the saddle. She eats quickly and finds a spot on a sleeping pallet at the far end of the hall, while Hogni and the others drink late into the night.

On the third day, they leave the farm behind them and continue south, past an enormous dry lake basin. They ride across the sandy bottom of the lake, and at its far end pass through two narrow lava crags, before emerging onto a vast green plain, where they pause to rest and graze the horses. After a few more hours, the grassland gives way to lava shield, its black and jagged surface disguised by blueberry and willow and dwarf birch. Hogni stops and surveys the land around them. "Now we are close," he says with an approving nod. "Just a few hours more." Fulla smiles gratefully. The horses pick their way carefully across the lava, until she catches sight of an enormous lake shimmering in the distance. "Laugarvatn," says Hogni. They reach the edge of the shield, from where she can see the entire plain of Thingvellir laid out before her.

"Look," says Hogni, pointing into the distance, "the Rift Rock of the People." She surveys the two enormous gashes in the rock, where the earth has torn itself asunder and the river Oxnare snakes its way through the valley. She can see the enormous basalt cliff that forms the backdrop for the lawspeaker, and the grassy plains in front, studded with hundreds of encampments. Her heart races at the sight of it. Without realising, she smiles.

"So," says Hogni, eyeing her. "The Althing at last. You've waited long for this."

"Eleven years," she replies, without once taking her eyes from the scene.

"Has it been that long?" Hogni muses. "Come. Our booth will be ready."

They begin the descent into the valley, and as they approach the encampment, find themselves the object of much scrutiny. Hogni nods to those he recognises and stops to greet a few old friends warmly. But it is Fulla, with her long hair and pale complexion, who draws the most attention. She quickly sees that men outnumber women at the Assembly by far. She feels a flutter of apprehension and excitement.

They ride around the outside of the encampment until they reach the northern edge. Hogni then works his way slowly through the crowd with Fulla close behind. They pass dozens of tents and booths, each stuffed with provisions and people of all ages chatting amiably, and women stirring pots over campfires. She had forgotten the sheer scale of the event. There are hundreds of people here, perhaps thousands – never has she seen so many assembled in one place.

Hogni comes to a halt in front of their booth, set low against a hillock, the last but one in its row. Fulla slides off her horse and surveys the camp. Like the others, the booth has been made of solid rock foundations and thick turf walls. Across its ceiling is a broad canvas of saffron-coloured sailcloth. The late afternoon sun casts a pale yellow glow into the booth's interior. "Well?" says Hogni.

"It's perfect," she replies.

Hogni beams. Inside, his men have already organised their provisions for the days to come. Fulla steps inside and sees the jugs of beer and mead, smoked meats hang-

112

ing from the rafters, sackcloths of grain and wooden barrels of skyr. At the rear of the booth, the sleeping pallets are stacked one upon the other to the ceiling. At night, they will be laid out side by side, covering almost the entire floor.

"Greetings, Hogni!" Fulla turns to see an old man wearing a broad felt hat and a shaggy fur cloak clasp her grandfather warmly.

"Ari," exclaims Hogni, "it is good to see you!"

"And you, my old friend. Your journey was uneventful, I hope."

"Brief by comparison to your own."

Ari shrugs. "A man must endure a bit of hardship for the greater good," he says with a smile. "You've brought a companion," he says, turning to Fulla.

"Fulla, meet my old friend Ari. From the Lake of Light in the north."

Fulla smiles. "The Lake of Light is very far, is it not?"

"I was two weeks coming," he explains. "It is a great pleasure to finally meet Jarl's child."

"The pleasure is mine," she replies.

"You must keep a close eye upon her," he says to Hogni. "She'll have few rivals here."

"Then we will have no trouble in our mission," says Hogni.

"Grandfather," she admonishes, blushing.

"Betrothal is an honest business, Fulla. One need not be ashamed."

"And you need not be so pointed in your address," she scolds.

"Come. There will be plenty of time for quarrelling," says Ari. "Now we must celebrate your arrival with a drink."

They have barely set aside their packs when Ari leads them through the crowd to his own booth. Along the way, they pass young boys wrestling in the tall grass and men playing draughts on rough hewn log benches. At one corner, a small group has gathered to hear a recitation by a skald. The poet is tall and dark, with thick bristly eyebrows that jump animatedly while he speaks.

Finally, they pause in front of Ari's booth, and an older woman immediately comes out to greet them, her face plump and criss-crossed with tiny lines. She and Hogni embrace warmly, then she turns at once to Fulla. "We have waited long to meet you," she says with an engaging smile. Despite her age, she is a handsome woman. She wears a gown of finely spun moss-green wool, held in place at the shoulder by two elaborately cast bronze brooches. Between them hangs a string of amber-coloured beads. "She is the image of Jarl, is she not?"

"She is far prettier," says Ari. He hands them each a cup of ale and beckons them to drink. A moment later, a youth emerges bleary-eyed from the back of the booth.

"Ah," says Ari. "Hogni, meet my brother's grandson."

The youth smiles sheepishly at them, still rubbing sleep from his eyes. His face is wide and heavy set, and his nut-brown hair thick and tousled. "Greetings," he says. "You must forgive me. I rode all night to get here."

"From where have you come?" asks Fulla.

He looks at her with interest. "From the far north, near Axafjord."

"I've heard of it."

"You've not been there?" he asks.

"No."

"The north has a beauty all its own," he says. "You should visit us one day."

"I should like to."

"Cold," says Hogni shaking his head. "Too cold for my liking."

Ari slaps him on the back. "You're not invited! But Fulla is welcome anytime," he jests.

"What news of Thangbrand and his men?" asks Hogni.

"They arrived yesterday. They're in a separate encampment to the east."

"How many?"

"A few hundred. Or more. The lines were quickly drawn. They nearly came to blows yesterday. But the lawspeaker intervened. It is now up to him to decide. Both sides have agreed to abide by his decision."

Hogni frowns. "Where is he now?"

"In seclusion. He has shut himself within his booth, under his cloak, since yesterday afternoon."

Hogni raises his eyebrows in disbelief. "Is he alive?"

"Of course he is! He is merely taking his time. A great weight rests upon him with this decision."

"The weight of an entire country! When will he emerge?"

"Who knows? Soon, I hope."

Hogni grunts. "I see we've missed a great deal."

"Perhaps not. His decision is what counts."

Hogni finishes his drink and hands the cup back to Ari's wife. "Come, Fulla," he says decisively. "We must unpack our things. Who knows when the lawspeaker will emerge from under his cloak? Or what the result will be?"

∾⊛⊛∽

They bid farewell and return to their booth, where they spend the next hour unpacking and organising their provisions. Hogni stops frequently to greet old acquaintances, and after a time, Fulla wanders out into the

115

crowd on her own. She makes her way towards the law rock, where a barrel-chested man speaks passionately about matters relating to land law. She listens for a time, eyeing up the crowd, made up mostly of old men. There is a mood of distraction in the air, as if the entire crowd is waiting. After a few minutes, she grows restless and turns to go, but as she winds her way back through the crowd, she sees an excited throng form just ahead of her. She sees Thorgeir the lawspeaker standing in front of his booth, his face creased with a frown. He still wears the woollen cloak wrapped tightly around his shoulders. His long grey hair hangs loose and his face seems taut with strain. The crowd continues to gather around him, until he finally moves off purposefully towards the direction she is coming from. The crowd heaves all around her. With a grim face and a resolute air, Thorgeir walks straight past her towards the law rock. Behind him, the crowd surges and jostles her along. She casts a backward glance in the direction of their booth, but does not see Hogni in the crowd. Before long, she and many others have been buoyed along and pushed up against one side of the rock wall, where she manages to perch upon a ledge a few feet off the ground.

Thorgeir advances to the law rock and quickly claims the attention of all those around. He turns and stares out over the crowd, waiting for the throng to settle. After several moments, a hush falls across the valley floor. Taking this as a signal, Thorgeir clears his throat and begins to speak. "I bring you greetings," he begins slowly. "And my most fervent hopes for peace." He pauses meaningfully. "Many years ago, the ground beneath our feet was rent by forces beyond our control. Whether you believe the fate of this valley lies in the hands of one god – or many – I urge you to listen. Just like the rocks we stand upon, our country is at risk of being torn asunder by two opposing faiths. Until now, our great strength as a people has been that we have been united by a common belief, and more importantly, by a common law. If we divide the law, we must then divide the peace. Discord and hostility will prevail, and Iceland will be ruined." A wave of noise erupts from the crowd. Thorgeir pauses, allowing time for the throng to settle. Fulla glances around her uneasily.

"We must, as one people, embrace one solution to this conflict. Violence should not be the means by which we find this solution. We must not let those prevail who are most eager to go against each other, but let us mediate the matter between the two sides so that each may win part of his case. I therefore propose that the Assembly allow me to strike a compromise – that we all have one and the same faith, and one and the same law." Thorgeir pauses again, allowing his words to reverberate across the valley floor. Fulla hears the crowd stir and murmur. She sees a number of heads bobbing vigorously in assent. "Hear, hear!" calls a man standing several feet away. "Let the lawspeaker pronounce!" A cry goes up from the crowd. Thorgeir nods and raises his hands to silence them.

"I have pondered long and hard, and the choice is not an easy one. But I have come to the conclusion that the key to our preservation is change. I proclaim that from this day forward, we shall all adopt the Christian faith. Those who have not yet received baptism shall do so here and now, before the Assembly adjourns." Again the crowd stirs, and a number of angry voices can be heard. Thorgeir moves to silence them. "However," he shouts loudly above the din, "the old faith may still be practised in the privacy of one's home. And the old laws shall stand to protect these practices insomuch as they are carried out in secret. But severe penalties shall be imposed on

117

those who publicly flaunt the old ways." He pauses, allowing his words to sink in. "Let this be my decision," he says finally. Then he steps down from the law rock and makes his way through the crowd, his face set, his eyes directed forward.

Fulla scans the throng but does not see Hogni, and wonders whether he has heard the lawspeaker's pronouncement. She dreads his reaction, for he is bound to be angry. As her eyes sweep across the crowd, they alight on the men of Skallagrim's clan. Her eyes focus on the small knot of men and finally come to rest on Vili. From far across the crowd, he is staring intently at her. She feels her face redden and instantly looks away. In the next second, she ducks through the crowd, her heart beating hard.

The booth is empty when she reaches it, but after a minute Hogni arrives with Ari, deep in conversation. She sees at once from the grim set of his face that he has heard. He barely acknowledges her as he enters the booth. "Is our faith rotten to the core?" He says angrily to Ari. "Or are we just indifferent?"

"Neither. Come Hogni, you must see: Thorgeir made the only choice he could. One that allows us to continue our way of life without interference."

Hogni scowls, his eyes sweeping the tent. "I need a drink," he grunts.

Fulla moves to him. "Let me, grandfather." She finds two ceramic cups and fills them with ale from a cask in the corner, handing one to each of them. Hogni takes the cup and downs it in one long gulp, wiping his face with the back of his hand.

"Perhaps," he admits with a sigh.

"It was necessary – both to prevent bloodshed and preserve our independence. That is what matters most! Iceland must remain free from outside interests."

"Yes," Hogni concedes. "Perhaps you are right."

Ari reaches for his arm and holds fast to his wrist. "It was bound to happen," he says intently. "Things could not remain the same. Come! You knew this deep inside."

Hogni meets his gaze with a frown, and the two men stare at each other silently for a long moment. Ari lets go of his wrist. "It need mean nothing for you personally, Hogni," Ari continues. "You can still worship any way you choose. Besides, it is just a bit of water splashed about the face," he says, breaking into a smile.

"You'll not catch me ducking my head in the freezing waters of Laugarvatn!"

"You can stop at the hot springs on the way home," laughs Ari.

Hogni manages a conciliatory smile. "Who would have thought we'd come to this?" he says, shaking his head. "Not in my lifetime." He slaps his hand upon the table forcefully. "Come! Let us refill our drink and toast what we have left." He raises his glass. "To independence."

"Here, here," concurs Ari.

"Let us forget the matter of worship," says Hogni. "And concentrate on more important business. Such as Fulla's betrothal."

Ari turns to her with an approving smile. "Indeed. We must find you a suitable match."

"I already have one in mind," says Hogni triumphantly.

Fulla's eyes widen with alarm.

FREYA

ach will have a night with me. That is our agreement. Some would think me mad. But the Vanir are a practical race. We do what must be done. No sooner had Grerr rolled the stone back in place to conceal the Brisingamen than I felt a twist of pain at its absence. I pine for it even now, like a lost love.

Still, there is something about the bartering of flesh that unsettles me. I have been with many men in the past, have given myself freely. I am neither proud nor ashamed of that history. I've discovered that the body and mind can operate independently of one another, if necessary, and that this is a blessing. But I wonder whether I will regret the price paid in future. Whether it will somehow taint the necklace. Or me.

A night is just a speck of time, I tell myself. And while Grerr may be unpleasant, the other two are not. I confess I feel a small stab of guilt when I think of Berling, for he is barely on the cusp of manhood. But this fades when I remember the necklace and its warm weight of gold in my hand. I know that I would do far more, if necessary, to feel that weight again.

Anyway, it is too late for doubts, as one of them is already waiting. I prepare myself carefully: make myself a bride. Grerr is to be first. The order has been worked out between them, and was the subject of some deliberation. Alfrigg will be second and Berling will be third, because the one they call Dvalin is away. They do not know when he is expected to return. Apparently, I must wait, if I am to have the necklace. I can only hope his sojourn does not run to years.

Now it is Grerr who waits, mottled with anticipation, like an overripe fruit. As I approach the cave where he lives, I am suddenly apprehensive. I have washed and scented my hair with sprigs of lilac, and wear only a light chemise held together by two simple bronze clasps, each bearing the figure of a gripping beast. Charmingly, the cloth for the dress has come from Berling. He delivered it this evening, blushing. It seems it is a gift, though I wonder now where he obtained it. (Did he steal it from his mother?) Earlier, as I returned from bathing, I passed them both in the tunnel. I recognised her at once, for Berling has been carved in her image. She is quite attractive, in a maternal sort of way, with abundant honey-coloured hair and eyes that flash at you, though I can tell from the way she carries herself that her spirit is over-burdened. She hesitated when she saw me, as if waiting to be introduced, and Berling blanched. Apparently, she knows nothing of our arrangement. I did not wish to embarrass him, so I smiled and carried on.

When I arrive at Grerr's cave, he stands in the door-way expectantly. He gives a curt nod of greeting and motions for me to enter, but his expression remains guarded, as if he doesn't quite believe that I will stay.

"So you've come," he says, his voice laced with suspicion.

"Of course," I reply, spinning around to face him. "Did you think I'd change my mind?"

He raises an eyebrow in response. I turn to survey his home, aware of his scrutiny. It is as if he is weighing up my integrity even now, measuring my worth. The room is small and neat and sparsely furnished, not far from what I had imagined it to be. The floor is covered with a rush woven mat, and two oil lamps provide a modest amount of light, together with a small fire in the corner of the room. There is little adornment, except for an array of ancient tongs that hangs along one wall. I cross over to examine them.

"These are your tools?"

"Not mine," he answers gruffly. "My father's and grandfather's. And his father's before him. All three were skilled goldsmiths. Masters of their trade, just as I am. The tools are my inheritance." He runs his eyes over the tongs, then takes a step forward and gingerly lifts one off the wall. I can see at once that it is the oldest. The metal is rusted and has begun to deteriorate. He runs his hands along its length.

"A tool like this has a life of its own," he says fervently. "It has its own power, its own skill. Even its own destiny." For a moment it seems as if he will place it in my hands, but then he changes his mind and returns it to its hook on the wall. "When a goldsmith dies, his tools are revered, just as he was."

He turns to face me and I do not ask who will revere his. Instead, I examine the room's other contents. There is a crudely built wooden table and two chairs, and in the corner, a raised bed strewn with the shaggy skins of an animal I do not recognise. A curious musky odour lingers in the air. In spite of the fire, the room is cold. I regret not wearing more, though it occurs to me that soon I shall wear less.

"Sit down," he says, motioning to the chair.

"Thank you." We sit opposite each other at the small rough-hewn table. He hands me a drinking horn filled with mead. I take a demure sip, then return it to him. He drinks deeply, emptying it. When he is finished, he lays the horn on its side on the table. His eyes are red and have begun to water. He makes no move, only stares at the horn. I wonder fleetingly whether we are to sit at table all night.

"It took us four years to make the necklace," he says slowly. The mead has affected him, for his speech has suddenly thickened. He must have been drinking before I arrived.

"It is a fine achievement," I say cautiously.

"It is more than fine," he snaps. I do not reply. We have not even completed our transaction, and already he regrets it. He looks at me with eyes steeped in anger. "A night for a year, does this seem equitable?"

"You do not have to sell it."

"Perhaps I won't." Our eyes lock. My heart beats wildly at the thought that he will change his mind, though I dare not let him know it. I want to lunge at him, grab his stubby beard and throttle his undersized life away. After what seems like an eternity, he takes a deep breath and looks into the fire. "Or perhaps I will," he says finally.

I feel the numbing tingle of relief.

Grerr continues speaking slowly. "It's as if we've borne a child who has spurned us."

"What do you mean?"

"We made it," he says. "It came from us. But it is better than we are." Even as his voice hardens, I see a lone tear roll down his cheek and lose itself in the coarse silver hair of his beard.

He is right, of course. The Brisingamen is sublime. And dwarves are not. There is little I can say to comfort him. "You still have me," I offer.

He nods. "Tonight at least," he says, "I have you." His tone is no longer pitiable, but that of a man who, though only four feet tall, knows exactly what he wants. His entire demeanour suddenly alters: his chest swells and the look in his eye is almost swarthy. He makes his move then, swift and purposeful, crosses to my side and takes me in his arms in a way that is surprisingly fluid. He is a man like any other, I think. I close my eyes and try to relax into his kiss. It is tense and overwrought, but not unlike others I have known. He pulls frantically at my chemise, and I hear the brooch on my left shoulder burst free, the pin springing from its delicate clasp. Before long, we are both naked, and it is only when he climbs on top of me that I am briefly, and unwisely, tempted to laugh. For there is something utterly incongruous about our bodies, as we have difficulty achieving a lover's fit. I wonder if he too senses this, or whether desire has eclipsed his brain. But when I open my eyes, I see that he is not concerned with our respective sizes.

It is over quickly. When he has finished, Grerr pulls his tunic and trousers hurriedly back on. He appears oddly self-conscious of his nakedness, while I do nothing to hide my own. I recline on the bed while he rises and walks to a small oak casket in the corner to replenish his horn of mead. He drinks deeply, this time offering me none. And when he looks at me again his gaze is no longer camouflaged by lust. Now it is my turn to feel self-conscious, for without lust, my purpose here has vanished. I quickly reach for Berling's cloth and cover myself, though it is too late for modesty. Grerr senses my discomfort and turns away.

"You can go," he says over his shoulder.

I raise my eyebrows in surprise. "One night was the arrangement. Would you not prefer me to stay?" I ask.

He shakes his head. "You'd best leave now," he says curtly. He does not need to explain. Soon he will begin to ache for the Brisingamen. Before long, the ache will bloom into an agony of loss. He does not wish me to be present when it starts.

"You are an honourable man," I tell him.

"No," he says bitterly. "I am not."

I gather my things and depart quickly, lest he change his mind. But I needn't worry, for when I turn to look at him one last time, his gaze is lost inside the fire's flickering flames.

I leave the cloying atmosphere of the caves, find my feathers and fly straight to the nearest thermal waters. It is a ritual cleansing I'm in need of, though I am uncertain whether it is my body or my soul that needs purifying. It is almost midnight when I reach the deserted spring, set deep in the mountains. A nearly full moon sits low on the horizon. It lights the black face of the water, enough to see the steam rising from its surface in treacherous wisps. I throw off my feathers, sit upon the ring of stones and lower myself into the warm, dark pool. In spite of the heat, a shiver runs right through me. For if the Brisingamen can bring a grown man to tears, what else is it capable of?

～✿～

The next morning, Berling blushes uncontrollably when we meet. "Thank you for the cloth," I say. "It served me well," I add mischievously.

His entire face glows pink. "Actually, " he stammers, "it was a present from my mother."

"Your mother?"

He nods. "She wishes to meet you."

"When?"

"Whenever you like."

"Before or after tomorrow night?" I smile at him and the colour drains from his face.

"No!" he whispers hotly. "My mother knows nothing! She must never know —" he breaks off in horror.

"Then rest assured I will not tell her, Berling." He

nods, evidently relieved. "I will meet her whenever you please."

"Today then," he says. "This evening. You can dine with us before –" He breaks off once again, his eyes dropping to the ground.

"Before I visit Alfrigg," I continue. He nods. "Very well, then," I say. "This evening it will be."

What does she want with me? I wonder, as I make my way towards Berling's cave that evening. Perhaps there is an affair of the heart she wishes to discuss. Or perhaps she is just curious. They are waiting for me when I arrive. Gerd is flushed with anticipation, while Berling wears the haunted eyes of a sick animal. I smile at him reassuringly, but this only seems to make him more nervous. I turn my attention instead to Gerd, clasp her hand warmly in greeting.

"How good of you to come," she says, inviting me to sit. The table has already been laid. A large earthen pot sits squarely in the centre, surrounded by several smaller wooden serving bowls.

"You've taken much trouble," I say, indicating the food. There is stewed hare, pickled onions, roast gull's eggs, fresh whey and a large, flat loaf of coarse-grain bread.

"Not at all," she says modestly, beginning to serve out the meat on wooden trenchers. "I wanted to meet you. We have few visitors here."

"Berling has told me." Berling flashes me a pained look, as if to say: do not bring me into this. I smile back at him, and he looks down at his feet.

"Besides, anyone who can make Berling's stepbrothers part with the Brisingamen is doubly interesting. They have been obsessed with the necklace for years."

"It is worthy of their obsession."

"Is it?" she asks. She turns away towards the fire. "I wouldn't know." She crouches down, poking at the embers for a moment, then returns carrying another serving dish, which she places in front of me.

"You've not seen it?" I ask, incredulous.

"No one has, but you." She freezes, the serving spoon in her hand. We stare at one another for a moment. Berling coughs a little awkwardly.

The idea stuns me. "I didn't realise," I murmur.

"Perhaps you'll show it to me," she says more lightly. "Now that it's yours."

"It isn't mine yet," I add quickly.

Gerd looks with surprise at Berling. "But I thought terms had been agreed." Berling's eyes widen slightly. I can almost hear the thumping in his chest.

"Not quite," I explain. "We are waiting for Dvalin."

"Oh," she says. She stops serving food for a moment. "Yes, of course," she says. "The necklace could not be sold without his consent."

"I am sure the terms will suit him," I say lightly. Berling chokes on his beer just then, sending a small spray of liquid onto the table. Gerd looks at him askance, then turns back to me.

"Dvalin is a sound man," she says a little too intently. "He is not attached to worldly things. If the terms are fair, then I'm sure he will agree to them."

I meet her gaze for a moment. "I don't think he will object," I reply, reaching for my cup of beer. I empty it in one go. There is something about this woman that makes me want to behave excessively, for she tethers her own manners too tightly.

"Would you like some more?" asks Berling, indicating the jug.

"Go and fetch some wine from your uncle's house," says Gerd. Berling stares at her dumbly for a moment. "Go on, then," she says pointedly. He nods but seems reluctant to move for a moment, then finally excuses himself and dashes out the door. Once he is gone, Gerd turns to me expectantly. "Why have you *really* come?"

My heart skips a beat. "To Nidavellir?"

"Yes."

"To find the necklace." The words sound hollow.

She considers my response. "The Aesir have long known of the existence of the Brisingamen. Why now?" Her tone has hardened. I see at once that I have under-estimated her.

"The time was right." I have no wish to divulge my true concerns.

"Something has happened."

I shake my head. "No."

"But something will."

I hesitate. Truly there is more to this woman than meets the eye. "Perhaps," I say.

She scrutinises me for a moment, then slowly utters the words that haunt my dreams. "*I see beyond the future*," she recites, "*the mighty doom of the triumphant gods.*"

"You are familiar with the prophecy?"

She smiles. "My husband was a king. And a poet. He knew the *Voluspa* well."

"And the words? Did he believe what they foretold?"

"Perhaps I should ask you the same."

I stare at her uncertainly.

"That is why you've come, isn't it," she continues. "To save your people from destruction."

It is not a question. So I do not answer. After a moment, she picks up a knife and begins absently to scrape the blade against the hearthstone, as if to sharpen it. Her fingers are slim and delicate, unusual for her

128

race, and the sight of them, together with the slow ring of steel against stone, mesmerises me. At length she pauses and looks up at me.

"It is only a necklace," she says.

"Perhaps," I answer. "But I will have it just the same."

She holds my gaze for a moment, then glances towards the cave's entrance.

"He is a fine young man," I say of Berling. "You must be very proud."

"To me he is still a child," she counters. "But yes, I am."

"His father died some years ago?"

"Seven," she says.

"You did not remarry."

"No. My first responsibility was to Berling. And you?"

"I was married once," I reply. "A long time ago."

She raises an eyebrow. "I'm sorry."

"I prefer to be alone."

She considers this, but does not reply.

"You must have loved your husband very much," I offer.

"It was not love I felt, but loyalty." She glances again towards the door, and her voice drops slightly. "Now, it seems as if a vast fog has settled between me and that other time." She pauses for a moment, gathering her thoughts. "Sometimes I feel that I am trapped inside it, that I will suffocate if I cannot be free of it."

"Free of what?"

"The past," she replies.

Berling enters the room just then, startling us both. He carries a small earthenware jug, which he holds up to me. "Will you take a cup of wine?" he asks. I look at him, and what I see is neither man nor boy. And then I look at his mother, and what I see is a woman fettered by the fruit of her womb.

I drink too much at Berling's house, unsettled by his mother's words. By the time I reach Alfrigg, the world is suffused with a pale yellow glow. Alfrigg himself seems lit from within, though whether that is the effect of the wine or due to his own excitement, I can't be sure. He has tidied himself for the occasion. His few strands of hair are freshly oiled and combed, and his face has been scrubbed to a burnished pink. When he comes to the door, he smiles with delight. I cannot help but smile in return. This he anticipates as a kind of exuberance on my part, but I am so drunk I do not care. "Come in, my dear," he twitters, presenting me with a small bouquet of field flowers. I raise them to my face to inhale their sweet scent, but already he has whisked them from my hands, and is steering me towards his bed. It is vast and misshapen, made of several layers of dried moss inside a wooden frame, and covered with coarse linen cloth. It reminds me of an animal's bier. Alfrigg sinks down into it and pats the space beside him. I clamber on and am surprised by how comfortable it feels. He turns to me and proceeds to unwrap me like a gift, chortling throughout. When he unpins my chemise, he lingers momentarily over the bronze clasps, admiring their fine craftsmanship. Then he lays them gingerly to one side, before removing Berling's cloth with a flourish.

At the sight of my naked breasts, he nearly swoons with delight. "Oh my!" he exclaims. "Oh my, yes!" He addresses them separately, fondling each in turn, the way one might attend to a small animal, or a pair of young children. When he judges that my breasts have had enough attention, he turns his ministrations to the rest of me. He leaves no part of me out: no digit, no curve, no lobe, not even a blemish (for I have a few) escapes his attention. He delights in all of it, in all of me. And perhaps because of the wine, I do not mind the slightest bit, am even flattered. Who would not be?

Then it is his turn to undress. Unlike his brother, he does so with pride. How pale and round and hairless his body is! Each plump part seems to disappear into the next. When he is naked, he pauses momentarily, as if awaiting my approval. I cannot help but smile, whereupon he claps his hands once and leaps onto the bed. He is an ardent lover, eager and thorough, and when we finally finish my body feels like a well-kneaded piece of dough. He grins at me afterwards, like a well-fed dog, and we both fall into a deep sleep. I do not wake until dawn, when I am eventually roused by his gentle snores. I dress quickly in the half-light and plant a light kiss upon his shiny brow before creeping away. When I turn to look at him one last time, his entire body seems suffused with a smile.

Alfrigg's attentions leave me exhausted. These Brisings may be small, I think, as I make my way towards the hot pool once again, but they are no less passionate than ordinary men. It is a good thing there are but four of them, I decide. My goal is no longer spiritual cleansing but recuperation, and once there, I linger for hours in the warm sulphurous waters.

But each time I close my eyes, I cannot help but see the necklace. The longer I wait, the more it preys upon me.

THE NORNS

Beneath the lush grass of Hekla's flanks lies layer upon layer of ash, the legacy of her temper inscribed into the earth. Hekla is a conduit. She has one purpose: to channel heat and gas and molten rock from the centre of the earth. In future generations men will come to regard her as the gate to Hell. Though she is but one of many here, Hekla is the most unpredictable, and the most violent. For now, she lies dormant, gathering her strength. Beneath her arched spine, like the giant back of an enormous whale, a huge chamber slowly fills with molten rock. Eventually, the long ridge of her spine will tear asunder, as if someone had drawn a knife across the belly of the earth.

FULLA

ulla stands mutely eyeing the man in front of her. He is not at all what she expected. When her grandfather said that he was widowed, she assumed that he meant old. But Rolf is far from ancient. Though older than her by many years, he is still youthful: tall and broad-shouldered, with a thick head of raven hair flecked through with tiny spots of silver. His features are large and finely crafted, his eyes a startling blue. What is even more disconcerting is the manner in which he looks at her, as if challenging her to meet his gaze.

"It is a great pleasure to meet you," he says.

Fulla cannot find her voice. She smiles and gives the ghost of a nod instead.

"Rolf is an old friend of mine," says Hogni. "Indeed, I knew his father for many years before he died." He turns to Rolf and smiles. "He was a fine man. And a good fighter."

"He also held you in high regard," says Rolf.

"Fulla is Jarl's only child," explains Hogni, laying a hand upon her shoulder. "The last of our line."

Rolf turns back to her. "You've been to the Althing before?"

"Only once," she says. "As a child."

"Ah. I thought I had not seen you last year."

"Grandfather did not wish me to come."

Rolf smiles. "Afraid of losing you too soon."

"Exactly," laughs Hogni.

"And is it as you remembered?" asks Rolf.

"It is bigger. And more crowded."

"Indeed. The Althing seems to double in size each year."

"But otherwise, yes. It is much as I remembered."

"Come," interjects Hogni heartily. "Sit with us and share a horn of ale."

They seat themselves on logs about the fire and pass the silvered drinking horn from one to another. When Rolf hands her the horn, Fulla fumbles and spills some of the contents across his leg. "I'm sorry," she says quickly.

"It's nothing," he replies. He smiles at her reassuringly. There is nothing hasty about this man, she thinks. His bearing is strong and measured. He displays none of Hogni's excitability and none of the awkwardness that seems to afflict men of her own age. She watches his mouth as he converses easily with Hogni. His voice is low and resonant, and the words roll smoothly from his lips. Hogni drinks quickly, his face soon flushing. Rolf passes the horn more than he drinks, and speaks to them both solicitously, though his gaze returns frequently to her. After some time, he places his hands upon his knees and rises, turning to her. She and Hogni quickly stand. "I am very pleased to have met you, Fulla."

"And I you," she replies.

"Please be my guests this evening, both of you, after the games."

"An excellent idea. We must make the most of our brief time," says Hogni pointedly. Fulla flushes. Hogni takes Rolf's arm and steers him outside while Fulla watches. Upon his return, Hogni looks at her expectantly. "Well?" he says.

She takes a deep breath. "He is not unpleasant."

"He is perfect! As fine a man as we could hope for.

And wealthy too. He owns half the Western Fjords! You will lack for nothing. And he is keen. You have caught his eye, there is no doubt. We must move quickly."

She hesitates. "The Western Fjords," she says tentatively. "They are a long way from Laxardal."

He steps forward and plants a kiss upon her brow. "Fulla. I will not be here for ever."

"But you're here now."

He shrugs. "Who knows for how much longer?"

They spend the afternoon and early evening at the games, watching young men test their skill at various contests. Fulla spends as much time looking at the crowd as the contenders; here and there she recognises a few faces, but nowhere does she see the men of Skallagrim's clan. At length, the games conclude and Hogni steers her towards Rolf's booth. It is close to the Law Rock, as befits a man of his stature, and the booth is already crowded with visitors when they arrive. Rolf immediately moves towards them with a welcoming smile. He introduces them to several kinsmen, and Fulla senses that he has told them of a possible betrothal, for she feels their scrutiny keenly. Rolf invites her to sit beside him and hands her a horn of mead.

"You enjoyed the games?" he asks.

She smiles. "We've seen many spears thrown."

"Ah. Young men's pursuits. Did they distinguish themselves?"

"A few. Most missed the mark."

"I am glad to hear of it," he says heartily. "I hope they did not catch your eye."

"Not at all," she assures him with a laugh.

"As a young man, I rarely excelled in such contests.

Though I had no equal in draughts," he adds.

"You were not a keen rider?"

He shrugs. "I can sit a horse competently, if that's what you mean."

"Hogni said your father was a skilled fighter."

"He was. And I can wield a sword if need be." He pauses. "But I prefer not to."

"I am glad," she says. "Did you travel much when you were young?"

"A fair bit. My people came from Denmark and from there made their way to Norway. I have been all through Scandinavia, and have sailed as far as Orkney and the Faroes. But I prefer my own shores to that of any other."

"The Western Fjords."

"Yes. Have you been there?"

"No."

"My farmstead is at Barder." He hesitates, as if reading her mind. "It is two days' sail across Breidafjord, then another day's ride to Laxardal."

"I see." He watches her closely as she takes in this information. "You've been to Laxardal?" she asks.

He nods. "I've travelled through there on a few occasions. I passed a night at your grandfather's farm once."

She smiles self-consciously. "Forgive me. I do not remember."

"You were but a tiny child," he says gently.

"Oh." He hands her the horn, and she drinks deeply, hoping to erase the unease she feels. She should not feel odd about their respective ages, yet the fact of it arises more often than she would like. Rolf clears his throat, then addresses one of his kinsmen across the booth. The two men exchange jests. Fulla sees that Hogni is deep in conversation with Rolf's uncle on the opposite side of the fire. As she looks about, she catches the eye of an older woman wearing a violet gown and an elaborate headdress seated beside Hogni. The woman smiles, and at once rises and crosses over to sit beside her.

"I find women's talk far preferable to that of men's," she says with a mischievous smile. "But perhaps you are still young enough to be enthralled by deep voices."

"Not at all. I too prefer the company of women, but find myself surrounded by men most of the time."

"You've no sisters?"

Fulla shakes her head. "No. And my mother died when I was born."

"You've been unlucky."

"Perhaps."

"But now," the older woman nods towards Rolf and drops her voice. "Rolf is a fine man. He will make a good husband."

Fulla flushes. "I can see this," she says. "Did you know his first wife?"

The older woman smiles. "She was my sister."

Fulla flushes again. "I'm sorry," she murmurs. "I didn't know."

"No need to apologise."

"When did she die?"

"Two summers ago. Just after the Althing."

"You must miss her."

"I do. Very much."

"What a shame they were not blessed with children."

"Indeed. It was her great regret. She was ill for much of her life, you see. I think it was a relief for her to die in the end. Perhaps for all of us." She casts a darting glance at Rolf. As if sensing their talk, Rolf shifts his attention from the others back to them.

"You've met Edith, I see," he interjects. "My late wife's sister."

"Yes."

"Fulla says she prefers the company of women to

that of men," says Edith.

He looks at her with a bemused smile. "Oh?"

"I only meant...I have so little opportunity...there are few women in our small household, so I welcome their company."

"There is no need to justify your words. Whatever you said, I am certain it was meant well." He casts a meaningful look at Edith. The older woman rises at once.

"Please excuse me," she says nodding to Fulla. "I am promised elsewhere."

Fulla and Rolf stare after her as she makes her way out of the booth. "I'm sorry," she says to him.

"No need. Edith has a way of wreaking havoc with her words. What else did she say?"

"She said your wife suffered from ill health during much of her lifetime."

"It's true," he says earnestly. "She was unlucky. Ill health plagued her all her life." He turns to her and looks at her intently. "Perhaps we could take a walk down by the lake and speak in private."

She feels a small surge of panic. "Yes, of course," she says. "If my grandfather doesn't object."

"I've spoken with him already," says Rolf.

They both rise and quietly take their leave of the others, walking out into the cool night air. Darkness has begun to fall, and most people have retreated to their booths for the night. As they stroll through the encampment, she sees small knots of people gathered around open fires. They speak in low voices, punctuated by occasional outbursts of laughter. Neither she nor Rolf speaks for several minutes, until they reach the edge of the lake. Once there, they are alone, except for a few men off in the distance fishing from the shore. Rolf turns to her.

"Fulla, may I speak plainly? You are young and desirable. You could have your choice of many men."

"The decision is not merely mine, as you know."

"But I wish it to be."

She hesitates. "What do you mean?"

"That I desire you to choose freely and of your own accord – not simply follow the wishes of your grandfather."

She considers his words. "You are an honourable man," she says carefully.

He sighs. "I have the advantage of experience."

She looks out upon the lake. The moon has risen just above the horizon; its reflection shimmers in a line across the water. "Did you love your first wife?" she asks quietly.

Rolf hesitates. "I respected her."

"That is not the same."

"No. It is not."

"Why did you marry?"

He takes a deep breath and exhales slowly. "Because as a young man, my heart was set towards another. She married someone else, according to her family's wishes. And eventually bore two children before she died."

"I'm sorry."

He smiles. "It was a long time ago."

"Do you think that I...that we..." She hesitates.

"I think that when two people enter into marriage with an open heart, anything is possible. Love can be nurtured, but the heart must be willing."

"And is your heart willing?"

"Very much so." He turns to her. "Is yours?"

"I think it might be," she says. "But I'm not certain."

He pauses, his expression growing more serious, then reaches for her hand. She feels his fingers close around her own. His hand is large and warm. He gives a small squeeze. "Fulla," he says, choosing his words with care, "I have had one loveless marriage. I do not want another. You must consider carefully."

She nods. "I will sleep upon the matter, and give you my decision in the morning."

He smiles and releases her hand. "That is as much as I can ask for. Tomorrow it shall be. I will come to your booth first thing."

✁✁✁

On the way home she evades Hogni's probing questions. He has drunk a vast amount during the course of the evening, so does not press her overly. Once they have retired, sleep eludes her. She lies awake listening to the snores of those around her, and ponders her decision. Rolf is a fine man; that much is obvious. Thus far, she has seen nothing in his character to object to. But neither does she feel the excitement of a new bride. Would love grow between them, as he claims, given the right conditions?

Part of her resents the responsibility he has conferred upon her with the choice. A different part of her sees the possibility of a new life in a distant place, with a man who will do his best to love her. She knows that his proposal is not one to be trifled with. But it has come so soon – before she has even grown accustomed to the idea of marriage.

She sleeps eventually, but when she wakes at dawn, her body is still exhausted. Hogni lies to one side of her, and the other men are ranged across the floor. She takes in the stillness of the morning, and finds to her dismay that her mind is no clearer. As quietly as she can, she rises and pulls on her overshift and shoes, before creeping across the booth to the door. Once outside, she turns to survey the encampment. A small handful of people have woken around her. They crouch beside their camp-fires tending the delicate first flames. She makes her way across the field towards the edge of the encampment, and finds the path cut into the wall behind the law rock that will take her to the top of the escarpment. She climbs quickly, breathlessly, her mind concentrating on the jagged steps cut into the basalt wall beneath her feet. At length, she reaches the top and walks a little further inland, so she cannot be seen from below. The dawn sun sits squarely on the horizon. She walks without purpose, lost in thought, until she eventually reaches the great rift that tears the rock in two. She peers down into the crack, which drops for many metres below her feet.

"They say it widens each year by the span of a man's hand."

With a gasp, she turns to see Vili standing not ten paces away. He has come from behind her, without her realising. Did he follow her from the encampment? She looks down at the rift. "How can such a thing be possible?" she says.

He shrugs and moves a bit closer to where she stands. They both stare into the crevasse. "For the past three years I've measured it. But it is difficult to tell."

"Perhaps it is we who alter each year," she offers. "Rather than the rock beneath our feet."

He looks at her and smiles uncertainly. "The new religion preaches forgiveness. The old one retribution. Who are we to believe?"

"Maybe neither."

He looks at her intently. "Do you hate me for my father's crime?"

She shakes her head. "No."

"And my kin?"

She hesitates. "Hate is too strong a word," she says.

He sighs. They both look out across the valley floor. "There is talk of a betrothal," he says after a moment. She turns to him with a frown.

"I am not yet betrothed."

"But you will be."

"Perhaps," she says.

"To a man twice your age."

"Rolf is a worthy man," she says defensively. "With a fine reputation."

Vili raises an eyebrow. "His wealth is equally reputable."

"If wealth is a crime, then I am not aware of it."

He considers her for a moment. "Then what is it you seek? Is it his purse? Or the wisdom born of age?"

She feels her face start to burn. "You've no right to say such things!"

"No," he says. "Perhaps not. Who am I but the son of an outlaw?" He flings the words at her, his cheeks two spots of colour. "I wish you both great happiness," he says. Then he turns and strides quickly across the rock towards the steps, never once glancing back in her direction. Fulla stands motionless, long after his figure has disappeared over the crest of the escarpment. Anger gathers like a storm inside her. She is stunned by his outburst. And by the doubts he casts upon her motives. She had not yet made her decision. But now perhaps she has.

❧

Once back at the booth, she feels newly calm, as if the path ahead has been suddenly cleared of obstacles. She smooths and straightens her dress, attaches her best brooch, and combs her hair in preparation for Rolf's visit. The others have risen and are busy with their morning labours. Two of Hogni's men are dispatched to

144

fetch water; another is sent to check upon the horses, grazing at some distance from the camp. Hogni himself seems buoyant this morning, as if last night's celebrations are still carrying him along. He hums a little tune as he ladles out some skyr for breakfast, holding up the spoon to offer her some. She shakes her head. A few minutes later, an old friend stops by to greet him. The two men stroll out of the booth together, and Fulla is left alone. As if on cue, Rolf sticks his head round the door.

She smiles at him. "Come in. The others have just gone."

"I know," he says. "I watched from a distance, as I wished to find you on your own."

She laughs. "Do you manage everything so easily?"

He shrugs good-naturedly. "I try to." He hesitates, then steps a little closer to her, lowering his voice. "Have you considered my offer?"

She nods. "I have."

"And?"

"I accept."

He breaks into a wide smile and takes another step towards her. "You are certain?" he asks.

"I believe so, yes." She laughs. "Yes," she says again with more emphasis.

He too laughs. "Then all is well. We shall be happy. I promise you. We must wed soon. In the early autumn. Just after haymaking, when food is plentiful. I'll speak to Hogni."

"Yes, of course."

He reaches for her hand, and suddenly, despite his age and self-assurance, they both sense the awkwardness of his touch. He carefully folds her hand into his own, then gives it a tentative squeeze. "Already I feel ten years younger!" He gives a small self-conscious laugh. "Twenty, even!" She smiles up at him. He stops short then, and leans down, lightly pressing his lips against hers. She feels her heart racing, and catches his scent as he draws near. His lips are thick and warm once they are upon her, and the coarse hair of his beard brushes against her chin. She feels a strange sensation, as if her mind and body are somehow detached from each other. After a moment, he pulls away, looking down at her. "You have graced me with your favour, Fulla, daughter of Jarl," he murmurs softly. "I will not disappoint you."

"I know this," she replies. "And it is I who have been fortunate in this match."

"What's this then? A match we speak of?" They turn to see Hogni standing in the doorway, a twinkle in his eye.

"She has consented to marry," says Rolf.

"Thor's blessing on you both," says Hogni heartily. He crosses over to them and plants a kiss upon Fulla's brow, before clasping hands warmly with Rolf. "You've made an old man quite content."

"Two old men!" says Rolf. They both roar with laughter.

FREYA

fter my night with Alfrigg, I do not return to the caves until late in the afternoon. It is Berling's evening, and the arrangements are more complicated. Berling has told his mother that his stepbrothers need him to tend the forge overnight. We are to meet in Dvalin's cave, since he is away. Grerr devised this plan. He seems anxious to conclude the sale, and grows increasingly irritated over Dvalin's absence, as if it is some sort of personal affront. When I asked him whether Dvalin was expected to return soon, he almost snarled. "Dvalin comes and goes as he pleases," he said bitterly. "He has no regard for his responsibilities here." Berling, on the other hand, adores him. When the boy speaks of Dvalin, it is with a kind of zealous devotion. The fact that Dvalin is frequently absent only serves to heighten his allure, for young Berling is obsessed with the world outside Nidavellir.

That evening, I follow Berling's directions to Dvalin's cave. It is some distance from the others, down a narrow, dark side tunnel. This does not surprise me, as he is by all accounts a private man. There is no sign of Berling when I arrive, and the air in the cave is thick with cold. Despite the chill, the room exudes a strong sense of its owner. For a man who apparently does not care for worldly things, he certainly has a lot of them, I think. The cave is cluttered with objects of all kinds. A trio of battered wooden chests lies along the wall nearest me, together with piles of old horse tack. There are furs of every animal scattered about, as well as old woollen blankets, most of which are tattered and moth-eaten. In the corner is a mass of carved wooden staves covered in runes, and at the base of his sleeping platform lies a pair of vast, red-veined granite stones painted with images of idols. There is no table for eating, only two long, low benches by the fire. Beside one of these sits a large earthen bowl filled with glass beads of all shapes and sizes and colours. I sit by the hearth and run my fingers through the beads, wondering where he obtained them. Is he a raider? Or merely a finder of things, a hoarder of the past?

I am surprised to feel some warmth in the fire's ashes, so I set about relighting it with bits of straw and kindling from a pile on the floor. After a few minutes' effort, I succeed in coaxing the ashes into flame. Berling's voice comes from behind me. "I lit it yesterday."

I turn to see him standing in the doorway. "I didn't hear you."

"Sometimes I come here when Dvalin is away," he adds a little sheepishly.

"Does he know?"

"Yes, of course." There is a false note in his voice. I raise my eyebrows. "Actually, no," he admits. "But I don't think he would mind."

"Then why not ask him?"

He shrugs. "He's not here for me to ask," he replies.

"I see." By now I've managed to light a small bundle of straw and the first spiral of smoke begins to rise. I add a few pieces of turf to it. Berling comes forward and kneels down beside me. With the softness of a lover, he places his palms upon the ground and leans in towards the fire, gently blowing. The flames surge. After a few moments, he rocks backwards on his heels. We watch the fire spark and spread. I spread some furs out in front of the fire and seat myself, patting the space next to me. Berling hesitates, blushing.

"Sit," I order. He does.

"I meant to come earlier," he says apologetically. "My mother needed me."

"No matter. I enjoyed meeting her last night."

"And she, you."

"Nonsense. She did not approve of me."

"Why do you say that?"

"Because I'm alone."

He shrugs. "So is she."

"No, Berling. She has you."

"Oh." He blushes a little.

"Besides, I think she harbours an affection."

"An affection? For whom?"

I shrug. "Whom indeed?"

Berling frowns. The idea clearly unsettles him. "I wouldn't know," he says, after pondering a moment.

"And what of you, Berling?" I enquire teasingly. "Do you harbour an affection?"

"Not me," he says a little grudgingly. He picks up a stick and probes the fire.

"You've not been with a girl before."

He shakes his head, continuing to prod at the fire in little jabs.

"But you've dreamed of it," I continue.

He shrugs. "Who hasn't?"

"You've made a start, then," I say reassuringly. "Besides, anticipation is half the pleasure." He looks at me askance, as if this latest information is deeply worrying. I laugh. "Maybe not half. Perhaps one-quarter." Berling sighs. He practically radiates discomfort. "So you have no one special, then," I say gently.

"Not really." After a moment, he fixes me with a pointed look. "Do you?"

I laugh, surprised. Berling waits expectantly for an answer. "I was married once," I say cautiously.

"And?"

"And now I'm not."

"What happened?"

"My husband had a restless nature," I say. "He found it difficult to be tethered to a place. Or a person. In the end, marriage proved too settled an existence for him. So he left. I suppose I was just a brief stop on a much longer journey." I think of Od: of his easy smile and his warm grey eyes and their unfathomable remoteness. I have come to understand that he was never really present in our life together. A part of him was lost to me from the beginning.

"Where is he now?"

"I don't know," I reply simply. For it is true.

Berling frowns. "Did you love him?"

How can you love a shadow? "I thought I did," I say. "But I was young. And very foolish." I smile. "So the answer is no. No, I did not."

"But you were sad when it finished."

This last is not a question. Berling looks at me intently and I wonder how he knows. "Yes," I say. "I thought somehow that I had failed."

"Do you still think that?"

"You ask too many questions, young Berling," I reply.

He blushes. "I'm sorry," he offers apologetically.

"Let us speak of you now. What is it that you most desire?" I ask. He glances up at me, and a look of confusion mixed with panic crosses his face. "What is it you have dreamed of?" I ask more gently.

Berling stops prodding the fire, but does not take his eyes from it. "I should like a kiss," he says finally. He gives a small, embarrassed smile.

"A kiss it is, then," I reply. With deliberate slowness, I lean forward, until my lips are but a breath away from his. Berling does nothing, neither moves towards me nor away, but remains frozen. I move my lips to one side of his, allow them to trail lightly across his cheek, follow the line of his jaw, then down his neck to his throat. He swallows. I look him in the eye. "You see?" I murmur. "A kiss is not so very difficult." He is breathing deeply, for I can see the rise and fall of his chest, and can almost hear the warm rush of his blood. I lean towards him again, and this time I let my lips brush up against the softness of his own. I let them linger for a few moments. Berling's eyes are closed now and he responds slightly with his body. I feel the weight of him move towards me, feel the parting of his lips. I let my tongue just touch his own. A jolt runs right through him, as if I've burnt him with an anvil from the fire.

At once, he stops and looks at me, his eyes wide, his chest heaving. "I'm sorry," he says. He rubs his hand across his face.

"Are you all right?"

He nods. He takes a deep breath and lets it out slowly. "Do you think," he says then, "that we could...talk?"

I smile at him, surprised. "Of course."

He exhales, his relief almost palpable. "Thank you," he says, a little hoarsely.

"You are very welcome." An embarrassing silence stretches out between us. Berling concentrates his gaze on the fire and his expression turns serious. "You must be careful with the necklace," he says after a moment.

"I will guard it with my life," I say facetiously.

He shakes his head. "You don't understand. It's not the necklace I fear for. It's you."

"What do you mean?"

151

He pauses for a moment, struggling to find the words. "The necklace can do things."

"What sort of things?"

"It can make things happen." I look at him with scepticism. He chews one lip uncertainly. "The night we cast the gold for the pendant," he begins, "there was an explosion in the furnace. I don't know what caused it, only that the fires were very hot. I was loading more fuel into the furnace when it happened. Suddenly, there was a tremendous bang, and the fire leapt out at me. I lost consciousness for a few minutes, and when I woke, I couldn't see. Everything was blackness. Dvalin was with me. He carried me home, and my mother bathed my eyes with cold compresses for two days and nights. It was a terrible time. I can still hear the sound of her sobbing. On the third morning when I woke, my vision had returned. I was overcome with joy, although I noticed at once that the world looked different. Colours didn't seem as vibrant as before, almost as if they'd been washed away. Still, I was so relieved I didn't say anything. Later that day, I went to the workshop to see what progress they'd made during my illness. I was amazed when I saw the necklace, for the colour of the gold had been altered by the explosion. The metal had been exceptionally pure to begin with, but now it had the most extraordinary lustre, a wonderful sheen that I'd not seen before. It was almost as if the fire had been trapped inside it." Berling pauses then. "I think the Brisingamen stole something from me that night," he says softly. "A part of me stayed with it. Even now, the world does not seem as bright a place as it once was."

"Berling, I'm sorry. But surely it was just an accident?"

"Don't be sorry," he says quickly. "I'm not. If the Brisingamen has taken something from me, then it was worth it. For now you have come and changed the course of things."

"What do you mean?"

"Our lives will never be the same. I can feel it."

"Because of me?"

"Not you," he says shaking his head. "Because of the Brisingamen."

I stare at him and ponder his words. Is that not why I came here? To change the course of things? "I hope you're right," I say slowly.

"Trust me. I am."

I raise my hand to brush a lock of golden hair out of his eyes. "I'm very happy to have met you, young Berling," I say. "And I *do* trust you."

He smiles. "Then you will not deny me one more pleasure."

I laugh. "Of course not. Isn't that why we're here?"

"Not that," he says quickly, his face turning pink.

"Then what?"

He leans towards me. "Tell me of the outside world."

I smile at him in disbelief. He is quite serious. "What is it you wish to know?"

"Your people, tell me about them."

"The Aesir?" He nods emphatically. Where do I begin? With our deceit, our jealousies, our failures? Or with our own imagined triumphs, the heroic tales we've told each other for so long we now believe them to be true? I look at Berling. His eyes practically shimmer with excitement. "Yes, of course," I say finally. He beams and stretches out upon the wolfskin, his head propped up on one hand.

I do not have the heart to give him damning truths. So instead, I tell him the myths of my people, tales invented long ago as a means of consolidating our power. I speak of Odin and Thor and Loki, of magic hammers and eight-legged horses and ships that fold themselves away into your pocket. I tell him of Valhalla, the Hall of the Slain, and of Niflheim, the world of the dead, and Nidhogg, the dragon that devours corpses.

But even as I speak, I realise that the lines between truth and falsehood have long ago become blurred in my mind. For the names are real enough. And so are many of the places. It is the stories themselves that have been embellished over time. They have been told and retold so many times that it is no longer possible to say which parts are real and which have been imagined. And my own part in the myths, what can I say of that? I know what is said of me, and I know what is true. But I do not know who I am without them. And neither do my people.

Berling listens intently for what seems like hours. It is as if having satisfied the man inside him, I must now feed the little boy. And all the while, Gerd's words ring inside my head. Perhaps he is a child after all.

❧

We sleep finally, exhausted by words. The stories have disturbed something deep inside me, a grave of memories I thought I'd laid to rest. Even when sleep takes me, the Aesir crowd my dreams and will not let me be. I dream of Odin's great hall, and of my father and brother. They are all there: Nord and Freyr, Odin and Loki, Odin's wife, his son Balder and countless others. They are holding a feast, a celebration of some kind, and I am the last to arrive. No one notices my entrance. They are all engaged in drinking and merrymaking. I make my way through the crowded room towards the fire, where a goat roasts upon a spit. I freeze in horror. Flanking the goat on two smaller spits are my cats. I recognise them instantly, for unlike the goat, they are still alive. They are trussed tightly to each spit, but I can see their wild eyes dart about, and their tails lashing frantically from side to side. I lunge forward with a cry, but as I do my brother Freyr emerges from the crowd to grab my arm. He grips it so hard that I wince with pain. We struggle for a moment, until I scream. At once, the room falls silent. They form a circle around me. Odin's wife steps forward with a stern look upon her face. "What is it?" she demands.

"Please," I say, pointing to the cats, "Let them go."

"Cover yourself Freya!" she snaps. I look down and see that I am half-naked, my dress torn during the struggle with my brother. Freyr drops my arm and turns away in disgust. My father shakes his head slowly from side to side. Loki looks at me and smiles.

I wake in a sweat. Berling and I lie side by side next to the hearth. The fire has died to no more than a handful of embers. Apart from their dull glow, the room is black, the torches having burned down hours before. I sit up quickly. Berling sleeps soundly. I can just make out his form next to me, his breath deep and regular. But it is the other sound I hear that unnerves me, for I sense another presence, a third heartbeat, in the room. I turn and quickly scan the shadows, but can see nothing in the darkness. "Who's there?" I demand. My voice sounds oddly strangled. It bounces back at me, followed by a silence so great that it seems to swell and envelop me. I wait for what seems like an eternity. And then I hear the faintest sound of footfall near the door and the soft pattern of steps retreating in the darkness. I strain to listen until they finally disappear.

Afterwards, I cannot sleep. I lie awake, disturbed by thoughts of the Aesir and the twist of fate that brought us to Asgard in the first place. We were a bribe, my family and I. An offering of peace, designed to quell the unrest between two races. We will come and live among you, said my father. Share your bread and drink your wine and prove that we are one. But we were never united, even as a family. Freyr was everything I was not: responsible, diligent, earnest. We fought constantly as children, but never left each other's side. Did we really emerge, hand in hand, from the womb? My father said it was this that killed my mother. Freyr and I would not be parted, even in birth.

I wake Berling at dawn, so he can return to his mother's without raising suspicion. He is difficult to rouse at first, but eventually comes to a bit sheepishly, yawning. He looks even younger this morning. The ease we felt last night has melted, and we exchange only a few words. Berling seems embarrassed. I too am uneasy, troubled by my dreams and by the strange presence in the night, though I do not speak of either to Berling. We leave together, but once we reach the main tunnel we separate.

The caves oppress me. I do not think I will be able to endure their stultifying air much longer. Once again, I feel an overwhelming need to escape, and when I am finally outside I am enormously relieved. Again, I fly over the mountains to the thermal springs. It is light now, the sky a vast plane of grey. From high in the air, I see a lone horse grazing nearby and a man in the water. I am surprised to find the springs occupied, for the area around is largely uninhabitable. Perhaps he is a traveller, though few people pass along this route. I land at some distance and stow my feathers underneath a bush, before climbing the slope to where the spring lies, tucked beneath the face of the mountain. The man has emerged and is just finishing dressing, his back to me, when I approach. He hears me coming and turns around. He is small, perhaps my own height, but squarely built with broad shoulders and muscled forearms. His hair and eyes are dark, almost black, and his jaw is wide and square, with just the thinnest of beards. He wears a tunic of plain brown cloth, but his cloak, though worn with age, is made of rich green velvet. When he sees me, he stops short. The look on his face is one of complete surprise.

"You," he says, incredulous.

I am certain I have never laid eyes on him before. "Have we met?"

He shakes his head slowly. "No."

"Yet you know me."

He studies me for a moment. "No," he says finally. "I was mistaken." He turns away and whistles for his mount. The horse raises its head in the distance, then comes towards us at a brisk trot. I watch as he ties his bedroll onto the back of the saddle, his hands pulling hard on the leather straps. I see that his fingers are thick and calloused, with knuckles twice the size of my own. The hands of a labourer, I think. Or a craftsman. And with a start, I realise who he is.

"Dvalin," I say. He turns back to me, one eyebrow raised. I see the taut line of his jaw pulse.

"So it *was* you," he says slowly. "Last night. In the caves."

I feel a lump rise in my throat. His eyes sweep the length of me, and I know that he is thinking of Berling. I feel my face flush with embarrassment, and it renders me speechless. We stare at each other for a moment, then he turns back to his horse and climbs into the saddle. He nods very briefly, then nudges his mount and rides past me without another word.

I spend a few restless hours in the hot springs, uneasy over this first meeting. The man was not at all what I expected. I am beginning to doubt whether I will gain possession of the necklace after all. The thought is agonising, and by the time I leave the baths I am almost ill with apprehension. It is noon when I return to Nidavellir and Berling is waiting for me when I arrive, his face shiny with excitement. "Dvalin is back!" he says. "He's only just arrived. Come, you must meet him!" He grabs my arm and pulls me along the passage, but even as he does I have a strong sense of foreboding. In a few minutes, we reach a natural opening in the caves where the horses are stabled. Dvalin is there brushing down his mount, and when he sees me, he stops.

"You again," he says, this time a little wearily. "How did you —" His eyes drift down to the falcon cloak I am still carrying. He stares at it for a moment and swallows. "I should have known," he says quietly, turning back to the horse. Berling steps forward eagerly.

"Dvalin, this is Freya."

Once again he stops. "Freya," he repeats. "From Asgard."

"Yes," I answer.

He drops the brush and leads the horse past us to a bucket by the wall, securing the lead to an iron ring driven into the rock. He picks up a broom and begins to sweep the area clean. Berling hops excitedly about, dodging Dvalin's broom. "So much has happened since you left," he says. "You've seen Grerr?"

"I've seen no one."

"Then you know nothing of the agreement?"

"No, Berling, I told you, I've seen no one," says

Dvalin. "And I'm very tired, so perhaps you'll excuse me." He puts the broom in the corner, then bends down to retrieve his saddlebags.

"We sold it," says Berling impulsively. "We sold the Brisingamen." Dvalin straightens up slowly, the saddlebags hanging limply from his hand.

"You sold it?" His voice is deliberately flat, the emotion concealed just beneath the surface.

"Yes! Well, no. Well, partly. We were waiting for you. We couldn't sell the necklace without you."

Dvalin says nothing for a moment. He looks from Berling to me, then back to Berling. "To her?" he asks finally.

Berling nods proudly. Dvalin says nothing. He looks down at the saddlebags with a sigh. In the silence that follows, Berling's face begins to crumble. "Dvalin," he begins pleadingly.

"Perhaps I should explain," I say quickly.

Dvalin looks at me. "Perhaps you should."

"Is there somewhere we could talk in private?" I ask.

"My cave is private. Or used to be."

"Very well, then," I reply. I turn and walk in the direction of his cave. Berling starts to follow, but Dvalin raises a hand to stop him. "It's all right, Berling," I say. "I'll speak to Dvalin alone." Berling nods, his face ashen.

Dvalin follows me silently to his cave. When we reach the door, he turns to me with a raised eyebrow. "But of course, you've been here before," he says.

"Only for the night."

"I trust you made yourself comfortable."

"Yes, thank you. Your brothers offered," I add.

"Half-brothers," he says. "How generous of them." He indicates that I should enter. Once inside, we stand facing each other awkwardly. "What else have they offered?"

159

"We've come to an agreement. Subject to your approval, of course."

"For the sale of the Brisingamen."

"Yes. But you seem like a reasonable man."

"Don't be fooled," he replies evenly.

"The sort of man who keeps the word of his brothers," I say.

"Half-brothers."

"Blood kin, nonetheless."

He drops the saddlebags on the floor and removes his cloak, throwing it on the bench by the fire. He picks up an iron poker and stoops down to flatten the still-warm coals into a bed, and puts two large squares of turf on top. My eyes are drawn to his forearms, for they are as thick as two stout saplings, and covered with fine, dark hair. The turf smokes for a moment, then bursts into flames. He prods expertly at the fire, before standing and turning to me. "I think it would depend on the word in question," he says. "So tell me, what idle chatter have my brothers engaged in during my absence?"

"It was hardly idle chatter."

He shrugs. "Gossip. Boasting. Rude oaths. Silly jests. Between them, my brothers excel in all manner of speech-making."

"Half-brothers," I say. He smiles for the first time. "I can see you think highly of them," I add.

The smile disappears. "What I think is my business,"

"What if I told you they made a contract?"

"A binding contract? In my absence?"

"An agreement, then."

He smiles. "And what trinket have they accepted in return?"

I start to speak but feel my throat tighten, as if the words themselves will choke me. It is too late to change my mind, I think, for the deal has already been done. I take a deep breath. "Me," I say, in as loud a voice as I can muster.

He looks at me, and when he speaks, his tone is one of complete disbelief. "You?"

I nod. "For one night each." I feel my face redden, curse the hot tide of blood rising up in me. My entire body feels alight with embarrassment. Where was this man when I arrived?

"So the Brisingamen is to be traded for a few nights of debauchery?"

"I would hardly call it debauchery."

"What would you call it?"

I stare at him. Pleasure, I think. Passion. Love of a certain kind. These are not evil words, but I cannot bring myself to speak them.

"The Brisingamen is a sacred object. You profane its very essence with your offer," he says intently.

"If you don't like the price, then you are free to name another," I say quietly. "I don't think your brothers would object. Their own demands have already been discharged."

He looks at me in complete astonishment, then throws back his head and laughs. "Discharged? The three of them? And you?"

"Not at the same time," I say grimly.

"What kind of woman trades herself for a..." He hesitates, searching for the right word.

"A trinket? You said yourself the Brisingamen is a sacred object. Powerful. Mysterious. The embodiment of beauty and perfection."

"You forget one aspect of its nature," he says slowly. "Dangerous."

"I forget nothing," I snap back. We stare at each other for a long moment. Finally, he turns away. He crosses over to his saddlebag, removing a wineskin from one side.

He pulls out the stopper and takes a long drink, then wipes his mouth with his sleeve.

"It's clear your brothers underestimated your attachment," I say carefully. "As I said before, if you do not like the price, then you are free to name another."

"And if I refuse?"

"You own but a quarter of the necklace. The rest is already mine."

He shakes his head, slowly. "Then I have no choice," he says.

I shrug. He takes another long drink of wine, then crosses over to the sleeping platform and sits down upon it heavily. He rubs his eyes with one hand, clearly exhausted by the journey. Finally he looks up at me. "My price is this: not one night, but three."

Now it is my turn to be incredulous. "Three?"

He holds up his hands. "Three nights. That is my price."

I stare at him for a moment. "It could prove difficult," I say haltingly. "Perhaps you ought to confer with your brothers."

"Why?" he asks. "They did not confer with me. You accept this price, or we do not have a sale."

I look at him and what I feel is fear. I do not know why. He is a man like any other, I tell myself. What harm could come of it? "I accept," I say finally.

"Fine," he says wearily. "Make ready your things. We leave tomorrow at dawn."

"Leave? To where?"

"Jotunheim. There is something I must do there."

"But what of me?"

"You will help me."

"How?"

"You will see."

"And afterwards?"

"The necklace will be yours," he says simply. "We'll take it with us if you like," he adds. He throws the empty wineskin on the floor and lies back upon the bed, closing his eyes. "I am extremely tired," he says.

I do not move. After a moment, he raises his head and looks at me. "You *do* have somewhere to go?" he asks. I nod. He closes his eyes again and sighs deeply. "Good. I prefer to sleep alone, if you don't mind." He rolls over onto his side, away from me. I turn to leave. "Perhaps one of my brothers will accommodate you," he murmurs.

THE NORNS

The Norns are not immune to beauty: we understand why gold occupies the high seat in the minds of men. Gold is the noblest of metals. It cannot be eroded and is impervious to attack. It does not dissolve easily, nor tarnish, nor lose its brightness, and can reflect light rays humans cannot see. Though it is rare, traces of gold are everywhere: in the crust, beneath the oceans, and deep within the core. But gold must accumulate in order to be found. It congregates in ancient fault lines, deposited by the movement of warm fluid through fissures in the rock. As mountains shift and sheer over time, these veins are exposed, enabling gold to migrate from the centre of the earth into the hands of men.

DVALIN

He dreams of Menglad. They are alone together in a dense pine forest. The ground is soft underfoot, a spongy floor of moss and aromatic pine needles. The forest is eerily quiet. No birds call, no animals can be heard rustling through the undergrowth. Menglad walks ahead of him, choosing her route with care. His eyes are fixed upon her slender frame. She wears a long, pale blue tunic that washes around her legs with every step. She pauses from time to time to gather something from the earth: a handful of leaves, a few fragments of moss, the blossom of a tiny flower. She stows each in a small pouch that swings freely at her side. Each time she stops, he finds his own feet frozen to the ground, as if she controls both of them with her movements.

Finally, she turns to face him. He sees at once that she wears the necklace he made for her, a delicate choker of elaborately woven gold and silver threads. Her neck is long and creamy; his eyes are drawn to the way the necklace clings to the base of her throat. She smiles at him, raising a hand to finger the necklace. "You see?" she says. "I wear it always. Just as I promised." She reaches for his hand. At the touch of her he feels a searing pain. He jerks his hand free with a gasp. They both stare down as blood flows freely from a wound in his palm. Her face creases with concern. "You're bleeding," she says.

She kneels down and presses her lips to the wound. When she raises her head a moment later, the wound is gone. There is no trace of blood upon his hand, nor on her lips. Still clinging to his wrist, she applies the slightest pressure and pulls him down to the ground, until he kneels opposite her on the forest floor. She leans forward, her mouth just brushing his ear. "I can heal you," she whispers. He feels dizzy suddenly, disoriented. Now that she is so close, he can see the intricate design of the necklace. The fine strands of metal seem to writhe and twist in front of his eyes, like tiny curling tendrils of a vine. Menglad slips the tunic from her shoulders. It pools about her knees. He tries but cannot see her nakedness, can see only the glint of gold and silver at her throat. She leans forward to kiss him, her body pressing closer to his own. He wants desperately to feel the warmth of her lips, but the necklace bars her mouth from his.

And then he wakes, his heart beating hard in the darkness. He turns in his bed, half expecting to see Menglad lying next to him, but there is nothing. He takes a deep breath. He feels her dream presence slip away from him, and knows that it will soon be gone. He closes his eyes to recapture it, but she is lost. He opens them and stares out at the dying embers of the fire. He must not think of her. He will go to see her; he has promised Idun that much. But he will not succumb to the lure of her again. Besides, he thinks, she will be married now. Bound to the man she had sworn herself to when they first met. He is not in the habit of pursuing other men's wives.

He does not know how long he has slept. His body still aches from the journey, and the air in the caves is cold and damp. Each time he returns to Nidavellir, he wonders why. Unlike his brothers, he prefers life above ground. He rises and stirs the embers in the fire, loading on more turf, then climbs back into bed. He can tell from the stillness that dawn is some way off. As much as he dislikes the caves, he does not relish the prospect of another long journey. Even less does he like the idea of travelling with a woman. But he needs Freya for protection. They will not harm him in Jotunheim with one of the Aesir by his side. For all their strength and might, the giants who live in Jotunheim remain in awe of the Aesir. They would not risk incurring their wrath for such a trifling prize as his head. Still, Freya is bound to slow him down on the passage over the mountains. On the other hand, he thinks, to have a woman by his side when he reaches Menglad is perhaps not such a bad thing. Particularly one whose beauty rivals hers. He will not feel such a fool. The thought brings him a small measure of comfort.

He sleeps again, this time too long, and when he wakes his head is heavy and his mouth is dry. He rises quickly, his mind already crowded with preparations for the journey. His horse has thrown a shoe; that will need tending straightaway. And he must organise a mount for Freya, as well as provisions for them both. He packs a dry set of clothing and an oilskin for warmth, then adds a second one for her. She may be capable of flight, but he hopes that she can sit a horse. He would sooner die than use the falcon suit.

When his pack is ready, he goes to the stables. Berling is already there, brushing down the horses. The boy casts a shy glance in his direction. "You're not angry?" he asks.

"With you? Of course not. Why would I be?" Dvalin pulls up a small wooden stool and sits down beside his horse. He takes an iron pick out of his pocket and lifts up the animal's foot.

Berling shrugs. "You seemed cross about the necklace."

"I was only surprised that a decision had been taken in my absence. But I do not blame you, Berling. At any rate, the deal is done. Pass me that knife, will you?"

Berling's face lights up. He hands a small iron blade across to Dvalin. "Then you've agreed to the sale?"

Dvalin nods. "In principle, yes." He carefully trims the horse's hoof, allowing the pieces to drop to the ground. After a moment, he pauses. "Berling, why are you so keen to sell the necklace?"

Berling considers this. "I don't know. It seems the right thing to do, I guess." He shrugs. "Besides, I like Freya."

Dvalin smiles. "I can't imagine why."

Berling colours. "It's not because of that. It's just, she's different."

"Different from what?"

"From other people."

"What kind of people?"

"I don't know Dvalin! Our people." The boy makes a face.

Dvalin stands up, having finished trimming the horse's foot. "Of course she's different. She's one of the Aesir. Build up the fire, will you? I need to shoe this horse." He walks over to the other ponies and selects one for Freya, leading it out from its stall.

"Are you going somewhere again?" says Berling.

"Unfortunately, yes," says Dvalin. Berling watches him bridle the second horse.

"Who is that for?" he asks hopefully.

"Her."

"She's going with you?"

"Yes. The fire, Berling." The boy stands there frowning, then comes to all of a sudden and begins to load fuel

170

into the fire. He takes up the bellows, and starts to fan the flames. The fire leaps to life under his hands. Dvalin steps forward holding a pair of iron tongs. He clasps the shoe and holds it in the flames while Berling watches.

"When will you return?" asks Berling.

"Four days. Five maybe."

"Will she come back with you?"

"She doesn't live here, Berling."

"I just thought..." He breaks off with a shrug.

"Why would she?"

"She likes it here. She told me."

"She wants the necklace, Berling."

"Oh."

Both pause for a moment as Gerd approaches in the passage. Her gown is of a golden hue that sets off her complexion nicely. Dvalin smiles at her, and her face lights up in response.

"Welcome home, Dvalin," she says warmly.

"Thank you."

Her eyes travel to the bridled horse. She turns to him with a look of surprise. "You're not off again, are you?"

"I'm afraid so."

"To where?"

"Jotunheim."

"Another long journey! Your feet have hardly touched the ground."

"It can't be avoided."

"And when will you return?"

"Within a week, I hope."

"You have provisions?"

"Yes, of course."

She turns to the boy. "Berling, go and fetch a cheese from the storeroom. And a loaf of bread." Berling hesitates.

"Really, Gerd. It isn't necessary," says Dvalin.

"Nonsense. You have to eat. Go on then, Berling!" They both watch as Berling trots off in the opposite direction. When he is out of earshot, she turns back to him intently. "Take Berling with you," she says quickly. Dvalin opens his mouth to speak but Gerd interrupts. "Let him see the outside world. He is desperate here. I cannot bear for him to be raised in the caves any longer. It will smother him! It will smother both of us."

Dvalin sighs. "Gerd. You said yourself: this is a long journey. And arduous."

"He is old enough."

"It could be dangerous, Gerd," he says emphatically. She frowns. Dvalin shakes his head. "This is not the right time. Nor the right journey. But I swear to you: I will show Berling the outside world soon."

Gerd regards him doubtfully. "When?" she asks.

"The next time."

"Is that a promise?"

"You have my word."

She sighs and raises one hand to stroke the horse's nose. "He is devoted to you."

"And I to him."

She laughs. "He can speak of little else when you're away. Sometimes I think you are more of a father to him than his was."

Dvalin stops what he is doing. He steps forward. "Gerd, my father found it difficult to show his feelings. But he loved Berling as much as he loved any of us, I promise you."

She nods. "I know."

"In truth, he was a better leader than a father," says Dvalin. "His strengths lay elsewhere."

Gerd hesitates a moment. "In truth, he was a better leader than a husband."

They stare at each other for a moment. "Then you did

well to stand by him."

"I did my best," she replies. Dvalin smiles at her a little awkwardly, then picks up his tools again. He takes a seat and continues to work on the horse.

"It is better than my own mother managed," he says lightly. "She fled the confines of his kingdom as soon as she was able. I think she grew to hate him in the end."

Gerd gazes down at him thoughtfully. "I never knew this."

Dvalin shrugs. "Their marriage wasn't meant to last."

"Many aren't," she says quietly. She watches him for a moment. Berling comes running along the passage, bearing the cheese and a loaf of bread.

"I've got them," he says breathlessly, stowing both in the saddlebags.

"Thank you," says Dvalin to both of them.

"You must travel safely," says Gerd. "And *return*."

"I intend to," he says lightly. All three of them look up to see Freya come along the passage. She is dressed for the journey and carries a satchel of provisions, together with the falcon suit.

"Good morning," she declares to all of them. She walks over to the horse he has bridled for her and pats its side. "Is this one mine?" she asks, turning to Dvalin.

He nods self-consciously. Gerd looks from her to Dvalin, her eyebrows raised.

"When do we leave?" says Freya. Dvalin does not answer. Gerd looks at him pointedly for a moment. He can feel her anger gathering. Finally, she turns and walks away without a word. He watches her disappear down the corridor, then turns back to Berling. The boy's eyes are wide.

"Now," he says wearily.

FREYA

I will not sleep with him. Whatever else he asks of me, I will do. But I will not share his bed. He is arrogant and rude, especially when you consider his size. Which is not great, though admittedly, he is not as small as his brothers. He will tell me nothing about the journey, neither our final destination nor our purpose.

We set off soon after Gerd left us. I do not know what he said to her, but she was clearly affronted. He showed no sign of remorse. He merely handed me the reins and mounted his own horse without so much as a backward glance. "Keep up," he said over his shoulder. Then he set off at a brisk trot.

I turned and looked at Berling, who gave me an apologetic smile. "Wish me luck," I said. The boy nodded, unable to speak. I could not help but feel sorry for him as I rode off. He cut such a forlorn figure as the one left behind. When I was almost out of sight, I turned back to see him. He was still there watching us, and gave a sad little wave.

❧

We head straight for the mountains to the north. I cannot see their tops, as they are ringed in low-lying cloud, though I know we must cross them somewhere. Dvalin rides at a fast pace and I quickly fall behind. After an hour, the gap between us has widened considerably, so I spur my horse into a canter. When I am near, I let the horse relax its gait and give myself a moment to recover. Only then do I pull abreast of him. "You do realise we could fly," I say, as casually as I can. He does not even turn his head in my direction, though I am certain he has heard me. "It would be much quicker," I add.

"Who said we were in a hurry?" he replies lightly. His eyes are fixed on the mountains. Before I can answer, he gives his horse some subtle sign and it breaks into a fast lope. I am left choking on his dust.

After some time, we pause to rest and water the horses at a stream. We have reached the foothills of the range now, and the mountains rise up in front of us like a giant tidal wave of granite. The horses lower their heads in unison and drink noisily. He stoops down and cups some water from beside them, then stands again, wiping his mouth with his sleeve. Then he reaches in his saddlebag and withdraws a goatskin, crouching down again to fill it from the stream. "You'd do well to do the same," he says, nodding towards my bag. "Unless, of course, the Aesir do not thirst," he adds. I scowl at his back, then retrieve the empty goatskin from my bag. When I have finished, he points to the route that we will take. "The pass is up there," he says. I follow his line of vision, and can just make out a trail that zigzags almost impossibly up the side of the mountain and disappears within the cleft of the nearest peak.

"Will we make it over before dark?" I ask.

He slings the saddlebag back over the horse's saddle and gingerly alights. "I will," he says, turning the horse towards the trail.

Our progress slows now that we are on the mountain. The horses thread their way up the steep slope, occasionally losing their footing and sliding sideways. Behind us, loose gravel skitters down the hillside. It is hard work for the horses. Within a short time, their shoulders are lathered and their ears are laid back with the effort of the climb. Dvalin and I do not speak. He does not appear to be capable of ordinary conversation. Or perhaps he is just preoccupied, for he is all the time scanning the range for something. I wonder what he is looking for, but I do not ask. When we near the top, the track becomes too steep even for the horses. He dismounts, motioning for me to do the same.

"Now what?" I ask.

He points to the cleft. "Now we walk." He starts up the slope, leading his horse, and after a moment, I follow. I do not relish being immediately behind a half-ton animal on a steep incline, but I have no choice. If he were a man of better breeding, he would have let me go first, I think with irritation. We pass into the shadow of the mountain, and the temperature immediately plummets. The ground is icy here and the wind bites at my face. I lower my head and follow the hooves of his horse for what seems like an eternity, until we finally come to a halt. When I raise my head, I see that we have almost reached the top. The track ends right in the side of the mountain. Above us, the peaks rise up almost vertically. There is no obvious way forward. I look at him in exasperation. He points to a narrow ledge butting the right hand flank of the peak just ahead of us. It is perhaps the width of a child's shoulders, and it meanders crookedly across the front of the flank and disappears around a corner.

"After you," he says with a smile.

I stare at him, astonished. "You must be mad."

"That is the route."

"I'd sooner die."

"You will, if I leave you here." As soon as he says this, his eyes flick toward my saddlebag, where the falcon suit is stowed.

"That is unlikely," I say smugly.

"Have it your way," he answers "But you'll not get the necklace."

"Why?"

"Because I need you and your horse over that mountain."

I snatch up the reins and lead the horse right past him, but I hesitate when I reach the ledge. I call back to him over my shoulder. "It's not me I'm worried about," I lie.

"The horse will be fine," he says. "Just do it."

I take a deep breath and step out onto the ledge. To my surprise, the horse requires little coercion. It follows me easily enough, stepping daintily along the narrow shelf of rock. I move at a steady pace and soon I have reached the corner where the ledge turns. Once around it, I see with relief that it is only another dozen steps. Beyond that, there is a wide gap in the peaks and a clearly visible trail over the top. I can hear Dvalin and his horse behind me, though I keep my eyes fixed on the ledge in front. All at once, I feel faint. I stop and lean down, bracing myself with one hand against the rock face. Black spots dance in front of my eyes, and I realise that I've not been breathing. I pause for a few moments, taking in some air, until the spots finally disappear. When I straighten, I feel a lone drop of sweat trickle down my side. I hear his voice call forward to me.

"Just a few more steps and you'll be there."

Is he coaxing me? I think crossly. For I do not need it. Quickly, I take the last few steps, and when I finally step onto proper ground I feel my knees buckle. The horse snorts exuberantly and trots a few steps up the hillside. I do not turn to watch Dvalin finish, though I can hear that he is right behind me. Instead, I walk over to my horse and calmly remove the flask of water from the saddle-bag. Irritatingly, my hands tremble when I remove the stopper.

"You did well," he says, reaching beneath his horse's belly to tighten the cinch on his saddle. After a moment, he crosses over to my mount and does the same. "People often die here," he adds, yanking hard on the leather strap. Then he looks at me and gives a broad grin.

≈≈≈

The north side of the slope is easier, and we descend quickly. The sun has almost set when we reach the lower elevation, though Dvalin shows no signs of stopping to make camp. We continue riding through the last rays of light, until the hills around us are no more than dark shapes, and the first few stars have appeared in the night sky. Eventually, I see a light in the distance, and make out a small farmhouse tucked behind a copse of birch trees. He is clearly headed there, though he saw no need to inform me of his plans. When we reach the house, he dismounts.

"Do you know this place?" I ask, climbing down.

"I've stopped here in the past. The farmer and his wife are hospitable enough."

"They'd have to be," I murmur. For truly we are in the middle of nowhere.

At that point, an old man appears in the doorway carrying a torch. He raises it high. "Who stops there?" he asks in a hoarse voice.

Dvalin steps forward. "Friends. Seeking a warm hearth for the night."

The old man peers at Dvalin, then swivels his gaze around to me. I can just make out his features by the torchlight. He is thin-faced and balding, and slightly bent with age. "What are you called?"

"I am Dvalin, son of Ivaldi, from Nidavellir."

"Nidavellir?" The old man frowns. "You're not dwarves, are you?"

Dvalin hesitates. "No." The old man looks at me. "This is my wife. She is Barga, daughter of Thorgood." I scowl at him in the dark, but he does not see.

"You'd best come in," the old man says. "The horses can go in the stable." Then he turns and shuffles back inside. I wait while Dvalin unsaddles the horses and leads them into the stable. He crosses back towards the house and motions for me to follow.

"Barga?" I say to him in a low voice as we enter the house.

"Say nothing," he replies. "Do not draw attention to yourself."

"I'll do as I please," I mutter back.

"Then you can forget the necklace."

The house is small and damp, made of turf and a crudely cut timbre frame. A turf fire burns in a pit in the centre of the hard mud floor. They have little furniture and even fewer adornments. The old man and his wife stand to one side as we enter. She is a small, bird-like woman, with a pinched face and wary eyes. She nods cautiously in welcome, and beckons us over to a bench by the hearth. "You'll be wanting some supper, I expect."

"We'll not take food if you're short," says Dvalin.

"We're not short," she answers. "You're welcome to any that's ours. Though it isn't much, I can promise you." She serves us each a bowl of dried shredded fish mixed with butter, and a cup of ale brewed from fermented whey. As we eat, the farmer and his wife watch us in

179

silence. When we are finished, the farmer clears his throat.

"Where are you headed?" he asks.

"North. To the Hill of Healing."

"Ah," he says with an understanding nod. He and his wife exchange a knowing glance. "You intend to pass through Jotunheim?"

"We have no choice."

"There has been much fighting there of late," says the farmer. "Between rival clans." His wife nods vehemently. "Be careful you do not get caught in it."

"We will certainly try not to," says Dvalin.

The farmer's wife looks at me with renewed interest. After a few moments, she leans forward and pats my arm reassuringly. "Know this," she murmurs in my ear. "*She* will help you." I smile politely. Perhaps age has robbed her of her reason.

Dvalin clears his throat. "We would not keep you from your sleep any longer."

The farmer nods and stands with a grunt. He and the old woman retire to their bed closet, leaving Dvalin and I alone beside the hearth. I watch as he unrolls his bedding and spreads it by the fire. He looks up at me.

"What is it?" he asks.

"The Hill of Healing? Is that our destination?"

"Yes."

I look at him askance. "But it is for women."

"Yes."

"Then why do you go there?"

"For reasons of my own."

"Yet you need my help."

He scrutinises me for a moment. "I need safe passage through Jotunheim," he says finally. "I am not greatly loved there," he adds.

"Why?"

He frowns into the fire. "I killed a man there once," he explains. "Two, in fact."

"You killed two giants?" He nods. I am impressed, but I do not let it show. "I did not take you for the fighting sort."

He shrugs. "I was provoked."

"Remind me not to get on your bad side."

"You already are." He gives a small half-smile, then stretches out upon the bedroll with a sigh. I think this is his first joke. It must have tired him, for he closes his eyes, giving me the distinct impression that our conversation has ended. But after a few moments, he speaks again. "They raped my sister," he says bluntly.

I stare at his outstretched form. His eyes remain closed. "I'm sorry."

"So were they. In the end."

"And your sister?"

He opens his eyes and looks at me. "Married now. But childless."

"So you are here on her behalf?" He nods. "And I am here on yours," I add.

"They are not fools enough to risk war with the Aesir."

"Let's hope not."

"I'm sorry to put you in danger. It was necessary."

"For your safety," I say accusingly.

"For Idun," he replies.

"Idun?" I repeat, surprised. It is not a common name. "Idun, wife of Bragi?" I ask.

"And daughter of Ivaldi," he counters.

I have known the woman he speaks of all my life. We played together as children and came of age at the same time. Indeed, we met and married our husbands within a year of each other. I attended her wedding, and she mine. But I do not remember him.

"You are Idun's brother?"

"Is that so difficult to believe?" He is clearly annoyed.

"I don't understand."

"Our mother was a swan maiden."

"One of the Aesir?"

He nods. "She was my father's second wife. Before Gerd."

"And your father was?"

"Ivaldi," he says with slight exasperation, as if speaking to a child.

"A dwarf?"

"A king," he says emphatically. "My father was a great leader of his people, by any standard."

"So you are half-man, half-dwarf."

"I am both man and dwarf," he says tersely. "As are my brothers."

"Yes of course, I only meant –"

"I know what you meant." An awkward silence spreads between us. "In the eyes of other men, I am a dwarf," he says. "That is what counts."

We both stare in silence at the fire. His resentment is so strong that if I put my hand out it would bite me. "And in the eyes of women?" I say, trying to lighten the mood.

"The women of Asgard do not often cast a glance in my direction," he says coldly.

"Perhaps even less than you cast a glance in theirs."

"I have no time for pointless talk," he replies, lying down once again. Then he turns on his side away from me, signalling that the conversation is definitely over. I choose a spot on the opposite side of the hearth and make up my own bed upon the floor. I close my eyes and listen to the spit and crackle of the flames. So it was not me he wanted, but my presence. I am to be his protector.

When I wake, it is morning. The fire has burnt to ashes and the room is empty. Dvalin's bedroll is gone. I rise and pull my outer clothing on, then quickly roll up my own bedding. When I emerge from the farmhouse, the sun is already bright. The horses have been saddled and wait patiently in the yard. Dvalin rounds the corner carrying a bucket of grain. He lowers it to the ground by the horses. "You slept well," he says with a raised eyebrow.

"You could have woken me."

He shrugs. "I needed time to ready the horses." He fishes a small round loaf out of his bag and hands it to me. "Here," he says.

The bread is coarse and dark and full of husks. I break off a piece and take a bite. It crumbles in my hand and is dry and salty to the taste. "Where is the farmer?"

"Gone to the fields."

"And his wife?"

"In the barn."

"We should thank them."

"I already have." He finishes tying on the saddlebags, then hands me my reins.

"You've thought of everything," I say coolly.

"I usually do."

He mounts his horse with a grunt and turns it around.

"How long will it take us to get to the Hill of Healing?"

"We should be there by nightfall. As long as there are no setbacks."

"Setbacks?"

He shrugs. "Interference."

"Is that what happened last time?" I say as he rides past me. "*Interference?*"

"Last time was retribution," he says over his shoulder.

He urges his horse into a trot, and I watch as they disappear over a small hillock. Reluctantly, I mount my own horse, though my entire body protests from yesterday's riding. I glance longingly at the feathers spilling from my saddlebag. We are fools not to fly.

For the next few hours, our pace is rapid. I have never been to Jotunheim, and the landscape is truly beautiful. We pass through rolling wooded dales and broad undulating pastures criss-crossed with sparkling streams. There is more forest here, and the trees themselves are taller. To my relief, we meet no one. At noon, we break to rest and water the horses. Shortly after we have stopped, we hear the jingling sound of a harness. An oxcart comes into view, driven by a man and boy and pulled by two horses. They watch us silently as they approach, the boy's expression openly curious, the father's more guarded. As they draw near, I am reminded of the sheer scale of these people. The man is three or four heads taller than Dvalin and I, and even the boy, though hardly more than a lad, would look down on us. Apart from their height, there is little to distinguish them from ourselves, though I can see from their clothing that they are poor yeoman farmers. As the oxcart passes, the farmer gives the barest hint of a nod, while the boy merely stares at us open-mouthed. I can feel Dvalin's relief once they are gone. We set off once again, hoping not to meet anyone else.

But our hopes are soon dashed. The trail enters a dense pine forest and after several minutes of winding our way through the trees, we chance upon an encampment in a clearing. Three woollen tents have been pitched in the clearing, and half a dozen horses graze amongst the trees. A campfire spews a small spiral of smoke. Beside it lies a pile of dead wood and branches from the forest. At our approach, the nearest horse lifts its head and snorts. We halt and Dvalin glances around us quickly. He raises a finger to his lips and turns his horse in the opposite direction. I start to do the same, but my horse takes several steps backwards, the dry brush crackling loudly beneath its weight. Dvalin frowns at me as I try to get my horse under control, but no sooner have I done so than a bearded man pokes his head out from the nearest tent. He calls to his companions, and within a few moments, five enormous men have tumbled forth in various stages of dress. They have clearly been asleep, as they are bleary-eyed and yawning. One carries a sword, the other a small hatchet. The others are unarmed. The first steps forward.

"Greetings, travellers," he calls out. Despite his words, his tone is unfriendly, and I am instantly wary.

"Greetings," says Dvalin cautiously.

"From where have you come?" He eyes us closely. "The far side of the mountains, by the look of you."

"From Nidavellir," says Dvalin. I glance at him. The line of his jaw is rigid. The man walks slowly towards us. He has dark, curly hair and a large, coarse beard with a touch of auburn in it, and when he reaches us, he is tall enough to look us in the eye, even though we are mounted.

"We do not often get your kind up here. What is your business in Jotunheim?"

"We are merely passing through. On our way to the Hill of Healing."

The man swivels around to look at me. "The Hill of Healing," he says, stepping closer to my horse. He raises a large bony hand to its nose. His skin is tanned and weathered; I can see the cracks in his lips. "And who are you?" he asks me.

"I am Freya, daughter of Nord, sister of Freyr, from Asgard." I speak as loudly and clearly as I can, though my voice betrays a tremor.

The man smiles and turns to his companions. A rustle of laughter runs through the group. "The very one! Come down off your horse, Freya, daughter of Nord, and let us see you. For we've heard your beauty is so great that the sun itself would halt its journey across the sky to get a closer look."

I glance at Dvalin, who nods almost imperceptibly, so I slide off my mount to the ground. Now the man towers over me. He peruses me for a moment, then turns to his companions.

"Perhaps a little rough around the edges. Bruised from the rigours of your journey."

At that moment, we hear a crackling in the undergrowth, and all of us turn towards the source of the sound. A boy emerges from the trees. He is much younger than the others, and though quite tall, he is beardless. Perched on his arm is a small hawk, its claws tethered to his wrist by a leather thong. The boy stops short when he sees us, his eyes widening. The others laugh. The man we have been talking to motions to him. "Come closer! We have visitors." He gesticulates towards us.

The boy steps forward, eyeing us cautiously. The leader turns to us with a wink. "The lad cannot speak, but fancies he can fly." The others laugh, while the older man places a hand on his shoulder. The boy fixes his eyes on the hawk, his cheeks colouring. I glance at Dvalin. He is staring intently at the boy.

The leader turns to me. "But we have heard that you can fly. Is this not the case?"

"Today I ride," I say.

"What a pity. I should like to see you with your wings."

"I have a feather form."

"Feathers then! Why don't you show us?"

"Not today," says Dvalin.

The man turns to him with a dark look. "You did not say your name," he says slowly.

Dvalin hesitates. "Dvalin. Son of Ivaldi," he replies.

The man frowns. "Dvalin," he repeats. "The name is known to me, though I am not sure why." He looks from Dvalin to me. "One from Asgard. One from Nidavellir. The two could not be further apart," he remarks. "Tell me, Freya, daughter of Nord, what do you see in him?" He turns to his companions with a raised eyebrow. "Surely not his stature." The men laugh. I do not look at Dvalin. "Perhaps his attributes are of a different nature. Perhaps they are the sort that remain hidden from the eye," he continues suggestively.

"A finer man you will not find amongst you," I say coldly.

He laughs. "Is that so?" He looks at Dvalin sceptically. "High praise indeed, coming from one of the Aesir."

"We are betrothed," I add. I do not know what has prompted me to say this. Dvalin blinks with surprise. The man claps his hands together.

"Betrothed! I see! But..." He turns to me with a curious look. "You are already married, are you not?"

I feel myself redden. Truly, I have always hated giants. They are a suspicious and disgruntled people, their blood thick with envy. "I was," I say finally.

He turns to Dvalin. "A well-oiled bride! For a very short groom!"

I glance at Dvalin. His entire body seems to swell with anger. "Time to go, Freya" he says tersely, his dark eyes locked on the giant's face. I turn back to my horse

187

and climb into the stirrup, when I feel the bearded man's enormous hand fall upon my shoulder.

"No need for haste," he says, pinning me to the ground, his hand a dead weight upon my shoulder. "We've barely met." This time, he makes no effort to disguise the threat in his tone.

I turn around and he smiles at me lewdly, but before I can speak, Dvalin draws his knife and leaps straight from his horse onto the man's head. His weight throws the man backwards and they both tumble to the ground. The other men rush closer until they form a circle, though they do not intervene, clearly regarding it all as great sport. The boy with the hawk does not move, though a look of alarm registers upon his face. He shields the hawk's eyes with one hand.

We watch as Dvalin and the bearded man roll back and forth in the dirt. I am at a loss for how to help, as we are greatly outnumbered. But even as I watch, the giant begins to get the better of Dvalin. Finally, when I can stand it no longer, I do the only thing that I can think of. I snatch the feather form from my saddlebag and in the next moment, I am airborne. The men who are not fighting immediately lift their heads to gawk at me, forgetting the two wrestling at their feet. The boy with the hawk lifts the bird up towards the sky, as if they both intend to follow.

I rise steadily upwards, until I am circling at a great height, then I dive down towards the ground and grab Dvalin, pulling him upwards with me into the sky. The effort of lifting Dvalin aloft is almost too much for me. Still I manage, and we are soon soaring high over the forest. I can feel him struggling in my grip, but I continue to climb. Far below us, the men stand and gape helplessly.

I fly a short distance to a different part of the forest,

then lower us both to the ground. We land heavily, which I cannot help. Dvalin tumbles to the ground, then turns away from me and immediately vomits. Out of politeness I avert my eyes. When he is finished, he turns back to me, his expression furious. "Never do that again!" he says.

"I saved your life!" I reply, indignantly.

"You were the one in danger!"

"They would have killed you! Are you completely mad, taking on five men?"

He takes a deep breath and lets it out slowly. One eye has begun to twitch and the line of his jaw pulses against his cheek. "And what would they have done to you?" he says finally. Without waiting for an answer, he turns away and walks into the forest, whistling long and low for his horse.

Presently, I hear a crackling in the undergrowth, and within a few moments, his horse appears through the trees, running at a brisk trot. My own horse trails behind.

Dvalin greets his horse with affection and quickly mounts it, turning it around without another word. I glance back uneasily towards the direction of the camp, but evidently the giants have decided not to pursue us. I climb upon my horse and follow him north.

THE NORNS

The first settlers to land upon these shores had no compass to guide them. Instead they navigated by the sun and stars and the flight of ravens. They did not know of lodestones, nor that the earth is shrouded in a transparent veil of magnetism that is embedded in her rocks. Deep inside the earth is a ball of spinning iron, which transforms the core into a vast magnet. The pull of its force extends far into space, guiding the migrations of animals across the face of the planet. But the earth's magnetism is capricious: it wavers like the point of a compass. Thus North and South, from one eon to the next, trade places like players in a dance.

FULLA

ogni and Fulla wind their way through the crowd until they reach the vast field where the horse races are held. At one end, a clump of youths await the start of the next race, reining their mounts in tightly. Two men are busy setting out stakes at the field's halfway point. Fulla watches as they tie a gull's feather to the top of each stake. She has seen this race before: each rider must pluck a feather from a stake at full gallop, then loop around a single stake at the end, before racing back to the finish. Fulla's eyes roam restlessly about the crowd. It has been two days since her betrothal to Rolf. Each time she thinks of it, she feels a sudden lurch deep inside.

"Ari's nephew races today," remarks Hogni, eyeing up the contestants.

"Who?"

Hogni nods at the riders. "You remember. We met him that first day."

Fulla settles her gaze on the contestants, feigning interest. There are eleven brawny young men in all, including Ari's nephew. Her eyes drift slowly down the line. With a start, she sees Vili. How could she have missed him the first time? She glances sideways at Hogni, but he does not appear to have noticed. Vili is at the far end, the last but one in the line. She watches as he positions his horse at the starting mark. Even from a distance, she can see the mare is bursting with the desire to sprint. Vili leans low into the horse's neck and speaks into her ear. Then he straightens and awaits the signal, his eyes directed ahead. When the flag drops, the horses surge forward. Immediately three riders pull ahead, Vili one of them. As they pass the stakes, the feathers vanish in a blur of motion. The crowd cheers wildly. The remaining riders reach the stakes a split second later. Two miss the mark and are immediately forced to turn their mounts back. The others gallop hard towards the lone stake at the far end of the field. As the three frontrunners converge upon the stake, Fulla hears a strangled gasp from a woman by her side, followed by the shrill scream of a horse as it slips sideways, hitting another. Both horses go down in a flurry of dirt and hooves. The third horse leaps over the previous two, narrowly missing the riders, and those behind veer wildly in all directions. Fulla cranes her neck to see. With dismay, she realises that Vili is one of the two that have fallen.

The race is now in disarray. Five riders gallop towards the finish, while three have come to a standstill beside those on the ground. After a moment, one of the fallen horses rolls unsteadily to its feet. Its rider too stands up. He turns and waves a little sheepishly towards the crowd. Now only Vili and his horse remain on the ground. He kneels next to the mare, his back turned, bent low over the animal's neck. He signals to one of the other riders nearby, and the lad quickly dismounts and joins him. Hogni frowns. "Bad luck," he remarks. Fulla realises that he has still not recognised Vili.

Two older men come trotting across the field. Thorstein too emerges from the crowd, his face grave. He walks over to where Vili kneels and crouches down, laying a hand upon his shoulder. Fulla sees one of the men run his hands carefully across the horses flanks and legs, checking for signs of injury. After a minute,

Thorstein urges Vili to his feet and nods to the other men. As Vili turns, Fulla sees that his face and clothes are smudged with dirt, and one arm is folded protectively against his chest. As Thorstein guides Vili across the field towards the edge, Hogni finally recognises them. "It's Ranulph's lad," he mutters. Then he turns and scrutinises her face. "But perhaps you knew this already."

Fulla shakes her head. "I only just realised," she replies. Hogni looks back at them. The remaining men now confer beside the horse. Every now and then, she sees the mare try to lift its head. Presently, one of the men steps forward, drawing his dagger.

"Aach! Don't look," says Hogni suddenly, grabbing her arm. But it is too late, for she has already seen the man kneel and lift the horse's head, severing the vein in its neck. She utters a cry and turns away, but the sight of blood spurting forth is trapped inside her. She glances quickly to see where Vili has gone, but he and Thorstein have already melted into the crowd. Hogni shakes his head in disgust. "A race is not worth the life of a horse," he says bitterly, turning away. "Come. I've lost my appetite for sport." He leads her through the crowd, while a cluster of men drag the mare's body to the far edge of the field.

That night, they dine with Rolf and his kinsmen. After the food has been eaten, there is much toasting. Again and again, they pass the drinking horn in her honour, until her face is flushed and her head begins to swim. At length, Rolf notices her discomfort. He leans towards her. "You are quiet. Are you unwell?" he murmurs.

"I am fine. Only a little tired. Perhaps I will return ahead of the others."

"Shall I walk you to your booth?"

"No," she says quickly. "Please, you stay. It will only

195

draw attention if you come." She smiles at him.

He leans in close, his face flushed with drink, and presses his lips against her forehead. "As you wish," he says. "Sleep well."

She squeezes his hand gently. "Tell Hogni I have gone." She slips quietly out of the booth into the cool night air. Once outside, she pauses, breathing deeply. She decides to walk the long way round in order to clear her head before sleep. The night is cool and the stars look as if they have been flung across the sky. Craving solitude, she makes her way to the perimeter of the encampment, then walks through the long grass, now slick with dew. Before long, her dress and shoes are damp, but she welcomes the sensation, for it takes away the numbness brought on by the ale. She walks for several minutes, concentrating on the feel of the earth beneath her feet. Eventually, she realises she has walked too far. She returns to the main path that links the booths, and sees that she has already passed Hogni's, and is now halfway back to where she started.

She turns around and sees Vili standing in the darkness several paces away, his arm in a leather sling. She draws a sharp breath. Vili walks over to where she stands.

"Are you all right?" She nods towards his injured arm.

"It's nothing. Only a sprain." He hesitates. "Trika did not fare so well." His voice falters. "We had no choice. Her leg was badly broken."

"I'm sorry."

He shakes his head. "The blame is mine," he says grimly. "I acted foolishly and rode too hard."

"You were unlucky," she insists.

"No," he says, cutting her off. "I was keen to impress." He hesitates for a moment. "I saw you in the crowd," he confesses. An awkward silence follows. Vili glances around a little nervously, then takes a step towards her and lowers his voice. "Fulla, you are betrothed now. Everyone has said so."

"Yes," she murmurs. She cannot bring herself to look at him.

"I am sorry for the things I said upon the rift. I had no right. Rolf is a fine man. It is a good thing that you favour him." Vili pauses, awaiting her response. Fulla raises her eyes to him and tries to speak, but no words come. He looks at her intently. "You *do* favour him?"

She closes her eyes for a long moment. She knows that she must speak, but cannot think of the answer. Finally, she gives a small, almost imperceptible shake of her head. Vili steps forward, until his face is only a breath away from hers. Then he leans in past her and his lips brush her ear. "Then do not marry," he whispers. And it sounds to her like a prayer.

She moves her head a fraction closer to his. "I must," she murmurs. But in the next instant she feels his lips on hers, silencing her. His kiss is soft and warm and urgent; nothing like the ones she has exchanged with Rolf. His arms circle her waist and draw her in tight against him. His face is smooth like hers, his body lean and wiry: a young man's body, she thinks, and in that instant, she knows that she has erred in her decision. She kisses him with hunger, aware now of what she has been lacking, desire welling up from deep inside.

"Fulla." A deep voice shatters the darkness.

They both turn at once to see Rolf standing on the main path, not ten paces away. After a moment's hesitation, Fulla frees herself from Vili's grasp and steps backwards. Rolf's face is dark with anger. He moves towards them, his chest heaving, then turns to Vili. "To kiss another man's betrothed," he says slowly, "is a punishable offence. Even *with* her consent." He stares at

Vili. "But you must know this."

Vili nods. "Yes."

"What is your name?"

"Vili, son of Ranulph, son of Skallagrim."

Rolf frowns. "I knew your grandfather," he says heavily. "Leave us now, grandson of Skallagrim. I wish to speak to Fulla alone."

Vili hesitates, looking at Fulla. She cannot bring herself to meet his gaze. Her eyes remain locked on Rolf's face. After a moment, Vili turns and goes. Once they are alone, Rolf takes a few steps towards her.

"I'm sorry," she says, her voice sounding hollow.

"Are you?"

She feels a tear well. "You are a worthy man. Too worthy for me."

"You have played me for a fool," he says accusingly.

"No," she replies, shaking her head. "You must believe me. It was myself I fooled. I wanted to be everything you asked for," she says. "But I'm not."

He stares at her for a long, agonising moment. "Perhaps," he says slowly, "the young are easily misled in matters of love." He pauses. "This man," he continues. "This...youth. For he has that advantage over me. Do you love him?"

She shakes her head. "It's of no consequence. There is no hope for a union. My grandfather would not hear of it."

"Nor will I accept you if your heart is fettered by another."

She hesitates. "What are you saying?"

"That I refuse you," he replies. He shakes his head slowly. "It is a sorry ending for us all."

Relief washes over her. "I can think of no other," she says quietly.

He takes a deep breath and exhales. "I'll speak to

Hogni in the morning."

"What will you tell him?"

"The truth."

Fulla takes a small step forward. "I've no right to ask anything of you..." Her voice falters in the darkness.

Rolf reads her meaning instantly. Silence follows. She can hear his breath as he ponders her request. "If you wish," he says finally, "I will contrive some other reason."

She places her hands upon his chest in a simple gesture of gratitude. "Thank you."

He stares down at her. "Am I never to love and be loved in return?" he says bitterly.

She shakes her head slowly. "I wish I knew."

"May the gods take pity on us both," he says. Then he turns away, leaving her alone in the dark.

❧❧❧

The next morning, Hogni returns from his meeting with Rolf lit with anger. He stands in the booth's doorway, his chest heaving. "Leave us," he says loudly to the others. His men hesitate, then scurry out of the booth in a matter of seconds.

Fulla rises and faces him. "What did he say?" she asks tentatively.

Hogni takes a deep breath, his nostrils flaring. "He said that you were not compatible. He said that in the end, he did not find you sufficiently agreeable. He said that when he looked for a young bride, he was not looking for a wife who clung so tightly to her own ideas, but one who would readily adopt his own."

Hogni's face is red, his forehead damp with perspiration.

"Tell me Fulla, which ideas are these?!"

Relieved, she shakes her head. "I do not know...I

199

merely spoke my mind. If I gave offence, I was not aware of it."

"You are sixteen! You have no ideas!"

"I am sorry."

"Sixteen! And already you have behind you a failed betrothal!" he blusters. He pauses then and scrutinises her, as if seeing her for the first time. "Tell me this: was there something in him that repelled you?"

"No," she protests. "Truly there was not."

"Then how are we to proceed in the business of marriage?" he explodes.

"I do not know."

"Nor do I," he says heavily. He sits down upon a log, his anger suddenly deflated. After a moment, she joins him. "We will leave this afternoon," he says glumly.

Fulla looks at him in surprise. "So soon? Before the Assembly closes?"

"Our business here is finished. If they wish to gossip, they can do so more easily once we have gone."

She hesitates. "I do not fear their gossip. Nor their ridicule."

He frowns at her. "Perhaps you should. At the end of the day, a man has only his reputation to speak for him." He shakes his head slowly from side to side. "A lone tree in an open field withers away, Fulla. You must *make* yourself compatible."

❧

They begin packing, and after an hour, Hogni leaves the booth to go and bid farewell to Ari. Once he is gone, Fulla pulls on her cloak and she too slips away, hoping to find Vili. She is not certain of the location of Thorstein's booth, so she makes a sweeping circuit of the encampment, all the time watching out for Hogni. Finally she spies Thorstein deep in conversation with another man in front of his booth. She approaches them uncertainly. When Thorstein at last registers her presence, he stops mid-sentence and stares at her.

"I am sorry to interrupt," she says quickly. "I was looking for Vili."

Thorstein frowns. "He's with the horses," he says slowly.

"Thank you," she says, turning to go.

"What business do you have with him?" asks Thorstein.

Fulla hesitates. "It's not important," she says, then hurries away.

The horses are kept in pastures near the lake, and as she walks along the path, she glances back in apprehension, for there are fewer people here and she feels suddenly exposed. When she arrives, she sees two men saddling their mounts and another in the process of shoeing, but Vili is nowhere. Frustrated, she walks slowly back to the encampment. Hogni has returned before her and though he raises an eyebrow when she enters, he asks no questions. After a few minutes, one of his men arrives with their horses and they set about strapping their provisions onto the saddles. "We'll need but one night's food for the return," says Hogni. "I've arranged to stop a night at Skokar." He finishes tying on the saddle-bags and ducks back inside the booth. Suddenly, Fulla feels a presence behind her and turns to see Vili. He looks at her beseechingly.

"Thorstein said you were looking for me," he says in hushed tones. His eyes drift to the horses with alarm. "You're not leaving, are you?"

Fulla glances anxiously inside the booth, then grabs his arm and pulls him off to one side, out of Hogni's line of sight. "We must," she says.

"And the engagement?"

She shakes her head. "Finished."

Vili takes a step forward, the curve of a smile forming on his lips. He reaches for her hand. "Then you're free to marry me," he says urgently.

Fulla shakes her head. "Vili, I can't. It's impossible."

"Why?"

"Because Hogni would rather see me dead than married to you!" she says. Vili stares at her in dismay. Suddenly, they hear a step behind them. When they turn, Hogni is standing there.

"She's right," the older man says, his voice thick with rancour. "But it's you I would kill."

"Grandfather!"

Hogni turns to her. "So this is why you were not agreeable?"

She takes a deep breath. "Please, you must believe me. I had no secret design."

"How could you even *think* of such a thing?" Hogni takes a step towards her, his voice incredulous. "Have you no shame, child?!"

Vili steps in front of her. "Hogni, please. Hear me out. I was only six when Jarl was killed," he says emphatically. "I do not even remember my own father's face!"

Hogni looks at him askance. "So you wish me to forget my son as well?"

Vili shakes his head. "Of course not."

"Then go back to your people, and leave us with the ghosts of our dead."

Hogni's tone is final. Vili takes a deep breath. He looks at Fulla, as if seeking her approval. She gives a small, almost imperceptible shake of her head. "Go," she says, close to tears.

So he does.

DVALIN

He regrets bringing her. She reminds him of his mother, and it is not just because of the feather form. She is too at ease with herself, too certain of her place within the world. Her confidence borders on smugness, as if her privileged birth was somehow deserved. It unnerves him, for he has never stood so comfortably in his own shoes. And now, to make matters worse, he is beholden to her. The idea rattles him. Perhaps she did save his life, but he still resents her interference. She was meant to ward off violence by her presence, not be the cause of it. She was especially not meant to rescue him once it had begun. He berates himself for having acted with haste and carelessness. They never should have stumbled onto the camp in the first place.

Something else bothers him. He thought he recognised the boy with the hawk as one of Idun's captors. There had been three of them altogether, the youngest only a lad. But more than six years had gone by, and he is only too aware that people alter over time. The memory of it all sickens him. And soon they will arrive at the Hill of Healing, where he must face Menglad once again.

He glances back at Freya.

She is some fifty metres behind him, a distance she has maintained carefully for the past two hours. She is clearly angry. Perhaps he should just give her the necklace and send her on her way. But not until we see Menglad, he thinks. Freya may be useful to him yet.

Already, the terrain around him looks increasingly familiar. He urges his mount up a steep slope, and when he reaches the top, he can see the Hill of Healing in the distance. The sight of it shakes him. Without thinking, he pulls his mount to, his eyes locked upon Menglad's home. When Freya reaches him a few moments later, he is barely conscious of her presence. She too halts her horse, and looks at him oddly.

"You've been here before?"

"Some years ago," he replies.

"For what purpose?"

"I undertook a commission."

"For Menglad?"

He nods. "Yes."

"What sort of commission?"

"A necklace. In honour of her betrothal."

"Is it true that she can heal?"

He shrugs. "So they say."

"You've not seen it?"

He hesitates. "I've seen her relieve the suffering of many who came to her," he admits.

"Many?" she asks.

"Most," he concedes.

"But not all."

"No. Not all."

"Let's hope that she can help Idun." She kicks her horse and it breaks into a lope down the hill. He watches her for a moment.

"Yes," he says to himself. Then he spurs his horse to follow.

∽◦◦◦∾

They reach the edge of her estate within a short time. A high stone wall encircles it, and at its entrance is a forbidding iron gate with an enormous lock. They dismount, and he hands her the reins, then proceeds to run his hands along the cracks in the wall. It takes him only a minute to find the key in its hiding place.

"The gate is certainly elaborate."

"She does not like unwanted visitors."

"Such as?"

"Giants. Raiders. Mercenaries. Anyone who is prone to fighting."

Freya raises an accusing eyebrow. He ignores her and unlocks the gate, swinging it open. She puts a hand on its ornate frame. "Did you fashion this as well?"

"Yes."

"It must have taken you some time."

"Some weeks," he says with a shrug.

"And you lived here throughout?"

"I was her guest, yes."

"You know her well, then."

"Well enough," he says crisply, banging the doors shut behind them. Just then, a pair of large black hounds come running towards them, barking furiously. "Easy," says Dvalin, stepping protectively in front of Freya. The dogs come to an abrupt halt only six feet from him, snarling. Dvalin slowly crouches down on his haunches and holds his hand out to them. "Hello, boys," he says quietly. "So she's kept you all these years, eh?" One dog slowly comes forward, sniffing at his hand. Its tail begins to wag, and after another moment, the other approaches. Soon he is petting both of them affectionately. After a minute, he stands and takes the reins from her and they walk through the yard towards the stable, with the hounds following at his heels. He leads the horses inside and ties them to a ring on the wall.

"When were you here?" she asks.

"Four years ago, five. I don't remember," he says,

loosening the girths on the saddles.

"Six." Menglad's voice washes like a wave right through him. He turns around. She stands in the doorway, the evening light behind her, so that he can barely make out her features, just the familiar outline of her presence.

"Perhaps it was," he says, as casually as he can.

"Now it seems like barely one passing of the moon." She walks towards him and kisses him on both cheeks in greeting. He freezes as she brings her face next to his, for he cannot help but take in the scent of her. She takes a deep breath and exhales, then turns to Freya with a smile. "You've brought someone to meet me."

"Menglad, this is Freya," he says belatedly.

"You are very welcome, Freya," she says.

"Thank you."

"You must be tired. Come inside and rest from your journey. You must partake of our thermal waters while you're here. They have wonderful properties and will revive you."

"So Dvalin has told me."

"My servant will show you to them now, if you wish. When you've finished, we will take some food in the hall." She calls into the yard and a young girl appears from outside. Freya turns to Dvalin with a look of uncertainty.

"The waters are for women only," explains Menglad. "They're of no use to him, I'm afraid."

"A cup of ale will do for me," says Dvalin.

"Come, then. Let us have wine in celebration of your arrival." She turns and walks towards the house. The servant touches Freya's arm, indicating that she should follow in a different direction. Dvalin nods for her to go. He watches her disappear around a corner, then turns and heads towards the house after Menglad. He already

206

feels uneasy, as if he is not in control of his actions. It is a sensation so familiar that it unnerves him. He passes over the carved wooden threshold of the house, into the main hall where a large fire is roaring in the centre of the room. Menglad motions for him to be seated in a throne-like chair by the fire. He sits, letting his eyes roam the tapestries that hang about the walls. He looks at each in turn, remembers the stories depicted in their threads, stories Menglad herself told him in the evenings by this hearth. A pungent smell of brewing herbs comes from somewhere nearby. Menglad disappears into a side room and returns a few moments later with a jug of wine and two earthen cups. She sets the cups on the table and carefully pours wine into both.

"You left it long to visit," she says finally, handing him one.

"Was a promise made? I do not recall it," he says evenly.

She takes a sip of wine, then turns away and walks towards the fire. "You no longer travel alone. I heard no news of a marriage."

For the briefest instant he is tempted to lie. "She is not my wife."

"I see. Your companion then. She is very beautiful."

"What of your husband?"

"Svipdag?" She takes another sip of wine. "Away. Raiding. As usual. It is a young man's pastime. I thought he would grow out of it. But he has not."

"You have children?"

She purses her lips. "No," she says. "I have my herbs and my healing. It is enough."

"Is it?" The words have uttered themselves. He feels himself colour in the semi-darkness of the room.

She turns to him with a dark look. "Why have you come, Dvalin?"

He takes a deep breath and begins to speak. He tells her of Idun, of barren wombs and waking sleeps, icy falls and raven-filled nightmares. He speaks slowly and carefully, anxious to convey only the facts, not conjecture.

"Why did you not bring her to me?"

"She is unfit to travel."

"Unfit? Or unwilling? The Hill of Healing is available to any woman who cares to make its ascent."

"And those who are unable?"

"I cannot help them," she says simply.

He feels anger rise within him. "There was a time when your greatest quality was compassion," he says.

"There was a time when your greatest quality was devotion," she replies in steely tones.

"It was you who sent me away."

"Because I was destined for another."

"Then the blame lies with your destiny," he says.

They eye each other fiercely for a moment. He can see the rise and fall of her chest. "What is it you want from me?" she says finally.

"Idun has three times lost a child in her womb. You have helped many others in her situation. Surely there is something you can offer from afar."

She sighs. "From what you say, Dvalin, her mind is unhinged. She dreams of ravens feasting on her entrails and hurls herself from icy cliffs. If she is mad, I cannot make her sane."

He stares at her a moment, then abruptly rises and crosses to the door. He is already outside when he hears her voice.

"Dvalin, wait!" He stops and turns around to face her. "I'm sorry," she says. "It is anger speaking. Not me."

He walks back into the house. "You've no right to be angry with me."

She hesitates. "Perhaps it is myself I am angry with," she replies, her voice dropping to barely more than a whisper. He sees a slight tremor in her lower lip. Slowly, she comes towards him, halting only inches away. She lays her hands upon his chest, so that he can feel the heat of her through her outstretched palms. She looks at him imploringly. "Dvalin, how could we have known what lay ahead?"

He says nothing for a moment. His mind casts back in time, to the feelings that bound them both like hostages, and the struggle that ensued. I knew, he thinks. And so did you. He looks down at her outstretched fingers and something inside him curdles. Suddenly, her hands are like a dead weight upon his chest. Unable to speak, he takes a small step backwards. Stunned, she drops her hands. Her face pales, and she turns away, crossing to the table. One hand comes to rest on its edge. She grips it firmly.

"There is a plant that may be of help," she says, her voice now flat. She does not look at him. "It must be used within a short time of harvesting. Otherwise, its powers are depleted."

"What is it called?"

"It's a type of mandrake. It thrives in boggy places. There is a small patch beside the lake not far from here."

He calculates. "It is two days' journey to Idun."

She shakes her head. "It would be worthless. It must be picked and consumed within the space of a day."

"Then it is no use," he says.

"What is no use?"

Dvalin turns to see Freya in the doorway, her damp hair curling in tendrils about her face, her pale skin glowing. She looks at him enquiringly, but in his mind's eye she has already taken flight, carrying the prospect of a child to Idun.

They agree that Menglad will harvest the plant at dawn, and Freya will depart as soon as she returns. Once they have finalised the details, an awkward silence ensues. Menglad's servant arrives with roasted squab, wild greens and unleavened bread. Freya eats hungrily, but Dvalin finds his own appetite lacking. Menglad too only picks at her food. Before long she rises, excusing herself. "I have remedies to attend to," she says with a nod to them both. "My servant will show you to your sleeping quarters."

After she is gone, Freya does not meet his eyes when she speaks. "I hope my presence has not been a hindrance to you."

"Why would it be?" he replies.

She says nothing, and they finish eating in silence. The serving woman clears the plates, then asks that they follow her. She shows them to a small bed closet off the main hall, of the sort shared by husband and wife. Freya looks at him quickly and Dvalin at once feels a flush rise in his face. "I'm sorry," he stammers. He motions to the outer room. "I'll sleep by the fire." He retreats hastily, leaving her alone in the bed closet. The servant closes the doors behind him, but not before he sees Freya staring out at him with a look he cannot decipher.

FREYA

I do not like her. The moods blow past her like spring storms. One moment, she looks at him with coal eyes, the next, with thinly concealed longing. They were clearly lovers at one time. But how did it finish, and by whose hand? Watching them, I cannot tell. Dvalin seems uneasy in her presence. Indeed, his manner altered even before we arrived. The past dropped over him like a shroud; it tempers his every move. But their pairing seems unlikely. I admit that she exudes a kind of earthy attractiveness, as if the trees themselves had somehow shed her. She is taller than I, and more generously proportioned. Her long, dark hair is horsetail thick, and her features exaggerated in their lushness: large, round eyes and lips like overripe plums. She is charismatic, but in a vaguely menacing way. She uses her gaze as a weapon, pinpoints you just long enough to unsettle, then shifts her attentions elsewhere.

I sleep uneasily in the bed closet and wake at first light. When I emerge, I see that Menglad is already awake, and is preparing to depart in search of Idun's cure. "Good morning," I offer.

She turns to look at me, clearly startled. She stares at me for an instant, as if she is trying to remember my significance. "I trust you slept well?" she says finally.

"Yes, thank you," I reply. "Would you like me to accompany you?" I ask.

She raises an eyebrow. "No," she says, as if the idea is

preposterous. "No, that won't be necessary." She finishes loading her tools into a leather pouch at her waist, then turns to go. At the door, she pauses. "Dvalin sleeps still," she says.

"I will not wake him," I reply.

She nods and slips out the door. For a moment, I am tempted to follow. But I do not. She is no doubt reluctant to reveal the source of her cures. She keeps a bevy of young women around her: servants, followers, admirers. But it is hard to imagine her disclosing her secrets to anyone. When I asked Dvalin who they were, he merely shrugged. "She collects people," he said. "They come to be cured and never leave."

"Why are there no men here?"

"Perhaps her husband prefers it that way." He grinned. "What man wouldn't?"

"But even he is not here."

Dvalin nodded but said nothing. Maybe he takes offence on her behalf. For my part, I am only too happy to be leaving. There is something about her, and about this place, which I find disquieting.

She is gone for nearly two hours. Dvalin rises an hour after she has left. He eats some porridge that the serving girl puts out for him, then scratches a crude map on a piece of rawhide, showing the location of Bragi's farmstead in the mountains. Afterwards, he paces by the fire, before eventually excusing himself, saying he must go and check the hounds. Perhaps it is the dogs he loved, and not their mistress.

Once he is gone, I am free to nose about the house. I find the room she shares with her husband, though there is precious little evidence that he lives here. The room smells of her, of pine needles and damp moss and forest floors. There is a low shelf in the corner with an array of small glass bottles in various hues. I uncork the first and smell the pungent scent of clove oil. Beneath the shelf is a wooden box with an ornately carved lid. At first, it appears locked, but then I discover that the lid slides backwards from the box. Inside is a small bronze brooch adorned with the figure of a lion, and a strand of coloured glass beads. Beneath them is a silk pouch of deepest indigo. I open the pouch and peer inside. It is her betrothal necklace. I recognise certain aspects of the style, for though it is not as fine as the Brisingamen, it is not dissimilar. There is something else under the pouch: a thin iron chisel, of the sort used by goldsmiths for the most delicate work. I take it out and examine it, and think of Grerr's words: in his absence, a goldsmith's tools are revered just as he was. The chisel must be Dvalin's. Did he give it to her, or did she steal it from him? And why does she keep it after all these years, when she is married to another man?

I hear a noise outside and quickly replace the box under the shelf, just as Menglad's serving woman appears in the doorway. She looks at me a long moment. I can think of no excuse to justify my presence, so I simply nod and walk past her out the door. When I reach the main hall, I see that they have both returned. Dvalin nods towards the pantry, where I can hear Menglad issuing instructions. After a moment, she appears carrying a small linen pouch. She crosses over to me and holds the pouch out. "These are the roots and new leaves," she says. "Tell her to pound them first, then make an infusion, which she should drink. Tell her not to delay, but to prepare them forthwith."

"I will see that she does."

Dvalin steps forward. He too hands me a small pouch. The instant it touches my hand, I know what it contains. Our eyes meet.

"You do not wish me to return?" I ask. For he has

given me the Brisingamen.

He shakes his head. "You have no further obligation. I will leave here soon after you do. There is another matter I must attend to, and it cannot wait for your return."

"You will travel through Jotunheim?"

He shrugs. "I must."

I raise my eyebrow. "Then take care."

He nods. I can feel Menglad's eyes upon us, so I take up my feather form.

"Tell Idun I will come to her as soon as I am able," he adds. "And that she is uppermost in my thoughts." I nod and turn to go, but not before I glimpse a faint shadow of irritation cross Menglad's face. Apparently, she is even jealous of his blood ties. When I leave, they follow me outside. They stand silently and watch me go, heads tilted back, each with one hand raised to shield their eyes against the morning sun. It is a fine day for flying. The sun shines and the biting wind that plagued us on our journey here has finally ceased. I circle once directly over them, then fly due east. I cannot help but think that Dvalin was anxious to be rid of me. Perhaps he was lying and intends to stay on here with Menglad, since her husband is so conveniently away. When I look down one last time, Menglad has disappeared inside the house. Only Dvalin remains, his face tilted towards the sky.

A few hours later, I reach Bragi's farmstead. The house and surrounding buildings are exactly as Dvalin described. From the air, I can see the glacial river he was forced to swim, its jade green current swift and treacherous. I land a short distance from the house and pause for a few moments to catch my breath. Then I gather up my falcon suit and walk towards the house. It is Idun I see first. She is outside in the yard, drawing water from a well, and when she sees me, she drops the bucket and claps her hands together with surprise. She rushes to me, her pale face lit with a smile. "It's Freya! Darling Freya!" She embraces me warmly, then shouts loudly over her shoulder. "Bragi! Come and see who is here!" Bragi emerges a moment later, wiping his hands upon a rag, a perplexed look upon his face. He too smiles when he sees me, though not as broadly.

"Well, well, Freya," he exclaims. "Welcome to our home. It is not often we have visitors from Asgard. We pride ourselves on being hard to find."

Idun frowns at him, then takes my arm and leads me to the house. "Your hands are freezing," she says. "Come inside and warm yourself."

"In fact, I've come from Jotunheim," I say.

Bragi raises an eyebrow. "Jotunheim! Even rarer!" Once inside I turn to Idun. "Dvalin sent me," I say quietly.

Idun's eyes widen. "Dvalin?"

I nod. "We've been to see Menglad."

"The Hill of Healing," she murmurs. "He promised me." She steers me towards a chair by the fire. I am already searching in my cloak for the leather pouch Menglad gave me. My hands brush against the Brisingamen. I've not yet looked at it, though I am almost painfully aware of its presence. I open Menglad's pouch and hold it out for her.

"She sent you this."

They both step forward and peer inside. Bragi frowns. "What is it?" he asks.

"A type of mandrake. You must first grind it, then make an infusion, which you must drink at once."

Idun reaches out and takes the pouch a little hesitantly. "Of course," she says. "I am very grateful to you."

215

"Isn't mandrake poisonous?" asks Bragi.

"The plant itself is poisonous. But the infusion is safe. It is known to help with conception. And it will strengthen her womb, so that she can carry a child to term."

I can tell from Bragi's face that he remains doubtful. But Idun is clearly pleased at the prospect of a cure. "Go now and prepare it," I say.

"Yes, of course," she says, disappearing into the pantry at the far end of the room.

Bragi turns to me. "You'd best be seated," he says a little grudgingly. "I'll fetch some ale."

Later that night, Idun and I are finally alone. The mandrake infusion appears to have had a positive influence, for she seems relaxed and happy. Perhaps it is the prospect of hope that has elevated her spirits, or perhaps she is pleased to have a female companion. Bragi himself retired to bed early, after drinking several horns of ale. Not for the first time, I am struck by the incongruity of their ages, for already he seems an old man, while she is still in the flower of youth.

"I never knew you had a brother," I say, once Bragi has gone.

"We were raised apart. But he is very dear to me."

"And your mother. Did she regret leaving him behind?"

"She refused to speak of the past. Up until the time she died, I never once heard her say my father's name. But I know she was haunted by thoughts of Dvalin."

"How?"

Idun shrugs. "She must have been. Any woman forced to leave a child would be."

216

I wonder whether she is right. "Dvalin told me what happened to you in Jotunheim," I say quietly. Idun stares at me for a moment, then looks away.

"I'm sorry," I add. "Perhaps I shouldn't have mentioned it."

"No," she says quickly. "It's all right. It happened some time ago." She smiles at me thinly. "Another lifetime." She glances towards the door and lowers her voice. "Even Bragi doesn't know all the details."

"Dvalin told me he killed the men involved."

She takes a deep breath and lets it out slowly. "He killed two men. There were three altogether. The youngest was only a boy. He did not..." Idun hesitates, "...participate. I could see in his eyes that he was terrified, for he never said a word." She shakes her head. "I was nearly eighteen at the time, and I remember thinking, 'This boy is only a child! He is too young to be a part of this.' The other two were his brothers. Dvalin killed them both in the fight that ensued. The boy escaped. Dvalin insisted on going after him, even though I begged him not to. I told him the boy had only watched, that he could not be held responsible for the actions of his kin." Idun's voice trembles at this last. She pauses for a moment. "But he was blind with rage. He caught the boy and brought him back to the house. They left him tied in the barn overnight, while they considered what to do with him. That night, while everyone slept, I crept into the barn. I spoke to him, and told him I did not hold him responsible. He never said a word, did not try to defend himself, nor apologise for what had happened. He just stared at me with the strangest look upon his face. In the end, I set him free." Idun looks at me searchingly. "Even though they were guilty, I knew that the deaths of his brothers would hang like a shadow over my life. I did not want to be the cause of any more violence. In the

217

morning, when they found the barn empty, they assumed the boy had escaped of his own accord, or been rescued by his kin. I never told them what I'd done." She hesitates. "I never told anyone."

"You did what you had to," I say reassuringly. But Idun does not hear. She is already lost within that other time. Something in her story snags my mind. A young boy in Jotunheim, I think. A boy who did not speak. And then I remember the strange look on Dvalin's face when we first encountered the mute. Perhaps this is the pressing business he was so anxious to pursue. I had thought that his distracted manner was due to Menglad. But the more I ponder it, the more convinced I become that he recognised the boy. For Idun's sake, he would feel obliged to pursue his earlier vendetta.

Idun is staring at me with a look of concern. "What is it?" she asks.

I smile at her. "Nothing. I am tired, that is all. The flight has made me weary."

"Of course it has. I will show you to your bed."

THE NORNS

No men dwell within the heart of this island, for at its centre sit enormous caps of ice. The ice has been here longer than us all. Each year new snow falls with the lightness of a feather, compressing that beneath it into luminous blue glass: the dense crystal heart of glaciers. When enough ice has gathered, the mass begins to creep under its own weight. It follows the landscape, flows down valleys and over cliffs, uproots and carries obstacles in its way. The people here must sometimes cross these ice caps, scarred by treacherous pits and crevasses. Many have been lost within. But the glacier always gives back what it takes: the ice inside it constantly circles, delivering up the bodies of the dead.

DVALIN

e watches until Freya disappears on the horizon, then follows Menglad inside the house. She is waiting for him by the fire and hands him a small cup of warm liquid.

He peers inside. "What is it?"

"A tonic."

He hesitates. The liquid smells vaguely of juniper. For a fleeting instant, he wonders whether he can trust her. Then he takes a small sip. It is sweet and pungent, but not unpleasant.

"The pouch you gave Freya," says Menglad casually, "what was in it?"

"A necklace."

She smiles thinly, perhaps remembering her own betrothal necklace. She no longer wears it, though Dvalin is not sure what this signifies. "Was it one of your making?" she asks.

"Not mine alone. My brothers and I fashioned it together."

She raises an eyebrow. "A necklace made by all of you. It must be very fine."

"It is."

"You spoke to her of obligations."

"She did me a favour, that is all."

"And earned your gratitude."

This is not exactly how he would have characterised their transaction. But he has no wish to discuss Freya or the Brisingamen with Menglad. "Yes," he says. He finishes the tonic and hands her the empty cup. She eyes him expectantly, and when he does not volunteer any further information, she motions towards the table. "Come. There is food."

"I haven't time, Menglad," he says. He has only just decided.

"You are leaving?" She looks at him, stunned.

"I must."

"I see." Her voice deflates. They both stand silently for a moment. "So," she says, turning away from him, "must I wait another six years before I see you?"

"Perhaps."

She smiles self-consciously. "I shall be old and decrepit by then."

"You could never be anything but beautiful," he replies.

Her smile fades. "Do we only get one chance in life, Dvalin?"

He shakes his head. "I don't know."

"The idea frightens me."

He hesitates, unwilling to offer her the reassurance she seeks.

"Well," she says finally, forcing a smile, "at least we have the past to dwell on. That is more than some have."

"Yes."

"I should like to know that you forgive me. For sending you away."

He wonders whether he is capable of this. "Of course," he says.

"Then I shall have to be content," she says, her voice thin.

"I must go now."

"Yes."

She follows him out to the yard, where she watches

him saddle the horses. Her hounds circle around him excitedly, their tails wagging. He pauses for a few moments to fondle each in turn. Then he mounts his own horse and attaches the reins from Freya's horse to his saddle.

"Goodbye, Menglad."

"Go safely," she replies.

◌◌◌◌◌

A numbness descends upon him as he rides away, as if he has been frozen by the past. He does not love her. Perhaps he never did. Maybe love itself is beyond him, an idea that tears at him. But the mute still lingers at the back of his thoughts, as does the task he has set himself.

He rides without stopping, hoping to reach the area where the giants are encamped well before sunset, so that he can find a safe hiding place. After a few hours, he begins to recognise the landscape around him. He pauses at a stream to water the horses and survey the territory. The land is sparsely wooded, with low-lying hills and craggy outcroppings of rock. He winds his way through the rocks in search of a sheltered spot where he can tether the horses, and after half an hour, finds a small cave in the lee of two hills. It is a half-moon-shaped outcropping that extends inwards by several metres, large enough for him to make camp in. He unsaddles the horses and stakes them to grazing leads, then sets about collecting firewood. Once this is done, he builds a small fire in the cave and waits for dusk to fall.

It is a clear, cold night when Dvalin eventually sets out. He saddles both horses by moonlight, and leading Freya's mount, rides in the direction of the encampment. He moves at a slow but steady pace through the forest. When he is still some distance away, he dismounts and tethers the horses to a tree. He continues slowly on foot, stopping every now and then to listen and memorise his route. After several minutes, he pauses and waits. Soon he is rewarded with the faint sound of laughter. He moves in its direction, taking care not to make a sound, and before long, he sees the glow of a campfire through the trees. He drops to the ground, taking cover behind anything he can, and steadily advances, until he can see the entire camp in the firelight. He sees four men sitting in the darkness. None of them resembles the mute, so he settles himself on the ground and waits.

The men are drinking. One of them stands and recites a poem, until the catcalls of the others force him to be seated. Mostly they sit in silence, with the occasional word or jest spoken. Dvalin makes himself as comfortable as possible, though the ground is cold and damp beneath him. After an hour, when the chill has truly crept into his bones, a fifth man pokes his head out of one of the tents and calls to his companions. It is the bearded leader Dvalin fought with. He exchanges a few words with the others, then withdraws into the tent. After a short while, two of the men rise and wish their comrades goodnight, before disappearing inside a second tent. Now only two men remain by the fire, and the young mute is nowhere to be seen.

Suddenly, Dvalin is startled by a noise behind him. He turns quickly, his heart racing, and sees the mute not forty paces from him, walking slowly towards the camp, the hawk still perched upon his arm. Dvalin crouches low, and the lad walks past him, unsuspecting. The men by the fire mumble greetings to him. The mute nods and drops to his knees in front of a small wooden cage on the ground. He opens the door and carefully places the hawk inside, making a clicking sound with his mouth. The hawk jumps from his arm onto a perch. The mute closes the door and covers the cage with a piece of cloth, before disappearing inside the tent where the bearded leader is asleep. Dvalin's heart sinks. Somehow, he was hoping to surprise the boy on his own. But he has missed his opportunity. Now he will have to contend with at least one other man. He waits for the last two men to retire. By the time they do, he has lost all feeling in his fingers, but the camp is finally quiet.

He forces himself to wait even longer, then creeps forward towards the tents. The fire still crackles and burns, and he cannot resist holding his hands up to it for a minute to restore their feeling, while he ponders what to do next. Not far from him is the hawk's cage. He crawls over to it and raises the cloth cover. The bird tilts its head at him fiercely. Dvalin eases open the cage door and reaches inside. He unties the leather thong that tethers the hawk to its perch and ties it to his own wrist. He holds his arm next to the bird and waits. The bird shifts its weight uneasily from one foot to another and looks at him. Dvalin scowls at the bird, willing it to jump onto his arm. The hawk blinks and turns its head the other way. He curses the bird silently, then remembers the clicking sound used by the mute. He imitates the sound, and immediately the hawk jumps onto his arm. He slowly withdraws his arm from the cage and stands, surprised by how weightless the hawk is. He reaches out his other hand to stroke its wing feathers, and as he does, he hears a noise from the leader's tent. He turns to see the boy crouching in the doorway, watching him with eyes full of alarm. Dvalin steps backwards immediately, still carrying the bird. A look of panic crosses the boy's eyes, and for an instant, Dvalin fears that he will wake the others. Instead, the boy takes a step towards him, one hand raised, his only concern for the hawk. Dvalin begins to retreat, motioning for the lad to follow. The boy takes a deep breath, looks behind him at the tent, then follows. When Dvalin reaches the edge of the encampment, he turns and walks briskly through the forest, all the time glancing behind him to ensure that the lad is still there. He does not stop until he reaches the horses. Then he turns to the mute, who is staring at the hawk with wide eyes.

"You remember me, don't you?" says Dvalin.

The boy hesitates, then nods. He swallows anxiously, then nods again towards the bird.

Dvalin points at Freya's horse. "Get on," he says tersely. "Do nothing but follow me, or I'll break its neck."

The mute blinks rapidly a few times, then moves to Freya's horse and mounts it. Dvalin climbs upon his own horse, still holding the hawk and turns it in the direction of the cave. Their pace is slow, owing to the bird. They reach the cave just as the moon disappears behind some clouds. Dvalin dismounts and motions for the boy to do the same. He orders him to secure the horses and follow him inside the cave.

"Sit down," he says, nodding towards the fire. The lad obeys, eyeing him anxiously. Dvalin ties the hawk to a log in one corner, then draws his knife and crosses over to the mute. "Hands behind your back," he says, "feet in front of you." The boy looks at the knife, then does as he is asked. Dvalin walks behind him and, putting the knife in his teeth, secures the mute's hands with two leather strips, then crosses back in front of him and does the same to his ankles. When he is finished, he takes the knife out of his mouth and sits down heavily with a sigh.

"Do you know why you're here?" he asks after a moment.

The boy hesitates, before shaking his head.

"Because I intend to finish what I started."

The boy blinks several times.

Dvalin takes a deep breath and lets it out slowly. It is well past midnight and he is exhausted. Now that he has succeeded in capturing the mute, he does not have the will to continue. He puts two logs on the fire, and unrolls his bedding right beside it. After a moment's hesitation, he fetches Freya's bedroll and spreads it out beside the mute. The lad looks at it, then wriggles onto it as best he can. Dvalin lies down by the fire and closes his eyes. After a moment, he raises his head. The mute is lying on his side, staring at him.

"Get some rest. You'll not die tonight." says Dvalin, before turning his back on him and succumbing to sleep.

⚬⚬⚬

When he wakes, the first thing he feels is the bone-chilling cold. His entire body aches from the hard rock floor. He closes his eyes and tries to lose himself in sleep. Only then does he remember the boy. He rolls over. The lad is still asleep. He looks even younger this morning. His head is thrown back at an awkward angle and his mouth is slightly open. Dvalin stares at the ceiling of the cave. Perhaps he should have let things be. He felt so clear in his purpose yesterday. Today his mind is frozen with doubt.

He rises and puts some wood on the fire, blowing at the still-warm embers. The noise wakens the boy, who sits upright quickly. The mute immediately glances in the direction of the hawk. Dvalin follows his gaze. He had forgotten the bird. It sits quietly upon the log staring back at them. Dvalin forages in his saddlebag for what little food he has remaining. A stale end of bread and the last bit of cheese. Not enough for one person, let alone two, though why he should be feeding the boy, he doesn't know. He takes up his bow and arrow and sees the lad

229

stiffen. Dvalin shakes his head. "I'm going out," he says, "for food." The boy looks at him and nods.

It takes him all morning to make a kill. In the first few minutes, he misses a grazing doe by a hair's breadth, then does not see another living creature for two hours. When he has almost given up, he spies a hare nibbling grass at the edge of a copse of trees. It is large and old and dirty grey. Just as he takes aim, the hare senses his presence. It stops eating and raises its head, ears twitching. The arrow thumps and the hare falls. Dvalin walks over to where it lies. The point has gone right through its neck. He picks up the warm carcass and heads back towards the cave. When he arrives, the mute is sitting next to the hawk. The lad eyes him nervously. Dvalin sits down with a grunt and begins to clean and skin the hare. He tosses the innards and the pelt to one side, then skewers the body onto a green stick he has brought from the forest. Using two more sticks, he fashions a crude spit over the fire and places the hare upon it to roast. That done, he glances over at the mute, whose eyes are fixed on the discarded remains of the hare. The mute looks at him, then nods towards the hawk. Dvalin picks up the hare's remains with the point of his knife and walks over to where they are sitting, leaving the carcass on the log. The mute flashes him a look of gratitude, then eases away from the hawk. The bird begins to tear hungrily at the innards with its beak. Dvalin returns to the fire and sits down to wait.

An hour later, he has untied the lad's hands and both sit in front of the fire, their mouths smeared with grease from the hare, which they ate in its entirety in a matter of minutes. The hawk has polished off the carcass as well as the innards. Only the tiny bones remain, though the lad has sucked the marrow from them. Dvalin takes a long drink of water from his flask, then hands it to the mute, who hesitates briefly before accepting it. His feet are still bound together at the ankles, but the leather thong has loosened over the course of the day. Dvalin notices it without concern. The boy seems disinclined towards escape. Anyway, he would not leave without the bird.

Dvalin is just beginning to contemplate a nap, when he hears the sound of a twig snapping outside. Within an instant, he has unsheathed his knife and grabbed the mute from behind, holding the blade to his throat. The boy freezes in his grip. Dvalin can feel the racing of his heart against his forearm. Both keep their eyes locked upon the cave's entrance. For a long moment, there is only silence. Then they hear the faintest sound of foot-fall, and in the next instant, Freya is standing there peering into the darkness.

"Dvalin, is that you?"

Dvalin releases the mute with a sigh. At once he feels both angry and relieved. "What are you doing here?" he asks.

"Looking for you. And him." She indicates the boy. She drops to the ground beside the fire. "I knew you'd come for him."

Dvalin stares at her hotly. He did not even know himself what he was planning. How on earth could she? The idea that she anticipates him is unbearable. "How did you find us?" he asks with irritation.

"I saw the horses. You forget I have the advantage of height." She is carrying the falcon suit and holds it up now as a reminder. Then she nods towards the mute. "You've not hurt him, have you?"

"That's between me and him."

Exasperated, she turns to the boy. "Are you all right?" He nods solemnly.

Freya flashes a look at Dvalin. "Good."

"We were doing fine without you."

"And what, exactly, were you doing?" she demands. Dvalin shifts uncomfortably under her gaze. "And how do you intend all this to finish?" she continues.

He stares at her for several seconds, then looks away. "I don't know."

"Revenge is a poison, Dvalin."

"And what of honour? Is that a poison too?"

She sighs. "Just look at him." They both turn to the mute, who seems to shrink under their gaze.

"He's more clever than he seems," says Dvalin. "He escaped me once before."

"He was set free," says Freya emphatically. "Idun cut his bonds. She told me herself."

Dvalin gazes at her in disbelief, then shakes his head. "No," he says. "She would not have done that."

Freya turns to the mute. "It's true, isn't it? The woman your brothers violated. She felt compassion and let you go, did she not?" The boy slowly nods, wide-eyed. Dvalin snorts in disgust. Freya turns back to him. "So what you do now is not in Idun's name, but in your own, and yours alone."

Dvalin says nothing. He picks up a stick and begins to poke at the embers. Freya watches him for a moment, then crosses over to the boy and kneels down at his feet, untying the leather cords.

"Stop it!" Dvalin lunges for her. He grabs her hands, and they both tumble over in the dirt. He manages to get on top of her and pins her down in the dirt, while the boy looks on in amazement, his bonds now undone.

Freya looks up at him, her chest heaving. "He is innocent and you know it!"

Dvalin stares down at her, shaking his head. "You must be mad," he finally mutters, rolling off her. Freya sits up, rubbing her leg where he has hurt her. Dvalin wearily wipes his face with a hand, then looks up at the lad. "Go," he says, with a nod towards the cave entrance. "You're free."

The mute gapes at him in disbelief. Slowly, he stands. He looks at Freya, who nods, then glances anxiously at the hawk.

"Take the bird with you," says Dvalin. "And do not cross my path again."

The lad nods and quickly crosses to where the hawk is tethered. He unties the thong and makes the clicking sound. The hawk hops onto his forearm. When he turns back to them, he hesitates, as if he would like to say something.

"If you bring the others here, I'll cut your throat," says Dvalin sharply.

The boy's expression darkens. He contemplates them for a moment, then turns and runs out of the cave. They watch him go. Dvalin turns to Freya. "Are you satisfied?"

"Are you?"

He sighs. "I had no intention of killing him."

"Then what were you doing?"

Dvalin sighs. "Teaching him a lesson. Remembering. Forgiving. I don't know."

"Perhaps it's you who needs forgiving."

He says nothing. They both gaze into the fire. After a minute, Freya looks outside, where darkness has begun to fall. "Do you think he'll make it back?" she asks.

"He'll find his way," says Dvalin. "The hawk will guide him." He hesitates, then looks at her. "What about you?"

"I'll finish what I started," she says evenly.

∾➷➻∾

There is no point in setting off in darkness, so they remain in the cave for the night. Dvalin gathers more firewood and water, while Freya lays out some provisions that Idun has sent, including a flask of wine. "How is she?" he asks, when they have finally settled for their meal.

"Better, I think. It is difficult to say."

"Sometimes I wonder whether it is her marriage that is blighted, rather than her womb."

"She made an odd choice in Bragi. But given her past, perhaps it was not such a surprising one."

"Perhaps not." He frowns into the fire.

"You did not fail her, Dvalin. Then or now." Freya watches as he takes a drink of wine. "She would be proud of what you did today. And grateful. For her, the punishment was worse than the crime."

"They took something from her," he murmurs. "Something that can never be returned."

"But she has kept her dignity, and her faith in others. Surely that is what matters."

He shrugs.

"And she has Bragi. For all his faults, he is a devoted husband," she continues.

"Yes. Bragi is more faithful than a hound."

She smiles, watching as he loads more wood onto the fire. "Why are you not married?"

"Perhaps it wasn't my fate," he says lightly, snapping a branch in half over his knee. He tosses both halves onto the flames.

"Do you believe in such things?"

"No," he admits with a smile. "Do you?"

She hesitates briefly. "Yes." They are both silent for a moment. "What of Menglad?"

"What of her?"

Freya raises an eyebrow. "Your friendship struck me as... complicated."

Dvalin smiles. "Your words are apt. Menglad was

indeed complicated." He prods at the fire with a stick.

"And you were not?"

He laughs. "Maybe we both were."

"And now?"

He shakes his head, still poking at the fire. "That is for her husband to contend with."

"You knew her before she was married?"

He nods. "When Menglad was sixteen, she consulted an oracle. The oracle told her that one day she would marry a man called Svipdag."

Freya nods. "And when you met, she was already betrothed?"

"No."

Freya looks at him askance. "But she commissioned you to make her betrothal necklace!"

"Such was her faith in the oracle," he says dryly.

"And this man Svipdag, did she wait for him?"

"Yes."

"And he came?"

Dvalin pauses. "Yes."

"So the oracle was right."

"Only because Menglad believed her to be," he says. He frowns into the fire. "Anyway, the marriage quickly ran its course. And now she is trapped in a bitter union."

Freya considers this. "Perhaps that *was* her fate."

Dvalin raises an eyebrow, for this had not occurred to him. "Perhaps," he admits.

"Anyway, from the oracle's point of view, there was your fate to consider."

He laughs. "But I don't believe in fate."

"Maybe it believes in you," she says jestingly.

He shakes his head, still smiling. "And you? What of your past?" he asks.

She stares into the fire for a moment. "I was married," she says philosophically, "and now I'm not. "

"You are content to be alone," he says.

She looks up at him. "Yes, I am."

"Then we have that much in common," he replies. She meets his gaze for a moment, until he feels himself flush and looks away. Embarrassed, he clears his throat and picks up another log, throwing it on the fire. He should not have drunk so much. The wine has made him heavy-headed and weary.

"You are tired," she says quietly. "We should sleep."

He looks at her and wonders how she finds her way into his mind.

When Dvalin wakes, he feels a cold knife hard against his throat. He looks up into the eyes of the bearded leader. The grey light of dawn stretches across the cave. He can see the lumbering shapes of the other men all around him. He flinches uncontrollably, and feels the blade almost pierce his flesh.

"If you move, you will die," says the leader.

"Where is Freya?" he asks through clenched teeth.

"Here."

Her voice comes to him across the room, though he cannot see her.

"Are you all right?" he asks.

"That's enough talk," says the leader. "Sit up."

He raises himself up in the darkness. At once, they bind his hands and feet, just as he had done to the mute. He quickly glances around the cave, but the lad is nowhere to be seen. Freya sits off to one side. She remains untied, but one of the men stands next to her with his sword drawn. He thinks of Idun and what she suffered at the hands of men like these.

"She had nothing to do with it," he tells the leader.

"Our quarrel is with you," he replies, "not with the Aesir."

"Then let her go."

The bearded leader smiles. "She is free to leave, if she wishes." He turns to her expectantly. Freya glances anxiously at Dvalin.

"Go," says Dvalin. Freya stares at him but does not move.

"Perhaps she is unwilling," says the bearded leader.

"Don't be foolish, Freya," says Dvalin quietly. Her eyes dart nervously between the bearded man and Dvalin.

"Perhaps she is not as fond of you as you thought," says the giant. "Perhaps she might even enjoy the spectacle of your death." He steps towards Dvalin with his knife drawn.

"Wait," says Freya. The men all turn to look at her. "There is something you should see." Dvalin frowns. Freya rises and reaches inside her tunic.

"Freya, no," Dvalin hisses.

Slowly, she reaches her hands back and unclasps the necklace, holding it up for them to see. The first rays of light have begun to filter through the trees, enough to set the Brisingamen on fire. For a long moment, there is silence. Then the bearded leader slowly walks over to where she stands. When he is a few feet away, she takes a step backwards.

"That's close enough," she says. "Let us both ride free and it's yours." The bearded leader nods and reaches a hand out.

"Not until he's free," says Freya firmly.

The bearded leader laughs. He turns and nods towards one of his men, who kneels down in front of Dvalin and cuts his bonds. Dvalin stands and rubs his wrists.

"Get our things," orders Freya, clutching the necklace tightly to her chest. Dvalin quickly moves around the cave, gathering up their supplies. Within moments, the saddlebags are packed and slung over his shoulders. Freya nods at him. "Now get the horses." Dvalin walks out of the cave, and returns a minute later with the horses. Freya waits while he readies them.

"All right," she says. "We are going to mount the horses. Then I will hand you the necklace and we will ride free. You must give your oath that you will not pursue us."

"You have my word," says the bearded leader.

Freya turns and walks back to where Dvalin waits. She takes the reins from him, and as she passes by, he breathes urgently in her ear. "Don't."

She mounts the horse, and urges it forward a few steps, until she is abreast with the leader. Then she reaches down and holds out the necklace. The instant it passes from her hands, she feels her throat tighten.

The giant smiles at her broadly. "How fortunate that fate enabled us to meet," he says.

Freya looks at him with disgust, then turns her horse around and leaves. Dvalin doesn't move. He and the bearded leader stare at each other. After ten paces, Freya reins her horse in, and turns around in the saddle. "Dvalin!" she calls sharply.

Dvalin turns his horse away from the giants and trots over to where Freya waits for him. "You foolish, foolish woman," he mutters as he rides past her. She watches him for a moment, her anger mounting, then spurs her horse to follow. It takes her a minute to catch up with him.

"I save your life a second time and still you do not thank me!"

"Thank you? You've just thrown away my life's work!"

He glances back quickly at the giants. "And we'll have the devil's job stealing it back," he says.

"I have no intention of stealing it back," she snaps.

"Don't be ridiculous!"

"It was a fair trade, and I intend to honour it!"

"A fair trade? You think these men know the meaning of honour? They are thieves and murderers. No doubt rapists as well."

Freya purses her lips. "It was mine to do with as I pleased."

"You debase us all with your actions."

"And you did not deserve to be saved!" She kicks her horse hard and it leaps forward. She urges it into a gallop, leaving Dvalin behind in her dust. Dvalin pulls his horse to and looks back. The giants are still in the cave, no doubt celebrating their good luck. Now he must decide whether to follow Freya, or take his chances and try to recover the necklace. He turns and looks at her. She is already some distance away, riding flat out. The necklace will have to wait, he decides, spurring his horse after her. He will finish what he started.

FREYA

saw him hesitate at first. He almost did not follow. I understand my own motivations with respect to the necklace, but I do not understand his. He parted with it easily enough the first time. Why would he not relinquish it a second time when his own life was in the balance? Now he rides behind me, at a distance. We have been travelling several hours, with only a few brief pauses to rest and water the horses, interludes during which we do not speak. I have had plenty of time to consider my actions. To come all this way and return empty-handed seems pointless in the extreme. But I had no choice. I was not prepared to see blood spilt for the Brisingamen. Such a thing would taint it, surely. Even Dvalin must agree, and yet he refuses to acknowledge that his life was in danger.

It is late afternoon, the sun low in the sky, and I am already bone-tired. The mountain looms ahead of us. Fortunately, we've encountered no one else today. I can tell that we are nearing the farmstead where we stayed on our journey here. We pass over a hilltop, and the small turf house appears in the distance. It looks cosy enough, with its thin spiral of dark smoke. But I do not think I can bear the probing stares of the farmer and his wife, so I ride on. Behind me, I see Dvalin pause momentarily when he reaches the house, then continue. We ride for another hour, until the sun has almost set. We are still some distance from the pass, so we will have to camp. I stop beside a small grove of birch trees. A stream runs nearby, trickling over rocks and dark green moss beds. I dismount and unsaddle my horse, turning it loose to graze. Then I clear a space for a fire and start to gather wood. After a few minutes, Dvalin appears. Wordlessly, he dismounts and begins to help with the fire. I see that he has shot a mallard, the dead carcass slung across his saddlebag. "When did you get that?" I ask.

He shrugs. "Earlier."

Apart from what is necessary, we say nothing. He cleans the duck, while I build up the fire and unpack the remaining provisions left from Idun. The bird is small and thin, and cooks quickly. We eat it just as darkness falls, the silence heavy between us. After dinner, Dvalin broods into the fire. I cannot tell whether he is angry or simply mourning the loss of the Brisingamen. I also feel a kind of quiet desolation. Without the necklace, Dvalin and I are stripped of our connection. We are two strangers on a hillside in the darkness far from home.

The last of Idun's wine does little to ease the awkwardness. It only serves to make me angry. He should never have returned for the mute, I think darkly. He must realise this by now, even if he is unwilling to admit it. The night is cold and the frost comes quickly. We seek refuge in our bedrolls, laid out on opposite sides of the fire. I stare up into the sky. A thousand stars shine down upon us, and on the northern edge of the horizon, a ragged curtain of light dances. Dvalin lies with his back to me, so I cannot see his face. We will cross the pass tomorrow and go our separate ways. And neither of us will possess the thing we most desire.

Eventually, sleep takes me. It is shallow and fretful, troubled by dreams of the Aesir, and by images of bearded giants who ride rings around us in the night. In the early hours of the morning, I am woken by a noise. I sit up quickly and listen to the sound of horse's hooves not far from where we sleep. I turn to see Dvalin already crouched beside the now-dead fire, his knife and sword in hand. He raises a finger to his lips and we wait. The horse's hooves slowly draw near: the sound of a lone rider. We strain to see through the darkness. Suddenly, the young mute emerges from the trees upon a horse. He halts at once when he sees us. The hawk perches in front of him, tied to the saddle.

"What the?" Dvalin murmurs. He draws his sword, advancing towards the mute.

"Wait," I say behind him.

He pauses. The boy slides off his mount, eyeing us, and reaches into his saddlebag, withdrawing something that we cannot see. He then walks slowly towards us, and when he is ten paces away, he stops and fumbles for a moment in the darkness. Eventually, he pulls the necklace free and holds it up. Dvalin turns to me and laughs. It is a joyous sound, one that echoes deep inside me, for I too am delighted. I quickly move past him towards the boy and extend my hand for the necklace. It feels warm and solid in my palm. "Thank you," I say. He nods once, then turns and walks back towards his horse and stands beside it, watching us. One hand reaches out to stroke the feathers of the hawk. Dvalin crosses over to me and stares down at the necklace, shaking his head with surprise.

"Do you think he stole if off them?" I ask quietly.

"I hardly think they let him walk away with it."

"Perhaps he persuaded them to give it up."

He looks at me askance. "By what means?"

I frown. He is right. Without words, it is unlikely the lad could make a case for its return. But then a thought occurs to me. "Do you think they'll come after him?" I ask.

"Possibly. Men have died for less, that is certain."

We both glance at the mute. He remains by his mount, calmly stroking the hawk. "Then we will have to take him with us," I say quietly.

"What?" Dvalin practically shouts. The boy looks up quickly in alarm. I place my hand on Dvalin's arm and lean towards him.

"We might as well just slit his throat right now," I whisper, "than leave him behind!"

Dvalin sighs. Once again, he looks at me as if I'm mad. "He goes with you," he says finally, "for I'll not have him."

I smile at him and beckon to the boy.

✺

The lad is exhausted. Dvalin offers to keep watch until dawn. With luck, the giants lie deep in drunken sleep somewhere, and have not yet discovered his absence. Dvalin builds up the fire, and the boy lays his bedroll next to it. Sleep takes him instantly. I wrap my bedding around me and sit on the opposite side of the fire. Dvalin glances over at me several times.

"What?" I finally ask.

"You were right about him."

We both look at the boy. "It was Idun who was right."

We watch in silence as the first fingers of light reach across the sky. The atmosphere has eased between us, and Dvalin seems more content than I have known him. I wonder at this, because it is I who have recovered the Brisingamen, not him. But I say nothing. Eventually, he rouses the mute from a deep sleep. We cannot afford to leave him any longer. The lad sits up and rubs his eyes, then quickly turns and looks towards the hawk, which is tethered to a log nearby. He packs his bedroll, glancing at us nervously from time to time. "We'll cross the pass in a short while," I tell him, pointing towards the mountain. His eyes travel upwards, widening. "The men you were with may try to follow, so we must hurry." I turn away from him, but he grabs my arm. He shakes his head, frowning. "What is it?" I ask. He shakes his head again. "They will not follow?" I ask. He nods.

Dvalin stops what he is doing and crosses over to us. "Why not?" he demands. The boy hesitates, then rolls his eyes back and tilts his head to one side, his mouth hanging open. "You killed them?" asks Dvalin, astonished.

The boy quickly shakes his head. Then he raises his hands in the air and makes a long sweeping motion. Dvalin and I exchange a puzzled glance. The boy makes the sweeping motion again. "A landslide?" I murmur to Dvalin. The boy grabs my arm and nods emphatically.

Dvalin looks at him in disbelief. "Are they dead?" he asks. The boy nods, more slowly. "All of them?" The boy shrugs and nods again. "Where were you?" says Dvalin. The boy points to the mountain, then mimics looking down on his companions.

"Above the slide," I say. The boy nods, this time more slowly, and suddenly his eyes betray the horror of the experience.

Dvalin lays a hand upon his shoulder. "I'm sorry," he says gently. The boy blinks, then lowers his head and stares at the ground.

Dvalin turns to me. "How on earth did he recover the necklace?"

The boy raises his head and touches Dvalin's arm. Then he points to the hawk. "The hawk got the necklace?" asks Dvalin, incredulous. The boy nods. Dvalin shakes his head in amazement, then laughs. The lad gives a small smile, and Dvalin claps him on the shoulder. "Well done," he says heartily. "To the both of you."

We take our time now. Dvalin offers to procure fish for breakfast. He takes up his spear and walks along the stream until he finds a small pool. He settles himself on the bank to wait, his spear upraised. Three times we hear the water splash, followed quickly by Dvalin's muttered oaths. At length, the boy wanders over to the stream. He chooses a spot slightly downstream from Dvalin. We both watch as he rolls up his sleeve and lies face down on the bank, stretching his long arm deep into the water. He remains this way for several minutes, until with a sudden movement, he flips a live fish out of the water and onto the bank, where it flaps about helplessly. Dvalin stares at the fish, astonished. The boy smiles shyly and stretches his arm back into the water.

In all, he pulls five small trout from the stream. Dvalin guts the fish and skewers them on sticks. We roast them whole over the fire and devour the flesh between us, while the hawk feasts on the innards with zeal. When we finally set off, the sun is nearly overhead. We cross the last plateau and begin our ascent, riding single file. Dvalin leads and the boy follows, with me at the rear. It is only then, with the horses scrambling for balance, and shingle rocketing past me on its way down the slope, that I remember Berling's warning. *The Brisingamen can do things.* I raise my eyes to the pass ahead of us. Can it bring down a mountain, I wonder? Is this what happened to the giants? My horse stumbles suddenly and I fly forward, grabbing its neck. All at once, I feel the hard weight of the Brisingamen trapped beneath my chest, as if it is reminding me of its presence.

We cross the pass without incident, much to my relief, then continue down the mountain. It is late afternoon when we reach the place where the three of us must part. Dvalin and I have already agreed that he will return to the caves with the horses, while the mute and I will use the falcon suit to fly to Sessruminger. When I explain this to the lad, his eyes grow round as dates. He takes a deep breath, then glances at the hawk with concern. "Don't worry," I say. "When we fly, the bird will follow." He frowns, then unties the leather thong which binds the bird's feet to his wrist and raises his arm to the sky. He makes a noise with his throat, and the hawk takes wing, rising above us in circles, until it is no more than a dot in the sky. The lad watches it, blinking into the sun, then turns to me. "Are you ready?" I ask. He nods. I cross over to where Dvalin stands beside his horse, the other two already roped behind him.

I choose my words. "There are things I still don't understand," I say. "About the necklace. And you."

"Perhaps too much knowledge is a bad thing," he replies. His eyes linger on mine, and I feel the heat rise in my face.

"Go safely," I say.

"And you."

I walk back to where the boy waits and don the falcon suit. "Put your arms around my neck," I tell him. As he does, I feel his body tense. I lift us both into the air. We climb upwards, tracing the hawk's circular flight. The wind buffets us gently. After a minute, the boy relaxes slightly. I glance over my shoulder and see his eyes shine with wonder. He has waited all his life for this moment. Perhaps inside he has always known the joy of flight. I look down at the ground. Far below us, Dvalin recedes quickly. He stands staring up into the sky, his expression already lost to the wind.

THE NORNS

Animals understand the secret whisperings of the earth. When the crust prepares to rearrange itself, it is they who take heed: hens refuse to lay, bees flee their hives, and fish jump out of rivers. The slow constant movement of the crust produces stress that rocks cannot withstand. Eventually a fault occurs: opposing sides of rock fracture open, are thrust together or wrenched past one another. It is not a graceful process. The crust judders and jumps, resulting in a quake. The energy released is enormously destructive: it radiates outwards in waves from the centre, wreaking havoc on the land. Volcanoes are not immune to these forces. A few hours before Hekla erupts, she will begin to tremble. As magma reaches the surface, she will burst open and the ground beneath her will vibrate almost continuously, like the strings of an enormous earth-bound instrument.

FULLA

ulla hands Hogni a wooden bowl full of pale brown gruel. "What is this?" he asks suspiciously. It is three days since they returned from the Althing. His mood has been sour throughout.

"Porridge. Made from barley," she says. "A trader passed by yesterday."

He raises an eyebrow. "Your grandmother was fond of barley." He sniffs at it. "Is there no butter?"

Fulla rises and retreats into the storeroom, returning a moment later with a lump of yellow butter. Hogni grunts his appreciation, stirring the butter into the porridge, while Fulla seats herself again beside him and begins to eat.

"Was she a good cook?" she asks.

Hogni nods. "She was good at everything. It was her biggest fault. Perhaps her only fault," he adds.

Fulla smiles. "I'm sorry I did not know her."

"She too would have been sorry."

"How did you meet?"

"At the Shyling Festival. She didn't approve of me at first. I don't know why, but it was obvious from her manner. She thought I was impulsive. And high-minded. Perhaps I was. I certainly remember being impatient at that age." He takes a bite of porridge and chews methodically, the fleshy corners of his mouth moving slowly up and down.

"How did you win her favour?"

"Every day for a week I walked up to the high meadows and brought her a bouquet of flowers. She refused them for the first four days. On the fifth day, she said, 'If I accept them will you stop?' 'Probably not,' I told her. On the sixth day, she laughed and asked if there was nothing else I could present her with. So on the seventh day, I brought her a wheel of cheese. She told me that she preferred flowers. 'Woman, you are difficult to please!' I said. Then she looked me in the eye and said, 'Yes. I am.'"

Hogni pauses, smiling at the memory. "She was right," he continues. "In marriage she was exacting. She held me to higher standards than I held myself. We worked hard. And laughed too seldom. Though perhaps we didn't realise it at the time." He frowns. "Love eluded us for a time. And then it came upon us suddenly, like a spring storm. When it was almost too late," he adds slowly. "She became pregnant with our second child, and for a brief time we knew great happiness. But the birth proved too much for both of them, and Jarl and I were left alone." His voice dwindles to a hoarse whisper. He stirs the remaining porridge in his bowl. "For a long time, I could not reconcile myself to the idea that it was love that killed her. Perhaps if we had not found it so late, she would still be here today."

Fulla lays down her bowl. "Why did you not remarry?"

"I thought of it. Many times in the first few years. But her memory clung to me. And in the end, I could not."

"It is a blessing you found love with her, then."

"But it took time," he says, eyeing her. "Love is not like a spring flood, Fulla. It comes to us in tiny increments. And there are many things that masquerade in its name." He pauses. "I do not believe that you would have found love with Skallagrim's grandson," he continues.

"The men of his clan are not like our own."

"But he is not like his kin," she protests quickly.

"How do you know?" Hogni says emphatically, cutting her off. "You have spent how much time in his company altogether? Three hours? Four?"

"I knew Rolf even less," she counters, "when you offered me as his bride."

Hogni shakes his head slowly. "I have known Rolf and his kin all my life. He is a good man. He could have made you happy."

"How do you know?" she echoes his words.

Hogni sighs. "I never had a daughter," he says wearily. "Only a son. And now, not even that."

"I never had a mother," she replies evenly. "Only a father. And now, not even that." Her words are wounding, though she does not know if she intended them to be. In that instant, the gulf between them seems to widen, until it is a vast expanse they cannot cross.

The following afternoon, a quartet of riders appears on the horizon. Hogni is in the stable yard when he sees them. He pauses in his work and walks out to greet them. Two of the men he has never seen before: they are dressed in coarse brown cassocks and wear crosses around their necks. The third is Gizurr, a godi he knows from the neighbouring district, and one of the first to take the oath of conversion. The fourth rider he recognises from the Althing as the missionary Thangbrand. Both Gizurr and Thangbrand wear vests of chainmail over their tunics and carry swords and shields. The four riders come to a halt just in front of him, but do not dismount. "Greetings," he calls to them.

"Greetings, Hogni," says Gizurr. The other men nod.

"You are welcome to stop and rest."

Gizurr shakes his head. "Thank you, but we'll pass by. We hope to reach Husafell by nightfall."

"As you wish."

"You left the Althing early," continues Gizurr.

"Aye."

"Too early to take the sacrament of baptism," he adds.

Hogni looks from Gizurr to Thangbrand, then back again. "We forgot," he says flatly. Thangbrand's eyebrow shoots up in response.

"Then you can have no objection to receiving it now," he interjects.

Hogni turns to him. "I bathe when it suits me."

"We have been told to ensure that every man receives the sacrament of baptism."

"By whom?"

"The lawspeaker."

"And if I refuse?"

"Then under the law you can be prosecuted."

"Christian law."

"The law of our country. The only law."

"As I said before, I will enter the waters at a time of my own choosing," Hogni declares. He and Thangbrand eye each other for a long moment.

"Obstinate minds cling fast to their beliefs," says Thangbrand slowly.

"Better obstinate than indifferent." Hogni shifts his gaze to Gizurr. "I'll not abandon my faith at the first puff of opposition."

"Yet sooner or later, you will have to," says Thangbrand.

"Then let it be later."

Thangbrand narrows his eyes. "As you wish," he says after a moment's consideration. He turns to his companions and addresses them. "After all, one does not reach the summit in leaps; one mounts it step by step." He turns back to Hogni. "We ride east now to Husafell. We will pass through Laxardal again in a fortnight. Be prepared to take the sacrament then." He does not wait for a response, but turns his horse around and nudges it into movement. The others follow. Gizurr nods coldly to Hogni, who merely raises an eyebrow in response. Fulla steps forward to Hogni's side, and they watch the figures retreat into the distance.

"Grandfather, you risk your freedom with these men," she says once they are out of earshot.

"I worship whom I please."

"But you will have to submit to what they ask."

"Perhaps," he says, turning away. "But not today."

∾≈∽

The next morning, when Fulla returns from her ride, she sees a strange horse tied up in the yard. She enters the house where Hogni is deep in conversation with a tall heavy-set man she has never seen before. The man is grey-haired but younger-looking than Hogni. He is rich-ly dressed in an elaborate dark green cloak, its borders decorated with silver thread. They sit by the fire, each with a tankard of ale, and they both turn and look at her expectantly when she enters.

"I'm sorry," she says quickly. "I didn't mean to intrude."

"Not at all," says the stranger, standing. Hogni too rises to his feet. She sees at once that his mood has lift-ed. His face is slightly flushed with drink, and his eyes sparkle with anticipation.

"Fulla, this is Gunnar. He's a very old friend of mine."

Gunnar smiles at her. "I am pleased to meet you," he says in a heavy accent.

255

"And I, you," she replies politely. An awkward silence follows, and Fulla realises that she has interrupted their business. She excuses herself and the two men sit down again in front of the fire. She goes to the scullery, where Helga is busy over preparations for a stew.

Helga hands her a bowl of onions and a knife. "Peel." Fulla takes the bowl and pulls up a small stool, seating herself.

"Who is he?" she asks quietly, nodding towards the other room.

Helga shrugs. "Norwegian, from the accent. I've not set eyes on him before."

"What business do they discuss?"

"It's no concern of ours," Helga admonishes, picking up a knife. She begins to briskly chop a head of cabbage. After a moment, she lays down the knife. "Though I did hear mention of a ship's passage," she says, without raising her eyes.

Fulla frowns. "Ship's passage? To where?"

Helga shrugs. "Who knows?"

Fulla finishes peeling the onions and hands the bowl to Helga. She stands and returns to the main hall, in time to see Hogni and Gunnar shake hands warmly.

"Safe journey on your return," says Hogni.

"Are you leaving?" asks Fulla.

"I must. I sail tomorrow back to Norway," Gunnar says with a smile, "where I shall carry the most favourable of reports from Laxardal."

His words make her uneasy. She watches as Hogni walks Gunnar out into the yard to see him off. The two men clasp arms affectionately. When Hogni returns, she confronts him. "What reports are these? And who is he reporting to?"

"Gunnar is an old friend of mine," says Hogni in a placating tone. "It was his ship that brought me here

256

from Norway as a young man. I have known him all my life."

"And?"

"And…he brings us news of our kin at home. Good news. It seems our family prospers there."

"I thought this was our home," she says distrustfully.

Hogni ignores this last comment. "My cousin is a wealthy man now. As a youth he was unpromising. But he inherited a huge landholding south of Bognor, and it seems that he has managed it wisely." Hogni pauses. "His eldest son now seeks a wife. It appears they've heard reports of you. They asked Gunnar to enquire whether you are spoken for."

Fulla hesitates, her heart racing. "Am I?" she asks.

Hogni turns towards the fire and thrusts his hands out to warm them. "I'm told he is a fine man of good character. He will, of course, inherit his father's lands."

Fulla stares at him. "I saw you clasp hands with him," she says slowly. "You've come to an agreement, haven't you?"

Hogni turns to face her. "What I do, I do solely for your well being," he says.

"Please answer me," she says urgently.

"He is kin, Fulla. There can be no better match than this one."

She shakes her head, incredulous. "You did not even consult me," she says accusingly.

"I did not think it necessary," he replies sternly.

"Because I do not merit even the smallest amount of consideration!"

"Because you refuse to display even the smallest amount of reason!"

"Yes," she says, her eyes lit with anger. "Reason is indeed beyond me. Though hatred is still within my grasp." She pushes past him out the door.

DVALIN

With two animals in tow, the journey back to Nidavellir seems endless. Each time he glances behind him, the sight of the riderless horses jars him. He does not feel as he should, heading home. He should feel elated, or at the very least relieved. Instead, he feels empty.

By the time he arrives, night has fallen, hastened by a sudden lowering of clouds. The dark membrane of storm appears over the jagged tops of the mountains and within minutes, has slid across the entire ceiling of the valley, where it huddles low, anticipating. Dvalin draws his horse up outside the cave's entrance, just as the first rush of gale reaches him. The wind leans him hard into the mare's side, and she sidesteps nervously. Freya's mount jumps backwards. He grabs hold of the leading rein.

"Steady." He cups a palm against the horse's nose and pushes his forehead into its cheek, as he reaches under with the other hand to untie it. The animal's hide is wet with effort from the ride.

A crunch of stone sounds from inside the cave. Grerr materialises out of the darkness, as if he has just passed from one world to the next. Dvalin sees at once that he is agitated. His eyes wear a frenzied look like one who has not slept in days.

"The necklace?" he asks intently.

"I left it with her." Dvalin lifts the saddle from his

horse and lays it upon the stone ledge, then turns to Freya's mount. The pony tosses its head and snorts. Grerr narrows his eyes suspiciously.

"She paid for it?"

Dvalin stops for a moment and meets his gaze. "Yes," he says firmly. He finishes unsaddling the horses, then turns them out onto the grass. The horses move off to join a clutch of others grazing nearby. Dvalin turns towards the cave, but Grerr blocks his way.

"I don't believe you."

Dvalin pushes past him. "Suit yourself."

Grerr follows him and grabs his arm. "You never had her." The words fall slowly, thick with disdain.

Dvalin's face tightens. "The choice was mine," he says stiffly.

"The price was four nights. One for each. She owes us still."

"She owes us nothing. I set my own price."

"A coward's reckoning."

Dvalin shakes his head. "Call it what you like," he says wearily. "But it's none of your business."

"She is not all you think her to be, brother."

"Maybe not." Dvalin shrugs. "Maybe she is more."

Grerr throws back his head and bellows loudly, his laughter bouncing off the stone. "Let me tell you something: the night she came to me she was smiling."

"You're a fool."

"A fool who knows the wetness of a woman's want."

Dvalin says nothing. Instead, his body seems to swell slightly in the gloom.

Grerr leers. "I tasted hers, brother."

Dvalin grabs him by the shirtfront, hoisting him onto his toes, until their noses almost meet. His teeth are tightly clenched. "It was the necklace she wanted, you foul maggot!" he hisses.

Grerr waves his arms like an insect, his face slowly reddening. He splutters and chokes, but a triumphant smile forms upon his face. He spits the words out in half-strangled gasps. "You said it, brother. We're all maggots of Ymir's flesh. You. Me. Our father's father. His father before him. Grasping dwarves who dwell in darkness. Did you really think she'd want one of our own?"

Dvalin releases him suddenly, tossing him to the ground. "I care not," he says flatly. Grerr lands heavily in the dirt, his arms splayed behind him. Dvalin turns away. He walks towards the cave's entrance. Berling, his face ashen, stands watching from the shadows just inside. Dvalin brushes by him.

"Dvalin!" Berling calls after him, his voice beseeching. But Dvalin has already disappeared inside the cave's darkness.

❧

Later, they sit beside the fire in Dvalin's cave. Berling crouches next to him, his knees drawn up tight beneath his chin. He traces a circle on the ground with his forefinger. "Was it truth you spoke to Grerr?" His voice is small, that of a child. Dvalin feels a stab of regret.

"What is truth, Berling? I myself do not recognise it."

Berling frowns. "This is how I see it, Dvalin. We are small. And we dwell below the earth's surface. These things are true. But we have a home. We have a place within the world."

Dvalin sighs. "Yes, of course."

"And a purpose. We have that too."

"Yes."

"And knowledge. We have our knowledge of all things past. That is more than some are blessed with. And our skill as craftsmen, that as well."

"Yes, Berling." Dvalin spans his hand across his temples, as if to hide from Berling's words. The ache in his head does not recede.

Berling entreats him. "Does this not amount to something?"

"Of course it does."

"Then what did you mean?"

"Sometimes, I do not know myself. The words flew out before I had a chance to stop them."

Berling gives a rueful smile. At once, his face floods with compassion for the man next to him. "Small birds of truth, eh Dvalin?"

"I suppose so."

"In the eyes of the world, we are low."

"Yes, we are."

Berlings laughs self-consciously, then gives a small shrug. "Of course I knew this. But one does not often hear it said in these dark walls."

"Perhaps it is best that way."

"Yes," he says doubtfully.

Dvalin frowns. "Berling," he says, "what matters most is what your own eyes see. That is what you need to know."

"Yes, Dvalin."

Berling's face swells with doubt, however. Dvalin closes his eyes, the pain scratching once again at the places in his head. He utters a silent oath for his earlier outburst. The boy needs nothing of stone-cold truths; he must focus only on his own survival, evade the harsh web of the world. Dvalin opens his eyes. Beside him, Berling's expression has eased. He toys with an ember that has landed at his feet. He taps it with a stone, turning and tapping until the last glow of red is gone and only dust remains. Not for the first time, Dvalin wonders when Berling will reach manhood.

Berling looks up at him with a wistful expression. "Do you think we'll see her again?" he asks.

Dvalin frowns. "I don't know." He hesitates. "Berling, you didn't...you're not in love with her, are you?"

Berling shrugs. "I just liked her, Dvalin. Is that a crime?"

"Of course not."

"The caves are dull without her here."

Dvalin looks at him. He has tried not to think of what went on between Freya and Berling, though the idea gnaws at him. "Berling," he says finally, "did you..." he breaks off.

Berling looks up at him. "What?"

"Never mind." He picks up an iron poker and prods the fire. The flames leap to life.

Berling stares at him thoughtfully for a moment. "No," he says then. "The answer is no." Dvalin meets his gaze for an instant, before a noise startles them both.

"What was the question?" says Gerd good-naturedly. She has entered silently and is standing a few feet from them, smiling. They both turn to look at her, speechless.

Dvalin jumps to his feet. "I'm sorry, we didn't hear you."

"Are you home for good now?" she asks.

"Yes," he says.

"And your journey? How was it?"

"Unremarkable."

"Excellent," she smiles. "We must celebrate your return." She turns to Berling. "Berling, go and fetch a jug of wine from your uncle."

Berling moans. "Must I?"

"You must," she says. Berling sighs and rises to his feet. They both watch him go, then take their seats by the fire. "And Freya?" she asks, turning back to him.

"She's returned to Asgard."

"With the Brisingamen."

"Yes."

She nods thoughtfully. "I never saw it," she remarks.

Dvalin shrugs. "It was only a necklace."

She hesitates, measuring the truth of his words. "Yes, of course," she replies. She picks up a piece of kindling and throws it upon the flames. After a moment, the fire crackles. "I had a tiny fear you might not return," she says self-consciously.

"Why?"

"It sometimes seems as if only part of you is here with us," she says. "And another part of you dwells somewhere else."

"Sometimes I feel that way myself."

"Where is that place, Dvalin?"

He smiles and shakes his head. "I wish I knew."

She turns and looks at him. "Dvalin, have you never thought that you and I...?" She lays a hand upon his arm. "It makes sense, doesn't it? For Berling's sake. And for our own?"

Dvalin casts his eyes down to her slender fingers. "Gerd," he says softly, "you are my father's wife."

"*Was*," she says emphatically. "Am I to be a widow forever?" Her voice contains the barest tremor.

Dvalin shakes his head. "Only to me."

"Your father was a great man. Full of passion and committed to his people. But I have passions of my own, Dvalin. I am still young." She looks at him intently.

"I know this, Gerd."

"We needn't be alone, you and I."

"I know this too," he says quietly. His gaze falls to the ground. Gerd's fingers slip from his arm. He can think of nothing else to say. He cannot love her, though whether it is for the reasons he has given, he isn't certain. Gerd's face slowly drains of expression, as if he has torn the life from her. Her eyes drift across the room. The silence spirals out between them. Dvalin berates himself.

They hear footsteps in the passage, and in the next instant Berling rushes in, carrying a jug and a pair of wooden cups. "Wine," he announces breathlessly, flopping down beside them. He holds up the cups and looks at them. Something in their manner alerts him. His smile fades, the cups fall to his side.

His mother takes a deep breath. "We'll have that toast then, shall we?"

FREYA

've called him Sky. I thought it fitting. He cannot tell me his real name, so there was no point in asking, but he seems content with this one. The hawk followed us here, just as I knew it would, and the two of them have adjusted with surprising ease to life in Asgard. The boy spends his days roaming the hills around Sessruminger. Each time, he brings me something he has found along the way. This morning, it was a beautiful piece of rose quartz. Yesterday, it was the tail feather of an arctic tern. The day before, a giant seed pod. He gives these things to me without fanfare, as if he is quietly repaying me for the life I have bestowed upon him.

He was nervous at first. The cats alarmed him. I don't think he'd come across such animals before. He froze with terror the first time one leapt into his lap. Now he seems to like them, though I've noticed that he doesn't handle them in the presence of the hawk. I've encouraged him to let the bird fly free from time to time, as I cannot bear to see it tethered. He was reluctant to do so at first, but when he realised that it would return of its own accord, he grew more willing. Now the hawk flies free each morning, accompanying him on his rambles.

He gains a little in confidence each day. I wish that I knew more about him. When I first asked his age, he seemed uncertain, and for a moment, I thought he didn't know. Then he picked up a piece of charred wood from the fire, and carefully drew thirteen marks upon the hearthstone. "Thirteen," I commented lightly. "No longer a child. Not yet a man." At once, I regretted this remark. His eyes flickered with dismay, and I realised then that perhaps he had never been a child in the true sense of the word. Had he ever lived without the burden of responsibility? I wondered. I felt guilty then, as if it was I who had snatched away his youth, and not circumstance.

Gradually, I've learned a few details about his past. His parents are dead. And Dvalin killed two of his brothers, though I do not speak of this. He confirmed that the men he was with when we first came across him were kin. But whenever I question him about his family, his manner instantly alters and he retreats even further into silence. Does he mourn all those he's lost? I wonder.

∾≈∾

This morning, my father surprises me with a visit. I've not seen him in some weeks. His own house lies to the east, and though it is only an hour's ride, neither of us makes the journey often. The bond between us has never been an easy one. When Freyr and I were young, my mother's death hung over him like a shadow. Rather than bring him closer to us, it somehow pushed him further away. Freyr and I responded in kind, by maintaining a childish alliance that we excluded him from. But as we grew older, Freyr and I moved apart. As he drifted towards manhood he became more and more like my father, inheriting certain aspects of his personality, especially his distrust of those outside his circle.

I walk out to greet him in the yard. "Father. It's good to see you," I say as he climbs off his horse. In truth, I am surprised by the state of him, for he has aged these past few months at an alarming rate. "Come and rest from your ride."

Once inside, he takes stock of me in his usual peremptory manner. "You look thin," he declares. I immediately feel the warmth of the necklace against my breast. I readjust my clothes, to make certain it is well hidden.

"I've been travelling."

"So I've heard. What's all this about Nidavellir?"

"One of many places I visited," I say evasively.

He gives me a piercing look. "You've not seen Od again, have you?"

"No, Father," I say, relieved. "Od is dead, as far as I'm concerned."

"Good." My father has long regarded my marriage as an illness that might recur. He was set against Od from the beginning. He could not fathom my decision to marry outside the Aesir. "Why choose bread made of barley, when wheat is your due?" he asked me. The question typified him. He lived his own life as an allegory, never daring to confront its harsher truths. When his second marriage fell apart, he endeavoured to explain its failure in purely geographic terms. He could not live without the sea, he told me earnestly, while his new wife was firmly tethered to the mountains. "I cannot bear the ceaseless baying of wolves," he said. "And she cannot endure the endless lapping of waves." The fact that they could not abide each other's voices was lost on him.

Like me, my father had married outside his own. His second wife, Skadi, belonged to the race of giants. She was young and beautiful, and had been lured into the alliance through deceptive means. In fact she'd been betrayed by the beauty of his feet, for it was these she'd seen first: small for a man, perfectly proportioned, with pale crescent moons upon each toe. Her own father had been slain in battle by the Aesir, and they had offered her a choice of husbands from among them as a concession, with the only stipulation that she must choose them solely by their feet. Those men who were eligible were assembled, my widowed father among them, and cloaks were thrown over their bodies. That summer, it was rumoured that Skadi was infatuated with Odin's son Balder, he of the smooth-faced smile and dark, lustrous eyes. Who could blame her, for I too had been tempted by Balder's innocent charms. How unfortunate for her, then, the state of his corn-ridden feet. In the end, it was my father she unwittingly chose. Not surprisingly, the marriage went quickly awry.

I watch my father stroll restlessly about the room. He has put on weight this last year, and while he has always been a handsome man, his looks have filled out to the point of bloatedness. His hair is the colour of grey ice, though unlike many men of his age, he has it in abundance. His features are large and overly expressive, and they go hand in hand with his manner, which tends to be extravagant.

"What of you?" I ask. "Have you and Skadi reconciled?"

He gives an irritated wave. "I've not seen her in months. She refuses to leave that cabin of hers in the mountains. I don't know what she does up there."

I smiled. "She hunts and skis. It sounds very pleasant." He narrows his eyes at me. "And what news of Freyr?" I ask.

"Still in Sweden," he says distractedly. "Uppsala, I think. The farmers there adore him. To excess, I fear. They'll be the ruin of him." Freyr has a devoted following in Sweden. In Uppsala, every household has a shrine to him, in hopes that he will favour their harvest.

"Perhaps not," I venture. "Our world is changing, Father. You must know this."

He raises a sceptical eyebrow. "I know what I've seen. Men with wooden crosses who roll off their ships and plant themselves among us like bad seeds. They will never thrive here. Their ideas will not take hold. You will see." He gives a dismissive wave of one hand.

Sky enters the room then, having just returned from his morning ramble. The hawk perches quietly upon his forearm, and when he sees my father, he stops short and looks at me uncertainly. My father also turns to me with a look of alarm, as if to say, who is *this*, then? "Father, this is Sky," I offer. Sky nods at him shyly. "He doesn't speak," I add.

My father looks him up and down. "Can't or won't?" he asks, frowning. Sky looks at me worriedly.

"He is mute," I say quietly.

"Oh," he replies, embarrassed. "Greetings, son." Sky nods briefly, then turns and walks out of the house. My father turns to me with a raised eyebrow. "What kind of name is Sky?"

"One of my choosing," I reply.

He makes a face. "Where did you find him?"

"Jotunheim."

"Well, that explains his height," he murmurs. "But I don't understand: why is he here?"

"Because I invited him," I say. "His kin are dead." My father raises a dubious eyebrow.

"Do you employ him?" he asks tentatively.

"No, Father, he's a guest."

"A guest." My father repeats the word, somewhat disbelieving. He crosses to the door and peers outside, where he can see Sky standing in the garden. "Well, at least he's quiet," he says, turning back to me.

"Why have you come?"

He looks offended. "Must I have a reason?"

"Of course not. But you usually do."

He sits down heavily in an armchair with a sigh. "If you must know, there's been talk," he says with a little flourish of his hands.

"Ignore it," I say.

He frowns, clearly annoyed. "What's all this about a necklace, Freya?"

I shrug. "Idle gossip."

"And dwarves," he says, more pointedly.

I look him in the eye. "Lies."

He squirms uncomfortably. "Freya, in case you've forgotten, we have a certain position to maintain here in Asgard. You, me, your brother. We have a function to fulfil."

I stare at him. The Aesir have no purpose other than to bring about their own destruction, I think. But my father does not see this. Perhaps he was not meant to. I walk over to the doorway. Sky sits upon a rock wall in the garden, while the hawk wheels high overhead. Behind them, Hekla smoulders patiently. "Hekla is uneasy," I say, changing the subject.

My father comes up behind me and peers over my shoulder. "Hekla has always been this way," he says, frowning. "For as long as we've been here."

I shake my head. "No. Something is different. I am certain of it."

I watch him weigh my words. "If this were true, then we would know," he says finally, dismissively. He turns back to me. "So there is nothing you wish to tell me?"

I have tried, I think. "No," I reply.

He takes a deep breath and lets it out slowly, his nostrils widening. "What will become of you, Freya?"

"What do you mean?"

"Your marriage has failed. You rarely see anyone.

You've only the cats for company. Except for…bird-boy." He waves his hand in the direction of the garden.

"Sky," I correct him.

"It isn't healthy."

"I am content, Father."

He sighs. "Very well. I can see you don't want my interference."

"I'm grateful for your interest," I say in a conciliatory manner. "But I can manage my own affairs."

"As you wish," he says wearily, rising to go.

All at once, I do not want him to leave. It is a fleeting childish moment, but the feeling is so powerful that I cannot shake it free. "Please," I say, my voice breaking, "don't go."

He turns and gives me a curious look. "I'm afraid I must," he says. "The weather's unsettled. They'll be making offerings at sea, with no one there to receive them," he explains earnestly. He takes up his cloak and turns to me one last time. "Do use some sense, Freya. Remember who you are." And then he disappears out the door, leaving me alone.

Almost without thinking, I pull the Brisingamen out from beneath my dress and squeeze the pendant tightly in my hand. The feeling of panic slowly ebbs, and a veil of calm drops over me. There is no need to worry, I think. Skuld would not let me down.

❧

The next morning, the first thing I see when I open my eyes is the bird looking down at me, its head tilted to one side, its gaze characteristically fierce. Sky stands beside my bed, with the hawk perched upon his arm. He looks exhausted; his eyes are ringed in shadow, and he seems desperately unhappy. I sit up at once, pulling the

271

bedclothes over myself. "Sky, what's wrong?" I ask. He blinks a few times, his distress obvious, then motions awkwardly towards my chest. I do not even need to look down, because in that instant I know that it is gone. The realisation pierces me like a fine steel blade: I feel a sharp pain somewhere deep inside.

"What happened?" I ask in a paper-thin voice. Sky shakes his head a few times, then with his free hand, mimics a complex set of motions that end in the hand flying away. "I don't understand," I tell him. He hesitates, pursing his lips. He tries again with his hand: this time he makes only the flying motion. "A bird?" I ask. He nods earnestly. "A bird took my necklace?" I say, incredulous. His nod is long and slow, and his eyes apologetic. I glance at the hawk. "Your bird?" I ask. He shakes his head quickly, emphatically.

Later, after we've been over it several times, I am no wiser. Bird or man, whoever entered Sessruminger has left no trace behind. There is no sign of forced entry, nor of escape. Sky remains agitated. He refuses to go on his morning walk and will not leave my sight. Finally, I realise that he is afraid I will suspect him of the theft. I lay a hand upon his shoulder in reassurance. "I know it wasn't you," I tell him. He looks anxiously towards the hawk. "Either of you," I add. Relief washes over him. He smiles tentatively. "But I wish that you could tell me what you saw," I add. His smile melts, replaced by a look of uncertainty. He turns away. "Don't worry," I say. "The necklace will find its way back to me, just as it did the last time."

I wish I could be more certain of these words. Perhaps the necklace was not fated to remain with me, after all. I persuade Sky to rest, then walk outside for some fresh air. It is a cold grey morning. The temperature has plummeted during the night, and the wind bites at my face. A light rain has begun to fall, and as I look out across the mountains, I see a dark curtain of storm drifting east. Once again I remember Berling's warning. At the time, I was uncertain whether his concern was for me or for the necklace. Now I think he meant us both. In the next moment, I see a lone rider appear in the distance, and before long I recognise one of Odin's servants. I wait while he approaches and watch him dismount. His coarse linen shift is wet through, and his hair is a tangled dark mass. He turns to me with a look of weary resignation, his lips pale with cold. "Odin wishes to see you," he says.

"Come inside and warm yourself," I reply. He nods, following me inside. A large fire blazes in the centre of the hall and the servant walks straight over to it, thrusting his chafed hands towards the flames like an offering. His long, dark hair is plastered to the back of his neck. Beneath it, the skin is angry red from exposure. "Why did he not come to me?" I ask.

He shifts uncomfortably and shrugs. "I don't know."

❧❧❧

I wait for the rain to stop. It has been some months since I've been to Odin's homestead. It sits high up near the centre of Asgard, with a commanding view over the surrounding mountains. His buildings are all large and well tended. No grass grows in these roofs, I notice as I approach. The main hall is especially grand. The roof timbers have ornate carved wooden ends, and the large front door is magnificently cast in polished bronze. As I enter, I am reminded of his penchant for order. The hall is unnaturally bright, its walls whitewashed to perfection. It is lit by dozens of oil lamps suspended high around the perimeter. The flames dance eagerly, and the walls glisten like the pearly innards of a fine shell. I am unused to such brightness indoors. He is profligate with fire, I think, as I cross the wide stone floor. It is warm underfoot, and I remember that it is heated by thermal water diverted from a nearby spring. It courses like blood beneath the stone. I have a sudden feeling that the room itself is alive; that at any moment it will wake and stir beneath my feet.

At the far end of the hall, Odin perches in a chair, wearing a long robe of woven brown wool and a dark patch over one eye held in place by a leather thong. His coarse grey hair hangs below his shoulders and his face is bronzed and weathered from many years' exposure. The eye that sees is of a brilliant, youthful, cobalt blue. When I meet his gaze, I am reminded with a sudden lurch why I lay with him all those years ago.

He is flanked by two smaller chairs, one occupied by Loki, his constant companion these past few years. The man is like a second skin he cannot shed, and his influence over Odin is rumoured to be very great indeed. As I cross the hall, Loki rolls his eyes at the sight of me. He leans in towards Odin and murmurs something as I approach, even while Odin waves him away with an irritated hand. Loki's mother was a giant and he has inherited her height. His long, thin frame is elegantly draped in an ivory cloth shot through with silver threads. His jet-black hair is combed straight back from his wide, pale brow, and despite his fine features, his skin is unusually ashen. He still retains the colouring of his tribe, I think with satisfaction, even if he has managed to shed their vast bulk and ungainly manners. I have never liked Loki, for a multitude of reasons. Even less have I trusted him. Now I ignore him, turning instead to Odin.

"You sent for me."

"I have an errand I should like you to undertake."

"Since when am I a servant?"

"We are a brotherhood Freya. We must all earn our keep."

I nod towards Loki. "What does he do for his?"

Loki straightens. "I steal things," he says with an insouciant air. His voice rings out across the room.

I look at him and the Brisingamen forms in my mind. He rewards me with a mocking smile. Loki is a shape-changer. He can assume the form of any animal at will: a tiger, a flea. Even a bird. I am a fool. I feel a warm rush of blood rise to my face. I turn to Odin. "And what is it you do to earn your high seat?"

"I make others do my bidding. And it is not as easy as it seems." Odin's tone is forceful, but underneath it lies a trace of weariness. I wonder whether his words conceal some hidden meaning.

"The Brisingamen must be returned," I say.

"Of course."

"And you must give your word it will not go missing in future."

"Your attachment to it is very strong," he replies with a raised eyebrow. I say nothing, refusing to be baited. "Perhaps because you paid so dearly," he continues. Loki smiles knowingly. I purse my lips. There are no secrets in Asgard. But I am past the point of caring about my reputation. And Odin's is hardly untainted where matters of the flesh are concerned.

"What is it you require?" I ask.

"I wish you to procure something on my behalf."

"You have one thief at your disposal already."

"Ah, but this is much too precious to entrust to an outsider," he says. Loki stiffens at this slight. Odin toys with him, I think, though I do not know why. I have never understood the nature of their relationship.

"There are few objects more precious than the Brisingamen," I say.

"This is no object. It is a child." I raise an eyebrow, as if to suggest that his depravity knows no bounds. "She is my daughter, in fact. And my reasons are entirely just. The girl is an orphan. Her mother and the man she knew as her father are both dead. She is being raised by her grandfather. He is planning to take her abroad soon in preparation for marriage. I prefer that she remain within these shores. This does not seem unreasonable to me, but her grandfather does not recognise my claim. The child's mother was most discreet, it seems. She never breathed a word of our affair to anyone, not even on her deathbed. So I am left with no entitlement regarding the girl's future."

"What can I do?"

"Find the girl and take her to Sessruminger. Treat her well and guard her closely, for her family has much influence and is certain to come after her. Introduce her slowly to our ways. But do not speak of me. Once she has had a chance to adjust to life among the Aesir, I will come myself to Sessruminger and tell her everything. At that point, she will be free to choose."

"A grand gesture on your part."

"I would not force her to remain among us."

"You are certain she is your child?"

He hesitates. "Yes."

I do not reply at once. Odin shifts uncomfortably. I can see my silence tears at him. When I finally speak, my tone is one of condescension. "So the world of men is littered with your offspring."

"Just as the world of dwarves may one day be littered with yours," he retorts.

"You forget that if a seed is sown, I will be the one to watch it grow."

"You are fortunate to have a choice."

I look at him askance. "There was a time when you relished the absence of such burdens."

He shrugs. "My interests have changed over time."

So he admits to growing old, I think. "You surprise me," I tell him.

"Sometimes I surprise myself."

"What makes you think the girl will recognise your claim?"

He hesitates. Perhaps this had not occurred to him. "Unlike her grandfather, she has nothing to lose by acknowledging me," he says slowly.

"Only the memory of the father who raised her," I offer.

Odin frowns. Loki leans forward. "A dead father for a live one," he offers. "Which would you choose?"

"The one who earned my love," I reply.

"Enough," says Odin to both of us. "We will wait and see what she decides. But I expect no interference. From either of you."

They are both mad, I think.

FULLA

he day Fulla disappears, Hogni is cleaning out the tanning shed. Since his decision to return to Norway, he has thrown himself into preparations for the journey. He and Fulla will take relatively little with them, apart from what is most valuable, but he wishes to leave the farm in good working order. After all, it is his only legacy, apart from her. He has built the farm up from almost nothing, and it has made him a wealthy man. But over the years life has soured him against its abundance. For it was land-lust that killed his only son.

He stares down at the rusted blade in his hand. No man should outlive his own offspring, he thinks wearily. He drops the knife and wipes his hands clean upon a rag. When he comes out of the tanning shed, the sun is high and he suddenly feels hungry. As he crosses the yard towards the house, an odd sight confronts him. In the distance, the lumpen shape of Helga jostles up and down on a fast-moving pony. Behind her, Fulla's horse trails on a leading rein. But Fulla herself is nowhere. He feels his gut twist. He begins to run at a lope towards her. As Helga draws near, the expression on her face confirms his fears.

Helga halts her horse and looks down at him. "Fulla?" he asks desperately. She shakes her head in response, barely able to speak. She slides off the horse and collapses onto his shoulder.

"She's gone," Helga says breathlessly, her large frame heaving. "They've taken her."

"Who?"

Helga looks at him in despair. "I don't know. It happened so quickly. We were at the baths, and she was in the water. I left them only for a second, and then I fell and hit my head, and when I woke, they were gone." She breaks off.

"Left whom? Who were you with?"

"A woman."

"What woman?"

"I don't know. A stranger."

Hogni stares at her. "Come into the house," he says finally. He helps her inside, but not before glancing back at the empty plains behind them. *They've taken her*, he thinks. First Jarl, and now Fulla. Silently, he curses the ghost of Skallagrim.

Hogni gets no more useful information out of Helga. He leaves her in the care of a young serving woman and, taking three able men with him, rides east towards Skallagrim's farm. It is mid-afternoon when they spot the vast collection of buildings in the distance. As they approach the farm, Hogni searches the yard for signs of danger, but sees nothing unusual. In one corner, a woman washes clothing in a large wooden bucket. And outside the stable, a farmhand is breaking in a horse on a leading rein. Both look up as he and his men ride into the yard. The farmhand halts what he is doing and calls towards the barn. A moment later, Thorstein appears. He stops short when he sees Hogni, then walks slowly towards him. Hogni halts his horse several feet away, but does not dismount. One hand drops down to the hilt of his sword. Thorstein, instantly on his guard, calls into the house for his brothers, and within moments, two more men emerge. They all stare at Hogni expectantly.

"Fulla has been taken."

Thorstein exchanges a glance of surprise with his brothers. "Not by us."

"Where is the boy?" demands Hogni.

"At home, where he should be," says Thorstein cautiously.

"I want to see him."

Thorstein hesitates, then nods for his brother to fetch the boy. The man trots towards a house at the rear of the yard, and after a minute, returns with Vili. When he sees the boy, Hogni swells with anger. He climbs down off his horse and walks up to him.

"Where is she?" he demands.

Vili shakes his head in confusion. "I've not seen her."

"You're a liar!" Hogni pulls a knife and rushes towards him. He grabs the boy by the shoulder and spins him around, putting the knife to his throat. Thorstein jumps forward, then stops himself.

"You think I'd harm her?!" cries Vili.

"I think you're a villain, just like your father was," Hogni snarls.

Vili's face contorts with anger. With one hand he reaches up to grab Hogni's wrist, then throws his other elbow hard into the old man's side, winding him. Hogni grunts and doubles over, and the boy wrenches frees from his grasp. At the same time, Thorstein leaps forward, his own knife drawn. He sinks it into Hogni's shoulder in a flash. Hogni drops his own knife with a cry. His men spring forward to defend him, but Thorstein turns on them, the knife still in his hand. They stop short when they come face to face with Thorstein's knife, still wet with Hogni's blood. For a moment, no one moves.

"Stop!" cries Vili. He steps between Thorstein and Hogni's men. Then he turns towards Hogni. "She isn't here," he says intently. "But we'll help you find her." The boy bends down and retrieves Hogni's knife, and holds it out to him.

Hogni looks at him, breathing hard. One hand clutches his shoulder; blood oozes through his fingers. He hesitates, then reaches out with his good hand and takes the knife. "We'll find her ourselves," he says hoarsely.

He crosses to his horse and, with the help of one of his men, struggles onto its back. The others follow. Vili watches in silence, as Hogni turns his horse around and rides out of the yard.

Upon his return, Hogni dispatches men in every direction to search for Fulla, as well as a messenger to Nidavellir to alert Dvalin. He can think of no other action to take, and the sense of helplessness overwhelms him. His instinct tells him that Skallagrim's grandson has nothing to do with Fulla's disappearance, though in his darker moments, he has drawn and quartered the boy in his mind.

"Sit down," orders Helga, "and let me dress this wound." Hogni settles himself gloomily by the fire, while she carefully washes his shoulder. He spends the rest of the evening fretting. One by one, his men return in the darkness, having found nothing.

When he wakes in the morning, he is flushed with fever. Helga examines the dressing anxiously. The wound is badly inflamed. She forces him to remain in bed. He sends his men out again to search for Fulla, though this time they do not move so quickly, for they already know that she is gone. At noon, Helga brings him soup made from sorrel. He shakes his head when she appears in the doorway.

"Drink it," she orders. "It will do you good!"

"I'm not hungry," he insists.

"You're no use to her dead."

Hogni eyes her sullenly, then grudgingly accepts the bowl. He lifts the spoon to his mouth before pausing. "Is it possible she ran away?"

"On foot?"

Hogni shrugs. "Or by some other means. A horse hidden elsewhere?"

"By whom?"

Hogni stares at her and thinks of the boy Vili. Perhaps he was lying after all. Perhaps they planned to meet at a later date, when he was no longer under suspicion. "Helga, did she say anything at all to you? Anything that would suggest that she was leaving?"

Helga looks at him askance. "She *was* leaving. With you."

He sighs and looks down at the soup. Has he brought all this upon himself? When he raises his head, Helga regards him thoughtfully.

"It isn't your fault," she says. "What's done is done. She's out there, somewhere. And now we have to find her."

❧

Dvalin arrives at noon the next day. At the sight of him, Hogni feels a sudden surge of hope, the first he's felt since Fulla's disappearance. Dvalin kneels beside the bed and clasps his hand warmly. "I came as quickly as I could," he says, frowning at the dressing on Hogni's shoulder. "Are you all right?"

The old man gives an irritated wave with his good arm. "It is nothing."

"When did she disappear?"

"Two days ago."

"Is Thorstein responsible?"

"Perhaps. But I don't think so."

"You've seen him?"

Hogni raises his eyebrows, indicating the wound. "He took offence at the suggestion."

"And you believe him?"

"I don't know. But with each passing day, I fear for her life."

"Who was with her?"

"Helga. They rode to the baths, as was their custom. A woman approached them there, a stranger, and joined them in the water. They spoke for a time, then Helga got out to relieve herself. When her back was turned, someone forced a hood over her face. She struggled and fell, and lost consciousness for a moment. When she woke, Fulla and the woman were gone."

"Who was the woman?"

Hogni shakes his head. "A complete stranger, by all accounts. Helga had never seen her before."

"I must speak with Helga."

"Of course. But you'll be none the wiser."

∽≈∾

Dvalin finds Helga seated on a bench in the scullery, washing an enormous bunch of leeks in a wooden tub of water. There is a small turf fire in the centre of the tiny room, its heat surprisingly warm. The air is dense with the smell of burning peat and the scent of pickling preserves. The walls of the room are lined with earthen jugs of all shapes and sizes, each containing foodstores.

Dvalin pulls a wooden stool up and seats himself next to her, watching as she slits each leek neatly up the centre with a knife. Helga's face is more bloated than usual, her eyes ringed with dark circles.

"Helga, you must think hard. That day at the baths, are you certain you saw no one else?"

"I saw nothing. They came from nowhere."

"They struck you from behind?"

She frowns. "No. At least, I don't think so. I've no wound."

"Then how did you lose consciousness?"

"The cloak. It unbalanced me."

"What cloak?"

"They forced a cloak over my head, and then I fell." Helga pauses for a moment, her face confused. Her hands are full of leeks, and she stares down at her fingers, as if they belong to someone else.

"You fell over?"

"No," she says, shaking her head slowly. "I fell a long way. As if I'd been pushed from a great height."

"And when you landed?"

"There was no landing. I fell and fell, and then I woke."

Dvalin frowns. Helga exhales heavily and plunges the leeks into the water, throttling them vigorously to clear the dirt from their layers. "Tell me more of the cloak," says Dvalin slowly. "What colour was it?"

She shakes her head. "It had no colour."

"Wool or flax?"

"I cannot say."

"Tell me *something*, Helga!"

Helga sighs and pulls her hands from the water, throwing the leeks upon the table. She sits back and dries her hands on her apron, then looks up at him. "I remember only how it felt, for it was as soft as down, and had the lightness of a feather."

Dvalin stares at her. "The woman," he says, his voice dropping low. "Describe her."

Helga looks at him imploringly. "I have tried and

tried, but I cannot see her face. It is as if she robbed me of my senses, as well as the child." A single tear forms and slides down her cheek. She wipes at it with the heel of her hand, then looks up at him in despair. "I remember only the softness of the cloak," she murmurs, the tears coming again. "And how it carried me away."

Dvalin tells Hogni that he wishes to see for himself where Fulla disappeared. He rides east to the baths, a place he has not been to in many years. But they have changed little during the interim, and as he descends the hill of dwarf birch, he cannot help but think of Jarl, for as teenagers they often rode here together when a day's work was done, to soak in the soothing thermal waters and contemplate the future. As young men, it did not occur to them that their lives would not run in tandem. But that was before Dvalin's father had died, when he was forced to return to Nidavellir, and before Jarl's marriage to Fulla's mother, events which altered the course of things and severed them from each other. Dvalin climbs down from the horse, breathing in the familiar smell of sulphur. The day is fine, and a cool breeze lightly roughs the surface of the water. Slowly, he walks around the pool's circumference, studying the ground for clues. He is not sure what he is looking for.

After a few minutes, he stops several paces from the stone bench. He stoops down to retrieve something in the grass. Small, brown, weightless, unthinkably soft: a falcon feather. With a lurch, he realises that the woman he is seeking is Freya. And though he cannot conceive of her motives, the idea that his fate will once again be yoked with hers unsettles him even more than Fulla's disappearance.

At home, Hogni lies in bed cursing the pain in his shoulder. Like most men of his generation, his body is a small map of scars. But each wound seems to heal more slowly than the last. Right now, he can feel the fever raging through his body like a bush fire. He calls for Helga, his voice rasping loudly. She comes in after a moment, wiping her hands on her apron, before reaching forward to feel his brow.

"I need a drink," he says.

"You need more than that," she murmurs. She leaves the room and returns a moment later with a large jug of water and a cup. He empties the cup and hands it back to her. She refills it and sets it on the table by his bed. Then she pours the water into a small soapstone basin and soaks a cloth in it, wringing the excess out before laying it across his forehead. Hogni unfolds the cloth and spreads it across his entire face.

"That's better," he murmurs, breathing in the cool, wet fibre.

"I've got to tend the fire," she says. She leaves him, and before long, the coolness has evaporated, and the cloth is warm and cloying on his face. He is too tired to remove it, and he lies in the fading darkness of the room, his eyes and nose shrouded. After a few minutes, he hears a noise just outside the room and gives a small cough.

"Helga, is that you?" he wheezes. He listens to the silence for a moment. His mind drifts towards sleep. And then he hears the unmistakable sound of footfall by his door. He jerks upright with a spasm of pain and whips the cloth from his face, only to see Vili standing in the doorway. "You!" Hogni cries. The pain shoots through his shoulder, and he gingerly eases himself back down. "What on earth are you doing here?" he gasps.

"I came to find Fulla."

"Did Holstein send you?"

Vili shakes his head. "No."

"Do they know you've come?"

Vili takes a step forward. "No."

"That's far enough," says Hogni tersely.

"Your shoulder." Vili nods towards the wound.

"What of it?"

"I can smell the infection from here."

"I'm an old man," replies Hogni staunchly. "I heal badly."

"I'm good with wounds."

Hogni eyes him sceptically. "You must be mad," he says, incredulous.

"Perhaps I am." There is a hint of challenge in the boy's voice.

Hogni sighs and leans back, eyeing him suspiciously. "What are you waiting for?" he says finally.

Vili advances slowly towards the bedside. When he reaches Hogni, he carefully peels back the dressing on his shoulder. The wound beneath is small but angry-looking. Yellow pus has crusted around its edge, and the surrounding skin is red and swollen. "You need a poultice," he says. "If we don't stop the infection, it will spread to the arm."

Hogni eyes him. "How do I know Holstein hasn't sent you here to kill me?"

"You don't. But either way you'll die."

"Then get on with it."

Vili turns and disappears from the bedchamber. He returns after a few minutes laden with supplies. He works quickly, laying out on the bed beside Hogni a small selection of ingredients he has ransacked from the scullery and the garden. The old man watches as he prepares a thick brown paste from rendered lard and herbs, pounding it vigorously in a mortar and pestle. A sharply pungent smell fills the air as he works. "What is that?" Hogni sniffs at it suspiciously.

"Comfrey roots. Camomile. Angelica. It will lessen the inflammation and help bind the wound." Once finished, he washes the area thoroughly with clean water, then smears the salve directly onto the wound.

Hogni winces. "Ow!"

"Hold still. I'm nearly finished."

"It burns like the fires of hell!"

"The pain will lessen in a minute." Vili dresses the wound carefully with a clean piece of linen, while Hogni looks on.

"Where did you learn this?"

"My grandmother was a healer. She taught my mother. My mother taught me."

Hogni raises an eyebrow. "Your mother is dead now?"

"They both are." Vili carries the soiled dressing out to the larger room and flings it onto the fire, then returns to Hogni's bedside. He picks up the water jug and refills Hogni's cup. "Here," he says, holding it out. Hogni takes the cup, draining it noisily. He hands the cup back to Vili.

"Tell me what you know of Fulla," says Vili abruptly.

Hogni glares at him, now indebted. "I know nothing. She disappeared from the baths."

Vili weighs up the old man's answer. At length, he lowers himself onto a chair by the bed. For the first time, Hogni sees how tired he is.

"I've done nothing but scour both our farms for the past three days," says Vili. "She is nowhere."

Hogni nods. "We've come to the same conclusion."

"Where did she go? And with whom?"

"I wish I knew." Hogni stares at the boy. He is obviously in torment. Yet he knows nothing of their plans to leave for Norway. Hogni feels a sudden rush of guilt. They hear a noise in the hall, and a second later Helga appears in the doorway. Her mouth forms a circle of astonishment.

"Who's this?" she says. Vili leaps to his feet uncomfortably.

"It's all right," says Hogni. "He's made a poultice." Helga walks over to the wound and peeks under the dressing with a frown. Hogni winces. She sniffs at it suspiciously, then turns to Vili.

"You've not poisoned him, have you?"

Vili shakes his head. "No."

"Hold your tongue, woman! And fix the boy some food. Can't you see he's starving?"

Helga makes a face at him, and leaves the room with a clucking sound. Vili turns to Hogni. "Thank you," he says. Hogni gives a flick of his good hand, before lying back down and closing his eyes.

∽৪৪৶

An hour later Dvalin returns. When he enters the hall, he does not notice the boy sleeping soundly on a pallet near the fire. Dvalin crosses the room and enters Hogni's bedchamber. The old man stirs at once and sits up in the darkness. "Dvalin," he says.

"Let me light a lamp." Dvalin lights a small oil lamp with a piece of kindling from the fire. It casts an eerie glow about the room. He seats himself on the edge of the bed. "How are you?"

"Better," says Hogni. "What have you learnt?"

Dvalin pauses. "I have an idea who the woman was."

"Yes?"

"It's only a theory," he says cautiously.

"Don't be coy, Dvalin," Hogni says with irritation.

A noise startles them both. They turn to see the boy standing in the doorway, his face bleary with sleep. Hogni nods to him. "Vili, leave us, if you please."

Vili hesitates, then turns away and crosses back to his pallet by the fire. Dvalin turns back to Hogni, dropping his voice. "Who is he?"

"Skallagrim's grandson," says Hogni grimly.

It takes a moment for Dvalin to realise the significance of his words. His eyes widen. "Not the son of –"

Hogni raises a hand to silence him. "He is not like his father."

"Why is he here?"

Hogni takes a deep breath. "He and Fulla...are friends."

"Friends."

"Well, something more, I suppose." Hogni concedes.

Dvalin stares at him in disbelief. "That is why you are taking her to Norway," he says slowly.

"No," protests Hogni. Dvalin looks at him sceptically. "Well, in part, yes," he admits. "But it is not the only reason."

"Where you have betrothed her to your cousin."

Hogni shrugs.

"Against her will," continues Dvalin.

Hogni nods reluctantly.

Dvalin eyes him. "And now she has run away," he says.

"She was taken! You spoke to Helga!"

"It is all beginning to make sense," says Dvalin.

"You do not understand. She knew she could not make a life with this boy!"

"Did she?" Vili's voice comes to them from behind. Both men turn and see him standing in the doorway. He takes a step into the room. "She said this?" His eyes lock onto Hogni's.

"She knew this in her heart," Hogni says slowly. "Even

if she was not prepared to admit it."

Vili stares at him angrily. "You have no right to dictate our future," he says accusingly.

"I have every right!" Hogni says furiously.

Vili glares at him. "Then I should not have saved you," he says hotly. He turns and flees the room.

Hogni turns to Dvalin with a guilty shrug. "My plans have all gone awry," he says gloomily.

"Perhaps they were meant to," admonishes Dvalin. He stands up. "You must rest now."

"What of Fulla?" demands Hogni. "You know where she is, don't you?"

Dvalin looks down at him with a frown. "I have a fairly good idea."

"What will you do?" asks Hogni cautiously.

"First I will find her. Then I will let her choose."

Hogni regards him for a moment, and lies back with a sigh. "Then luck be with you," he says wearily.

CRECR

The next morning, Dvalin rises before dawn and saddles his horse in the darkness. He wants an early start, partly so Hogni cannot send his men after him. On his way out, he finds two loaves of bread and a cheese by the door, together with a flask of ale. A parting gift from Helga, he suspects. As he leads the horse out of the yard, he hears a footstep behind him. Vili steps out of the last stall, where he has clearly spent the night. There are bits of straw hanging from his clothes and hair. "Where are you going?" asks the boy.

"To find Fulla."

"Take me with you."

Dvalin hesitates. "If I take you with me," he says slowly, "then your people are sure to follow." The boy considers this, frowning. "Let me find her first, Vili. I will bring her back to you." Dvalin starts to lead the horse out of the stable.

Vili steps into his path. "Please," he says urgently.

"If you love her," says Dvalin, "you will stay here, and make peace with her kin."

Vili takes a deep breath, then nods. Dvalin leads his horse out into the yard, where the first hint of ragged light has appeared along the edge of the mountains. He mounts the horse and walks it out of the yard, leaving the lovelorn figure of the boy behind him.

THE NORNS

The first men landed here by accident, blown off course by stormy seas. They were mystified by what they saw: snow in midsummer, a midnight sun that never set, and smoke that rose without fire from the land. They also found hot water bubbling straight out of the ground — the island's secret source of warmth. They did not know that Iceland sits atop a plume of magma that pumps an endless supply of heat into its rock. The volcanic bedrock beneath her is like a sponge. Rain falls from the sky and trickles down to settle in the bowels of the earth, where it is heated by the core, then rises back up through cracks in the rock. As it nears the surface, the water searches out weak points in the crust, where it eventually escapes in the form of a spring. When the water remains trapped deep beneath the ground, a ghost of steam appears — as if the earth has just exhaled.

FREYA

he girl was waiting to be stolen. I felt the restlessness in her at once, like the trembling of water just before it rises to the boil. I could see as well that she was unhappy. A thin, almost imperceptible veil of loss hung over her. But she was too proud to parade her discontent. It lay smothered beneath her sense of duty and obedience. These things I divined from observing her, both alone and with her maidservant, together with the more obvious fact that she was uncommonly beautiful. Perhaps she really is Odin's daughter, I thought, watching her slide into the waters like a nymph.

She was drawn to me. She approached me at once and introduced herself. I did not tell her my name. Not at first, anyway. We spoke of her grandfather's land, and of the baths and their setting, and the storms that had passed only recently. Idle conversation, though she listened intently and regarded me throughout. After a time, we ceased talking and lolled about in the warm thermal waters. I waited for an opportunity to present itself. Before long, her maidservant went to relieve herself, and I too slipped away. The girl did not take much notice, for the day had turned sunny, and she was leaning back upon the rock with her eyes closed. A few minutes later I returned alone. She opened her eyes and looked at me.

"Where is Helga?" she asked.

"Asleep," I replied. It was only the tiniest of lies.

The girl frowned. "How strange," she said.

"Perhaps she is tired."

She looked at me curiously. "Where are you from?"

"Asgard."

"Asgard," she repeated slowly. Her eyebrows shot up like tiny arrows. "Do you mean, in the sky?"

All men think that Asgard lies in some distant heavenly realm, a notion the Aesir put about long ago. They do not realise that we all walk the same earth, breathe the same air, drink the same water, as they do. "Not exactly," I said. "But over the mountains, yes."

"How did you get here?"

"I flew."

She smiled with disbelief. "How?" she asked.

"I have a cloak made of falcon feathers."

Her expression changed. "I've heard of such things," she murmured. "But I didn't know that they were real." She looked at me intently. "Who are you?" she asked.

"I am Freya."

A slow smile spread across her face. "You've come to help me." It was not a question, and I scarcely knew what she referred to. But I did not dissuade her.

"I've come to take you away," I replied.

"To Asgard?"

"Yes."

She hesitated a moment. I could see her mind working quickly. She glanced briefly at the trees. "Now?" There was a hint of challenge in her voice.

"Yes."

She stood, and the water ran in streams down her naked body. She leaned across and reached for her clothing, which she hastily pulled over her head. Then she turned to me expectantly, her face slick with wet. "We must go quickly," she said.

I understood at once that I was not stealing her. She was running away.

⁂

That was three days ago. Already she has settled well here. Sessruminger appeals to her, with its dramatic setting and views of Hekla. She continues to surprise me, with her blunt-spoken ways and her impulsive manner. But she is not without regard for others: she has an intuitive sense of those around her, and is strangely trusting of me, though I am not sure why.

Only a few times has she mentioned her kin. I can see that it disturbs her to think of them, for she must know the worry her disappearance has caused. She told me that her parents are both dead, and that her only living blood relation is her grandfather. Though she did not say it, I got the sense that she was already anticipating his passing and the time when she would be alone. Still, she mentioned nothing of his plans for her: neither of her impending marriage, nor of his intention to take her abroad. And I was left wondering what her own intentions had been. Had she planned to run away before I arrived?

Sky intrigues her. He is taller than her by two heads, and three years younger, though she treats him as an equal. She plies him with questions: about the bird, about Jotunheim, about his size. He answers as best as he is able, through a combination of gesture and mime. At times, her boldness shocks him. Yesterday, when we were eating, she looked at him and said: "Have you always been mute, or did it come upon you suddenly?" Sky nearly choked on his food, and there was a long awkward silence while she awaited his response. His eyes darted briefly to me, then back to her, and his Adam's apple bobbed as he swallowed. Finally, he nodded. I think she realised she had erred then. "It is ill luck," she said gently, "though you wear your silence bravely." Sky flushed, embarrassed by her comments.

She accompanies him each morning on his rambles. The first day, he seemed uneasy when she suggested it, but this morning he waited patiently while she readied herself. She has already overcome his natural shyness. I see her chatting amiably to him as they climb the slope behind the house. It is good for him, for the boy lives too much inside himself, and it is impossible to do so in her presence.

I've not yet spoken to her of Odin. In truth, I am uncertain what to say. I did not expect to grow so fond of her. She reminds me of a younger version of myself, before I was flung out in the world to experience all its failings. We were both raised without mothers, and thus without a model of the women we should be. And she is blessed and hampered by her beauty, just as I was. But her spirit is pure, like a bone bleached white by the sun.

Perhaps because of this, I realise now that I must tell her the truth. Odin may arrive at any time. I do not want his sudden appearance to alarm her, nor jeopardise the bond that she and I have formed. But the prospect makes me uneasy. Since our return, I have tried not to dwell on the Brisingamen, and have endeavoured to separate the necklace and the girl in my mind. But I feel its absence acutely, like a lost limb. And I hope that the chain of events I have set in motion has a purpose. Otherwise, I could not justify my deceit to this girl. Most of all, I remain anxious over Hekla. Since our return, she continues to smoulder, occasionally belching forth great clouds of smoke and dust.

When Sky and Fulla finally return, they are ruddy-faced and mud-splattered. Fulla leads the way energetically, while Sky trails several paces behind in his absent way. The hawk wheels high overhead. "Sky took me to a waterfall," she says a little breathlessly. "It was the most beautiful place I've ever seen. There were giant ferns growing out of the top, and great clouds of steam billowing up from the bottom."

Sky stands in the doorway, the hawk perched upon his arm. I glance at him and he nods briefly. "Come in and warm yourselves," I say. "I've made some soup." We eat in silence and afterwards, Sky excuses himself, for he seems to understand that his presence is suddenly a burden. I am beginning to realise how extraordinary his perceptions are, as if his muteness heightens his other senses.

I turn to her once he is gone. "I have a story to tell you," I begin tentatively. She looks at me with interest, and I feel a clench of apprehension deep inside. "Some time ago, there lived a great leader. He was a man of many abilities: he had infinite knowledge of all things past and perfect powers of persuasion. The man travelled widely, and he was trusted and admired everywhere he went. The people did his bidding, and on the whole, they benefited. But he was not without his failings. Like many men, he was governed by his passions, so although he was married, he was often unfaithful. One day, he met a young woman with whom he became infatuated. He wooed her incessantly, and in the end, she submitted to his claims. They had a passionate affair. Not long after, she fell pregnant. As she was already married, she banished him for ever and resolved never to disclose her child's true paternity to her husband.

"Sadly, she died giving birth to a daughter. The child was raised by her father and cherished as his own. But

301

tragedy struck again, for he too was killed when the girl was only young. She was taken in by his family and, despite her misfortune, she flourished and grew into a beautiful young woman." I pause.

Fulla is no longer smiling. She listens intently, her head at an angle, her dark eyes unreadable. I take a deep breath. "Until the day her real father decided they should meet. He sent someone to fetch her and take her to a secret place, where he ordered them to await his arrival. This they did with little trouble, for the girl was of a trusting nature and easily misled. But after a brief time, her captor began to regret her actions, for she'd grown fond of the girl and no longer had the heart to deceive her. So she told her the truth, and bade her make a choice."

My voice trails off. Fulla sits before me, immobile, though I can see the rise and fall of her chest. The silence in the room swells, threatening to consume us both.

"Is this a joke?" she asks finally, her voice barely more than a whisper.

I shake my head. "No."

She swallows. "How can you be certain?"

"Your father is many things, but he is not a liar."

"Who is he?"

I hesitate. "I would rather let him tell you."

She frowns. "And the choice you spoke of?"

"To stay here with me and wait for him. Or return to your home." She looks at me, weighing up her answer.

"I chose to come here," she says pointedly. "Of my own accord."

"I know this," I reply. "I also have an idea why."

She regards me uncertainly.

"Your grandfather intends to send you abroad."

"Yes."

"And you do not wish to go."

She takes a deep breath and exhales, her nostrils flaring slightly. "No," she says. I wait to see if she will tell me more. "May I ask you something?" she says finally.

"Of course."

"Have you ever been in love?"

The question startles me. I look at her and see the tangled rod of emotion that runs through her, can feel the hot radiance of her youth. I realise that I am no longer capable of such feelings. I am as strong and pale and cool as the moon.

"No," I answer.

It is only the tiniest of lies.

Afterwards, she retires to her bedchamber, and does not emerge for the rest of the day. Once again, I feel a deep sense of loss. Any connection between the girl and me now seems severed. Evening falls, and Sky and I take our meal together in the hall, as is our custom. More than once, he glances towards Fulla's room with a questioning look, but I offer no explanation. Finally, when he has gone to bed, I venture towards her door. I knock softly, then ease the door open. The room is dark. She sits upon the edge of her bed, like a prisoner awaiting a sentence.

"Fulla?" I speak softly.

She turns to me.

"I thought you were sleeping." She shakes her head. I take a few steps towards her. "Are you hungry?" She looks away, does not even glance in my direction. With a sigh, I move to the bed and sit down beside her. "I am sorry if I deceived you."

"Your deceit is the least of my concerns." Her voice is flat.

"You have two fathers, not one. Is that such a bad thing?"

She looks at me with a frown. "And my mother?" she asks.

"Your mother gave you life. And sacrificed her own."

"He loved her, until the day he died. He never loved anyone but her."

"He loved you."

She considers this for a moment. "But I was not even his."

"You think that mattered to him. Then or now?"

Her lower lip trembles slightly. "I don't know." She looks around the room. "I am no longer certain of anything."

"Love is not an offering that we choose to bestow, Fulla." The words surprise me, once they have been uttered.

"I don't know what love is," she says bitterly. "Did my mother love my father?"

I shrug. "She may have. Constancy and love do not always walk together."

"They ought to," she replies hotly. Then she takes a deep breath and lets it out slowly. "I thought I loved someone once," she says. "Now I do not know." Her voice trails off.

"Then stay and meet Odin. Afterwards, you can decide your future."

Too late, I realise my mistake. She looks at me with surprise. "Odin?"

I pause before replying. "He is a man like any other, Fulla. No more, no less."

"When will he come?"

"Soon." I hesitate. "Will you be here?"

She looks me in the eye. "Yes."

DVALIN

efore he died, his father had told him how to find Asgard. He was an old man by then, and his breath came in short bursts. His voice had deepened and was gravelly with age. "There is a pass through the mountains," he confided. The old man paused briefly to clear the stones from his throat. "Its entrance is concealed by water," he continued, raising his hand high up in the air, then letting it swoop gently down like an eagle. "The water falls from a great height, and it cleaves neatly into three rivers at the bottom. Each one takes a different direction." With the same hand, he cut cleanly through the air as if he was chopping wood: one, two, three. "That is how you will find it. Look for the join of three rivers."

"Why are you telling me this?" Dvalin had asked.

His father frowned. "I thought that you might want to find her," he replied.

Dvalin pursed his lips. He had no desire to see his mother. "You were wrong."

"Do not banish her from your heart, Dvalin. She loved you, as best as she was able." He looked into his father's eyes, now watery with age, and wondered how he knew this to be true.

They did not discuss it again. But since that day, Dvalin's dreams have been disturbed by the confluence of rivers. Already he can see them in his mind. And when he finally sets out to find them, he knows they will be there. It takes him most of a day to reach the mountains. He camps beside a small stream just as dark is falling, and is so tired that sleep takes him instantly. When he wakes in the morning, the sun has nearly crested the horizon. He packs his things and heads north along the range, but does not hurry. He knows that Fulla is safe. And Asgard will wait for him, just as it has always done. By noon, he is riding beside a river, and before long, he spies a second stream of water running parallel to the first, at a distance of several hundred paces.

The river winds through a small forest of fir trees, the interior cool and deathly still. When he emerges, he sees the third river in the distance, a long shimmering silver snake. Beyond it, he spies the source of all three, an enormous cascade of water falling out of the mountain. He stops short. The sight unnerves him. The cataract is taller than any he has ever seen, reaching high up to the crags, the top obscured from view. The water plummets in a thick, furious froth, and as he draws near, the sound of it blots out all others. When he is twenty paces away, he climbs off his horse and leads it forward by hand. The horse shies, and he covers its head with a blanket to muffle the sound and erase the view. The plunge pool at the bottom is deep and treacherous, and is surrounded by a ring of massive boulders. He peers closely at the flow of water, but can see no opening behind. Only when he leads the horse right up to its edge, so that they are both quickly soaked in spray, does he see the mouth of darkness concealed there. He realises with a sinking feeling that they must cross through the edge of the flow to gain access to the opening. He climbs upon the horse and bends low over its neck, speaking quietly but firmly into its ear. The horse sidesteps nervously when he urges it forward, so he allows it to turn away and retreat a safe distance.

He spends nearly an hour contemplating what must be done. All the time he reassures the horse, speaking to it calmly and continuously, lulling it into obedience with his voice. Finally, when the horse has adjusted to the sight and sound of the water, he kicks it swiftly into a gallop and heads for the edge of the cascade. At the last moment, he fears the horse will falter. He can feel its muscles tense beneath him, can almost hear the silent scream of its nerves. He urges it forward, and in the next instant, time stops. He is moving weightless, through the air, the great bulk of the horse beneath him, the water a vast wall of white ahead. He feels himself nearly lose his seat, and then there is the hard slap of water, followed by the sudden jolt of landing. The horse stops at once, breathing hard in the darkness. Dvalin slips from its side and hangs his arms around its neck, speaking to it reassuringly. The cave is cold and clammy, the thundering curtain of water now behind them. A foul stench emanates from the walls, which are bearded by a shaggy coat of moss. Here and there, water runs in tiny streams down the sides and along the floor. He takes a minute to allow his eyes to adjust to the darkness. When he can see the path ahead, he leads the horse slowly forward. The cave twists and turns, and at one point narrows so much that he fears they will not be able to pass, but then it widens out and he sees daylight ahead. Both he and the horse move quickly towards it.

They reach the opening with relief. He sees that they are half way up the mountain, a wide green valley spread beneath them. The massive, snow-clad cone of Hekla towers in the distance, ringed by a lesser range of craggy peaks. He surveys the land laid out before him. It is lush, green and wild. Magnificently untouched by the hands of men. The way things ought to be, he thinks ruefully. Perhaps heaven is a place defined by man's absence.

He descends the slope and heads across the valley following a southeast trajectory. Freya told him once that Sessruminger lay south and east of Hekla, and that her farm occupied one of the highest elevations in Asgard. She spoke only sparingly of her home, but each word she offered is burnt into his mind. For the rest of the afternoon, he follows the southern contour of the range that skirts the glacier.

It is dusk when he catches sight of it: a high stone wall clinging dangerously to the side of the mountain in front of him. He can just make out the line of a carved wooden roof behind it. His insides tighten, for he knows with certainty that she is there. He scans the side of the mountain. A thin trail zigzags up the slope and circles back out of sight behind the wall. He begins the ascent, just as the sun erupts in a hot sphere of colour behind him. As he climbs, he feels increasingly exposed, as if he is being watched from above. Freya once told him that Sessruminger was impregnable to outsiders. Now he understands why. Because it is impossible to approach without being detected from above.

When he reaches the top, he follows the line of the wall until he locates the opening. He passes inside without pausing. The house sits in front of him, with two smaller buildings flanking it. Between the gate and the house is a courtyard planted with flowers and paved with grey stone. At its centre is a small circular pool, fed by a spring. He dismounts and leads the horse over to the pool to drink, then stoops down himself to cup water from the spring. He rises when he is finished. Freya stands motionless in the doorway wearing a pale green pleated dress secured by two silver brooches on each shoulder. Her face is deathly white, as if the blood has just been drained from it. He looks for the necklace, but cannot see it. "Dvalin," she says, her surprise plainly evident. She takes a step forward.

He does not speak, for he finds that all the words of anger he rehearsed have flown like starlings from his mind. He had forgotten quite how beautiful she was. More beautiful than any woman ought to be, he thinks now. The sort of beauty that clouds one's purpose.

"What are you doing here?" she asks. Her face is a changing landscape of emotion. He watches each one blow past: surprise, confusion, disbelief.

"I have come for Fulla," he says.

"Fulla?" Her expression turns to one of complete bewilderment.

"She is the daughter of my oldest friend. Did she not tell you?"

Freya shakes her head. "How did you find us?" she asks.

He walks slowly towards her. "You forget I am my father's son," he says, regaining his purpose. "We dwarves understand all manner of things. The sound a cat makes when it moves. The breath of a fish. The roots of a mountain." He pauses just a few feet from her. His words have silenced her. She regards him uncertainly.

"You knew she was with me," she says.

He reaches inside the pocket of his cloak. "I found this at the baths." He holds up the feather. Freya's eyes fix on it. "Where is she?"

"She is well cared for."

"Her family is anxious for her return."

"Perhaps she does not wish to go."

"Is that her talking? Or you?"

"You can ask her yourself."

"I intend to." He takes a deep breath and regards her for a moment. "Am I to believe that you befriended her and brought her here of her own bidding?"

"It was not that simple," she says evasively.

"Nothing ever is."

She hesitates. "What if I told you that Odin is her real father?"

"I would say that you were wrong."

"Are you certain?" she asks.

"Her father was my oldest friend," he replies.

"And her mother?" Freya raises an eyebrow.

Dvalin pauses. He takes a deep breath and lets it out slowly. "That is a different story," he says finally.

"Then perhaps you should start there."

Dvalin frowns at the memory. "She did not love him," he says slowly.

"Yet you doubt me now?"

He thinks of Jarl's wife: elegant, proud, imperious. When it suited her, she was capable of great charm. But her coldness had unsettled him. And she brought Jarl only a small measure of happiness during their life together. "The marriage was a troubled one," he says. "She was unhappy at Laxardal and often journeyed home to her father's estate. She forbade Jarl to accompany her, and took only her maidservant and a farmhand as an escort." His voice trails off.

"So it is possible."

He frowns. "For three years, they did not conceive a child," he says slowly. "Jarl was beside himself with worry. She began to treat him with disdain. When she finally fell pregnant, he was overjoyed. But she took to her bed and refused to see him during her confinement." Dvalin shakes his head. "Jarl was so happy at the prospect of gaining a child. He did not realise he was losing a wife.

"When the labour came, it was very difficult. Each time Jarl went to her bedside, she sent him away. When Fulla was born, Jarl rushed to her side. He told me later that when he entered the room, she turned her face to the wall. I think he realised then that their marriage was over. That night, she caught fever, and two days later, she was dead. Jarl was left alone to rear the child." Dvalin stares at Freya. "Fulla was the sole achievement of his life. She was the only thing Jarl could truly call his own."

"He knew nothing of his wife's infidelity?"

Dvalin shakes his head. "I don't think so. At least, he never spoke of it."

"Odin learnt of her grandfather's plans to go to Norway. He wanted to meet her, but in a neutral place. He wanted to introduce her to Asgard, to show her that she has a place here among us, should she want it."

"So you offered to help him."

Freya hesitates. "He stole the necklace. I had no choice."

"You bartered the necklace for Fulla?"

"You make it sound worse than it is."

"I do not need to," he says accusingly.

"He only wishes to meet her!"

"And then?"

"She is free to return, if that is what she chooses."

"With the memory of her parents forever altered."

Freya says nothing. He sees her nostrils flare slightly in anger, and then she turns away. She crosses over to one side of the garden, staring down at the flowers with enmity. "I did not know of her connection to you," she says bitterly.

"He was my oldest friend," says Dvalin. "And on his deathbed, I vowed I would watch over her. So I intend to take Fulla back with me. With or without Odin's consent."

Freya glares at him. "Then it is her consent you should seek," she says coolly.

They hear the sound of footsteps. Both turn to see Sky and Fulla come through the gate, their faces shiny with exertion. Fulla stops short. "Dvalin," she says uncertainly.

"Hello, Fulla."

She takes a few steps forward and glances quickly at Freya. "How did you find me?"

He raises an eyebrow. "Fulla, your grandfather is sick with worry."

She takes a deep breath. "I'm sorry."

"Is that all?"

She stares at him. "What is it you would have me say?"

Dvalin raises an eyebrow. "That you'll return with me. At once."

She shoots a look at Freya. "I cannot do that. I intend to stay and meet my father."

"Fulla, the man who raised you is the only one who has the right to that title. If Odin wishes to see you, then he should come to you on his own terms," continues Dvalin, "not steal you like some outlaw."

Fulla hesitates, the blood mounting in her face. "He did not steal me," she says then. "I ran away. And I have no intention of returning." She pushes past him and disappears inside.

Dvalin looks at Freya. "You've done your work well," he says dryly.

"What work is that?"

He looks around at Sessruminger. "Persuading her that she belongs here."

"We are fond of her. And she of us. Is that inconceivable to you?"

He does not reply. They stare at each other a moment, then Freya turns and walks to the door.

"You can leave in the morning," she says coldly. "With or without her."

VILI

ili watches Dvalin until he is no more than a dark speck on the horizon, then walks slowly back to the house. He crosses to the door of Hogni's bedchamber. The old man lies still in the darkness. The bitter stench of sweat and sickness hits him, together with the pungent smell of herbs from the poultice. Hogni shifts in the bed and Vili catches the glint of an eye. The old man is not asleep as he'd thought. He takes a step into the room, and the two men eye each other uneasily.

"He's gone," says Vili.

Hogni struggles up into a sitting position. "He will find her, if anyone can." The old man begins coughing and Vili steps forward to help him, picking up a rag from the small table by the bed and handing it to him. Hogni takes the rag and holds it to his mouth. After a moment, the coughing subsides. He looks up at Vili, his eyes watering, and nods his thanks.

"I hope you're right," says Vili.

"Never underestimate a dwarf," says Hogni. Vili looks at him with confusion. Hogni grunts. "You didn't realise. Many people don't. He hides it well. Though he has nothing to be ashamed of. His father was a great king. His people have knowledge and skills that lie beyond the scope of ordinary men."

Vili frowns. "I thought that he was merely short," he offers.

Hogni smiles. "He is that as well."

313

"Dwarves," murmurs Vili. "My father used to speak of them." His voice trails off. Too late, he realises his error. The air in the room suddenly thickens. Hogni shifts uncomfortably.

"I need water," he says grumpily.

Vili turns and goes out of the room, returning a few moments later with a jug of water. He pours a cup for Hogni, who drinks it noisily. "You should eat," says Vili.

"I'm not hungry."

"Did Dvalin say where he was going?"

Hogni shakes his head. "He refused to tell me."

Vili frowns. "Do you trust him?"

"More than anyone alive."

"Then I suppose I'll have to."

"You have no choice."

Over the next few days, the old man and the youth minister to each other's needs. There is little else for them to do but wait, a situation that frustrates them both, but eases the course of their friendship. Vili tends to Hogni's wound with care, changing the poultice every morning and cleansing the wound. Slowly, the infection subsides, and the old man gradually regains the use of his arm. They pass most of their time within the dark room, playing chess and nine men's morris.

On the third day, Hogni feels a pang of guilt that he has not told Vili of their impending trip to Norway. It is evening, and a thin shaft of dying light comes through the slit in the wall, throwing an orange rectangle upon the bed. They play chance, a game they have only just taken up that morning, having exhausted all the others. Hogni can see the restlessness in the lad's face. He yearns for Fulla and for his life to begin, while Hogni knows that his own life is nearly over.

"Vili," he says quietly. "There is something I must tell you." The boy looks up at him, his face a question. Hogni takes a deep breath. "We were leaving, Fulla and I. We were due to sail for Norway in a fortnight."

"Norway?"

Hogni nods. "My home. Our home."

Vili frowns. "Fulla has never been to Norway," he ventures.

"No, but it is part of her. Just as it is part of me."

"She agreed to this?"

Hogni hesitates. He feels the guilt rise up in him like bile. "Yes," he utters.

Vili's face sinks with dismay. "I didn't know," he murmurs.

"There's something else," says Hogni. "She is betrothed."

"Betrothed?" For the first time, his voice is sharp. "To whom?"

"Does it matter?" asks the old man quietly.

Vili looks at him for a long moment. "I suppose not," he says finally. He stares down at the playing pieces in his hand. Carved from the antlers of deer, they are small and worn and smooth. "Then there is nothing left for me here," he says.

"What do you mean?"

"Since the death of my mother and my grandfather, I have no wish to remain."

Hogni frowns. "What of your kin? Your uncles and their families?"

"I feel no bond with my father's brothers," he says bitterly. "Their lives are governed by the sword. I do not wish to live by violence and greed, as they have done. It was violence and greed that tore apart my family. And yours." Vili pauses. The silence stretches out between them. Both men think of those who are absent: Vili, of his father, Hogni, of his son.

"You are a fine young man," says Hogni, laying a hand upon his arm. "A man to make any father proud," he adds.

"If Fulla is to marry, then perhaps I too will go abroad and seek my fortunes elsewhere," says Vili half-heartedly.

Hogni nods. What else is there for him to say? The two men sit in silence. The orange rectangle slowly slides across the bed. After a few minutes, they hear a commotion outside: the sound of riders and men's voices shouting. Hogni rises a little unsteadily, just as Helga rushes in. "It's Thorstein," she exclaims. "Together with his men." She glances at Vili. "They've come for the lad."

Vili looks at Hogni. "What is it you would have us do?" asks Hogni urgently.

"I will go and speak to them," says Vili uncertainly.

He turns to go, but Hogni grabs his arm. "You do not wish to return to your uncle's people?"

Vili shakes his head. "No."

"Then you are welcome to remain here."

The boy hesitates. "Are you certain?"

Hogni nods. "Go quickly and hide. I will deal with them." Vili bites his lip, his eyes filled with alarm. "Go now!" urges Hogni.

Vili nods, then ducks out of the room and disappears into the scullery. Hogni pulls on his cloak and boots and crosses to the door. Outside, the sun has dropped to the horizon in a dark circle of red. He sees Thorstein and his men, six in all, fully armed. Four of them remain on horseback. Thorstein and his brother stand in front of the house. When Thorstein sees Hogni, he steps forward, halting only a few paces away.

"We've come for the lad."

"He's not here," says Hogni.

"We've heard otherwise," says Thorstein.

"The boy was here earlier this week. We sent him on his way."

Thorstein eyes him suspiciously. He turns to his brother. "Go and look in the stables." The man runs off to the stables, while Hogni and Thorstein wait, scrutinising each other. After a minute, the man emerges leading Vili's horse by a rope. Thorstein turns back to Hogni.

"I see he left his horse."

"He stole one of our mounts."

Thorstein takes a step forward. "And you're a bloody liar!" He draws his sword and advances towards Hogni. At that moment, Vili emerges from behind the house.

"Wait!" he shouts.

Thorstein stops and turns to him with a frown. "Vili!"

"I'm here," says the boy defiantly. "But not against my will." He walks towards Thorstein, stopping just in front of him. The older man stares at him a moment, then draws his arm back and slaps him hard across the face. Vili doubles over from the blow. When he straightens up, his cheek is bright red and a welt blooms just beneath his eye.

Hogni steps forward. "Leave him," he says. "He's with us now." Hogni nods towards two of his farmhands, who draw their swords and advance.

Thorstein looks from Vili to Hogni. "With you?" he says in a mocking tone. "A grandson of Skallagrim? I'll be dead in the ground first." He lunges towards Hogni, and this time the sword finds it mark, deep in the old man's abdomen. Too late, Vili leaps forward with a cry. He grabs hold of Hogni just as he crumples to the ground, his mouth open but silent. Blood seeps forth from the wound in his gut. Hogni's men move to defend him, but find themselves instantly outnumbered by the others. A sharp moment of silence follows. No one moves. Vili slides to the ground, cradling Hogni in his arms. He looks up at Thorstein.

"You fool," he says bitterly.

"It was his time," says Thorstein. He wipes his sword clean upon the dirt, then replaces it in its scabbard, turns and walks back towards his horse. Vili watches him for a split second, his face twisted with anger, then grabs the knife from Hogni's belt and leaps to his feet. Thorstein has only just begun to turn when Vili rushes at him, stabbing him in the neck with such force that both men tumble to the ground. Hogni's men rush forward to defend Vili, their swords drawn, and Vili too spins around towards his father's other brother, the bloody knife still in his hand. He holds it out tauntingly.

"Come on!" he shouts, his chest heaving. He is crying now, the tears streaming down his face. "We'll finish what he started!"

Vili's uncle stares at him in alarm, then slowly shakes his head. He calls to the men behind him to lay down their swords. After a moment, he steps forward to Thorstein's body and kneels down, feeling for a pulse. He motions towards one of the men behind him for help. Together they lift Thorstein and carry his body to his horse, slinging his lifeless form over the saddle. He walks back to Vili.

"One life for another," he says grimly. "No one can say that justice has not been meted out this day." He turns to go, then hesitates. "You have severed the bonds of your kinsmen. Henceforth, let no one call you by the name of Skallagrim." With that, he returns to his horse and mounts it. He nods to the others and they turn the horses, walking them slowly out of the yard. Vili watches them go, before returning to Hogni's side, where Helga crouches anxiously, one hand cradling her master's head.

"Does he live?" asks Vili.

"He has a pulse still. But the wound is deep. I fear it has entered his stomach."

"Let's get him inside." Vili turns to one of Hogni's men. "Bring a blanket!" The man disappears inside the stable and returns a moment later with a woollen horse blanket. They lift Hogni onto it and carry him inside, where they lay him out upon the bed.

"Quickly! We must bind the wound," says Helga. She rushes out of the room and returns with a bundle of old linen and a knife. Frantically, her hands trembling, she begins to tear the cloth into strips. Hogni moans. Vili kneels at his side. The old man's pallor is grey. His eyes flutter briefly, then open. It takes a moment for his gaze to focus.

"Boy," he says weakly.

"Save your strength," urges Vili. "Do not leave us!"

Hogni shakes his head slowly. "I am cold."

"Please, Hogni, you must try. For Fulla's sake, if not your own."

Hogni's eyes wander towards the ceiling. "Fulla," he whispers. He raises a hand and drops it on Vili's arm. "Promise me that you will take her away from here. From all this death," he sighs.

"I promise."

Hogni takes a deep breath, his body shuddering from the effort. He licks his lips. Vili reaches for a cup of water by the bed and raises it to the old man's mouth. The water trickles down Hogni's chin, and he coughs. "Vili," Hogni whispers. Vili leans in closer. The old man swallows, his chest heaving from the effort of speech. "Take her to Norway," he says. "That is where her future lies."

Vili stares at him, uncomprehending. The old man's gaze has become glassy and unfocused. But he can feel

Hogni's death-grip upon his arm, surprisingly strong. "Do this for me," Hogni says urgently. "And you will secure my blessing."

Vili hesitates, then nods. "Of course."

Hogni takes a deep breath and releases his arm. Once again, his eyes wander upwards, as if searching for escape.

Vili leans forward urgently, sensing that the old man is sliding into death. "Hogni," he shouts. Hogni looks at him and shakes his head, his eyes rolling backwards. Suddenly he falls still. Helga steps forward, a small cry escaping from her lips. Vili stares at Hogni's lifeless body in horror, his own chest heaving with emotion. After a moment, he feels the weight of Helga's hand drop upon his shoulder. He turns to her. "He's dead," he whispers.

"There was nothing we could do," she says. Vili turns and folds himself into her embrace. They cling to each other in the darkness.

At length, Vili straightens. "Helga, the promise I made, about Norway. What did he mean?"

Helga shakes her head. "I wish I knew."

DVALIN

valin sleeps badly under Freya's roof, despite being worn out from the journey. He wakes before dawn, at once conscious of her presence, as if the timbers overhead contain some kernel of her essence. He tries without success to sleep again, but his mind is strewn with thoughts. Eventually, he rises, pulling on his clothes and going out into the large hall, where the fire has burned to only a handful of embers. The house is still, except for the occasional creak of the wooden rafters. He can hear the faint whistle of the wind outside. He lays several squares of turf upon the fire and picks up a bellows to fan the embers into flame. Soon the smell of peat smoke fills the room, and the flames crackle into life. As he lays the bellows to one side, he hears a noise behind him. He turns to see Sky standing in the doorway, the hawk perched upon his arm. The boy regards him closely.

Dvalin smiles at him. "Don't worry. I'm not set against you." Sky doesn't move, but stands watching him intently. Something in his manner causes Dvalin to pause. "Perhaps it is you who are set against me," he says slowly.

Sky does not respond.

"Come. Sit with me," says Dvalin.

Sky hesitates, then crosses the floor to where Dvalin sits upon a bench by the fire. He takes a seat next to him. "You are happy here," says Dvalin.

The boy nods.

"Freya has been good to you."

Sky nods again.

Dvalin says nothing for a moment. He picks up an iron poker and prods at the fire. "So you do not intend to return to Jotunheim." It is more a statement than a question, and Dvalin does not expect an answer. Instead, his attention is focused on the fire. He does not see the boy open his mouth to speak.

"No," says Sky.

Dvalin turns to him, wide-eyed. "You speak?"

The boy nods cautiously.

Dvalin shakes his head in amazement. "Do you mean that all this time you've been silent out of choice?"

The boy nods again.

"Answer me!" Dvalin says.

"Yes," says Sky. His voice is slightly hoarse.

Dvalin stares at him a moment, and gives a short derisive laugh. The boy eyes him uneasily. Dvalin wheels on him. "I should thrash you!"

Sky leaps to his feet and backs away.

"Sit down," says Dvalin with a shake of his head.

Sky hesitates, then returns to his seat. His fingers move to stroke the bird, but it ducks and bobs away from his hand.

Dvalin glares at him. "Why?"

The boy takes a deep breath and lets it out slowly. "I could not," he says finally.

"You would not," corrects Dvalin.

"Would not," admits Sky.

Dvalin scowls and turns back to the fire. Sky watches him intently. "I saw things," he says. "Things I did not wish to speak of." Dvalin turns to face him, his eyes narrowing.

"What things?"

Sky hesitates. "I saw you kill my brothers."

322

Dvalin frowns. "That is not the only thing you saw," he says.

"I hated them for what they did that day," Sky replies evenly. "But I hated you as well."

"They got what they deserved."

"Perhaps." Sky looks away into the fire. "Most of all, I hated myself," he says then. "For I did not have the strength to oppose them. Not that day, nor any of the others..."

"You were only a child."

Sky shakes his head. "Silence is the path of cowards."

Dvalin lays a hand upon his shoulder. "You are too harsh. Your brothers' sins were not your own," he says intently.

"Maybe not," the boy says, "but I still feel their shame."

They hear a noise outside. Dvalin drops his voice. "Do the others know?" Sky gives a quick shake of his head, just as Fulla enters the room. Dvalin glances quickly back at Sky, who pleads with him silently. Dvalin rises and turns to greet Fulla.

"May I speak with you?" she asks Dvalin.

"Of course."

Sky jumps to his feet. He nods to them and turns to go, and Fulla gives him a smile of thanks. She seats herself on the bench where Sky had been only moments before. "The lad is fond of you," says Dvalin.

"And I of him. He is like a brother to me. I am very fond of both of them."

Dvalin nods. "I know this."

They both stare at the fire for a moment. Fulla takes a deep breath and turns to him. "It was wrong of me to run away. One always knows, deep inside, what is right from what is wrong." She pauses, gathering her thoughts. "I feel as if my entire life has been lived inside the shadow of death. First my mother. Then my father. And now… now my grandfather wishes to return to his homeland, in order to die. Dvalin, I am too well acquainted with death and its ways not to recognise this. And though he has provided for my future, it is not one of my choosing."

"You do not wish to go to Norway," he says.

"No," she says emphatically.

"Then you must tell him."

She shakes her head. "He does not understand. I've spoken to him. And we do not agree…" She breaks off.

"And Vili? What has he to do with all this?"

She looks up at him with surprise. Her voice drops sharply. "How do you know about Vili?"

"He waits for you at Laxardal. I left him tending Hogni's wounds."

Her face creases with alarm. "What wounds?"

"Hogni is fine," Dvalin says reassuringly. "He was stabbed in the shoulder."

"By whom?"

"Thorstein."

She stares at him, aghast. "Because of me," she utters.

"Yes. But you could not have foreseen it."

"Nonetheless, the blame is mine! Had I not run away…"

"It might have happened anyway," he interjects. "There was bad blood between them long before, Fulla. Remember this."

She shakes her head. "Hate has poisoned all of us," she says.

Dvalin sighs. "Perhaps."

She looks around the room. "I must go to them."

Dvalin hesitates, suddenly riddled with doubt. "But what of Odin?"

"As you said, he will have to come to me." She rises

324

to her feet. "We must leave at once. I'll speak to Freya and ready my things." She turns and hurries from the room.

Dvalin crosses to the small bedchamber and begins to stuff his few possessions into a satchel. When he is finished, he folds the bedclothes they have given him to sleep upon. Freya stands silently in the doorway watching him. "She is leaving," says Freya.

He turns around, startled. "Yes," he admits.

"You were very persuasive."

"The choice was hers."

"Perhaps it is the right one."

Dvalin says nothing.

"I did not expect her to remain with us for good. Sky will be disappointed, however," she adds. "We are his family now."

Dvalin wonders briefly whether to speak of the boy's revelation, but decides against it. "What about the necklace?" he says instead.

"It remains with Odin."

"You would surrender it that easily?"

"What choice do I have?"

Dvalin ponders this. "You are its rightful owner. Odin must know this. You must persuade him to return it."

She frowns. "By what means? Would you have me debase myself with him as well?" she says tartly.

He colours. "Of course not," he stammers. "I only meant..."

"Maybe I was wrong to put my faith in the necklace, for it has done nothing but cause strife since it came to me."

The words hit him bluntly. "Perhaps you are right," he says. "Perhaps it was not meant for you."

"Perhaps not." She stares at him, and the gulf between them seems to widen. "It is time for you to go," she says.

"I'll see that your horses are made ready." She turns to leave, and they both see Sky standing by the fire like a ghost. Without a sound, he flees.

FREYA

Was it truth I spoke about the necklace? The words came from nowhere, but once they'd landed in the space between us, I felt the harsh weight of them. I saw a flash of something in Dvalin's eyes when I uttered them: whether it was anger or regret I cannot say. I do not know why Skuld sent me to retrieve the Brisingamen. Nor whose purpose it was destined to serve. But it has done little to alleviate Hekla's anger since my return. The mountain continues to behave in strange, unpredictable ways. One moment, she spews forth acrid clouds of smoke, the next, she is menacingly quiet. I do not trust her silence nor her outbursts, and I am beginning to believe that my faith in the necklace was misjudged. In the end, the Brisingamen has merely succeeded in dividing us. And a part of me now feels relieved that it is gone.

So let them return to their people. Sky and I will contend with Hekla on our own.

But a short while later, when they are about to leave, Sky is nowhere to be found. We look for him at length, calling all around the house and grounds. Finally, we are forced to abandon our search. Fulla turns to me with dismay. "I wanted to say goodbye," she says.

"Tell him we're sorry," says Dvalin. I shoot him a look, but he seems sincere.

"Will you visit me?" asks Fulla.

I force a smile. My quarrel is not with her, after all.

"Perhaps," I reply. I hardly think her grandfather would welcome me, however. I cast my gaze briefly towards Dvalin; his expression is remote.

"We must go, Fulla," he says then.

She embraces me, before turning to her horse. Dvalin holds the reins while she mounts, then climbs upon his own. I do not say goodbye to him, but when he has brought his horse around towards the gate, he turns and nods to me, just once. Our eyes meet, and I realise that I cannot read the darkness in them. The man is unknowable, I think, as I watch them both ride out of the yard.

After they have gone, I return to the house, feeling empty. Where is Sky? I wonder. And why did he disappear so quickly? My eyes roam restlessly about the room and eventually settle on the carved wooden trunk that holds the feather form. Without thinking I cross to it and lift the lid. The box is empty. Sky has stolen the feather form. I feel a sudden clench of fear deep inside: without the form I am powerless. I can do nothing now but hope that he returns.

I spend the rest of the day weaving. When my spirit is unsettled, the loom quiets me. Today I choose flax to weave with. My fingers caress the fine threads, feel the roughness of the cloth as it is formed. I shove the worn wooden shuttle back and forth, trying to lose myself in the rhythm of its dance. Every now and then, my feet brush against the polished stone circles that anchor the warp. Their weight reminds me that we are all tethered to one another, for better or for worse. I know that now, even if I didn't always.

When I finally stop, the late summer sun has nearly

finished its descent. I take up my cloak and climb the slope behind the house, my feet sending loose stones skittering down the mountain behind me. Eventually I reach a small crag and sit upon a rock ledge. In front of me, the dying sun is a vast orb of red. I watch it slip behind the mountains far to the west. To my left, Hekla sits squarely, her perfect cone emitting a dark breath of sulphurous smoke. She gives a little cough now and then, as if reminding me of her presence, and for the first time I see that one flank of her cone bulges slightly, like the puffed up bladder of a pig. Once again a dark curtain of fear sweeps through me. I have lived in Hekla's shadow all my life, but never have I seen her so alive. I reach for the Brisingamen without thinking, but my hands clutch at nothing. I pray that Sky returns, for I do not know how much longer Hekla will wait.

THE NORNS

The people here call it hraun, the burnt wilderness left behind when lava has grown cold. Much of the lava here is thick and rich in gas; it erupts infrequently but with enormous explosiveness. Gnarled and bumpy, this type of lava can flow at the pace of a snail, sometimes advancing only a few feet a day. It crumbles forward, glowing lumps breaking off and tumbling down the front edge of the slope, forming a surface that is ugly and impassable. When magma is less thick, it produces lava that flows in smooth, ropy channels like a flaming river. It quickly forms a hard skin on its surface. Red-hot lava runs beneath this skin, distorting it into coils like the pipes of an organ. These pipes direct the flow of lava away from the crater, sometimes over long distances. If a pipe empties at the end of an eruption, a cave forms. But all lava is savage in its treatment of the land: the ruined earth reclaims itself by degrees, often taking generations to recover.

DVALIN

They ride first to Nidavellir. It is dark when they arrive, and the caves are eerily quiet. Once they have fed and watered the horses, Dvalin takes up a torch and hands a second one to Fulla, then leads her through the labyrinth of twisting tunnels. The caves are clammy and the air is pungent with the smell of minerals. Fulla shivers and pulls her cloak more tightly around her. "Is it always this cold?" she asks.

Dvalin grins at her. "You get used to it."

"Where are the people?"

"Asleep mainly. Night comes early to the caves. There is little to occupy us after dark. Watch your step here." He motions towards a stream of water that cuts directly across their path, before disappearing down a hole in the wall.

Fulla steps across it. "Water is everywhere here," Dvalin continues. "The caves were formed thousands of years ago by underground rivers. The water is our lifeblood. Without it we would perish."

"So all those years, when you went away from us, this is where you returned to?" Her voice contains a hint of incredulity.

He laughs. "Yes, believe it or not."

"Did you bring my father here?"

"Only once. Once was enough. Jarl thought that I was mad to live in darkness, when I could have the sun and stars."

333

Fulla glances at him sideways. "But you are fond of it here."

He shrugs. "In spite of myself, yes, I suppose I am."

Finally, they reach Dvalin's cave. He stands to one side and motions for her to enter. Fulla wanders about the room with interest, pausing now and then to examine his things, while Dvalin kneels and lays a fire. When she discovers the bowl of coloured beads, she exclaims with delight, running her fingers through them repeatedly.

"These are lovely! Where did you get them?"

"They were my mother's. She collected them on her travels."

Fulla frowns. "Your mother travelled?"

"My mother was one of the Aesir. In fact, she was a swan maiden."

"I never knew this."

He shrugs. "Why would you?"

"A swan maiden," she murmurs. "Could she fly?"

He nods. "Yes."

"Like Freya," Fulla says.

Dvalin purses his lips. "Yes." He turns away and crosses to an oak barrel in the corner, where he decants two cups of ale. "Here." He hands one to her.

"How did she meet your father?"

"By chance. He came across her bathing in a river. In fact, it was her feathers he discovered. She was then bound to him, according to the laws of the Aesir."

"Bound to him?"

Dvalin nods. "For seven years. That was her punishment: the feather form was not meant to be out of her possession, even for an instant."

"So she returned with him to the caves?"

"Yes. They were married."

"And after seven years?"

334

"She left."

"She did not love him?"

He ponders this. "No," he says eventually. "I do not think so."

"Did he love her?"

Dvalin finishes the ale and sets the cup down. "Yes. Though I think he knew in his heart she would not stay."

Fulla frowns. "How sad." She runs her fingers again through the beads. She eventually chooses a small red one and holds it up to the light. "But she left these behind."

"Yes," he replies. "And me."

Fulla looks up at him with surprise.

"She took my sister with her. And left the stones and me with my father. I suppose we were her parting gift." He gives a wan smile.

"What a sorry tale," she says quietly. "But I suppose my own family did not fare much better."

"Life is full of such stories," he says.

She nods. "You look tired."

He smiles. "A fortnight on horseback will tire anyone."

"I'm sorry. The fault is mine. We should rest."

She looks around towards the bed. "You sleep there," Dvalin says. "I'll take a pallet by the fire. We've got another long ride tomorrow."

"Dvalin." She pauses. "I'm sorry for the trouble I've caused."

"Your father only wanted your happiness."

"Happiness is an elusive thing," she replies.

"I believe you made him happy."

"Perhaps. But we'll never know, will we?"

He sleeps deeply, without dreams, his mind and body desperate for release. When he wakes, he sees at once that Fulla has already risen. She smiles at him. "Good morning," she says. "You were sleeping so peacefully, I couldn't bear to wake you."

"I'm grateful," he says with a smile. He sees that her hair is freshly combed, and that she has lit a fire and even prepared a simple meal for him out of the remains of their food, which she has laid out neatly on the bench by the fire.

"Are you hungry?" she asks, motioning towards the bench.

"I'm famished." He rises and crosses to the bench, surveying her efforts. A tiny crease of pain runs through him. He has lived all these years without the presence of another, much less the deft hand of a woman. He smiles at her. "The man who wins your hand will be very fortunate indeed."

She laughs. "Why? Because I have the good sense to make a meal?"

Before he can reply, they hear footsteps outside. Berling enters excitedly, followed by Gerd. "You're back!" he says.

"Berling, Gerd. This is Jarl's daughter, Fulla."

Berling stares at Fulla, silenced by her beauty. "We're pleased to meet you," says Gerd warmly. "Indeed, we've heard much of your family all these years. Dvalin's loyalty has been sharply divided between Laxardal and Nidavellir."

"We're on our way back to Laxardal," explains Dvalin. "We arrived late last night."

"You're off again?" says Berling, disappointed.

"I'm afraid so."

"Have you forgotten your promise to Berling?" asks Gerd gently.

"Yes, Dvalin, you gave your word," says Berling eagerly.

Dvalin hesitates. "So I did," he says then.

"Does that mean I can come?" asks Berling.

Dvalin nods. "If Fulla does not object."

"Of course not. You would be more than welcome at my grandfather's house."

"We leave in an hour, Berling. Make ready your things," says Dvalin.

Berling beams with pleasure, before rushing from the room. When he has gone, Gerd turns to him. "Thank you, Dvalin. It will do him a world of good. He's been missing you. We all have," she adds pointedly.

"We'll take good care of him, Gerd."

"I am certain of it. How long will you be gone?"

"Three days at most. Enough time for him to get a glimpse of the outside world, but not so long that he becomes accustomed to it."

Gerd smiles. "Like his older brother, you mean." She looks at him purposefully, and he colours. "Very well," she says. "I'll leave you to your preparations. Goodbye, Fulla. Please thank your grandfather for his hospitality."

"Yes, of course."

After Gerd has gone, Dvalin returns to the bench and seats himself. Fulla eyes him for a moment. "She's a lovely woman," she remarks.

"Yes. A good mother to Berling."

"It's not my business, but...she harbours feelings for you, does she not?"

Dvalin stops chewing and looks at her. "She was my father's third wife."

"Oh." She frowns. She starts to speak, then hesitates.

"What is it?"

"Your father has been dead some years, and Gerd is closer to your age than his. Surely he would not begrudge a union now."

"Fulla," he says with a sigh. "I have no intention of marrying Gerd."

"I was only thinking of your happiness. It seems unfair that you have remained alone all these years."

"The choice was mine," he says.

She raises an eyebrow. "You choose to be alone?"

He shrugs. "Is that so hard to believe?"

"No, I suppose not."

"Perhaps it is a coward's way."

"I've never regarded you as a coward."

"Then perhaps I've fooled you." He smiles at her. "Now eat." He indicates the food with a nod. "We've a long ride ahead."

VILI

They build an enormous pyre, but do not light it. Neither do they move the body. After the second day, Helga closes the chamber door and locks it. There is little else for them to do but wait. Vili sleeps badly. At night, he dreams of valkyries, hideous women with long, dark hair and masks of death who ride screaming through the air on horseback. Each morning when he wakes, the same thought strikes like a coiled snake inside him. Had he acted differently, both men might still be alive.

Helga busies herself preparing food that no one eats. Her fleshy face has taken on the pallor of a turnip, and her eyes are permanently red from weeping. On the evening of the third day, they sit together by the fire, exhausted by grief. Helga has brewed a bitter-smelling tea from kitchen herbs, a recipe she claims is traditional, but one he suspects has been devised to mask the stench of death that has begun to seep from Hogni's bedchamber. They sit lost in thought, each hoping for Dvalin's return. The funeral pyre stands silently outside the house, waiting to claim Hogni's body. It took a band of men three days to scavenge enough wood for the pyre, a luxury in a country where few trees grow.

"We shall have to burn the body soon," says Vili, poking at the fire with an iron. Helga nods. She clutches a dirty rag tightly in one hand, he suspects without realising, for it has been there all evening.

"Perhaps tomorrow they will come," she offers. Vili prods at the square of turf with the iron, splitting it in two. The insides burst into flame. He has almost given up hope that Fulla will be found, and has begun to think that the man Hogni entrusted with her life is himself lying dead somewhere in a ditch.

Just then, a farmhand bursts through the door. Vili and Helga turn their heads in unison. "Three riders," says the man eagerly. "Coming from the south!"

Vili dashes to the door. He can just make out the riders on the skyline. He runs to the stables and quickly saddles a horse, intending to ride out to meet them. It is only when he leads the horse out into the yard that he realises he does not know what he will say. The thought halts him. He stands uncertainly, holding the horse's rein. If it is Fulla, does he wish to be the bearer of bad news?

As if reading his mind, Helga walks slowly out into the yard, twisting the rag in her hand. She links her arm in his, and together they wait. He feels a wave of gratitude towards this woman he has known barely a week. After a minute, they recognise Dvalin and Fulla. The third rider is a small boy they do not know. "It is them," she whispers hoarsely, digging her nails into his arm. His heart flails inside his chest like a trapped animal.

The pyre speaks for them. As the riders draw near, Vili sees Dvalin's face crease with concern. The older man's eyes are riveted to the pile of wood. Only Hogni is of sufficient stature to merit such a tribute. Vili looks at Fulla. She too understands, for her own face has gone deathly pale. Beside them, the young boy looks bewildered. Dvalin pulls his horse to a halt and slides quickly to the ground. He turns to Helga. "Hogni?" he asks anxiously. Helga nods her head wordlessly.

"Grandfather!" wails Fulla, her worst fears confirmed. The older woman rushes to her side, helping her down off the horse and wrapping her tightly in an embrace.

Dvalin turns to Vili. "What happened?"

"Thorstein came," says Vili. "There was an argument."

Dvalin's eyes glaze with anger. He takes a deep breath, then suddenly turns on his heel and starts for the horse. Vili rushes forward and grabs his arm.

"He's dead, Dvalin."

Dvalin turns around. "Thorstein?"

Vili nods. "I killed him," he says. "There is nothing more to do but grieve."

Dvalin stares at him for a long moment. "It is like the poets said," he murmurs. "'Brothers will do battle to the death, and sons of sisters will fight their own kin.'"

Vili shakes his head mournfully. "Come," he says, taking Dvalin's arm. "You must pay your respects to the dead."

Once inside, he has little chance to speak to Fulla. She views the body briefly, then shuts herself in her room with Helga for almost two hours. Vili and Dvalin sit silently by the fire, drinking horn after horn of mead, until the embers swim before their eyes. Dvalin is the first to sleep, while Vili remains awake, staring at the remnants of a family he has helped to ruin.

FREYA

his morning when I wake, the air is deathly still. I dress and go outside, climbing the hill behind the house. The dawn sun straddles the horizon, shrouded in a sickly yellow haze. The sky above me is a translucent shade of green. No birds sing. No insects worry me as I walk. I pause when I reach the top of the hill. The silence in Asgard is complete, as if every living thing has ceased to be. My skin has taken on an odd hue in the morning light; my arms look like the underbelly of a fish. I turn towards Hekla. She is eerily quiet, although the bulge in her flank looks more pronounced than ever.

I look down and see a tiny grey field mouse appear on the path in front of me. It emerges from behind a small bush and takes a few steps, then stops, panting heavily. I move my foot slightly, but the mouse does not retreat. It stands watching me for a long moment, turns and walks several steps, before halting once again and turning back on itself, as if dazed. I search the sky for predators; surely this mouse will not survive long in such a state. The sky is empty. When I look down, the mouse stands immobile on the path, as if it no longer has the will to live. I reach down and scoop it up in my hand. It does not squirm as it should, but sits impassively. I place it gently in the pocket of my cloak, where it lies quietly.

I turn and walk back towards the house, feeling uneasy. When I am almost there, I see two horses approach in the distance. Amazed, I realise that the first

342

carries Odin, the second, Sky. The feather form is flung across the saddle in front of Odin. I walk out to meet them. As they draw near, I see that Sky's wrists are bound in front of him.

"Odin," I say when the horses come to a halt, "what has happened? Why is he bound?"

Odin raises an eyebrow. "I thought it prudent."

I move at once to Sky's horse and reach for his wrists to unbind them. He holds them out for me glumly. "Where did you find him?" I ask Odin over my shoulder.

"I didn't. He found me." Odin climbs down off his horse. "He told me he had come to retrieve the necklace. He said that you were its rightful owner."

I stop short. Sky slowly raises his gaze to meet mine. "He *told* you?" I say, staring him in the eye.

"Yes."

"Is there something I should know?" I ask Sky quietly.

He hesitates. "I'm sorry," he replies.

"For which offence are you apologising? Lying or thievery?"

Sky looks at me, mortified.

"Sky," I say more gently. "What were you doing?"

"I thought that if I found the necklace I could put things right," he says slowly. "Between you and Dvalin."

"Me and Dvalin?" I ask, incredulous.

He shrugs.

"But I failed," he says miserably.

I glance at Odin. "I no longer have the necklace," he explains. "Loki took it. For safekeeping, he said." Odin looks surprised.

"Sky, go inside." Sky climbs off his horse and walks towards the house. Odin too dismounts.

"The girl is gone," he says, once Sky has disappeared.

I nod. "Yesterday."

He sighs. "I suspected as much."

"Her ties to her kin are very strong."

"Yes," he answers. "I knew this."

"Odin, she is not your daughter. Not in any way that is meaningful."

"Perhaps you are right," he says sullenly.

We turn and follow Sky inside, where I pour Odin a cup of ale. "Here."

He stares down into the cup for a moment, then looks back at me. "We were close once, you and I."

I smile at him. "Mountains have been born since then."

"We could be still."

I shake my head. "That time is past." I am no longer smiling.

Just then, the air is rent by three short sharp cracks, and the ground beneath us shifts violently. We stagger outside and gaze at Hekla. A tall column of billowing dark smoke shoots from her cone like an enormous fountain reaching up into the heavens. "What is happening?" I ask anxiously. He scrutinises the mountain.

"It's the beginning," he says.

"You knew this was coming?"

"I did not think it would be this soon."

"That's why you wanted to meet Fulla."

"Yes."

"There is still time."

He frowns. "Perhaps. Perhaps it is too late."

I hesitate, my mind running in different directions. "Where is the necklace?" I ask suddenly.

"Hidden in the sea at Singastein."

"Singastein?" I cry, aghast, for he speaks of an island, far away on the coast.

"It was Loki's idea. It is he who covets the necklace, not I. The man is like a cancer. I cannot rid myself of him."

"Where is he now?"

"On his way here, I suspect. He is never far away," Odin says.

"Singastein," I murmur.

"In a cave, by the sea." Odin turns to me, his voice now urgent. "You must go now. Before it is too late."

"To Singastein?" I ask.

He nods. "You must go and find the necklace now!"

"But...what of the boy?" Sky has just emerged from the house.

Odin shakes his head. "He'll be safer on horseback," he says. "I'll show him the way out of Asgard. If we leave now, there is still time." I glance at Sky uncertainly. "Freya, you must trust me," Odin says emphatically. "I'll see the boy to safety."

All at once, the prospect of the Brisingamen is too much for me. "Very well," I reply quickly, turning to Sky. "Do you understand? You must leave at once," I tell him. "Odin will help you." Sky nods, his eyes full of alarm. I cross over to Odin's horse and grab the falcon cloak slung across the saddle, hurriedly throwing it over my shoulders. I turn back to Odin.

"Go swiftly," he says intently.

Only then do I understand his meaning, for Hekla will not wait.

❧

Once in the air, I fly towards the sea, my eyes burning from the smoke. When I reach the coast, I fly south, until I arrive at the tiny island known as Singastein. By now the sky has grown even darker, the sun obscured by ash pouring from the volcano. The ocean itself is clearly disturbed by Hekla's activity, its surface a frantic chop of waves running in all directions like a crazed hen. I glide down close to the water, peering inside the caves that run beneath the island. Most have openings too small for me to enter, but one of them is larger than the rest. I fly inside and leave the frothing sea behind me.

Inside, the cave is eerily calm and dark. I perch upon a rocky ledge to rest. Beneath me, the water runs many metres deep. It is a brilliant cobalt blue, as if lit from below. Down through the water, I see rainbow stripes of algae along the rock walls, wonderful hues of green and yellow and orange. In one corner of the cave, light filters in from a spattering of tiny holes in the rock face, dappling the water like a handful of glowing pebbles thrown at its surface. When I look more closely, I see something glinting a few metres beneath the water. I crawl forward as far as I am able. And there I see the Brisingamen, nestled like a golden serpent in a crack along the cave wall.

The icy cold of the water squeezes my lungs, but I do not mind once the Brisingamen is safely in my hand. I swim towards the side of the cave and drag myself out upon the only ledge wide enough to hold me. The shock of the water's temperature has left me light-headed, and I pause to catch my breath, lying flat upon the cold wet rock. And then I hear an enormous blast, as Hekla finally loses all control. Even muffled by the cave, the explosion is deafening, unlike any I have ever heard before. It rumbles on and on, during which time I close my eyes and clutch the Brisingamen to my chest. When I open my eyes, the water in the cave has begun to roil, as if it too is terrified. Brilliant sparks dance beneath its surface. The entire cave begins to tremble then, jostled by a hidden hand. I stare down at the Brisingamen, wondering whether it will save me or lead me to my death. After what seems like an eternity, the earth's movement slowly ceases. The water halts its furious churning, though it still sways uneasily. I lie back upon the rock and close my eyes, afraid to discover what has happened to the world outside the cave.

My world: the world of the gods. The one doomed to fail.

FULLA

he sleeps badly, and wakes numb with grief. The morning sky is a strange shade of grey, a mirror of her own emotions. She blames herself for Hogni's death. She should never have run away to Asgard. Her place was here, by her grandfather's side.

But what of Vili? Last night, Helga told her that Vili had made peace with Hogni before he died, and had even avenged his death by killing Thorstein. What greater proof of loyalty could she ask for? She wishes she could know what Hogni thought of him in those final hours. Most of all, she wishes she could have secured his blessing.

She rises and dresses, choosing a sober-coloured gown that lies folded in the heavy wooden chest beside her bed. A moth flies free when she shakes out the cloth, and flutters aimlessly about the bedchamber. When she emerges from her room, she sees at once that Vili and Dvalin lie sleeping on pallets by the fire. She could hardly bring herself to look at Vili last night, overcome as she was with grief and guilt. Now she approaches his sleeping form cautiously. She kneels down beside him, studying his features openly for the first time. She notes a tiny scar beside one eye, a small mole on the side of his neck, and a hint of pale stubble on his chin. Otherwise, his face is smooth and bronzed from the sun, his skin like caramel. His long auburn hair lies in a tangled mass. She suppresses a desire to touch it. Her eyes drift down to his chest, to the small triangle of skin exposed by the opening in his shirt. This is where I would put my lips, she thinks, if I dared.

A noise startles her from behind. She turns to see Helga in the doorway, struggling with a large iron pot of water. Fulla jumps to her feet awkwardly, as Helga carries the pot over to the fire. The older woman exhales as she sets the pot down on the coals, then turns to Fulla with an expectant look. Fulla raises a finger to her lips, and the two women retreat to the pantry at the back of the hall. They duck beneath the small doorframe. Fulla sees at once that Helga has been awake for hours. The small space is full of chopped vegetables and half-made dishes, as if the older woman had thrown herself into preparations for a banquet. Helga raises a fleshy hand to move a wisp of hair from Fulla's eyes. Once this is done, she grasps Fulla's chin firmly in her hand and looks her straight in the eye. "Be brave. We'll light the pyre today. It's time to send him on." Fulla nods, fighting back tears. Helga sniffs and wipes her hands upon her apron, before turning back to the food. "You can help me with the bread," she adds, handing Fulla an earthen bowl full of freshly made dough.

Fulla stares down at the bowl. "Helga," she says slowly. The older woman stops and looks at her. "What will become of us?" she whispers.

Helga shakes her head. "I do not know," she says.

❧❧❧

As soon as everyone has woken, they assemble outside. Dvalin makes a short speech and, taking a torch from the fire, touches it to the ring of dead grass surrounding the pyre. The grass lights instantly, and they all watch as the flames gather and spread, leaping from one branch to

349

the next. Hogni's body lies atop a tall platform at the centre, his hands folded across his chest. When the flame begins to lick the bottom of the platform, Fulla turns and retches on the ground. She buries her face in Helga's shoulder, unable to watch the fire's progress.

When it is over, she climbs the hill behind the house. The sky remains a curious shade of grey, the sun hidden behind a thick yellow haze. The sharply acrid smell of the pyre is still strong in the air, though thankfully the wind has shifted away from the house. As she settles herself upon the grass, she hears three sharp cracks far off in the distance, like lightning. She studies the horizon, and thinks about her future. She has never met the man to whom she is betrothed and has never been to the country where he resides. Everything and everyone she has ever known and loved is here, on this small plot of land beneath her. She sees Vili come out of the house and watches as he walks towards the stables. She has barely said two words to him and could not bring herself to meet his gaze this morning. As he peers inside the stables, then turns and surveys the yard, she realises with a start that he is looking for her, and her heart begins to race. As if on cue, he raises his eyes to the hillside where she sits.

She watches as he climbs the short slope and drops down in the grass next to her. "Fulla, we must talk," he says abruptly. She opens her mouth to speak, but he raises a hand to silence her. "Hear me out," he says urgently, as if the words themselves will not wait. "All that has happened here is my fault and mine alone. I should never have sought refuge with Hogni, though he was generous to take me in. In the days before his death we spent much time together. And I believe he grew fond of me by the end. But I have done him, and you, an enormous injury by fleeing my kin. And for that I will never forgive myself." He pauses and takes a deep breath, staring down at the house beneath him. "Fulla, I swore an oath to your grandfather as he lay dying that I would deliver you safely to Norway. And I intend to keep it." He breaks off abruptly, and for the first time, turns to meet her gaze.

She looks at him, horrified. "But I do not want to go," she says.

Vili frowns. "He told me that you had consented."

Fulla looks down at the grassy slope beneath them. "He did not give me a choice."

Vili sighs. "Hogni showed me a great deal of kindness before he died. More kindness than my own people." He looks at her pleadingly. "I gave my word to a dying man on his deathbed. If I break my oath, then I forsake all my honour with it."

She gapes at him in disbelief, her throat tightening. Vili's eyes drift down to the grass, refusing to meet hers. After a moment, he rises to his feet. "I must go," he says hoarsely, turning away. She watches him recede from her, his lean form distorted by her tears.

She remains atop the hillside for another hour, and only descends when Helga comes into the yard calling her name. She walks slowly down the hill, and as she reaches the house, she hears the explosion. This time, she knows it is not lightning. Helga stands in front of her, her eyes wide with alarm. Both turn to study the horizon. Far off in the distance, they see a vast funnel of dark ash reaching high into the sky. At the same time, they feel the first shock waves, and the earth beneath their feet begins to shake. Instinctively, Helga reaches for her arm, just as Vili emerges from the stables, and Dvalin from the house. Within moments, the entire household is gathered in the yard, listening to the far-off sound of Hekla. The noise dies slightly after a minute, and the earth beneath them ceases to move. Fulla can hear the frightened baying of the horses and the incessant mooing of the cows. They stand and watch as an enormous black cloud slowly sweeps across the sky, obliterating the sun. Soon the first bits of ash begin to rain around them, followed by small pieces of pumice, some of them still warm. "Get inside," says Dvalin tensely. After a moment's hesitation, they all crowd into Hogni's hall. The sky outside is nearly black with ash. A young serving woman begins to wail, until Helga pushes her into a chair and forces a cup of mead into her hands.

Fulla crosses over to where Dvalin stands by the door. "Is it Hekla?" she asks tentatively. He nods, his face stricken with fear. They are both thinking of the same thing: the fate of Asgard and Freya.

Berling suddenly appears beside them. "Dvalin," he asks anxiously. "What of Nidavellir?" Dvalin shakes his head wordlessly and places a hand upon the boy's shoulder.

They spend the next few hours inside, waiting for the ash fall to subside. Towards late afternoon, they finally emerge into the yard. Everywhere around them, the ground has been coated with a thick layer of ash. Even the sheep and cows on the hillside are black with soot. Dvalin stares out at the horizon, his face set in a frown. After a moment, he motions to Vili, laying a hand upon his shoulder. "What should we do?" asks Vili.

"Stay here," says Dvalin. "Clear the ash from the yard and the garden as best you can. Give the livestock some hay, as the grass will not be fit for grazing. And make sure the water supplies are clear."

Vili nods. "What of you?"

"I will ride to Nidavellir."

"Is it safe?"

Dvalin hesitates. "I won't know until I get there," he says. "But I have to go."

Suddenly, Berling appears. "I'll come with you," he says fiercely.

Dvalin turns to him. "No, Berling. Your mother would never forgive me. I'll go alone and return with her as fast as I am able. Vili will look after you, and Fulla too. You must help them, as best you can." Berling swallows, then nods.

Together they watch as Dvalin gathers a few supplies and saddles his horse. He climbs upon his mount and waves to them, urging it quickly into a canter. The ash flies up around the horse's hooves, leaving a cloud of black dust behind them. On the horizon, the late afternoon sun struggles through the haze of darkness.

∽✱✱✱∾

Late that night, Vili is woken out of a deep slumber. Fulla crouches beside him, dressed only in a pale chemise. Her long golden hair hangs freely down her back. He sits up quickly, alarmed. "What is it?" he asks.

"Come," she says urgently. She takes his hand and pulls him to his feet, then turns and crosses to her bedchamber, glancing back to make sure he is behind her. After a split second's hesitation, he follows. Once inside the room, she closes the door and leans against it.

"What is it?" he asks. "Is something wrong?"

She shakes her head and takes a few steps towards him, until her face is only a breath apart from his. "I'll not be someone else's bride," she says intently. "If there is to be a first time, then let it be with you." She leans forward and kisses him fully on the mouth, her tongue searching for his own. Vili moans, his oath momentarily forgotten, and takes her in his arms.

353

DVALIN

hough he rides south to Nidavellir, his mind runs to Asgard. One thought persists: there is no way she could have survived the force of such an eruption. Not even the Aesir could withstand the might of Hekla. His own people, too, are at risk. Though Nidavellir lies some distance to the west, the force of the blast and the tremors that ensued could easily have destroyed the caves and everyone inside them. He could not have let Berling ride with him, for he does not know what he will find.

And Hekla's tantrum has not finished. Every few minutes, she rumbles into action, shooting more clouds of yellow dust and gas into the air. Once again, the ash begins to fall in earnest. It stings his eyes and clogs his nostrils, even finding its way into the back of his throat. His horse, too, is suffering, and he is forced to slow their pace. After one particularly large explosion, tiny bits of hot pumice begin to rain out of the sky. The horse is struck by burning pumice on its flank. The terrified animal screams and rears up. Dvalin clings hard to its mane. He himself is hit more than once on his face and arms. The burning embers leave red welts on his skin, like the angry bites of an insect.

All around him, the landscape has been altered. Though he knows the route well, he is forced to stop and check his bearings more than once. Familiar landmarks lie covered in ash everywhere he looks. As he draws closer to Nidavellir and Hekla, conditions worsen. He rides past huge lumps of smouldering molten rock, thrown vast distances by the first eruption. More and more, he worries about the fate of Nidavellir and his people, and counts his blessings that Berling was with him at Laxardal when Hekla blew.

But what of the others? And what of Freya? Again and again, his thoughts return to her. He does not know why. If he harboured feelings for her, he was not aware of it. Now he cannot banish her from his mind. The thought that she may have perished in the eruption sickens him.

As night draws near, he reaches the final plateau before Nidavellir. Exhausted by the worsening conditions, he and the horse slow to a walk. They are still an hour's ride from the caves, though he has begun to wonder if they will make it before nightfall. He does not know whether he can carry on in darkness. The smell of sulphur in the air is overwhelming and burns his lungs each time he draws a breath. A feeling of guilt washes over him. All his life he has fled the confines of the caves, and felt nothing but ambivalence towards his kin. If his people have been lost in the eruption, then he should have died with them.

Suddenly, another huge explosion tears the sky over Hekla. His horse rears up, and Dvalin flies backwards, nearly losing his seat. The horse breaks into a gallop, its nostrils flaring, and Dvalin struggles to bring the animal under control. A shower of hot pumice begins to fall, and the horse begins to leap frantically, its eyes white with fear. Dvalin is struck on the head by a rock the size of a fist, and in the next moment, he is weightless, the earth rushing up to meet him.

FREYA

t is some time before I can bring myself to leave the cave at Singastein. When I finally do, Hekla has grown quieter, and the earth no longer moves beneath my feet. But the sea is even worse than before. It churns like a cauldron, with waves running in all directions. As I circle the island from the air, I see an enormous wall of water gathering out at sea, rushing with great speed towards the shore. When it finally hits the coast, the water spills across the land as if hurled by a giant, destroying everything in its path.

I leave the sea behind me and fly towards Hekla, the air around me hazy with ash. It clings to my face and feathers, stinging my eyes and burning my throat. Far off in the distance, I can see a dark mass of cloud over her summit. More than once, I hear a faint subterranean groan, as if a demon has been trapped inside the earth. All the while Hekla beckons to me: I fly towards her, knowing that my life is at risk.

The air worsens as I draw near, and flight becomes almost impossible. I climb higher, until the atmosphere is so thin I can scarcely breathe. The ash is not as heavy up high, though beneath me is a dirty sea of haze. As I reach the valley to the south of Hekla, I struggle to catch a glimpse of the ground far below. With mounting shock, I see that the eruption has altered the face of Asgard completely. Nothing remains of Odin's home-stead, nor my own. The River Thjorsa rages across the valley, swollen beyond recognition, boulders the size of cattle tumbling furiously in the frothing waters. What ground has not been devoured by lava is already buried under several feet of dark grey ash.

And then a deafening explosion occurs: the sound swallows me, so immense I cannot discern its source, and I am billowed upwards by a tremendous surge of heat and wind. A huge white cloud shoots straight up from Hekla in front of me, soaring right above me. I watch as it climbs higher, then gradually halts, fanning out at the top in a feather of pale light. It hovers for an instant, then bends and falls, drifting down towards the earth with terrible beauty. As it does, a pall of black smoke billows outwards from the base, amid great tongues of fire. It spreads like spilled ink across the land, until a gust of wind scatters it away, and I catch a glimpse of the ground beneath. Hekla's spine has been torn open by the blast: a long jagged curtain of bright red lava shoots up along the ridge, where the earth has cleaved in two. The lava overflows in a myriad of hot red fingers down the sides of Hekla's flank, forming a web of bloody rivers against the blackened rock. The sight is both beautiful and terrifying, and for a moment I forget that all of Asgard has been decimated by her fury.

And then I realise that I am falling, as the earth rushes towards me. The ash is everywhere, clogging my eyes and nose and throat, and I am struggling to breathe. I try in vain to remain aloft, and feel my arms weaken as I drift downwards. I land hard upon Hekla's lower slopes in a bed of hot ash. Unable to move, I lie back, exhausted. The ground beneath me gives a sudden jerk, as another huge explosion rolls out of Hekla. Instinctively, I raise my arms to my face, as a wave of fire engulfs me. The earth and sky vanish. I find myself inside a sphere of heat and light and noise. In the next moment, a veil of red sweeps across the slope where I am lying, and a shower of debris hits me. I curl into a ball as the fiery torrent passes over me. It spills across the valley, devouring everything in its path. Behind me, a huge chunk of Hekla's side has been blown away. Nothing around me is recognisable. I close my eyes to the devastation. My home is gone, as are my people. Why have I survived?

∾ℰℰ℈∾

Some time later, I wake. I do not know how long I've been unconscious. My lungs burn as if they are alight, and my arms feel as if they have been pulled from their sockets. I sit up and survey the landscape. Behind me, Hekla continues to pop and hiss, but her violence has abated. With trembling fingers, I reach for the necklace at my throat. I owe my life to the Brisingamen: that is why Skuld sent me to find it. But I do not know why fate has chosen me to remain behind, or whether I wish it to be so.

Slowly, I stand and shake the ash from my feather form. There is a deep cut on my shoulder, but otherwise I am unhurt. I rise again into the sky and fly west towards Nidavellir, hoping that Fulla and Dvalin had moved beyond the caves by the time Hekla blew. There is little doubt in my mind that Nidavellir will have been destroyed along with Asgard. Even before I reach the vast plains that contain the caves, I see from a distance that the entire surface of the earth has collapsed inwards for many miles. Giant shards of rock jut out at every angle. Indeed, the entire plateau looks as though it has been dropped from a great height and trampled into pieces. Everywhere there is blackened ash, sometimes lying in drifts higher than a man's head. I circle twice around Nidavellir, but see no sign of life. I think of

Berling and his mother, and the girl with straw-coloured plaits who boldly greeted me that first day. I see the tunnels with their faint shafts of light, the rusted anvils, the bed strewn with shaggy skins, and the bowl of coloured beads. I realise that I am crying: my face runs with blackened tears. For my own people, for Dvalin's, and for all those who have survived.

As night approaches, I turn north and head towards Laxardal. I do not know where else to go and am so tired that my limbs are racked with pain. My entire body is caked with soot, and the intense smell of sulphur grips my lungs like a fist. I fly as long as I am able, until I spy a small cluster of trees beneath me. Miraculously, the ground beneath it is clear of ash. I land, endeavouring to catch my breath for a few minutes. Behind me, Hekla explodes again in anger. I feel the shock waves sweep across the valley, a force powerful enough to knock me from the skies, had I been flying. I reach instinctively for the Brisingamen at my throat. In the next instant, a shower of hot rocks begins to fall from the sky. I roll sideways into the base of a tree and curl myself into a ball. I feel the burning stones hit my back and legs, as if I am being struck by a staff. I wait until the shower subsides, then stand unsteadily. Night is falling fast now. I know that I must carry on, either to Laxardal, or somewhere closer, where I can shelter for the night.

And then I see it: a riderless horse running towards me at a gallop. The animal is half-crazed with terror, its eyes enormous blisters of fear. The horse runs straight past, blind to me. With a sickening feeling, I see that it is Dvalin's. I summon my strength and take to the skies, heading in the direction the horse came from. I fly for several minutes, searching the ground in vain, struggling to see through the mounting darkness. I have nearly given up hope when I see him. He lies face down, his body already covered in a thin layer of ash. I land next to him, and for an instant I am too frightened to move. I stare at the curl of his ear, the tangle of dark hair falling down his back, and feel my throat tighten. I reach out and lay a hand against the side of his neck. I feel the warmth of his body beneath my fingers and a faint pulse. With relief, I rest my forehead upon his shoulder, offering a prayer of thanks to whatever gods remain. Then I gently turn him over and wipe the ash from his face. His head is bleeding and one of his legs has been torn open just below the knee. I try in vain to wake him, then gather him in my arms and pull him up into the sky.

THE NORNS

Water abounds here. Twelve rivers and their offspring run in all directions, their names like stark warnings: Shivering, Crooked, Torrent. But rivers are as vulnerable as the land. Past Hekla's northern flank flows the River Thjorsa, swollen with run-off from the vast ice sheets of the central plateau. Like all rivers on this island, it is unnavigable, loaded with silt and gravel ground down by bedrock from glaciers far inland. When Hekla blows, the Thjorsa trebles in size with the debris of destruction: pumice, ash and snow. Hekla's venomous ashfall contaminates its waters, poisoning fish and carrying death to livestock further downstream, as the river finds its way back to the sea. But this is a fitting end to the cycle of eruption, for the sea gave birth to Hekla, and to the sea some part of her must return.

DVALIN

he first thing he sees when he wakes is the low ceiling of the cave. He sits up in the darkness, and the back of his head bursts with pain. At once, he falls back to the ground. He remembers the explosion and the stone that struck him, but nothing else. Slowly, he looks around him, his eyes struggling to see through the darkness. He does not know how he got here. The cave is long and narrow, its ceiling low. The entrance is a sliver in the rock at the far end, through which a tiny amount of natural light enters. A small pile of dead brush lies on the ground next to him. Beside it is something else. He peers at it closely: a pile of dirty feathers. His heart begins to race.

Once again, he pulls himself up, more carefully this time. After a moment, the throbbing in the back of his head recedes slightly. He looks around in vain. She is nowhere. He looks towards the narrow entrance. The opening is obscured by several thick leafy branches. His throat is parched and sore from ash, and for the first time, he sees that his leg has been wounded just below the knee. Someone has tied it with a strip of cloth. He can feel nothing, for the entire leg is numb. He lies back down again and waits, drifting into sleep.

The next time he wakes, she is there, crouching next to him. "You're back," he murmurs.

She smiles. Her face and hair are covered in soot. "Did you think I would abandon you?" she says. "I've brought some wood for a fire, and clean water. And something for a poultice. Your leg needs dressing."

She holds the goatskin up and helps him to drink. Then he watches as she sets about grinding leaves between two stones. "How did you find all this?" he asks in amazement.

"With difficulty. Everything is covered in ash."

"Hekla," he says, lying back down. She nods grimly and continues grinding. After a few minutes, she stops. "I think this will have to do." She carefully unties the bandage on his leg, exposing the wound.

"It's nothing," he says. "Only a flesh wound."

"It's deep and needs tending." She smears the poultice gently on the wound as he winces, then reties the bandage as best she can. "Let me look at the back of your head."

He raises his head slightly, allowing her to examine it.

She bends down closely to see. "You were lucky."

"We both were."

For the first time, she looks into his eyes. "I thought you were dead."

"And I you."

They stare at each other for a moment, until she turns away. "I must light a fire," she says unsteadily. She gathers a pile of dead leaves, then removes a flint from her pouch. He watches as she struggles with the flint, resisting the temptation to reach out to grasp her hand. Finally, a tiny flame sputters into life, catching on the leaves. Quickly she feeds the fire with small twigs.

"What of Asgard? And your people?" he asks.

She gives a brief shake of her head. "Asgard is destroyed."

He hesitates. "Did you fly over Nidavellir?"

She looks over to him and nods slowly. "I'm sorry," she says. "The entire plain has collapsed. I flew over it but saw nothing. No sign of life."

His eyes drift to the fire. "I did not think it would be spared," he says finally. He looks up at her and for the first time sees the Brisingamen around her neck. "The necklace!" he exclaims.

She stops and fingers it. "Odin sent me to the coast to recover it. I was there when Hekla blew." She looks down at it, then back at him. "I was wrong about the necklace. It saved my life."

"We were both wrong," he replies.

She continues feeding the fire until it is established, then sits down next to him. After a moment, she reaches back and undoes the clasp of the necklace, and holds it out to him.

"Here," she says.

He frowns. "What is this?"

"I'm returning it."

"Why?"

"Because it has done what it was meant to. I can ask nothing more of it."

He takes the Brisingamen from her and studies it. "I, too, am finished with it," he says.

"Why?"

"Because it represents all my faults."

She smiles. "What faults are these?" she asks teasingly. "I was not aware you had any."

"Oh yes," he admits, studying the gold. "Each one is here, burnt into the ore. You see this, at the top?" She leans towards him, peering closely. He shows her the ornate clasp that holds the chain together. "This here is the sin of pride."

She studies it. "There are worse crimes," she pronounces.

"And this," he continues, holding up the link between the chain and the pendant, "this one is anger."

She smiles. "Perhaps I was aware of that one."

"And this," he says, holding up the chain. "This represents the sin of solitude."

She looks at him askance. "Solitude is an offence?"

"It can be," he says.

"Then I, too, have committed it."

"Perhaps," he acknowledges. He takes a deep breath before continuing. "But the worst one is here." He holds up the pendant. "This one represents fear."

She frowns at the pendant, then raises her gaze to his. "What are you afraid of?" she asks slowly.

"Myself." He pauses and gazes at her. "You." Somewhere deep inside him, a tremendous force of longing is unleashed.

"You do not want the necklace?" she asks.

He shakes his head. "I want you."

Slowly, she leans in towards him, and brings her lips right to his own. He kisses her urgently, for he has waited much too long. He hears her whisper his name, her voice mingling with the desire in his brain. He lifts her up into the air with both arms and pulls her right on top of him, so he can feel the warm weight of her body atop his. This is where he wants her to remain, he thinks. Here with him, on the ground.

FULLA

short distance from the coast, Fulla and Vili meet an old man on the road riding a large white mare. He is modestly clothed in a dark red woollen cloak and wears a wide-brimmed felt hat, together with a leather patch over one eye. His other eye is of a startling blue, however. Fulla cannot help but stare at it. The old man appears from nowhere and smiles at them amiably. "May I ride along with you?" he asks.

Fulla and Vili exchange a bemused glance. "Of course," Fulla answers politely. She does not know why, but the old man strikes her as oddly familiar. Perhaps he is wary of travelling alone, she thinks, though he seems oblivious to danger.

"Where do you journey?" he asks.

"To the coast," answers Vili. "We intend to find passage on a ship bound for Norway."

"Ah, Norway," muses the old man. "A fine country. Full of trees, they say."

"You've not been there?" Fulla asks.

The old man smiles at her. "My home is here."

She meets his gaze for a moment, and something in it unnerves her.

"Do you go to visit or to live?" the old man asks after a moment.

Vili smiles at Fulla. "We intend to start a new life there," he says proudly. "We are newly betrothed, but will marry as soon as we arrive on Norwegian shores. It was her grandfather's last request that she should be married in Norway."

The old man nods thoughtfully. "One must respect the wishes of the dead," he says. "You are good to do so."

They ride along in silence for a time, until they reach the crest of a long hill. In the distance, the shimmering turquoise of the ocean comes into sight. "Look!" exclaims Fulla, pulling her horse to a stop. She smiles broadly at the vast expanse of water stretching endlessly towards the horizon. The enormous swell of it takes her breath away.

"This is your first journey across the water?" the old man asks politely. She nods.

He reaches in a small leather pouch hung about his neck and withdraws something, then advances towards her. "Here," he says, pulling his horse to a stop beside hers. "I should like you to have this." He leans forward and extends his hand. In his palm is a small gold ring.

Fulla looks at him with confusion. "No," she protests. "I could not."

"Please," he answers. "I am an old man. I might die tomorrow. It would give me great pleasure if you'd accept."

Fulla hesitates. She glances uncertainly at Vili, who raises an eyebrow almost imperceptibly. "Thank you," she says after a moment, taking the ring. She slips it onto her finger. It fits as if it had been made for her.

"I wish you well in your new life," says the old man intently. Without another word, he turns his horse in the opposite direction and rides away.

Vili watches him go, then laughs, shaking his head. He leans over, peering closely at the ring. "It is very fine," he acknowledges.

Fulla stares after the old man. "I did not even ask his name," she murmurs.

"What an odd thing to do."

"Yes," she concurs.

"Perhaps he was taken with your beauty," says Vili with a grin. He urges his horse back to a walk. After one last glance, Fulla follows. Every now and then she looks down at the ring. Already, it looks as if it has grown there. The sight pleases her. Without thinking, she reaches for the necklace hidden beneath her dress. She feels for the pendant and holds it for a moment. The old man seemed harmless enough. Perhaps he only wanted company, after all.

FREYA

It has been three months since Hekla blew. Each morning, Dvalin and I must contend with her legacy. Much of Hogni's land was destroyed in the aftermath of the eruption. Little pasture has been left that is suitable for grazing, and many of the crops have failed. Two-thirds of the livestock have perished from starvation. We have struggled to find food for the remainder, as well as nourishment for ourselves. Even the rivers are unsafe, their waters poisoned by Hekla's fury. It will be many years, perhaps generations, before order is restored. But we are alive and we are together. For these things we are grateful.

The weather continues to behave unpredictably, like an ill-tempered child. Each night, the sun sets with unearthly beauty, as if the heavens are awash with the blood of those who have died. We watch in awe and in sorrow. Berling remains with us and every day, he sheds another layer of grief, and of childhood. Death and destruction have made him wise beyond his years; he has seen enough of both to last a lifetime. He has grown to love life above the ground and spends hours exploring the land around Hogni's farm.

But he does not do so alone. Two days after Dvalin and I returned to Laxardal, a rider appeared in the yard outside Hogni's farm. He was unrecognisable, so black was his skin and hair from the ash. The horse appeared to be barely standing, its exhaused head nearly slumped

372

to the ground. I walked outside to greet this stranger, and when I looked into his eyes, I nearly fainted with relief. Sky gazed down at me with that same familiar look of hope and trepidation.

"Sky," I said. Slowly he slid off the horse, and I folded him into an embrace. The blackness of his skin came off on me. I felt his enormous frame tremble with relief. Eventually, he pulled back and looked at me. "Where is Odin?" I asked.

He shook his head. "He showed me the way through the mountain, but would not come with me." I stared at him, and understood that Odin had taken his own path.

Each week, Helga and the others quietly make offerings to Thor, even while the new religion spreads like wind-blown seeds across the land. Unlike the pagan gods of old, the new god they preach of is both faultless and pure. While Thor remains a symbol of both strength and protection, he must now yield to Christ in the eyes of many here. The godi have all been baptised now, and a bishop has been appointed to oversee the region. There are plans for a church to be built nearby.

I used to think that the people here laboured under false belief. Now I see that there is no such thing, for belief itself is as powerful and impervious as Hekla. I have come to understand that men are governed by their faith – whatever form it may assume. And it is faith that underpins both their identity and their purpose.

Long ago, the poets prophesied that a new world would arise after the storm age, ever green, and that all those who survived would meet again on the great plain to recall the deeds and ancient secrets of old. I know that the Aesir will continue to dwell in our stories and our memories. And that is how it shall remain for all time.

◈◈◈

The Brisingamen is no longer with us. We have given it
to Fulla, to keep her safe on her passage to her new life.
Now I do not fear its power, for it has proved its worth,
and I am certain it will serve Fulla well. Even the feather form is gone, the last vestige of my life with the Aesir.
Not long after we returned to Laxardal, I burned it in
the same spot where Hogni was cremated. Dvalin
seemed surprised, but did not argue. I think he was
relieved. Though the cloak saved our life more than
once, he prefers life upon the ground. Now we live like
ordinary people, who rise each day with the sun and
labour until dark.

Last night, as I drifted into sleep, I felt a quickening
in my belly. For the first time since the eruption, I
dreamt of Skuld. Asgard may be gone, but I am certain
the Norns remain, casting their long shadows over our
lives. In my dream, Skuld placed her hands upon my
stomach and smiled. "Two hands," she said. "One for
each child. Beautiful daughters, with names like jewels."

When I told Dvalin of my dream this morning, he
looked at me askance. "Twins?" He said with a raised
eyebrow. I laughed. He does not know it, but I have
already chosen their names. I shall name them after precious stones, according to Skuld's prophecy, for she has
never let me down.

And what do I think of love, now that it has caught
me in its grasp? I have come to understand its terrible
beauty, as well as its capacity to cleave the soul. But I also
know that love is a truth that must be learnt, rather than
taught. And that it should never be ignored.

AUTHOR'S NOTE

As the title suggests, this book is heavily steeped in the history, geology, mythology and ancient lore of Iceland. Norse myth, though drawn from all of Scandinavian culture, uses imagery that is unique to Iceland. In particular, the prophecy of creation and destruction *(Ragnorak)* which underpins the entire cycle of myths can only refer to the turbulent geology of that country. Thus, the tenacity of the book's central characters mirrors that of the Icelandic people themselves, who settled in this volatile land more than a millennium ago and refused to be driven out by its destructive nature.

Through the centuries, the Icelandic people have endured countless eruptions, some of them catastrophic. Mount Hekla, the infamous volcano at the centre of this story, first erupted in 1104. During that explosion, she deposited two and a half cubic kilometers of ash and rock upon her inhabitants. An entire valley was obliterated. None of the early farmers who laid claim to her flanks during the first years of settlement realised they were living atop such a beast. It is no wonder Hekla subsequently came to be regarded as the gate to Hell.

At the heart of the novel is Freya, the Norse goddess of love. The story is loosely inspired by the myth of the *Brisingamen*, which tells of Freya's quest for a magnificent gold necklace, and her decision to sell herself to the four brothers who created it. The myth has been widely embellished and reinterpreted over the centuries, but I have taken further liberties with it, altering both Freya's motivations and the outcome of her journey.

While Norse mythology is dominated by men, it is Freya who emerges as the most complex and intriguing of the pantheon. Although she represents romance and fertility, she herself is unlucky in love, having been deserted by her mortal husband Od. Freya suffers enormously when Od abandons her; indeed it is said that her tears flooded the earth with her sorrow. Yet she ultimately takes charge of her own destiny and lives independently outside marriage. Perhaps because of this she is often portrayed as a woman of dubious virtue.

Freya's portrait in the myths is consistent with ancient Icelandic society, where women had the right to divorce their husbands and be landholders. Many did just that. The Icelandic Sagas are full of tales of powerful women, such as the clever and formidable Gudrun of Laxardal, who outlived four husbands and became a legend of her own time.

But it is not just Freya's story I have borrowed from. The book draws on many other mythic elements: the story of Menglad and her betrothal necklace, Idun's rape by giants and subsequent fall into an ice crevasse, Nord's failed marriage with the young giantess Skadi, Odin's lecherous desire for Freya and his strange interdependence with the evil trickster Loki. All of these characters are based loosely on the mythic poems.

I was equally influenced by the *Icelandic Sagas*, that astonishing body of prose stories that forms the basis of our understanding of life as it was lived a thousand years ago. In these tales, which were recounted around open fires for generations before they were ever set down on paper, people argue, fight battles, fall in and out of love, commit infidelities, murder their relatives, set fire to their neighbours' houses, and confront ghosts in the dead of night. The *Icelandic Sagas* are as entertaining today as they were then, and they have no equivalent in medieval English literature. Just as Freya's story is underpinned by the myths, the character of Fulla and her forbidden love for Vili is inspired by the *Sagas*.

If there is a moment where the mythic poetry converges with the prose *Sagas*, it is around the theme of kinship. What attracted me to the Norse pantheon was not its fantastic element (though indeed the gods can change shape, throw spears of lightning and drive chariots across the sky). Rather it was their humanity (or relative inhumanity) that I was drawn to. The *Aesir* are portrayed as one large dysfunctional family, beset with lust, petty jealousies, envy, rivalry, corruption and malice of every kind. Despite their supernatural strength, they are morally weak, and it is this that brings about their destruction.

Kinship, honour and loyalty were the lynchpins of Viking society. Every individual was anchored by their obligations to those around them. The greatest punishment was outlawry: to be separated forever from one's loved ones was the worst fate a man could endure. And yet the sagas are full of tales of families torn asunder by feuding, and the myths themselves prophesy that just before *Ragnorak*, 'brothers will do battle unto death and sons of sisters will fight their own kin.' It is this point of thwarted kinship and divided loyalties that I chose to probe.

Asgard, the realm of the gods, is represented in the myths as a walled citadel above earth that can only be reached by crossing the shimmering rainbow bridge *Bifrost*. I have portrayed it as a mountainous region far inland where each of the gods occupies their own homestead, just as ordinary settlers did. Unlike elsewhere in Viking society, the Icelandic people did not settle in towns or villages until the eighteenth century. They lived in extended family units on large farmholdings, often in extreme isolation.

Despite this, they were a sociable people. They travelled frequently and came together often, for weddings, harvest festivals, governance and merry-making, which sometime lasted days. Their climate was a treacherous one. Hospitality and generosity were both essential and highly valued. If a guest pitched up on your threshold, it was your moral duty to furnish him with a warm hearth to sleep on and some form of sustenance. Winters were long, cold and dark. In the evenings, Icelandic farmers sought refuge in drink, poetry and story-telling.

True to their image, they were a violent people. Fighting and vengeance were part of everyday life: if you insulted your neighbour's wife then you had better not ride out unarmed, as someone would be waiting for you. Weapons were crude and dangerous, and the injuries men sustained were horrific. The *Sagas* are replete with gory descriptions of these brutal encounters.

Religion infused all aspects of life, but it had to coexist with the reality of survival. Daily life was hard. Nature was often cruel, and one couldn't afford to be complacent. If you were an Icelandic farmer you made offerings to Thor, and to a lesser extent to Freyr and Odin, and if you were a woman trying to conceive or get a husband, then perhaps to Freya. But you also worked hard and struggled for your livelihood.

When the first Christians came, the Icelandic people were bemused. It was only later, when Christian missionaries began to use violence, and King Olaf threatened to imprison Icelandic people abroad, that they were forced to make concessions. The story of Iceland's conversion, of the lawspeaker Thorgeir and his two-day vigil beneath a cloak at the Althing, is an astonishing one. I have simplified it slightly in the book, but it happened much the way I describe. No bloody wars. No massacres. Just a peaceful transition.

Above all, the Icelandic people were pragmatic; by the year 1000 they realised Christianity was inevitable. They valued their independence from the rest of Scandinavia, perhaps even more than their faith. The fact that they lived in isolated farmsteads and could continue to worship as they pleased made them all the more receptive. In reality, heathen beliefs and practices coexisted happily alongside Christianity for many centuries thereafter.

Finally, this is a love story. I began my infatuation with Iceland some years ago, and it continues unabated. Anyone who has ever languished in the warm thermal waters of an ancient ring of stones, staring out at a wondrously beautiful, seemingly benign yet potentially lethal mountain range will understand my affection for this amazing island and its stalwart inhabitants. This book is my love letter to Iceland and her people. May they long survive.

BETSY TOBIN
2007

ACKNOWLEDGEMENTS

Huge gratitude to my son Theo Sands, who first steered me in the direction of the Norse pantheon (and who remains my best reader); to Margaret Glover, who blew life back into this manuscript when it lay dangerously close to death; and to Ragnar Hjalmarsson for translating Icelandic geologic terminology. Many thanks as well to my lovely agents Felicity Rubinstein, Sarah Lutyens and Susannah Godman, for backing me over the long haul. And finally, an enormous gold star to the fabulous team at Short Books: Aurea Carpenter, Rebecca Nicolson, Emily Fox, Vanessa Webb and Catherine Gibbs, who make all good things possible.

In case of difficulty in purchasing any Short Books
title through normal channels, please contact
BOOKPOST Tel: 01624 836000
Fax: 01624 837033
email: bookshop@enterprise.net
www.bookpost.co.uk
Please quote ref. 'Short Books'